To Kit ♡

To faith to light / love of
Christ

Mary [signature]

9-29-13

Seventy
Times
Seven

Mary Ellen Wellbaum

Dedication

This book is dedicated to Jerry and all people whose faith inspires others to live better, to give genuinely and love when all else fails. To Robert and all the men and women who commit to changing their path in life for the better, thank you for inspiring the rest of us by example.

Acknowledgments

Special thanks to my husband, Michael, and our four boys, Patrick, Nicholas, Gregory, and Benjamin; to my editor, Geoff for his excellence in all things grammatically and conceptually sound; to my cover artist, Simone; to George for an enlightening interview; and to my friends and family who cheered this book on. Thank you for reading, listening, and encouraging this work to fruition. Charles thanks for the sound advice and the candid way in which you offered it; you have a wicked sense of humor. Thank you Jerry and Robert for inspiring me to write this story.

Prologue

I felt the metal point penetrate his flesh. It was a powerful feeling, flicking the sharp metal into his first, then second layer of skin; I waited a long time to catch this one, but I had him now. I held on to the grip, knowing the titanium in the metal was giving me maximum strength-to-weight-ratio. My adrenaline was pumping as I felt him jerk against the blade. He kept trying to slip out of my grasp so I had to force his head into the bend of my arm to secure my hold, adjusting my stance yet again.

Suddenly, he arched his back and began to flail with resistance, his whole body straining, as if he was using every ounce of strength he had left. I had to put more of my weight into the struggle, anticipating and compensating for his every move.

He was giving in. I could feel it.

I looked down at him when it was over. His eyes were looking past me into a landscape only he could see, his body no longer twitching, his chest no longer heaving or fighting. I rested the toe of my shoe on him while I worked the sharp metal free. Now that he was still and lifeless, I had a chance to stand back from him, taking in the full view. He was finally at rest on the wooden planks.

It's done.

Chapter 1

The shape of the shiny hook is enticing. The fish is drawn in by the light hitting it as well as the wiggly sustenance wrapped around it. It's only a matter of time before … gotcha.

Ryker James, Jr. – 2004

I's at the edge again, standin' on a cliff, lookin' down into a deep, wooded ravine. They's trees all the way down, but if I land right, I could hit and roll on impact.

Lookin' hard at d'fall, I tryin' to weigh my options. I could aim for the trees and let the branches break my fall. If I could grab on to somethin', I might could ease down the side.

I back off from the edge a little, draw in a deep breath and try to think. How'd I get back in this game? I guess it's the rush of it all. The high' as pure as it git.

I hear footsteps poundin' behind me, but when I turn to look, ain' nobody there. I can't tell if the danger all in my head or real. I just feel like jumpin', endin' it all. I look down again. Sometime I think it be better if I die.

Just as I step close enough to jump, they's a light that shine, blindin' me so I can't see to make my move. The light's warm and I'm so tired. I just want a stay in it; let the heat soothe my achin' body.

Bullets sound from a .45 and I want a run but I can't see anythang but the light. Waitin' for the bullets to hit my chest, I brace myself for the impact. Hollow points ain' gon' leave no chance a survival. That's why we use 'em. They shatter on impact.

More bullets come. I hold out my arms and prepare to dive off the edge blind. If I's lucky, the bullets will kill me on impact and I won't feel d'fall.

Oh my God, what am I doin'? I can't take the life you done gave me. How's that s'pose to fix thangs?

I look back; the bullets' a swarm a bees, ready to sting.

The fear come hard. I's lookin' at it full-on. Still, I ain' got the juice to jump. I want a end me, but I's frozen right where I's standin' and I know somethin' gon' kill me fo' sure. *Damn.* I ain' strong 'nough to end me, but the darkness behin' me ain' got no conscience.

I started prayin', *Lord, if you let me live, I'm 'on do ever'thang in my power to change this life I been livin'.*

Arms still outstretched, I 'member my .45, tucked in the backside a my jeans. I grab it with my right hand and turn so's I can step over the edge and start shootin' at what comin'. Before I could git off a round, I'm hit. Shards from the bullet stab through my heart. My chest' on fire as hot, dark liquid spread.

"Ryker! Open this door, boy! Ryker!"

Ryker leapt from the floor and held up his .45, aiming at the door. Releasing the safety, he pressed his finger against the trigger; he was ready. Sweat poured off him, his t-shirt soaked through. A chill sent cool air through his scalp. His coarse, black hair absorbed as much as it could until bulbs of sweat escaped and streaked down his face toward his neck. The trickles felt ice cold against his feverish body.

Where am I? He thought. Looking down at his chest, he didn't see blood. His chest was palpitating, the pain increasing with every breath, but there was no sign of the hits he took.

"Ryker!" the gravelly voice called out, this time more irritated. "Open this door. Now!" This time he recognized the voice. It was Ryker James Senior, otherwise known as Big R; his father. *That son of a bitch.*

He looked around, his head whipping in every direction. There was no ravine, no edge, no fall. Trying to focus, he started to put the safety on and then changed his mind. *What's Pop doin' here?*

Letting the .45 swing down by his side, his finger remained on the trigger. When Big R opened the door, Ryker swung the gun wide, shrugged his shoulders and popped his neck left, then right.

Big R saw Ryker's piece out of the corner of his eye, but it didn't register he was thinking of using it until he saw Ryker's eyes, smoldering like embers of searing, hot coals.

Ryker registered his father was in front of him, *or was he?* He suddenly felt five years old beneath his father's knitted brows, a mixture of confusion, no, trepidation brewing in his father's stare. Disoriented, Ryker met his gaze, trying to discern his intentions. *Real? Or, just a skewed image he fought in his sleep every night?*

This ain' real, he decided. *You a'ight. It's Pop. He ain' here to hurt nobody. Put the safety on. Chill,* he told himself. Seconds passed. His father's hands were still raised.

"Hey, Little R," his father kept his voice steady. "You a'ight?" He was still eyeing Ryker's piece.

Wiping the sweat from his brow, Ryker felt a twinge of anger at the way Big R was trying to handle him.

"What the hell you want old man?" He felt the weight of his .45, gripped it tighter, liking the power as he placed his finger on the trigger.

"They's a lot goin' down," Big R's eyes darted from the gun to Ryker and switched back. "Just, just tryin' to cover thangs," and he let his hands fall to his sides. "You gon' put that thing down?" *What set you on fire, boy?* He wondered, but didn't dare ask. Squinting, he decided to wait him out.

Little R had nightmares as a child and Big R remembered some of them stayed real, even after Ryker had been awake for a time. *Is he in it still?* Big R couldn't tell. He noticed beads of sweat dripped from his forehead, his clothes damp down to his bare feet. *It must a been a bad one,* he surmised. He wanted to reach out to him, but he knew better.

"No, I think I'll hold on to it," Ryker snapped, liking that he held the power. Blinking and feeling sweat trickle down his face, he felt an icy chill.

What is wrong with me? He blinked, a drip of sweat filtering through his dark lashes into his eye. *I'm burning up and freezing at the same time. This man in front a me ain' from my head. It's pop. Ain' it?*

Still trying to discern what just happened, his thoughts were interrupted. *Seventy times seven,* he heard someone say, or *did they?*

"What 'choo just say?" he asked, waving the piece.

"Nothin'. Ain' nobody gon' say nothin' 'til you calm down." Several minutes went by and Ryker's shoulders finally relaxed.

"Why you here?"

"I'm," he paused again, still not sure about the .45 Ryker was brandishing. "I'm 'bout to go down for possession. Jenkins done got me released on bail, but it ain' lookin' good. The police may have proof this time."

"Don't even go d'ere," Ryker said, as he sat down in the one chair in the room, knees spread wide, the .45 still hanging from his right hand. "You sayin' ole' Bennie Foster can't help you? Make a call old man, just like you always do," irritation lacing the edge in his voice.

"Foster dead," his words got Ryker's full attention. "Died this morning. The Cooper Police have hard evidence on me this time and Jimmy Earl say they ain' nowhere to hide."

James Earl Jenkins had been Big R's lawyer since Ryker was a baby. Six-foot-two with a slick shock of coarse, pepper hair with salt around the edges; he had a swagger that seemed to rule any court room he graced with his expertise. His sharp, silk suit commanded attention and his words echoed citations like he was born to defend. Yes, he knew his way around the courtroom and the law like no one else. If he said there was nowhere to hide, it meant the situation was dire.

Big R's face fell and Ryker saw a sliver of regret. There was no way to tell if it was grief or utter defeat relative to the charges he was facing, the likes of which could send him to prison for twenty or thirty years, depending. Big R knew he was going down for a long time.

What goes around is about to come down hard, Ryker thought. For years, his father had Bennie covering for him, looking the other way, helping him evade arrests and charges, but with Foster dead, Big R was vulnerable like never before.

"How'd he die?" the question sobered them both and brought clarity to Ryker's haze, giving him presence in the moment. His father appeared struck, both by morality and mortality.

"A stroke," his tone was blatantly resistant to the notion that it was true, though his face wrinkled in grief. Forcing himself to shake it off, he pressed on to the business at hand. "I need you to do something for me. I ain' got nobody else I can ax," he paused, raking his hands over his unkempt hair.

Here it comes. They's always somethin'. It all 'bout him.

"What the hell you think *I* can do? I ain' seen you in how long? You just comin' 'round now 'cause things done gone south, huh, old man?" Ryker knew he had a short fuse, but he didn't care if his words lit him up. He had honed *his* rage; he had control. And, the confidence in his right hand didn't hurt.

He considered telling his father the raw truth of things. *Why I always got to be here for you? You ain' never been there for me. You 'posed to be a father. You ain' never been that, not the kind I could count on or nothin'. It's the other way 'round. I's always taken cur a you. I's cleanin' up yo' messes and tendin' to the open wounds you leave behind. How come, just about the time I git to a good place, you come along and end me before I can git ground under my feet?* Ryker rolled his shoulders back, preparing for the fury he saw in Big R's eyes, his clenched jaw, his pursed lips; he considered adding more fuel to the fire. *Why not set him off? It'd give me reason to give it back to 'im. He done 'nough a that back in the day.* Just as he was about to pounce, his father surprised him; the rage on his face dissipating, leaving pain behind.

"You right. Things're bad and I wish I didn't have to come to you, 'cause Lord know I ain' got no right to ax for a damn thing. I don't *want* to end nobody," slivers of guilt lining his words even as he tried to shake them off. Foster's death hung like a lead cloud, tempering what used to ignite Big R's usual flash of impatience and indignation at what life had thrown him.

Big R had grown up with Foster. When he became mayor, Big R was his biggest supporter, as they had been friends for years. It wasn't merely about Foster covering for his criminal activity. It was about a bond they'd had since grade school. Foster knew his insides, good and bad; he understood his intentions, despite the means. He was family. It wasn't all about the cover up. Big R knew it. Ryker knew it.

Growing impatient with what was about to be the rest of his hard-sell, Ryker yelled, "Sure you do. If you goin' down, we all got to suffer some way. Ain' that how it is? 'Cause you ain' puttin' nobody ahead a yo'self."

"Now, hold on," his temper flickering.

"Naw, you hold on. I got to have time to process. I ain' gon' fall apart right here and jump to yo' rescue 'cause you hit me with Foster's death out a nowhere. I ain' nobody you can use or handle no more. Need? Want? It's all the same," he cut through the sentimental tactics, his words razor sharp against his father's vulnerable expression.

Big R cleared his throat, disappointed. He hoped being partners had changed their relationship for the better, perhaps bonding them where his lack of effort as a father failed. He thought back to when Ryker was expelled from Morningside Middle School in Fort Worth, Texas, years ago, and took off. He was living out of parked cars he broke into.

Even then, at thirteen, Ryker had grown up in so many ways. Big R knew a father-son relationship was something that had come and gone for them. He still cringed inside when he thought of how Ryker reared back, ready to throw a punch when he pulled him from a car, where he'd been sleeping. His dark skin winced at the flash of memory.

Looking in Ryker's eyes now, seeing him hold the .45 leveled at his heart not ten minutes ago, Big R could see the rage that lived there. He knew because if nothing else, Big R had planted that acidic seed deep. The boy had a fire inside, a rage Big R recognized because he held it in his own gut, the root of its source.

Ryker was just a toddler when Big R and his Mama used to get into it. Theresa Baggers James came at Big R with a vengeance that knew few bounds. Big R had to stop her when she unleashed on him, and the truth was, he didn't often remember what transpired when they fought each time, given his alcohol-induced stupor. Upon sobering up, he knew each time had been worse than the last, seeing the evidence all over her.

Unwilling to acknowledge his part, he left Ryker to tend her wounds. He had his own to nurse. The last time left a mark -- not just bruises and eyes swollen nearly shut, but a permanently recorded image of her hundred and ten pound black body covered in yellow, purplish-black hues that could not only be seen on her coffee-colored skin, but in the agony on her face. She was broken in two emotionally and Ryker knew there was no bandage, ice pack or antiseptic that could heal her numerous fractures inside.

At five years old, his mind simply shut down, in defense, but his subconscious brought it to the surface and forced him to feel it in his dreams. There was shock when he saw himself in the flashes of truth and horror, kneeling beside her. As he got older, the images stirred the rage and confused his judgment. He thought, *when I git grown, I'm on beat you. I'm on see how you like it.* Other times, he heard his mama's words in his head and thought, *I needs to take all this to God.*

Ryker becoming his father's partner in dealing drugs happened. Whether it was about beating him or simply surviving in the community he was born to, Big R chose to believe it was Ryker following in his dual livelihood -- hardworking-man-by-day and drug-dealing-criminal-by-night. Pride had him giving Ryker immediate control of his own game and any support he needed -- cash, living expenses, clothes, food, etc. Ryker agreeing to this life meant reconciliation of all that had transpired.

Big R gave him fancy clothes, a nice car, a black Labrador Retriever, cash for partying, his own room in the two-story ranch-style home they lived in on Farm Road 1528, and most important, he gave Ryker respect.

At thirteen, Ryker absorbed it all, breathing in the life, feeling the luxury of having. Ironically, Ryker appreciated the perks, but he used to stand, arms loosely rested on the fence around the barnyard, and watch the animals milling around, envying them their peaceful lives.

One day, he had been at the barn most of the day. His father came up behind him and asked if there was anything he wanted, special, that he didn't already have. Laughing, he said, "Besides a stallion of my own?"

Ryker had no idea Big R would go out and get one for him. It wasn't even a special occasion. He just came home with it a few months later. Ryker named the black horse Star.

As Big R thumbed through pages of Ryker's upbringing, he didn't understand how the gifts he gave turned from fond memories, treasured enough to be logged in a photo album, to shattered pictures he could not make whole. He speculated that being locked up from time to time -- the nature of the life -- had something to do with it, but it wasn't like he didn't tell Ryker the risks. Rubbing hard at his eyes, as if to press the pictures back together, he resolved to try again to make Ryker understand.

"Just hear me out. I need," Big R abhorred asking for help. "I need help with your brother."

"Stepbrother," Ryker corrected. The reminder of his father's infidelity was something he didn't often let him overlook. Big R had never divorced his mother. Neither of them would even discuss it. Ryker never understood it. *If he gon' move on with another woman, why not let Mama do d'same?*

His family was what it was. Though he didn't completely understand his father, cheating on his mother all the time, part of him held hope in the fact they didn't divorce.

Ironically, Doris, the mistress, and his mother were friends, of all things. Ryker could remember showing up at the house, to iron out business details, and his mother and Doris would be drinking together, laughing about Big R's bad habits. The only time they were not congenial was when Big R was in the room.

There was a thread, connecting every person who set foot on the farm. Acceptance often took precedence over grievances, for the sake of the business. Ryker didn't understand it, didn't pretend to.

Still, Big R brought few people into his circle of trust. Ryker was one. Big R knew, if he went down for possession, the only person he trusted to care for Junior was Ryker. This trust was both a compliment and a curse, as Ryker was witness to how dangerous and violent his father could be, from the inside out.

One of the hardest things he had to accept was Junior being given the same name as him; Ryker James Junior. Fortunately for Junior, he didn't experience Big R's dark side. He was spared the terror that crept into Ryker's dreams late at night. *I s'pose Pop got all his anger out on me and Mama. Junior ain' had to see d'at side a him. Junior git all the good and the rest of us live with the real. I ain' never want junior to see d'at side a Pop. Wouldn't wish d'at on nobody.*

"It's 'bout to go down in a few days," Big R's deep voice reminded Ryker of that side, even now. "Maybe even tonight. "The PD in Cooper suspect Foster was coverin' for me. With him gone and me facing charges, I'm lookin' at hard time, if the evidence' there." He sighed and scrubbed at his face.

"Junior' five years old. Ain' nobody I know can cur for him, 'xcept…."

"Me. What you tryin' to say is Junior can't be left with just anybody like Doris or any a yo' boys. I want a hear you say it Pop," he pressed all his buttons at once. "Tell me how you left Mama for a messed up junkie." He let the words hang in the air after spitting them out. "She can't even take cur a herself. Mama even make nice with her 'cause even she worryin' 'bout Junior bein' 'round her; she so crazy in the head. You know why Mama gon' do d'at? 'Cause Mama know Junior mean somethin' to me. Mama got a heart bigger d'an anything in this world. It's too bad she waste it on you. D'at's all kind a wrong Pop. But, what do you cur? As long as yo' *needs* is takin' cur of."

Big R was eerily quiet.

Ryker felt the weight of what he'd just said, gripping his .45 tighter still. He'd stopped being afraid of Big R long ago, but that didn't mean he'd risk the old man getting the drop on him. When Big R finally looked up, his dead eyes bearing down on his defiant son, Ryker returned the look, ten-fold, waiting for the explosion.

It didn't come. His ominous glare softened to understanding, resignation and if Ryker wasn't mistaken, a hint of fear.

"She still messed up," he admitted, reluctantly. He had tried everything he could think of to right her ways, but to no avail. He didn't quit the business, mind you, but he tried to get her help.

"Yeah," Ryker growled. Big R looked up, knowing it was about him hooking up with Doris, not long after he had nearly beaten his Theresa to death, leaving Ryker to deal. He knew Ryker had to tend his mama and his sisters, Tiffany and Neka. *He was how old?* Big R couldn't recall.

Theresa, the thought of her drew the corners of his mouth into the beginning of a smile, even now. *She stuck it out for almost twelve years,* he considered. She endured the fights and the drunken, violent episodes, but when it was all said and done, she left -- the danger, the drugs, and the criminal life. *She left,* he thought in defense of his actions. *Who was I s'pose to turn to? A man has needs.* She wanted to be with her children, free from *big, bad me,* he justified. And, *Doris was there.*

She was one of Big R's best customers. What happened between them was nothing more than a drunken haze that eventually cleared into a mutual connection. When she got pregnant, there was a part of him that hoped it might change them both for the better, offer them a fresh start. She played along, pretending Junior was his chance to raise a boy right, not like Ryker -- better. Big R bought into this. He wanted to be a father in ways he hadn't been before. Had she been sincere about getting clean, it might have worked, but when Big R caught her using, during her pregnancy, their paths changed drastically.

Ryker saw more of a change in his father when Junior was born. He spent time with Junior, talking to him, giving him guidance. Ryker didn't know his father was even capable of this.

Big R didn't change overnight, but he made an effort and Ryker filled in the gaps. Together, they had given the boy more than Ryker could have imagined having in his childhood.

"Junior. That boy lucky I'm around," Ryker reminded him he hadn't raised him alone. "If not for me, let's talk about where he'd be, Pop? You want a go d'ere?" They's a reason he look for me ever'time he woke up and Doris' wadn' in her right mind. You didn't think he lookin' for you, did you? Naw, if he look yo' way, it was 'cause I was somewhere in his line a sight. Just like now. He gon' be my responsibility 'cause you goin' down. You done put yo' greedy self in the slammer 'stead a thinkin' a where he gon' be if you go down."

Junior. Why we have to carry yo' name, Pop? He shook his head, tapping the .45 on the side of his leg. *It ain' never been 'bout us. It about us bein' you.*

"A'ight! That's enough," Big R yelled. "I'm clear I ain' done right by you. I got it," he took a moment to breathe Ryker's rage in and exhale it out. Ryker watched him, checking his stance. He was still a force to be reckoned with, his broad shoulders rounded by his toned muscles, his solid chest pushing out, as if to say he'd reached his limit, but his eyes were full of regret. Ryker hadn't seen this before. He almost felt sorry about coming at him so hard. "Look it, Junior' in her custody but if somethin' happen and I ain' around, I," his voice trailed off. He knew Ryker loved Junior, no matter how angry he was. He was counting on him doing the right thing. "I just don't want a go down and you not know the score."

"Nice choice a words, Pop." Ryker was losing patience with the conversation, what with seeing a new side to his Pop and all.

Besides, he knew the drill. When his family was living in Cooper, about twenty or more of them, it was understood that when someone went down for jail time, the rest of the family took care of any children who were left behind without a guardian. If his father hadn't asked him to be there for Junior, it would have been assumed on some level.

The reason he came in person was because he'd dropped out of sight when Ryker got sentenced to prison in Bradshaw State Jail in 1999. Even though it was common for Ryker's family to stay away, never visiting or communicating during incarceration -- not if they wanted to steer clear of being arrested because most of them had warrants out for *their* arrest -- Ryker still saw it as betrayal, regardless.

Thinking about Junior, Ryker relaxed his grip on the .45 and stood to place it on the window sill, turning his back on his father.

"You sayin' you want me to watch Doris, check she taking cur a him. Doris, who's messed up -- *she* gon' take cur a Junior. Like I gon' let d'at happen."

"Whatever it takes," Big R was relieved his tone was back to the logistics.

"Yeah, I hear you. Junior will be fine."

"Ryker ...." Big R's gaze was almost fatherly.

"Don't!" Ryker yelled. "Don't go d'ere! You all 'bout you," his jaw clenched, his heart hammering against his chest.

Big R let it go. After a long, awkward moment, when he'd finished swallowing Ryker's perception of him, he managed to rise above it and say, "With Foster dead, it's only a matter a time before it all hit. It was a good run a luck, but it's all changin' now. Just have to accept it and move on. I'm on try to git rid a what I can."

Ryker considered the past several years. He and his old man *had* been through a lot. When his mother walked them out of Big R's house twenty-five years ago, Ryker thought he would never see his father again. He didn't want to see him.

Time passed and Ryker needed money to help his mother care for his sisters, so he took whatever work he could find. One thing led to another, and he was stealing cars and selling parts on the street. Later, he learned to pack cocaine, cut it into scores, bag it for sale, and plan the meets. This was all before he partnered with his father. He had spent time with his uncles, Fast Buck and Honey, in Houston, and learned that if this was the only way to care for his mama and sisters, then he needed to know the down and dirty of how it all worked.

Even though he eventually ended up in his father's territory, it didn't mean he forgave him. He was still the same man who went after his mother, the two of them fighting like caged animals. The fine line between love and hate was still there, even if miniscule. Ryker remembered them tearing at each other, no matter how violent, no matter how bloody.

As early as five years old, Ryker wanted to protect her. Searing heat churned the acid in his belly every time they went at it. With every punch, anger stirred, causing rage to bubble up into his throat. He learned to shove it down, go somewhere else, whether it was spending the day at church with his mama's side of the family or simply going somewhere in his mind. He could do that no matter how bad things were. He simply imagined the life he wanted; saw himself living it, away from there. One day, he would escape, he told himself, but until then, he'd ensure survival. Sometimes, when it got to be too much, he and his friends used to ride their bikes to the top of the steepest hill in Cooper, release the breaks and ride the rush all the way down, nothing to break their fall should they lose control.

Even then, he wasn't afraid of death, should it claim him on the way down. The violence and destruction he saw in his everyday world was worse than death; he had witnessed his friends' parents being violently beaten to death, cousins gunned down in front of him, brothers on the street stabbed for pocket change. No. He wasn't afraid of death.

In his father's absence, he kept trying to earn enough money to care for his mom and his sisters. If he could make enough, they could stop living in fear and stop feeling helpless in the face of poverty.

When he couldn't make ends meet, he decided *he* would break the law, so they could get by on the cash he brought home. It didn't take long for him to discover the most lucrative way to make money was selling cocaine and weed. It wasn't about legal or illegal. It was about hard cash. At eight or nine years old, he could run errands, carrying liquor to and from the night club down the street and make a couple of dollars, working for his granddaddy, Daddy D, but that was a drop in a large bucket.

At age ten, he learned how to steal parts off cars and sell them for profit. Pay was limited, and when the car ring became lucrative, the leader cut him out of the profit. Ryker was worked hard and given little until he figured it out. Lesson learned. Check.

Drugs were the logical next step if he wanted to make enough to provide for his family. His father knew the business, but given they were not on good terms, Ryker let his uncles from Bloody Ward help him out. They were more than willing to teach him how to master the game so he could be his own boss.

Sure, he was curious about the effects of cocaine. He used on occasion, but more importantly, he was addicted to something that went much deeper. He thrived on the power he had over being defenseless and poor. He could take care of the ones he loved and be the one to make everything better for himself and his family.

In all the time he was dealing, from thirteen to thirty years old, it wasn't all about the steal or the drugs; more than anything, it was about the money. Greed for the green was a means to breed more of it, but ironically, there was a code, unspoken though it was. Without purpose, there was no justification for taking or dealing. It was about specific purpose.

If he stole a loaf of bread, he took just enough; no more, no less. Same with a score. If he needed to score a thousand, he did just that; the cash often flowed in a continuous motion, from his palm to another in exchange for food or shelter or medical help. He didn't need fancy clothes or nice cars. The scores paid the bills. He'd seen his father go through money like water and he was perpetually thirsty. When his dad bought him all the things he asked for, there was a part of him that felt guilty, knowing his mama was living day-to-day, and his sisters were left wanting.

Cigarettes were his Achilles heel. No matter how hard he tried, he couldn't quit, and he had to have the ones he liked -- Winstons or Salems. Being the man of the house meant providing, not flaunting his money for others to see. With his father still in Cooper, he felt more convicted to take care of his mama.

At thirteen, Ryker was bringing home the money for rent, food, and utilities. The criminal aspect was a small price to pay if it meant he could take care of everyone who depended on him.

He had been smart about it, too. His Uncle Honey, Fast Buck, and Roy coached him on how to handle selling on the streets. They taught him how to carry himself, how to learn people's weaknesses and set them up, steal their stash and walk away. Still, he only took what was necessary, and he became skilled at enforcement when necessary, should he have to engage with anyone who broke the rules. Rules were part of the game and there were consequences for those who broke them.

"If you gon' stay in control a the score, you got to walk the line ain' nobody gon' cross. You untouchable, man. You git what I'm tellin' you?" His uncles embedded this concept deep in his mind. During visits with them, he witnessed the line in action. Bloody Ward didn't get its name because the Red Cross had a place set up in Houston's Fifth Ward. Bloodshed was part of the life.

Ryker suffered a near-death beating once, when he tried to sell his first stash. He was lucky to be alive when it was all over. He saw them, through his swollen, deformed, bloody face. The taste of his own blood had him planning his revenge. When it was done, he could barely feel his heart beating, but managed to focus on their faces. *One by one, I gon' hunt you down. One by one, I gon' take you down*, he vowed.

A few weeks later, he did just that. From then on, he *was* untouchable.

He built relationships with his sources, established his reputation on the streets of Fort Worth, and proved he was a force with which to be reckoned.

Power was imminent in his future. Even so, not a day went by he didn't remember the night he took back his power from the boys who beat him so badly. He didn't enjoy giving it back ten-fold. Every blow punched at his own heart, broke his soul into pieces, killing the child God intended him to be. Honey told him it was necessary if he wanted to survive in their world. Angry he had already walked the line that forced his hand, he did not see it as a good thing, even if it meant saving his life and securing a way to bring money home for his family.

I felt like I's changin' into somethin' I couldn' never come back from, Ryker later said. *I had to stop it, somehow.*

One day, as he sat in the boys' locker room at Morningside Middle School, he came close to crossing a line he could not come back from when two brothers tried to get him involved in bullying a kid at school. Irvin Ross. He was a smart kid, but awkward, to say the least. Ox and Joe T. Black tried to provoke Ryker into joining their attack on this defenseless boy. As they slammed his head in the locker and flushed his head in the toilet, Ryker tried to stay calm. Flashes of his mother being slung across the room, hitting the wall and falling to the floor kept invading his thoughts, his focus.

He managed to find his voice, telling them to back off, but they kept on. Anger turned to heat, heat to sparks, sparks to fire, fire to rage and boom! Images flooded his head -- his sisters cowering under a hole-pocked blanket, his mother screaming, his father pounding -- and he was up and covered the twenty feet of ground in a few steps. Joe T. turned to see the flames in Ryker's dark eyes and smiled, thinking it was because he planned to join their tirade on this boy.

Instead, Ryker honed his temper, shoved down hard, and calmly took out his ballpoint pen from his jean pocket and clicked it out ... and in ... and out ... and in ... and, then out. Eyes vacant but for rage, he swung right and stabbed Joe T. in the neck, grabbed the boy's head out of the toilet and walked him out of the locker room. *No one need to be takin' from people too weak to fight for theyself,* he reasoned.

Ryker was expelled that day, but taking care of that boy was worth it to him.

"You just like your father, Lil' Man. What was you thinkin', son?" his mother screamed when he walked into the house. "You think it make you strong to hurt somebody like that? Do you? Let me tell you somethin'. They's strength in control. Control."

"Mama, please. They was a boy sufferin' and Joe T and Ox was hurtin' him bad. I had to do somethin'. I couldn't watch you get beat, not one mo' time. Not goin' there Mama, ever again." His voice, the one and only time she ever heard it so loud, was just like Big R's.

Silence filled the room. *He said he couldn't watch me get beat. He was seein' me when he stepped in front a J.T. Dear Lord,* Theresa thought. *This be on me.* Flashes of that night went through her mind. She saw his blurry face as she lay there, trying to make her eye blink so he would know she was alive. Her pulse had been weak and she could not answer him when he came to clean her up, like he had the times before. His eyes were filled with tears and rage. He was not a crier, *no, not my little man,* but this day, he let them spill over. She knew then she had to get them out of Big R's house, out of his grip. Little R's tears dripped into her blood, sending red rivers running. If she hadn't left, they might not have escaped. She looked hard at him now, his lips quivering, despite his effort to stop them. She saw a little boy's body of thirteen years, trying to contain a grown man's rage. The tears he let fall for the second time in his young life were evidence of the retribution that would one day come, she feared.

"Ain' no way I can argue with that, Lil' Man. Yo' daddy and I ain' been the best example for you. We damn near kill each other the night I decided to leave for good. I know you seen it, felt it. What have we done? Oh, dear Lord, what have we done? Lil' Man. Look at me. What have we done?" her tears streamed down her face when he couldn't look at her.

"Mama," he agonized, bowing his head further but trying to keep his voice calm, to soothe her somehow. He reached for her.

Pulling away fast, she said, "Lil Man, I don't know how to deal with you no more. I see you gots d'face of a boy I know God put here for me to love, but what comin' out a him ain' nothin' or nobody I want a know. How I s'pose to deal with you?"

"You don't," the words shot out. "I gon' deal with myself. I ain' proud a the way I handle Joe T., but, I don't know. I couldn't stop it. I seen your head slammin' 'gainst the wall when Joe T. had that boy in d'locker. I seen Pop grabbin' you 'round the throat and slingin' you 'gainst the wall. I was five years old in my mind, but my body grown and I had a strength I could use, Mama. At five, I couldn't stop it, but I could today and I done stopped it." His voice was slightly raised and he caught himself, cleared his throat and spoke as calm as he could. "I ain' sorry, but I know I ain' nobody you want a look at right now so," his voice dropped as he looked away. "I gon' go."

"What? Where you goin'?" her voice suddenly sending panic through her faster than she could stand. "Please. I didn't say I want you to go." She was crying hard, her chest heaving, her nose running. "You got to listen. Please," she hiccupped.

Ryker walked to his bedroom. He packed everything he thought he needed. When he came back to the kitchen where she had collapsed to the floor, crying, he said, "Maybe I am just like Pop. I don't know, but, if I am, I ain' gon' stay here with you. You done had a hard 'nough time with him."

He was gone before she could respond.

"Big R!" she cried into the phone when she heard his voice.

"Theresa? You a'ight?"

"No. It's Little R. He done stabbed some kid at school and he take it upon hisself to leave. He done run away and it's all yo' doin'. You done ruin d'at boy. No, *we* done ruin him. Now he gone and no tellin' what gon' happen to him. You have to find him."

"Calm down, Resa. I'm on find him. Just. Stop, now," he whispered, trying to soothe her. After all this time, he couldn't stand to hear her cry. It was one thing when she was screaming, but he could never stand her crying.

As he hung up the phone, her sobs tore at his heart. He grabbed his keys and turned them over in his hand. He had just walked in the door, fresh out of prison. Six years and Jenkins got him out on parole, free again.

What the hell's goin' on with Little R? He thought. He sat down on his brown leather recliner to pull on his black Lucchese, horn-back-caiman-tailed-cowboy boots. He buttoned his black, long-sleeved, Panhandle snap shirt and tucked it into his starched black jeans, finishing his look with his signature belt buckle, initials RJS.

Climbing into his black Ford F-150 from the flagship series in 1980, he gunned the V-8 engine and headed down the long, winding driveway toward Farm Road 1528. He could make it to his father's house, on East Powell in Fort Worth in about 75 minutes. With any luck, he might find Ryker at one of his hangouts in between Cooper and Fort Worth. He and his cousins sometimes frequented the Church's Chicken parking lot about half way between. He'd start there.

He ran into a few of his friends, but they hadn't seen him. So he got something to go and drove on into Fort Worth. The drive seemed to take forever. When he finally pulled onto South Sylvania, near the Red Cross building, he saw one of Ryker's friends looking into the window of a Lincoln Town Car parked alongside the curb.

Wiley's daddy drove a car like this, he remembered. *Was Wiley drivin' it now or was he tryin' to take it out without his pop knowin'?* He saw the boy about to knock on the window, which seemed strange if it was his, so he stopped, rolling his window down.

"Son, what're you doin'?" Big R had the boy jumping, nearly out of his skin with his deep, gravelly voice. Wiley looked up and realized it was Ryker Senior and immediately assumed an I-ain'-doin'-nothin' position.

"Don't move," he said, pulling over to the curb. As he stepped out of the truck, Wiley's eyes grew wide when he saw his ride, his clothes and Stetson hat, not to mention the boots. *Shit, man, where you comin' from?*

Big R walked past him and looked into the window of the Lincoln. Ryker was fast asleep in the backseat, not three blocks from his mother's home, across the street from Daddy D, otherwise known as Big R's father.

He forcefully pounded on the window next to Ryker's head. When Ryker didn't respond, he checked to see if the door was locked. In one motion, he swung open the door, grabbed Ryker by the back of his shirt and pulled him from the car. Ryker startled, broke free and reared back to pummel the intruder who had him by the collar.

It was in that moment that Big R saw his son was no longer a boy; his arms were strong and toned and he had grown, filled out. Looking at the fist Ryker was about to throw, Big R stepped back and held up his hands in surrender.

"What the fuck, Pop?" he spouted off, when he saw it was Big R.

Big R yelled, "Watch yo' mouth, boy."

"I ain' no boy, or ain' you heard?" Ryker shot back. "I'll talk however I damn well want. What the hell you doin' here?" he leaned down, squinting at the clock on the dash inside the town car. "It's 2 a.m."

"You first. What're you doin', sleepin' in this car?"

Ryker rested his hands on his hips, and raised his eyebrows.

"Your mama call me," he gave in. "She say you ran off."

"So," he countered. "You s'pose to be in prison."

"I'm out on parole," his voice got deeper.

Ryker eyed his father's appearance. He had just been released from prison and he was walking around in his gangster clothes, sporting his six-hundred-dollar cowboy boots and his custom-made Stetson. *How the hell you look like that straight from prison?*

He turned and started walking away; a little pissed his old man got the drop on him.

"Little R," Big R growled after him. When Ryker turned and shrugged his shoulders, Big R gestured to the car, "You checkin' out?" he looked over Ryker's shoulders, eyeing the other cars on the block. "You gon' make me guess the next car you plan on breakin' and enterin' or should I say, breakin' and sleepin'?"

"Why you cur, old man?"

Ignoring his attitude, he said, "You could come stay with me."

Ryker cocked a brow. "And, why you think I gon' do d'at? I ain' no boy you can order 'round no more. I ain' gon' let nobody run me, you feel me?"

"Git in the truck," he dismissed him.

"Oh, hell no," Ryker said, rolling his shoulders back, getting ready to defend himself. He had been too little the times he and his father had squared off before, but he'd grown to six feet now and he had some muscle on him. Big R looked to be a little on the heavy side and that made him slow. "What 'choo think? I gon' come live under yo' roof and obey yo' rules? Not happenin'. Not happenin'."

"A'ight then," Big R said and turned to walk back to the truck. Seeing his ride, Ryker started to follow and then turned from him and walked the opposite direction.

"Ryker," his father sighed heavily. "I'm just tryin' to help. I ain' gon' run you, boy. You your own man now."

Hearing those words, Ryker stopped mid-stride. *Who the hell is this man and what's he done with my Pop?* He wondered. When he turned to see his father, leaning on the driver's side door of his F-150, he shook his head, not knowing what to think.

"I got some Church's Chicken in the truck. You hungry?" Big R tried to lessen the seriousness of the mood.

Ryker lifted his head, "I could eat."

"C'mon, then. I'll take you to the house. You can decide your next move. The least I can do is let your mama know you safe for tonight, a'ight?"

A quick nod from Ryker answered his question.

From that day forward, they were partners in the drug-selling business. Ryker moved back to the farm in Cooper and as he stood before him now, in the apartment he'd just found through Inmate Services in Fort Worth, he knew his father wasn't just asking for help with Junior.

Ryker stared at him, trying to feel something for the old man, but he came up empty. Prison was part of the game. No one was exempt and though Ryker had escaped many charges in the twenty-something years he scored drugs, no one eased *his* plight. It was Big R who said, "When you done wrong, admit it, accept the consequences, and blame nobody but yourself. Then, move on."

Those gems were coming around to bite his old man in the ass and Ryker was fine with that. Standing there expecting Ryker to feel something was futile on his part.

Not this time, Ryker thought. *I's done.*

Chapter 2

*"The hook catches in my jaw. The straight end of
the shiny metal curves without warning, down and up
and before I can escape, the jagged point at the end of
the curve is violently yanked, pulling me this way and
that."*

Jack Lawrence – 2004

No one's going to believe this, he thought.

Sitting on the dock, about twenty feet from his Uncle
Pete's lake house, Jack was tossing a handful of pebbles into
Lake Worth, one by one, watching the water ripple. At
seventy years old, he thought he was ready to cash in, retire
and enjoy his golden years with his wife, Sarah. Why did he
have to go to church that Sunday and complicate things?

It had been a wonderful service at St. Timothy's Episcopal
that morning. He'd enjoyed the sermon and was in the
middle of the Prayers of the People when he felt it. It's hard
to put what happened into words, but suffice to say, he either
really heard someone say "help this man" or somehow the
notion took shape in his thoughts.

It didn't surprise Jack that he heard it or thought it, strange
as it sounds, because he'd been praying for the person for a
long time. His childhood had been difficult and he certainly
dreamt of having a healthy, happy life with a woman he could
love and a family to follow, but he couldn't have imagined
God blessing him the way he had. Then, when his first wife
passed away, he couldn't imagine filling the hole she'd left in
his heart, but once again, God had come through and he met
Sarah.

Twice God delivered and Jack was incredibly blessed, but as grateful as Jack was, it didn't seem enough to merely be thankful. He'd been praying God would show him someone who needed him, someone he could bless the way he'd been blessed.

Sunday morning, God answered him and Jack hadn't been able to think of anything else. *Did I imagine it?* He kept thinking. *Who is the man I'm supposed to help?* If he was indeed supposed to help someone.

Jack craned his neck around, hearing the footsteps coming up from behind.

"Hey, Jack," his Uncle Pete called out, as he walked onto the dock. "I didn't know you were down here. Anything biting?" Realizing Jack didn't have any gear, not even a cane pole, he teased, "Live bait's good, but fish tend to look for crickets or worms, not naked toes."

"Yeah." Jack nodded, watching the old man slowly make his way out to where he was sitting. "A pole helps too, maybe a hook. I just took a drive and ended up here. Been sittin' here thinkin' how lucky I am to have had such a good life."

"Planning on checking out?"

Jack blew out a breath and chuckled. "Not yet. I've got too much still to do."

"Anything you want to talk about?" Uncle Pete squatted down to sit with Jack. It was hard to believe he was a couple of decades older and still in good shape, agile. "You've got that look."

"Sometimes I wonder what would have happened if I hadn't come to live with you, all those years ago. Where I would be if it hadn't been for you and the guys," Jack said. Pete laughed.

"Well, I can answer that one. We'd have caught more fish. I'm still jealous of that twenty-seven pounder you caught that time," he nudged Jack's right shoulder. "No, I know what you mean. And, I think we all wonder that same thing from time to time."

"I had a lot of help, Uncle Pete."

"Yeah, well. So did I," Pete said.

"What?"

"Sure did. I think we all have to have someone or several someones to help us through. Sometimes parents do their best and…."

"Sometimes they do their worst," Jack finished.

"You can't truly know one unless you've experienced the other. What matters is you aspire to do better *because* you know better; not let mistakes give you permission to make more. If it's one thing I hope, it's that I leave this world a better place when I go."

"Did you ever feel like you should have done more with what was given to you?"

"Sure I did. I felt abundantly blessed and not so sure I deserved it."

Jack nodded, so grateful for the alignment of thought. He and his uncle always had that connection. When Jack used to come out for visits as a young boy, Uncle Pete seemed to be on his frequency within a few words of conversation. It was as if he could hone in on Jack's concerns and immediately know what to say to ease his pain.

"What did you do about it?"

"Paid it forward," he said, smiling and clapping Jack on the back.

Father Rayford put down his pencil and leaned in as Jack spoke.

"That's when I knew," Jack concluded. "I've been praying for this person since, well, since Sarah and I got married."

"Do you know who you're supposed to help?" Father Rayford asked, now intrigued by his story.

"No, but I aim to figure it out," he said. "We need to pray about this, Father. Then, I guess I have to find a way to meet him." Jack's confidence was evident in his tone.

Father Rayford sat back in his chair, moved by Jack's determination to jump in, virtually blind.

"You know, sometimes you don't have to go far to find someone who needs you. Often, they're kneeling right beside you. We have a group of people here at St. Timothy's who are trained to listen and encourage those who are going through difficult times or have, in some instances, lost a loved one.   The group is called the Stephen's Ministry.   Our director, Dr. Rick Stanley, assigns ministers to those who request it on the forms we keep in the pews; I'm sure you've seen them.

"This might be a good place for you to start.   Would you like to come for training here at St. Timothy's?   I think the first meeting is on the first Tuesday of every month, and training is usually on Saturdays."

"Sign me up," Jack grinned. "I'm ready."

"All right then. That's great. I'll give Rick a call."

Jack was thrilled.   He began training immediately and found it was quite similar to some of the prison ministry he had already been doing.   He began visiting prisoners a few years back, when he first met Sarah.   One of her sons was doing time in prison and Jack offered to go with Sarah to visit him a couple of times a month.

Until he walked into the facility, he had no idea what to expect.   Following the guard to the visiting area was disconcerting, to say the least.   The inmates yelled out obscenities and he couldn't help but think what it must be like for Sarah each time.   When he saw Jeb, he hadn't expected him to be resigned to serving his time.   There was no talk of getting out on parole or a lighter sentence, due to good behavior.   He seemed without hope like many of the guys inside.

After several visits, he got used to the vulgarity of the other prisoners, the demeanor of the guards and the despair. Jack focused on bringing hope with him.   Others heard about his visits and soon Jeb asked if Jack would be willing to meet with some of the guys on his cellblock.   Hence, Jack's prison ministry began.

Before he knew it, the group became an island amidst the chaos, just steps outside the room.   They met to talk about scripture and God's love for them.   Though Jack couldn't bring his Bible into the prison, he memorized passages he thought might lift their spirits.   At times, he wasn't sure if he was the one bringing the ministry or they were.   The insights some of them shared after hearing scripture often enlightened

Jack, bringing understanding to some of the darkness he'd thought was better buried in his own life. He had no idea how much he had in common with some of these guys. *I wonder if I might have taken a similar path and ended up here. What if I hadn't had Uncle Pete and the guys?*

Talks with Sarah helped. He felt instantly comfortable sharing about his difficult upbringing. Before, he'd thought it was somehow his fault. When Sarah mentioned she felt responsible for Jeb's choices, he'd heard himself say, "Shug, no one can make choices for us. There's always a choice," and the words rang true for him, as if they hadn't been said before that moment.

Things began to get more serious between him and Sarah and they weren't sure what to do about their place of worship. Sarah was a Methodist; they actually met at a bible study one morning, when several of Jack's friends talked him into coming. Raised in the Catholic Church, Jack had to adjust a little; he was used to the liturgy, communion every week and confession.

Sarah's brother Charles Brooks and his wife Elizabeth kept asking them to visit their church nearly every time they saw them, which was pretty often.

"It would be a wonderful compromise," Charles said. "You're going to fall in love with St. Timothy's, where we go. We've been there for several years and it just keeps getting better and better." With the constant encouragement, Sarah and Jack finally agreed to visit.

Knowing Charles and Elizabeth made it easy for Jack and Sarah to feel comfortable among the other parishioners. The liturgy was very similar to a Catholic service and likewise, not too far from that of the Methodist.

There were so many things that felt right about joining St. Timothy's, but what made it really special was the common bond the foursome shared; Sarah lost her first husband to a stroke, Jack lost his first wife to cancer, Elizabeth lost her first husband to heart problems and Charles lost his first wife to a brain aneurism. They'd enjoyed thirty plus years with their spouses and felt incredibly blessed to have found love again.

Jack was sixty-seven when he lost Anna to cancer. He was extremely close with her parents, Mama and Daddy Conner, as well. Sunday dinners, church gatherings, birthdays and anniversaries and the like, made their marriage and extended family as close as they could be. They even bought a farm together and ran it for twenty-something years.

Finding Anna had been life-changing for Jack. He had grown up with an alcoholic stepfather, who had violent, abusive tendencies and his mother didn't have the courage to leave until much of the damage was done. Jack felt God literally blessed him with the family he'd been praying for his entire childhood, when God brought Mama and Daddy Connor into his life; alongside Anna.

Aside from his Uncle Pete and his Aunt Rachel, Mama and Daddy Connor were the best parental figures he'd known; he cherished them.

Then one day, unexpectedly, Daddy Connor had a heart attack and died within a few days. Mama Connor was devastated, as were Jack and Anna.

Unfortunately, when he passed, Mama Connor wasn't far behind. Losing him had been harder on her than anyone knew. When Anna and Sarah would come by to check on her, the expression on her face was pure agony; it seemed as if she was in a perpetual state of supplication, that God would take her too. And, He did.

Incredibly, Anna and Jack had come from the doctor's office, where they'd learned Anna had cancer, when they discovered her mother had passed in her sleep. Within six months of her parents' deaths, cancer claimed Anna. Jack was overcome with indescribable loss and despair. If it hadn't been for his children, he might have prayed that God take him too.

At age sixty-seven, he figured there wasn't much opportunity to find love again so he dedicated his time and energy to being a good father to their four children: Janna, Amy, Kelly and Mark.

Still, the loneliness crept up late at night and in the early morning hours. He and Anna used to have coffee together and read the paper. When she was gone, he missed her so much he would often talk to her, sometimes asking her if she thought he should try to find someone else to love. He tried to imagine what she would have said, but it was hard to know. He began to pray about it and one morning in early spring, as he sat at the kitchen table, drinking his usual cup of coffee with her, in his mind, he felt it; the answer came.

Meeting Sarah soon after, he felt as if Anna gave him her blessing. Their families seemed to join together effortlessly. Sure, there were adjustments, as any family might have, but for the most part, the families were thrilled. Everyone took time to get to know each other, spending special occasions together and meeting for family dinners every other week.

When Jack learned Jeb had been incarcerated, he wondered if Jeb was the man he was supposed to help. Following his heart, he visited Jeb as often as he could and in time, he'd started a small prison ministry among some of the inmates; he felt incredibly blessed to serve them and God in this way.

Then one day he met with Jeb and he could tell he had something on his mind. After a few minutes he decided to ask him what was going on.

"Jesus told Peter he should look at his own life and decide how many times to forgive," Jeb blurted out. "When Peter asked if seven times was enough, Jesus told him *seventy times seven*. I can't even count how many times I've done wrong. I know I passed four hundred and ninety a long time ago and if I ever get out of here, I don't know that I could change," he paused and Jack could tell there was more. "I don't want to hurt anyone, Jack. I think maybe I'm where I need to be."

Jack took a moment to process. When he managed to speak, he was trying to think how he could refute Jeb's judgment on himself. He swallowed hard and made an attempt.

"Jesus called us to forgive our enemies and those who trespass against us. That's true, son," Jack tried to order his thoughts. Jeb seemed so resigned. *How can I change his mind?* He thought. Narrowing his eyes, he adjusted his glasses and pushed them back on his nose, buying some time. *Nothing was coming.* He drew in a deep breath and blew it out. And, there it was; he was suddenly reminded of something he'd heard years ago.

"You know, back when I was still at Lockheed, one of the guys at lunch said something interesting about that passage. We were having lunch together and I don't know how we got on the subject, but he said that Jesus didn't just pull those numbers out of thin air, seventy times seven. Seventy was the number of tribes that existed in the world at that time and seven was the number of days it took to create the heavens and the earth," Jack explained.

Jeb considered. After about thirty seconds went by, he looked up at Jack, "I don't follow."

"Well, some say Jesus was saying we should forgive *all* the people in the world *all* the time," Jack clarified.

"Forgive all the people, all the time," Jeb repeated. "Hmm. Maybe I got a shot then."

"I'd say so," Jack smiled; hope blooming in his heart as he saw evidence of it in Jeb's eyes.

Jack and Sarah talked about the visit on the way home. She smiled when Jack told her what he'd said. "Where'd that come from? I mean, who told you about the seventy tribes and the time it took to create the world -- the seven days? That's not in any of our Bibles, is it?"

"Nope," Jack said. "But the Messianic Jew who told me that saved me -- because it *was* in his bible." A smile pulled at the corners of Sarah's mouth. She could tell Jack was holding on to the hope that he'd gotten through to Jeb. In good conscience, she could not entertain the notion.

"I don't know," Sarah said, her lips thinning, her brows knitting. Jack braced himself, sensing what she was about to say. "I just don't know if he has it in him to change. Some people don't, you know. Oh, how it pains me to say that," her voice was almost a whisper.

I can't believe that. I won't, Jack thought, but managed a half smile and reached over to pat Sarah's arm, squeezing gently before he released her. Jack spent the rest of the drive trying to think how to bring Jeb around. When he and Sarah got to the house, it had been a six-hour drive, round-trip. He'd had a lot of time to think. He often prayed while he drove. It seemed an easy way to talk to God. This time, he was asking for direction.

When he put the car in park and turned to get out, a young man was standing on the front porch, his hands in his jean pockets. *Well, what do you know? Luke.*

Luke had not been to see Jeb since he was taken to prison. It wasn't that he didn't love his brother. If anything, he loved him so much he didn't think he could stand to see him locked up. At the same time, he couldn't really grasp who his brother had become. It was a terrible dilemma. Jack wondered if Luke had given any thought to their last conversation or argument, as it were. He winced at the last words he'd said. "The fact that you won't go see him doesn't hurt Jeb; it hurts you, don't you see? He understands. He doesn't expect you to accept what he did or forgive him. Don't you see? Forgiveness is just as much for you as it is for him."

Jack knew holding on to anger, resentment and regret didn't end well. He had hoped to save Luke the pain of finding out what he had; *it eats you up inside.* As he stepped out of the car, he couldn't help but hope he'd gotten through to him.

He eyed Luke as he walked up to the front porch. *If I could just convince Luke to go see him; offer him support. It'd be the healing they both need.* He could only hope.

◆

The day they went, it was about seventy-something degrees, a beautiful day for making the trip. Luke was wearing some khaki shorts and a nice, short-sleeved shirt. He looked good. He told Jack he'd been praying for Jeb since the day he was sentenced. Going to see him was a much bigger step. He couldn't stand the thought of Jeb thinking he didn't love him; that he couldn't forgive him, but at the same time, he couldn't reconcile how Jeb could commit the crime that put him there.

When Jack pulled into the driveway to pick him up, Luke suddenly felt his insides churn at the thought of seeing Jeb behind bars.

He steeled himself to the idea on the drive down, praying himself through what he was about to experience. By the time they arrived, he was starting to feel better, ready. He and Jack walked toward the entrance to the visitors' area, and with each step, Luke felt stronger. Just as they were about to walk through the gate, the guard standing outside the door stopped Luke.

"Sir, you cannot go past this point," he said, and he gestured for Luke to step back.

Jack, having already walked through, turned and raised his hands in confusion. "Sir, we're here to see my stepson. This is his brother, Luke. We have a letter that says we can visit today. Should we get it out of the car for you?"

"That won't be necessary," the guard waved Jack away. "This gentleman can't go in because he's not properly dressed." He gestured to Luke's shorts. "He has to have pants or jeans on."

"But," Jack blew out a breath. "We've driven three hours to get here, and there's no place within a hundred miles of here to get pants or jeans," his concern had evolved to irritation because no one said as much when he confirmed they were coming.

"I'm sorry, sir. I don't make the rules."

Dumbfounded, Jack and Luke were shaking their heads as they walked back to the car. When they were almost to the navy, four-door sedan Jack had driven to the prison, they heard someone say, "Excuse me. Excuse me. Sir?"

Jack and Luke turned and didn't see anyone. For a moment, Jack was worried it was only in his head, but Luke had turned to see where the voice was coming from as well. They shrugged, as if to say *nobody there,* and kept walking.

"Fellas, over here." This time they looked harder. A small, wrinkled hand waved to them at a distance. As they walked over, they came face to face with a tiny, shrunken old man. He stood by an old pick-up truck that looked to be older than him. "What size are you?" he asked Luke.

"What?" Luke didn't really know what this little old man was about and he turned to Jack for explanation.

"What size trousers are you, son?" he pressed, nodding and giving Luke a wink. Luke looked at Jack and saw a smile spreading across his face like a Cheshire cat. Jack nodded.

"32 by 34," Luke said, still looking from Jack to this old man, and back.

"All right," and he pulled a bag from the bed of his truck. "These should work, son. Go ahead, try them on." Luke looked at Jack and he nodded.

"Right here in the parking lot?"

"It's all right," the old man waved away his hesitation. "Go ahead and pull them on over your shorts. No need to moon anybody. I gave you a 33 by 34 so it should be okay."

Luke did as the old man said, all the while thinking, *who is this guy*? Pulling them on over his shorts, they fit just right. He turned to the man and said, "How did you ...." He stopped and looked at Jack, wondering if it was a stupid question.

"I'm here every week for visitation, young man. I see folks, like you, from time to time, who come to see someone they care about and they don't know they need pants in order to go in. So, I decided a year or so ago, that I would bring some extra pairs every time I come. No reason someone should be turned away because of the way they're dressed, right? Anyhow, I'm glad I could help you out today. Giving's a blessing to the giver too, you know? God bless." He turned to get into his truck.

"Wait just a minute, sir," Jack said. "Can we pay you for these?"

"Nope. You're doing your part." He pointed toward the prison.

"Wait a minute. You said you come every week and visit. Is there someone we could pray for or anything? You've been so kind."

As the old man smiled, Jack felt a gentle breeze wash over him, awakening his senses as he breathed it in. He was grateful, as the temperature had risen to about eighty degrees.

"You know, I don't have any relatives or friends in prison. Well, I suppose I have a few friends now, but I started coming here a few years ago when I felt like God was calling me to," he paused, smiling. "I can't explain it. Anyhow, I've seen a lot of people turned away just like you were today, and you'd be surprised at how few people make the effort to visit some of these prisoners. The men and women inside are the ones who lose big when people are turned away. They need all the visitors they can receive."

He put a hand on the partially rusted bed of his truck, nodded quickly as if acknowledging what people think of prisoners. "I know they were put in jail for a reason. Many of them have done unspeakable things, but forgiveness should come easier than it does." He stopped again and then looked Jack and Luke squarely in the eyes. "Seventy times seven -- you know that passage?"

Unable to speak for a moment, Jack stood there. When the silence hung in the air uncomfortably, the old man said, "I don't mean to preach at you. God bless." He climbed into his truck.

Before Jack could answer, Luke yelled, "No. God bless you, sir."

Jack and Luke visited Jeb that day. His face lit up when Luke walked into the visitors' room. He knew what it meant for him to take such an extraordinary step, given all that had transpired.

Though Jack knew their visit was about Jeb seeing Luke, he couldn't help but wonder about the old man they saw. He felt there was a reason, but he couldn't think what it could be. Maybe he was making more out of it than there was.

God called that old man to bring pants to people, of all things. Strange request, Jack thought, *but the old guy did it.* The joy in the old man's eyes, when he spoke of the people he had been able to help, was contagious, and Jack knew one thing. He wanted that feeling.

◆

As he knelt down for the Prayers of the People, Form VI on the following Sunday morning at St. Timothy's, he either heard the words or thought them, again. *Help this man. Help me.* The congregation responded to the liturgy, as did he, but he found himself looking around to see if someone might have said the words out loud.

When he saw everyone's head bowed, he turned back to the Book of Common Prayer, looking for the response he was supposed to be reading. The italicized words for the layperson response in his book were not the same as Sarah's, when he happened to glance at hers. He closed his book and saw he had picked up the wrong Book of Common Prayer. 1929. Isn't that a kick in the teeth? *I was born three years later in 1931*, he thought.

He quickly switched to the newer 1979 edition used at St. Timothy's for 10:30 Mass. Father Rayford read, "For those who are in danger, sorrow or any kind of trouble."

"For those who minister to the sick, the friendless and the needy," the congregation responded.

"For the special needs and concerns of this congregation...."

As they sat in silence, waiting for parishioners to add their petitions, Jack kept thinking about the words he'd heard. *Help this man. Help me.*

"Let us confess our sins against God and our neighbor," Father Rayford's voice echoed throughout the church.

Closing his eyes again, Jack thought of the little old man and the trousers. He thought about the blessings he had been given over the course of his life. This burning desire to give was festering, igniting somewhere deeper inside him. He thought of his Uncle Pete, Doc Sevrenson, Bob Leonard and Craig Jacobs.

His silent prayers turned to flashes of memories, rushing through his mind like a fierce undercurrent, pulling him back to his painful childhood, then forward into the present.

He thought about the elderly man talking about seventy times seven and the dialogue between Jeb and Luke when Luke tried to convince Jeb that life outside the prison walls was worth fighting for. Then his thoughts reached into the present, where he knew, without a doubt, he was supposed to help this man. At last, he was thinking of Uncle Pete's words "I paid it forward." *Lord, I just don't understand what it is I'm supposed to do here.*

Seventy years used to mean a man had lived a full life and was blessed to make it for a few more years, but today, longevity was taking people well into their late 90s, even early hundreds, barring those who fell prey to illness or accident.

Jack was strong as an ox, and healthy. He couldn't help but think there was a reason, especially now.

Seventy times seven. Jack kept turning the words over in his mind. *The old man. Jeb brought it up too. It can't be coincidence.* He opened the Bible in the pew and turned to the book of Matthew. Scanning the passages, he found where Peter asked Jesus how many times he should forgive his brother. "Seven times?" And Jesus said, "No, my son, seventy times seven." His mind wandered to what his friend at Lockheed said about forgiving all people, all the time.

I suppose I forgave my stepfather every day, as a child. I forgave him for beating me and my sisters, my mother. I forgave my mother because she wouldn't leave him. I tried to wake up every day, forgiving what had transpired the day before. I think I hoped he might realize what he'd become and change. I wanted a real father; someone I could love, count on, look up to; someone my friends thought was great. All it got me was more welts and more bruises. I wanted to wipe out the bad, start fresh.

Maybe I was confusing forgiving with forgetting.

Mother used to send us to church, two blocks down the street, on Sunday mornings to attend Sunday school and morning mass. The sermons and lessons often encouraged forgiveness; lightening your burden, letting go. It was a tough concept for a ten year old.

I was working by that time, delivering fruits and vegetables door-to-door, while my stepfather drank all day long. His behavior was so unpredictable. I didn't know if he was going to unleash on us or simply pass out. Beatings often won out.

Forgiving him meant never looking in the mirror, where the evidence shone on my face or my back, my chest; anywhere his belt could pop against me, not mention the scars he left on the inside — shame, fear, low self-esteem, weakness.

If not for Uncle Pete — I don't know.

He took me to the lake house as often as he could when things got bad. He taught me how to bait a hook with live bait, to catch my first ten-pound trout. Good gracious, I didn't even know what live bait was. He was always teaching me something.

That twenty-dollar-bill was something else. He stuck that thing under my arm, right in my pit, and told me to cast my line out as far as I could without dropping the twenty. He said if I could do it, he'd give it to me. That was like him giving me five hundred dollars at the time. It was 1942.

I did it, though. I worked at it until I could cast the line over thirty feet. I left the lake house with the twenty and an entry form for the next casting tournament.

Doc Sevrenson. I can't remember a time when he wasn't fishing with us. I used to go out on the lake with him and Uncle Pete on weekends when I was there. After I won my first casting tournament, they ribbed me a lot.

Possum Kingdom Lake was the best. Whole weekends of nothing but good fishing, good company and if we were lucky, a mess of good eating.

Possom Kingdom, he thought of the first time he learned of it. *I'd heard the guys talk about it and I wanted to go so bad. I was standing there beside Uncle Pete, wishing with all my might they'd asked me. They knew it, too. Doc said, "You know, Pete, Tony can't make it this weekend. Do you know anybody who can cast as well as he does?" Then, he winked at me. Uncle Pete cut his eyes toward me and I felt the hairs on the back of my neck stand up. He was thinking it; I could feel it, but the joker looked at Doc, gave a half-smile.*

"No, Doc. I can't say I know anybody who can cast more than twenty feet."

"That's too bad. We could sure use somebody that good." I was chewing the heck out of my bottom lip, trying not to yell out, "What about me? I can do it."

"I guess we'll have to ask some fellas at the Angler Club tomorrow."

That was it. They hit the button and the words flew out of my mouth like a rocket launched to the moon. "What about me? I, I can do it."

Silence. Nobody said a word. They looked at each other and then back at me, shaking their heads and stroking their chins. I was about to come out of my skin, waiting. Uncle Pete says, "I don't know, Jack."

And, Doc Sevrenson looked down at the ground. I remember this like it was yesterday. Doc says, "Well, if you're gon' a go, then you'll have to carry your weight, young man." Young man. I was eleven years old and he called me young man.

Young man. Mr. Bob called me that too. He was the one who hired me to wash dishes when I was almost thirteen. He heard about how I painted a fence for Craig Jacobs; I called him Mr. Craig. On his word, Mr. Bob hired me. That was the best and worst year of my life. Best because I got to move in with Uncle Pete; worst because it took me suffering a near-fatal beating from my stepfather to warrant the move.

Moving to Uncle Pete's put me within bike-riding distance of work and home. Uncle Pete suggested I ride my bike to work, catch the bus from there to school and the security guards at Leonard's Department Store would keep an eye on my bike in between times.

Mr. Craig was in and out of Leonard's all the time. When he saw how well I was doing, he and Mr. Leonard told me they wanted me in the sporting goods department. I sold more fishing rods and reels than anybody. I loved fishing. That's all there was to it.

Yeah, life before Uncle Pete and the guys was bleak; it still sends shudders through me, even now. Some days, most days, I stood on the area rug in the living room, between that monster and my sister, while he watched the evening news, threatening to beat us if we made a sound.

At six or seven, I thought I could protect everyone. I slept in front of my Mama's door frame at night, waiting for the bastard. I figured if he had to trip over me, then I could take the brunt of his anger before he could get to Mama.

Didn't matter. He beat me and still managed to beat the hell out of her. Mitchell Lawrence was a mean, violent drunk. The abuse made me want to get out of there the first chance I got and take my mother and sisters with me.

Mother took too long kicking him to the curb, but it finally happened. Choices. We all make 'em. Sometimes, we suffer for 'em and sometimes we're better off despite them.

He thought of the old man out at the prison – *he thinks God called him to give out trousers.* Jack chuckled, *wonder what's in store for me.*

I need to find this man.

Jack walked out of the service more convinced than ever he had to find him. The question was how.

Ryker James Jr., the same week

"Father Rayford, this is Ryker James," church secretary Marsha Ramey gestured to Ryker, standing with her in the doorway.

"Hello Pastor," Ryker put his ball cap in one hand and stuck out his hand to shake with Father Rayford, respectfully. "I wonder if I could git a few minutes a your time, pastor."

"Thank you, Marsha," Father Rayford said, nodding. "Mr. James, come in. Please. Have a seat."

"Thank you, sir," he sat, surprised to see Father Rayford make his way around the desk to sit beside him.

"What can I do for you, Mr. James," he said, breaking the silence.

"You can call me Ryker."

"Okay, Ryker. How can I help?" Father Rayford's eyes were kind and his half-glasses gave him a brainy-professor look; though, at the moment, with them a little askew, he looked like an absent-minded one.

"I been tryin' to change my life. I …." He ran his hands across the bill of his cap, rubbing the edge. "I done got a job at this place called Texas Marine."

"Yes, the boat place off Las Vegas Trail?"

"Yeah. And, uh, I can't git more than ten dollars a hour and I'm havin' trouble payin' my rent. I, I been out a prison for almost two years and I can't git a job d'at pay what I need for rent, utilities and food. I don't need much, but I can't see how to git enough. I been workin' double shifts and, I just. I don't know."

"Wow. I am really proud of you. It's not easy to get a job when you're just out of prison. What were you in for?"

"Possession," he said.

"Where are you living now?" Father asked.

"I'm in government housing off White Settlement, but I got a little brother I gots to look after. My dad just went down for possession. If I gon' make 'nough to take cur a Junior and me, I got to make mo' d'an I am. I'm tryin' to git a second job, but I ain' got it yet. So. I …."

"You need some help to get by," Father finished for him. "Ryker, stay here for a minute. I'll be right back, okay? Can I get you some water, a Coke?"

"Naw. I'm good, thank you."

Stepping out of his office, Father Rayford checked his discretionary fund and saw he could give Ryker about two hundred dollars. Knowing he had to get it from the bank, he checked his schedule with Marsha and determined when he could have it ready for him.

Returning to Ryker, he said, "Tell me where I send this check for your rent?"

"Uh, to Ms. Simpson at Inmate Services. She git me a deal so I could have a place to live while I gittin' another job. It's just d'at she didn't count on Junior livin' with me. D'at mean I can pay less 'cause I got a dependent, but since it just happen I's short what I owe this month."

"I understand. Do you have an address for her?"

"Yes, sir."

"Okay, when you see Mrs. Ramey on the way out, just write down the address and we'll make sure she gets the money. Now, how else can I help?"

Ryker looked at him, surprised. "Uh, d'at was really all," he hesitated, not quite sure what to say.

"How about we pray together?" Father Rayford said.

Ryker's whole body relaxed. "D'at be good 'cause thangs is," he paused, catching himself. *What am I doin'?*

"What should I ask for?" he raised his eyebrows at Ryker, as if to say *go on with what you were going to say.*

"I guess I need someone to guide me. Sometime I git off track, tryin' to help ever'body. I lose my focus. But, you don't have to say d'at." He wasn't used to being asked what he needed. "I should probably go."

"Ryker, you can talk to me, about anything."

Ryker met his gaze. He searched Father Rayford's eyes. He nodded. "Thank you. I, uh, I just feel like I tryin' to go against ever'thang. Ain' nobody understand what it mean to git out a the life I been in -- for good. If I do it, then I got to leave ever'thang and ever' person I's close to. I ain' gon' have nobody. I mean, God's there and truth be told, He enough, but I just, uh.

"It like, ever' time I think I gon' make it, somethin' happen and I be like back in it again, tryin' to start over. Like right now, I's tryin' to git out. I been working for two years and I can't catch no break so I can make enough to pay bills. It like I ain' got no way to git ahead a what behind me.

"I could do it if was just me, but it ain'. I been takin' cur a all my family since I can remember. If I stop now and do what right, I gon' go under." He stopped, realizing he had said way too much.

"It's okay to need help. All of us do. It's okay to ask for guidance," Father's expression was full of compassion, his eyes concerned, but void of pity or condescension. "I know you have been taking care of your family and friends and that's a good thing, but getting out is harder when you're carrying others.

"Don't be afraid to shift the weight; ask them to carry some of it. This way, you can stay focused. Remember, it empowers people when you allow them to help. They may resist, but it's only because they're afraid of letting you down. Assure them. Believe in them. Take it one day at a time. And… let yourself make mistakes. If you choose wrong, then you will know better next time. What is it people say? Don't sweat the small stuff?" He smiled and waved away the cliché. "Most important is how far you've come. Don't let the past paralyze you."

Nodding, Ryker wasn't sure what to say. The silence felt awkward and not, at the same time.

"Wow," Father Rayford was a little embarrassed. He hadn't meant to go on and on. "I nearly gave you a lecture. Forgive me. I doubt you were asking for that." He removed his glasses and placed them in his shirt pocket. *No one asked for advice and here you are heaping it on.* He started to get up. Just as he placed his hands on the arm chair to do so, Ryker spoke.

"Ain' nobody ever put it like that before, givin' people power to help theyself. I'm on try it," he said. Father relaxed, sat back.

"Well, good," Father sighed, relief evident in his expression. "You know, if I may, I want to… ah," He shook his head, realizing he was about to do it again.

"What?"

"I was feeling another bit of advice coming on," he laughed.

"Lay it down," Ryker said. "I can deal."

"Okay. Just this last thing and I promise I'm done. The Lord's prayer says, 'give us this day our daily bread' and I take it to mean every day brings choices. Choose to work, choose to sleep, choose whatever – you get to decide. Circumstances can make the choices confusing and people can complicate things, but there is always a choice."

"What if I choose wrong?"

"I hope you do, from time to time," and this had Ryker's head popping up to meet his gaze. "It's how you learn. Choosing wrong often brings the right decision into view." He paused, letting his words sink in.

"Like narrowin' thangs down 'til you know what's right," he summarized.

"Exactly," Father was thrilled at his insightful nature.

"Just wish I didn' have to git locked up to git it.

"How many times have you been incarcerated?" He knew he may be overstepping, but Ryker brought it up.

"Twice."

"Do you mind if I ask where?"

"The first time was half-jail-half-rehabilitation.

"The Substance Abuse Felony Punishment program," Father said, nodding.

"Yeah, that's it," Ryker stopped, grateful he knew it. "I was nineteen."

"And the second time?" Father pressed.

"Bradshaw," Ryker cut his eyes away.

"State jail," Father finished, confirming he knew it as well. "SAFP treats addiction. Were you addicted?" Father Rayford asked.

"In a way, but not so much physically as in my head. It's hard to change when scorin' all you know. I done what I had to, said what I had to. Ain' no way to git out a SAFP if you don't." He paused rubbed his index finger along his bottom lip. "I didn't let it work. It was easier to go back to dealin'. I's a lil' cocky. Ain' nobody in my world ever leave so I didn' think it could be done." He raised a hand to stop the lie. "Truth is I wadn' willin' to fail with so many eyes on me."

"It took Bradshaw."

Ryker's head snapped up; the white of his eyes a stark contrast to his icy gaze, capturing Father Rayford's attention. "Yeah, d'at's right. You don' mess around. You say it like it is, don' you?" A moment passed. His eyes softened a little.

"It's the real deal," he said, his eyes darting back and forth, as if remembering some of his time there. He stopped, closed his eyes and shook his head slowly.

"So, when you left SAFP, you knew the process for turning your life around. You'd been given a crash course."

"You make it sound like school," Ryker said, not sure what Father Rayford was getting at.

"No, I know addiction isn't that simple, whether it's physical or in your head. My guess is you were released from SAFP and you went back to your family, maybe looked for support from your friends."

"Yeah. Where else I gon' go?" he shook his head. "Ever' body in the life I's thinkin' a tryin' to leave.

"Well, not ever'body. My mama and my sisters ain' never been into drugs, but my dad and my uncles all sold 'em. So, when I wanted to git a real job, nobody git that. They thinkin' why I gon' work for minimum wage when I could score so much mo' in a day."

"A legitimate question," Father Rayford said. "What was your answer?"

"I know'd it wadn' me."

"Selling?" He nodded, his eyes confident, sure.

"Prison. It's a hell of a place."

"I know d'at's right. What I s'pose to do? I didn' have no job. All I know'd was how to sell, steal, break the law and pray. I pray ever' day." It was Father's turn to be surprised, but somehow he wasn't.

"It might be a surprise to you, but I like to work," Ryker had Father's head snapping up to meet his gaze now. "I like bein' useful. They's people who can lay 'round in they pajamas all day, smokin' weed and gittin' high, but that ain' me." He sighed, thinking there was no way to really explain it. "I'm all messed up. My mama the church-goin' type and so I'm used to spendin' three to five hours in church ever' Sunday. My daddy a gangster. He gon' work during the day at a real job and then, at night, he gon' sell the candy. He have ten-day parties with booze, barbeque, and candy.

"They's they own people, but I come out messed up."

"I don't think so," Father shook his head and searched the air for the right words to say. Unable to find them, he narrowed his eyes, searching Ryker's face.

"I loved goin' to church and I pray, ever' day," Ryker raised a hand, as if lifting it to heaven. Father did the same and smiled. "I love my family," he went on. "I know they do wrong and I can't change 'em, but I can cur 'bout 'em, pray for 'em, and be there. But, if I gon' be there, I got to know the places they spendin' they time and d'at gon' put me right where I don' need to be. People I cur 'bout dyin' out there and what am I doin'? Tryin' to leave 'em behind," he said, his voice lower and laced with shame. Father Rayford waited, knowing there was more.

"My mama git out, but she still need help 'cause she ain' been able to make enough money to keep food on the table and a roof over her head," he said.

"You said you have siblings."

"Sisters. They older," he said as he wiped sweat from his forehead. "I know in my heart that I ain' never belong on d'streets, sellin'. I know d'at, but I don't know how I gon' do different. Illegals' all I been taught.

"I'm gon' figure it out. It just," he paused. "I need," his voice trailed off, now sure that he'd said too much. On the street, he would be dead if people knew he was talking like this. "Wanting out" meant weakness.

He eyed Father Rayford hard and then looked out the window, thinking, *I guess if I gon' go down, God know it. They been 'nough times when I should a died and God didn' see fit to let it happen. Trustin' d'is priest ain' gon' be the reason I fall. 'Sides, it feel right.*

"You need help, guidance," Father Rayford said, breaking through his thoughts. "You also need time. Taking time to get there is good. It's good to hear that you pray; that you know God."

"All the choices that have set you back. Try to see them as steps necessary to find your right path. Think about the people who guided you toward the good times in your life. I don't mean all the dangerous, thrill-seeking, heady ones. Think of the times you felt most at peace with yourself, most relaxed, most happy. Those are the moments you want revisit. Figure out what led to those moments. Do you feel me?"

Ryker snorted a little at this white pastor using street talk. He thought it was nice Father was trying to meet him where he lived. Too many times he saw people hold onto to race, not because they were proud of who they were, but because they saw it as a license to judge; to breed shame instead of grace.

Father Rayford laughed too, knowing how lame he probably sounded.

"Yeah. Yes, I hear you." Ryker stood and almost put his hat back on, but remembering his manners, he stuck out his hand first. "Thank you, Pastor."

"My pleasure," Father Rayford said, taking his hand and holding on a little longer than Ryker expected, causing him to look up. "I'm here for you, son. Don't forget."

"Thank you. I won't."

Ryker walked toward the door and stopped, looking over his shoulder. "I got one more question, Pastor. I had d'is dream." He paused. "It was more like a nightmare. I kep' hearin' somebody say over and over, 'seventy time seven' and uh… ah, never mind," he said, stopping himself. He suddenly felt silly.

"Seventy times seven? That comes from one of my favorite verses in Matthew, chapter 18, verse 22. It's when Peter asked Jesus if he was supposed to forgive his brethren five, six, seven times." Father Rayford paused to see if Ryker knew the passage. When he didn't respond, Father Rayford continued. "Well, you may or may not know, but Peter was not exactly above making some bad choices himself," Father raised his eyebrows and it brought a smile. "Anyway, Jesus reminds him of his track record and tells him to consider his own transgressions – seventy times seven. Why do you ask?"

"That's four hundred and ninety times," Ryker said immediately.

"Yes. Yes it is, but I'm not sure Jesus was trying to confine it to an exact number. I believe he was saying forgive – lose count and simply forgive."

"So, I gots a shot?"

"Yes, yes you do. We all do." Father Rayford smiled. He started to ask Ryker more about his nightmare, but Marsha buzzed his intercom with a message. He turned his back for a second, long enough to write down the message. When he turned back, Ryker was gone.

Father Rayford sighed, disappointed they hadn't had a chance to pray. *So, I will pray for you, solo, Ryker James,* he decided.

Jack had not been able to shake the memories of experiences past. His dreams were random flashes of times he'd spent with Uncle Pete, Doc and Mr. Bob. His subconscious brought up some of the most pivotal times in his childhood; times when it was crucial that he make a good choice.

He remembered random things like the time Uncle Pete put him in charge of feeding the goats, as part of his chores around the house. He felt so proud at first, Uncle Pete affirming that he was becoming a young man; that he could trust him with such an important task, but he was quickly reminded he had a long way to go.

Uncle Pete's version …

Well, Jack was about thirteen when it happened. He had just gotten the job at Leonard's Department Store and he was making his own money, feeling really good about moving in with me and Rachel. I guess I just wanted him to have some responsibility around the house as well.

He was doing the usual stuff -- leaving his clothes on the floor in his room, not making his bed, getting careless with things in and outside the house. I wanted him to understand that making choices affects others and often influences whether or not trust is given or taken away.

Anyhow, I told Jack I wanted him to start feeding the goats every morning. It meant him getting up earlier and making sure to keep to a schedule so he wasn't late to school or to work. He had to: one, allow time for the dogs to go out and do their business, get *them* back in and two, tend to feeding the goats and cleaning up the pen a little.

Well, Jack thought he could consolidate those two steps and one morning, he had the dogs with him when he came to tend the goats. He thought it would be okay to let the dogs do their business, while he fed the goats. It probably would have been okay, but one of the dogs, Angus, got around him and ran into the pen, just as Jack was opening it up.

The goats went crazy. They took off in every direction, when Angus came barreling into the pen. And, here's Jack and his friend, Joey, getting a good laugh out of the whole thing.

The next day, Jack asked me to go with him to feed the goats. He said he had something funny to show me. As I rounded the corner and saw both dogs in the pen and the boys laughing, I was yelling at the top of my lungs, "Get those dogs out a there right now, Jack! Now!"

When Jack finally managed to catch Charlie, our lab, and Angus, our Australian shepherd, the goats had been severely traumatized, what with the two of them in there, cornering the weaker ones.

I was so mad I didn't trust myself to say anything until later that night. When I finally went into Jack's room to talk to him, he was sitting on the edge of the bed. He said, "Uncle Pete, I'm real sorry for letting the dogs into the pen. I really didn't mean any harm."

I didn't pull any punches with him. I told him the truth about what he'd done. Several of the goats were so scared by the incident their hearts literally burst and they died. I waited a beat, let it sink in; that a living thing had died because of his choice. He had a really tough time forgiving himself. I didn't soften the blow or sugar-coat it. He needed to know his actions had affected lives.

Later, I checked on him when I went to bed. I heard him praying about what happened. He asked forgiveness every night for some time. It was a hard lesson for him to learn, I suppose. He thought he was a grown-up, a man, working a job and going to school. He was thirteen and full of himself.

When the mistake cost us several of the goats, it jerked him up short and that was okay. We all need that, no matter how old we get. Ah! He was still a boy in so many ways, but that experience propelled him forward, I'd say.

Jack was still thinking about the goat incident when the phone rang. It must have rung several times because Sarah came into the den, where he was sitting.

"Honey, are you going to get that or not? I've got a pie in the oven and the ladies will be here any minute for our prayer group. I can't do everything," she went on, trailing off as she walked back into the kitchen.

"Uh-huh. What? Oh, the phone. I'm sorry, Shug." Jack scrambled up and went to the desk to pick it up. "Hello?"

"Hello, Jack," Dr. Rick Stanley's nasal voice gave him away.

"Hey there, Rick, how're you doing?"

"Doing well, doing well. I wondered if you…."

"I'm looking forward to the speaker next Tuesday," Jack jumped in, figuring he was calling to remind him.

"Well, good. Me too, but that wasn't why I called."

"Oh?" Jack got up to check the church schedule. He volunteered a couple of times a month to greet parishioners on their way into service. Sometimes, he ushered during the service. *Was I supposed to serve last week?* He scanned the calendar looking for his name.

"I've got a situation I think you could help me with," Rick began. "There's a young man, an ex-convict actually, who's having trouble finding a job and uh, well, haven't you've worked in prison ministry for some time?"

"Yeah, I sure have," Jack wasn't sure where this was going, but he kept listening.

"Well, this young man could use your help, if you think you might be willing," Rick's voice was hopeful. He liked to pair-up ministers with people who had common ground; it made for an easy time as far as having empathy and point of reference. Jack's experience in prison ministry seemed to make this particular situation a good fit.

"Well, I'd be glad to give it a shot."

Grateful, Rick continued with the details.

As Jack listened, he thought of the last few weeks. He'd been grasping at straws, trying to figure out who he was supposed to help. At first, he thought it was Mr. Carlson, who called, asking for help getting to the grocery store and back one day; and when Jack heard him say he struggled with other errands, he offered to be his chauffeur once a week. Retirement from Lockheed left him more free time than he really wanted so he was happy to assist.

Another elderly gentleman, Mr. Cotter, was having trouble getting to doctor appointments. Jack had heard about it at St. Timothy's coffee hour in between services. He put him on the calendar for help about three times a month as well. Even so, Jack wasn't sure it was that simple.

Maybe this young man is the one.

Maybe I'm just shooting in the dark, too, he thought, shaking his head.

"Sure, I can go over there," he offered. "I'll call 'em right now." If anything, at least Rick's call gave him a great excuse to go out for a bit. The ladies were coming for prayer group, and even if this man at Inmate Services wasn't *the man*, it would at least get him out of the house, no offense to ladies' prayer meetings.

"That would be great," Rick said. "I'll let them know you'll be calling. Really appreciate this, Jack."

"Okay, then."

After hanging up with Rick, he called the number he was given and got the director on the phone. As it turned out, the young man was in her office when he called.

"Listen, I could be there in about fifteen minutes, if you like," Jack told her.

"Mr. Lawrence, I can't thank you enough. We'll wait for you," she said. "You know, I knew Dr. Stanley was going to call you, but I had no idea I'd get to put you with Ryker this fast. Thank you, Mr. Lawrence. Thank you so much," she said.

"Call me Jack," he said.

"Thank you, Jack."

Remembering Sarah's group was coming, he quickly got shoes on and headed for the door. "Shug, I'll be back in a few. I need to run an errand. I'll explain later," he called over his shoulder, as he made his way to the front door.

"Oh," a sweet-faced woman gasped, when he opened the door and found her waiting.

"Hi Martha, c'mon in. Sarah's in the kitchen."

It couldn't have worked out better if he'd planned it. As he walked up to the entrance of Inmate Services, he had a good feeling about meeting this guy. He was directed to a conference room by the office manager.

"Hi. Mr. Lawrence?"

"Jack" he said, smiling and getting to his feet. He was a bit anxious as he looked past her, hoping to see the young man he was supposed to meet.

"Jack, yes, of course," she said. "I'm Karen Simpson, director of Inmate Services. Please, have a seat. I wanted to talk with you a moment about Ryker James, the man Dr. Stanley mentioned on the phone.

"Okay."

"It's important you know a few things about this man you're about to meet. He's going to tell you he's trying to reform, but you should know he has been incarcerated twice before and his record shows countless arrests for possession and drug-dealing. His family has a history of drug-trafficking, uh, his uncles used to sell on Bloody Fifth, in Houston. Are you familiar with the Fifth Ward?"

"A little."

"Originally, it was a decent area. Many African Americans purchased housing there, built small businesses. But, there was a terrible fire and it destroyed their homes and virtually their livelihoods. When it was condemned, the city didn't have a way to rebuild. This was about the time several drug lords took over what was left of the area. It was a pretty dangerous time and place," she trailed off, wondering if Jack was listening. "Jack?"

"What?"

"Are you with me?"

"Of course. I heard every word you said."

"Okay, good. Because he grew up around these dealers. Many of them connected to gangs. He's not a member, as of yet, but his family in Cooper has people in the Bloods, and his family in Fort Worth has people in the Crips. Am I scaring you yet, because this man has a past as dark as they come," her voice trailed off. Looking up from her notes, Jack was smiling.

Did you not hear a word I said? She stared at him incredulously, concern creasing her forehead. *You're what? Seventy or so? And, you're smiling like you're waiting for one of your grandchildren to come bounding through the door.*

"Jack, did you hear what I just said?" she wanted to shake him.

"Uh-huh, yes ma'am, I sure did," his smile was no longer as toothy. His eyes darted from the door to her with expectation, obviously impatient to meet Ryker.

"He's a career criminal," she said, pausing for a reaction from Jack. When there was nothing, she went over Inmate Services' policy with regard to Ryker.

She believed she had a responsibility to clarify as much as possible, disclose as much as she could. When she ran out of things to say, she looked at him again. *Still nothing,* she thought. Spreading her palms out to show she had concluded, she said, "Okay, then. If you'll wait here, I'll get Ryker."

She returned a few minutes later, saying, "Ryker James, I would like you to meet Jack Lawrence," guiding him into the conference room.

Jack stood, his chair noisily scraping the floor as he pushed it back. The young black man walked in and upon seeing Jack, removed his ball cap. When Jack put his pale hand out, a sprinkling of age spots covering the purplish veins on the top of his hand, Ryker immediately came forward, taking it in his. His dark eyes seemed to harbor a twinge of disappointment in them if Jack read him right. Jack smiled and nodded, trying to assure him.

"Mr. Lawrence," Mrs. Simpson continued.

"Jack," he interrupted, nodding kindly to Mrs. Simpson. "Jack is fine."

"Okay, *Jack*. Ryker's was released from prison in 2001 and he's had trouble finding a full time job. He's been able to make ends meet with part-time employment, but it's been hard for him to maintain his rent, utilities and keep food in the house. Dr. Stanley tells me you might be able to help him with applications and the interviewing process."

"I don't have a job at all right now," Ryker blurted out, feeling he should say something. Mrs. Simpson turned her head sharply as if to say she was not finished. At this, he added, "I been lookin' ever' day," and he looked down at his ball cap.

When Jack heard Ryker speak, he heard a plea in his voice. He took in his six-foot-something frame and his clothes, hanging off him. His dark skin was gaunt, especially in his face, while his hair was coarse and thick, now resembling the outline of his hat. He saw darker patches of skin on his arms, wounds that left scars perhaps, and his hands were like sandpaper.

He's a hard worker, Jack thought. Though he tried to focus on Mrs. Simpson's words, he angled his four-foot-six-inch frame so he could see both Ryker and her. Ryker was proud. Jack could tell by his stance; his chin squared and raised. He liked that Ryker looked him in the eye when he shook hands.

When everyone was seated, Ryker sat up straight, his shoulders back and down, confident. From what Jack could tell, he was on the edge of his seat, ready to do whatever it took to get this job.

"Ryker, do you have family here or, are they out of town?" Jack asked, when Ms. Simpson paused for a few moments.

"Both," he said. "My mama live on East Powell near my granddaddy house. I got two boys in Oklahoma City. They stay with they mama. Her name' Brittany Lang."

"Do you get to see them?" Jack was taken aback by the fact that this young man had children. He could not fathom having little ones to consider in the midst of the business he handled.

"Yes sir. I go there as often as I can, but without a job, it been hard. I miss 'em," he said, looking away quickly, as if to hide his emotion.

"What are their names, son?" Jack pressed, seeing him relax a bit when he inquired about them.

"Roco and Tavi," he said, a half smile forming. "We agree that 'til I git a good job, they gon' stay with her."

"I understand.   Does she stay with her family in Oklahoma?"

"Yes sir, her mama and daddy help with the boys," he said.

"So, you're doin' a good thing then," Jack said.

He looked from Ms. Simpson to Jack and back, his eyes moving slowly between the two. When Jack waited for him to respond, he said "I's tryin'."

"I know things are hard right now. I'm not tryin' to get in your business. I just want to help if I can. You tell me how to go about doin' that, okay?"

Ryker's head dropped and he looked hard at his ball cap. When he could answer, he raised his head and met Jack's gaze, tears on the edge of falling. "Why you want a go and help somebody like me?" he asked.

Jack wasn't expecting Ryker to be so direct. He took a moment, considering what Ryker was really asking. When he saw his dark, calloused hands were wet with perspiration, he could tell this boy needed more than just a glib answer.

"Because I believe in second chances," he said. The young man blinked, trying to hold back his emotions. When he said nothing in response, Jack said, "Do you?"

Several seconds passed, as Ryker considered the man before him and his dire situation.

"I want to," Ryker said, looking at his ball cap again, more intensely.

"Okay. Good enough," Jack said.

The young man looked up and met his gaze, expecting a "but" to follow. When it didn't come, he looked to Ms. Simpson, whose brow was furrowed and her expression grave. She said nothing.

"I do whatever it take to git a job," he said, hoping it was the right thing.

"Good to know, because there are a few things I'm going to need your word on. One, always tell me the truth. You'd be surprised at what I can handle, as long as it's true. Two, be willing to work. If you're not useful, then you're useless, not to me, but to you. And three, you have to stay sober. A clear head can solve problems, ward off trouble; keep your choices in plain view. If you aren't serious about these three things, I can't do much for you."

Ryker's gaze was steady and his mouth was pursed, as he blinked rapidly, trying to keep his composure. Jack waited for him to answer and after several moments, he said, "Can you do those three things?"

"Yes sir. I can," he managed. Clearing his throat he confirmed, "I will. Thank you."

"All right, then." Jack stood and shook Ryker's hand again. "Call me Jack."

"I go by Ryker, sir, but I like it when you call me son before." At this, Jack raised his brows in surprise. Despite his own determination to stay dry-eyed, he felt tears force him to blink. "But Ryker's good. Some a my family call me Little R. My Daddy be Ryker James Senior, or Big R, when we was in business together."

Jack appreciated the past tense. He hoped that was true. Regardless, Jack felt a smile creep into the corners of his mouth. He had seen God's grace take many forms, but not like this, not the way he had just felt it. When Jack reached the door, leading back out to the lobby of Inmate Services, he turned to look at Ryker once more.

It occurred to him that if they were going to get started as soon as possible, he needed an address and a phone number. "Ryker, where do you live?"

"Government housing, off White Settlement, apartment 103," he said.

"I'm gonna be at your place tomorrow morning. 7:30 sharp. Be ready. You'll need a phone number where employers can reach you, your address with zip code, your driver's license and any other identification you can scramble up. Okay?"

"Yes sir."

"All right then."

"Jack?" he called out, as Jack turned to go.

"Yeah?"

"Ain' you gon' ax me, 'bout what I done?"
"Nope. Did you want to tell me about it?"
"I just want a job, sir. A honest job," he said.
"Then be ready at 7:30, sharp."

Chapter 3

*I saw the food. It was floating in the water. As I
look toward the sky, now, twisting violently to get
free, I know it was a trap. I thought it was
sustenance and it was a trap.*

Ryker James, Jr.

Part a me want a tell Jack Lawrence what I done. They
was no judgment when he look at me and it make me want a
tell him the truth. After he left, I's glad I didn't. Ain' nobody,
old or young, ever been somebody I could trust. Ain' gon'
start now. Nobody git where I been. Half the time, I git it
but don't want to. Still, I's changin' inside and can't nobody
see it.

Being locked up what start me thinkin'. I's so busy bein' I
didn' think what I's becomin'. I's bein' smarter d'an the next
guy, bein' curful who I trust, bein' quicker to git d'drop befo'
I's dropped. I can't 'member d'last time I slept without
nightmares; somebody comin' fo' me and mine, wakin' up and
havin' a piece cocked in my face, findin' my chidren been hurt
somehow. When I's locked up, d'at's all I think 'bout.

I serve eight months in Delta County Jail 'cause a the
warrants they have out for my arrest. When the judge decide
he gon' sentence me to hard time in state prison, my Daddy
hire Jimmy Earl to plead my case. Jimmy Earl ax the judge
for lenience 'cause he say I addicted to cocaine and need
rehab. He full a somethin' there 'cause I ain' never been
addicted to cocaine.

Daddy said to go with it so I could avoid prison so I done
it. I didn't have no idea what Substance Abuse Felony

Punishment program meant when I went. I pictured a rehab place with rooms for people 'cause they all goin' through different stages a withdrawal. Wrong.

I's put in a room with 48 beds; 24 sets a bunk beds. The smell a disinfectant was ever'where, along with a mix a Clorox bleach and lice powder. The toilets be nasty. We got to do our bidness in front a ever'body. It no wonder people gon' fight when thangs like that.

We was assigned to bunks after we was processed. They sprayed us hard with a hose and told us to clean ourself with soap that dry out our skin. We had to wear white pants and white shirts; alla us have a number on 'em.

The guards be hard-asses, callin' out rules and expectations. The schedule they tell us we gon' follow didn't make no sense in my mind so I tune it out. I seen people already takin' toilet paper and messin' with the room. Cellmates' fightin' over they bed and who they gon' rape. I stare-down ever'body who even look at me wrong or otherwise. I's ready for whatever come.

"Pay attention!" I heard the guard saying and I slowly turned my head toward the voice. "You need to hear everything I'm telling you if you expect to get out of here. But, let me start by saying you can go to prison and take your chances there if this place isn't good enough for you. Take your angry ass to state prison and see how it works when you end up with a cellmate in prison who needs somebody to love, if you get my meaning."

Groaning and trash talk started and that was all it took.

"Shut the hell up!" Bam! A night stick came down on the bunk bed closest to me. Some of the guys jump and I glance up at 'em, not movin' a muscle. They was gon' have to do a lot worse 'an that if they wanna shake me.

"Let's get to it. Wake-up call is 5:30 a.m. We'll go straight to breakfast. After breakfast, we will shower, shave, dress, clean up the room and yes, you will make your bed. At eight o'clock, you are expected to meet with your counselor. At nine a.m., there's anger management; ten a.m., group session; eleven a.m., counselor recap; noon is lunch; one o'clock p.m., group encounter; two p.m. is group review; four p.m., counselor wrap-up; and five o'clock, dinner. As soon as dinner is over, head back to your cell for shower and shave before bed. Lights are out at nine p.m. There are no second chances here. Either get along or get thrown back into prison. Any questions? Good. I don't give a rat's ass about your questions.

"Oh, and one more thing. Those of you who are suffering from any kind of withdrawal, sweats, hallucinations, chills, headaches, whatever, here's some advice. Suck it up. It will only get worse before it gets better and no one here gives a shit how you feel about it."

I think this was the only time I smile. I done my share a cocaine but I could stop whenever I wanted. I had headaches but that was it. I looked 'round the room. They was people already shaking and agitated. Some was on they bed, covering they faces with they pillows, tryin' to keep from seein' hallucinations comin' on. They was several who was wide-eyed and jittery, like they could jump right out they skin. It was gon' be a long ten months.

The street ain' much different. If you smart, you take in all you can, use what help you survive and check the rest. The program was nothin'. All I done was regurgitate they words and I's done.

It all 'bout correctin' negative behavior that lead to incarceration. Counselin' sessions was 'bout my history a taking and sellin' drugs. They ax me to describe my home life, my friends, and my family. It ain' like they freaks, my family. My daddy a hard worker, always up at 6 a.m., working odd jobs 'round town. When he up, ever' body up. Ain' nobody layin' 'round, sleepin'. He always say "the sun's up and it's time to git on with bein' useful."

Mama worked hard too. She up, gittin' ever' body ready for the day. Mama always lovin' on us, tellin' us to be thankful for what we got no matter how little or how big. She come from a church-goin' family so she a big believer in God, prayer and good cookin'. She could make almost anythin' taste good. She had enough practice with it, as little as we had.

She always tryin' to keep peace in the house. It hard when they ain' no money and ever'body hungry and tired. It git to where keepin' the peace mean shutin' our mouths. Ain' nobody talk much, 'cause it easier than takin' a chance you gon' start somethin' that gon' end bad.

Daddy the one who brang drugs into the house. He had people who come and go at all hours, sellin', droppin' off they score. This when Mama stop stayin' quiet. She start gittin' up in his face and tellin' him she want it different. If he hadn't had the drink, he might a let things go, but the drink turn him mean in a quick minute.

How I s'pose to tell some SAFP counselor all that?

In anger management, I's axed to name specific things that trigger my anger. They say some people prone to violence when they drunk. That explain a lot 'bout Pop 'cause he always drunk when he beat my mother. I kept thinkin' alcohol s'pose to relax people, but it had a opposite effect on him.

It don't explain why he gon' hit my mama and not me or my sisters. He ain' never hit us no matter how mad he git. He be throwin' her 'gainst the wall but still pick us up and set us aside out a harm's way. The counselor axed me why I thought he did it and I didn't know what she want me to say. How I s'pose to know why people do things? He was 'posed to be the adult. I start naming whatever come in my mind. He know we couldn't defend ourself. He didn't hit us 'cause she stood in front a us. He didn't hit us 'cause he wore hisself out hittin' her. He didn't hit us 'cause we didn't matter d'at much. He didn't want social services sniffin' 'round." None of it make no sense to me. Anything I say be shootin' in the dark.

Group discussions was a trip. They was addicts of all ages, personality, and sobriety. The counselors' only way a controllin' the fights was sayin' we goin' to a real prison if we mess up there. Ain' nobody want that because it would a meant a longer sentence.

I faked-it. It wadn' easy. They real specific how you gots to do it, but it didn't take long to figure. Some time it was tricky. If a guard thought I's doing something that could trigger a set-back in rehabilitation, he gon' tell my counselor and the counselor gon' be all up in my face the next session. If I didn' say d'right thang, then I's back, startin' all over.

I feel what they sayin'. If I's havin' a smoke and hangin' with people packin' d'candy, d'en it gon' be hard not to sell. They sayin' I got to stay away from people who gon' be triggers for doin' wrong. D'at was funny to me. If I's gon' do d'at, I wadn' gon' be 'round nobody I know.

SAFP was the first place I realize how the law seen me. Nobody I know ever say doin' drugs wrong or sellin' 'em wrong. The police raid our house all the time and we didn' always know why. We all be hangin' out there, 'bout twenty of us. They come in, guns in the air, screaming to git down. We hit the floor and then my pop go in county lockup. Him and whoever else was of age. All us chidren git a free pass 'cause the adults to blame in the eyes a the law. Whoever didn't git caught know'd to watch the kids a the ones who did. It just the way we done it.

After bein' at SAFP, I start thinkin' maybe d'way I grow'd up wadn' normal. I blew it off 'cause ain' nobody normal. Ever' person gots somethin' or someone d'at's crazy in they life.

I done the program though. The guard say I's "too good" at it. She say I's just sayin' what they want a hear. She wadn' fooled by me, not even. She say one day, I gon' git it. It gon' hit me and then I git it. She right 'cause after Bradshaw, I did.

I change some after SAFP. I left town and tried to work thangs out with my boys' mama in Oklahoma City. Brittany and me was together before I went to SAFP. She was a single mother with a 6-month old baby when we met. She and I seem like we fit at the time. Then she git pregnant with my first child.

By the time I finish my ten months at SAFP, she had moved on, but she let me still be the boys' father. I was good with that 'cause I was still caught up in the life, driving the candy from Oklahoma City to Fort Worth and back to Cooper. I wadn' in no mind to take cur a the boys all d'time.

I's runnin' from the police. They had warrants for my arrest in three counties. I had people in ever place so I could hide when I need to, but it was catchin' up with me. My head wadn' in the game the way it used to be. I started losin' focus. I seen my little boys and it messed with my head. It almost like I wanted to git caught. And, I did.

Bradshaw was hard prison time. I had to step-up my game in there. Ain' no way to survive if you don't. I had to get somebody to spot me cash for sellin' cigarettes. Once I find the cash, then I had to git in with a guard for supply. I done it, but it take time and my sentence was for eighteen months. I had to work fast if I's gon' git the jump on the crazies in there.

That's when I start seein' the worst a what drugs do to people. I seen people die from the attack it put on they heart with some a the hard stuff. They be waitin' on medical attention and prisons ain' got the best medical help. I sat with one a my forty-eight cellmates one night. I seen him git the shakes and start convulsin'. Ain' nobody cur in the cell, but me. I watch him. I prayed he make it through the night. When the lights go out, I watch and I pray. About 3 a.m., he look like he dead, like my mama done the last time my daddy beat her so bad. I had to walk over to her and take her pulse to check she alive.

When I seen him, it take me back. I was five when it happen and Bradshaw make me feel like I's right back there.

The boy look like my cousin, D. Dominik a Blood now. He git hooked on crack when he 15. His daddy was beat, almost to death, in front a him one night. After that, he couldn't deal with the memory of it so he start usin' to 'scape. That's the thing. I seen a lot a kids who just want the pain they been through to stop. They ain' tryin' to kill theyself or git addicted. They just want to stop seein' the nightmares they livin'. I git that. It don't make drugs right, but I git that.

Anyhow, when I git out a Bradshaw, d'at when I decide I's gon' go straight. I seen more d'an I ever wanted to see in prison and I know'd for sho' I didn't want a go back there. So, when I git released, I had the bus drop me off at my granddaddy' house on East Powell. He say one a my uncles could help me git a job detailin' boats if I's interested.

That's how I git a job at North Texas Marine Company. I's just gittin' the hang a supportin' myself when Pop came along and axed me to cur for Junior. When I find out I's gittin' custody, I figure I's gon' *have* to go back to dealin' powder if I's gon' make rent; feed me and mine. I prayed for some way to git by without goin' back, but I was runnin' out a options. Kailey Overstreet the reason I made it 'til I could git to Jack. That's when I know'd prayer really work.

Kailey Overstreet was Ryker's immediate supervisor and at first, this didn't mean anything to Ryker. Having the job was enough. He felt lucky to have found work, given his record.

Kailey took an immediate liking to him. He thought it was a physical attraction, but she wasn't interested in him that way. She asked about his family, where he was from, where he wanted to be in a few years. She had an energy about her that awakened something he thought dormant in himself until he met her. She was relentless, twisting the view of the kaleidoscope that had become his life, pushing him to look for a better picture, one with more color and definition, less gray. He understood her immediately, intellectually.

Within the first few weeks, she learned her hunch was spot-on; he *was* more than his record. He had plans to get out of selling drugs. He hadn't told anyone he was thinking about it, but she put it together and he didn't say she was wrong.

He didn't like talking about himself and when she pressed him, he was a master at bouncing the subject back to talking about her life. That was being street smart, getting the mark to share as many details about themselves as possible.

"I feel like you're working me for information," she said once.

"Me? Naw. I's just passin' d'time."

"Then, tell me about you," she'd say.

"Ain' nothin' to tell."

"Okay, I'll tell you what I already know," she giggled, when he stood back, held up his hands in surrender.

"You make every car and boat that comes through here shine from the inside out. You're organized, methodical and you work, hard, from the moment you punch the clock. You don't drag around here like you have all day to get things done. You're driven, determined. And, the customers really appreciate you. What you do, you do because it's right and good, not because you're looking for compensation. You take great joy in going above and beyond," she held up *her* hands as if to say, "ta-da, I'm done."

His expression was unreadable. She waited a beat, not sure why her compliments would offend, but when they didn't bring even a hint of a smile, she had to wonder.

"How you know all d'at?" he finally managed.

"I pay attention," she met his gaze, head-on.

His tough, impenetrable venir cracked. Kailey saw through it and he had no words. She'd seen the good in him; what God had put there – until that moment, he had no outward acknowledgment that it even existed. It was like telling people he had captured a shooting star, but having no evidence to prove it. He'd felt he was someone special since he was a boy and the years had confirmed it in his heart, but until Kailey, there was no proof.

Ryker's Take

Kailey used to talk to me while I work'. She say I was a fanatic 'bout organizin' my work, making sure I done the absolute best possible job. To me, that was doin' it right. She know'd I needed hours bad so she bring me in whenever she can. The best part a workin' was bein' useful, changin' the look a things with a little polish and some muscle. Kailey respect my effort on the job and I think we git to be friends 'cause a that. She easy to talk to. She the first person I tell that I wanted out. She said right off she could see me makin' it happen if I's serious 'bout it. She feel me, just the way I mean it.

One night, she try to take me home 'cause I tell her my car not workin'. I kept sayin' she could just brang me back to the office but she push at me 'til I tell her my car ain' been workin' and it been parked on the street. She couldn't believe it when I tell her I was sleepin' there. I told her I didn't have no choice. I had to save my money so I could git it fixed and find a place to live. She wasn't havin' it so she put me up in a hotel for a month, close to the shop so I could walk to work.

That was crazy. I didn't see that comin'. I know'd she like me but I wasn't gon' be no kept man. So, I was workin' up to tellin' her it wasn't gon' happen when she cut through my stuff. She say she ain' after sex. She just see somethin' in me, somethin' she git. She say they ain' never gon' be strings for anythin' she give me. I waited for it. I stared her down, still waitin' for the catch. After a long time, she smile and say, "Don't be late to work." Then, she gone. I closed the door to my room and set down on the floor. I looked at the bed and the walls a the hotel room. I must a waited there for over a hour, sure she was comin' back to collect. People always comin' to collect, make they point, hold somethin' up to you, but she didn' come back.

I was so tired, I fell asleep by the door. For the first time, I had good sleep, too. No nightmares. When I woke about 3 a.m., I decided to take advantage of the best part of havin' a room in a hotel.

I stripped down, still thinkin' 'bout why she doin' this for me. I walked into the bathroom and turned the knob inside the shower. The water spray into the palm of my hand, the temperature gittin' warm each second d'at pass. I step in and let it wash over me.

I couldn't believe I's there. I's there for the next thirty days and I didn't see what she git out a doin' that, why she done it.

She didn't want me like I's used to women wantin' me. It wadn' like that. She give me a place to stay and her friendship and didn't axe for nothin'. Nobody never done anything like that for me. First, I git this job and then this place to stay. It felt like my prayers was bein' answered, one by one.

She check on me almost ever' day, even when she wasn't at work. I growed up bein' the one to check on ever' body else. It felt good to have somebody cur how I was.

Not long after that, Kailey helped me git a car. She found it on a used lot in Topeka, Kansas. She say all I got to do is go git it and it's mine. I done it and when I git back, she done worked out an apartment for me to live, but I couldn't pay the rent unless I could git a raise. She say since I been workin' double shifts and customers' so happy with my work, she gon' see if she can git me a raise.

It didn't happen 'cause she was transferred to another office out a state. Even so, she ax the new manager to consider it. He say no 'cause the job I's in don' git raises. When Kailey find out 'bout it, she call Ms. Simpson for me over at Inmate Services.

That was how come I's able to meet Jack. Ms. Simpson set me up with the place on White Settlement and she git Jack to help me, too. I have to check in, two times a week, pay rent bi-monthly and take urine tests to prove I ain' usin'. Kailey say it's better than what I's considerin' before. She know'd I's thinking 'bout goin' back to business with Pop and his people. It like a ever'day decision not to.

With him in prison, I could a cleaned up in scores. She know'd I's close to givin' up. It ain' as simple as people think it is. Ever'thing I ever known been in the drug world. Ever' thing I learn since I was born tell me not to trust nobody on d'outside. It go 'gainst ever'thang I know.

I went to Inmate Services though, like she say, 'cause I know'd she curred 'bout me, for me. She didn't ax nothin' in return. She want me git out a dealin', not 'cause it's wrong, but 'cause she seen who I really 'posed to be. They ain' no shame about it. She seen me and they wadn' no shame.

People in my world I know'd my whole life ain' seen me like she done. I told 'em a thousand times, but ain' nobody hear it.

Naw, Kailey was different. She down-to-earth, the real deal. I still don't know how she seen my heart. I didn't cur. It was a gift.

Ms. Simpson hook me up with Jack. Father Rayford help me with my rent and Jack say he gon' help me find a job. It all too much. I ain' sure what to think. Ever'thang I know say somebody 'bout to git the drop on me.

Chapter 4

*Once on the hook, getting off is unbearably painful
and hard. Most think when they see the hook going
in that it will hurt for a bit but if the pain is too
much, they can reverse their direction and slip off.
Not so.*

"I found him," Jack burst into Father Rayford's office at
St. Timothy's. "Oh," his face paled, when he turned to see
Father Rayford was in an executive committee meeting.

"Hey, Jack," Father Rayford said, standing up and taking
him by the arm to lead him into the corridor. Over his
shoulder he said, "I'll be back in a few, folks. This is
important."

The treasurer, Sandra Johnson, started to protest, but
thought better of it. Father Rayford had a habit of putting
parishioner's concerns before business and the last time she'd
tried to subtly object, she'd been the one uncomfortable.

Father Rayford took *pause* with parishioners, leaving the
business at hand for later when a situation warranted his
immediate attention; it was one of his most endearing
qualities.

On any given day, Father could be found praying in the
garden with someone who showed up unannounced, needing
to talk. If he wasn't taking time with parishioners, he might
be in the kitchen, an apron over his vestment clothes, cooking
burgers on the grill for the church picnic. He wasn't above
walking the trash out to the dumpster or sweeping debris off
the floor in the parish hall either; it was *all* part of being a
servant of God.

Parishioners tried to take on the jobs and send him on his way, but he insisted it was something he liked to do. He said, "It's my personal offering as a servant of Christ. I like it almost as much as celebrating a service or doing the foot-washing during the Lenten season."

Father Rayford's first love was God, his second was his son, Jesus Christ, and then he was all about tending to his parish, whether it meant the business of keeping the building and budget on task, tending the soil at the parishioner's feet or the nurturing the tendrils connected to their souls. Jack's "him" mattered to him and it was worth interrupting the meeting.

"Who is he? Tell me about him." Father Rayford said, wrapping his arm around Jack and guiding him to the empty parish hall.

"Well, I met him over at Inmate Services, Father. Do you remember me telling you about Luke and me visiting Jeb at the prison in Austin?" Father Rayford nodded.

"Yes, I do. You met someone who gave you trousers of all things."

"Yeah, that's the one. The old guy with the trousers and the truck." Father smiled, wondering if Jack had looked in the mirror in a while. *The old guy. What are you, twenty, Jack?*

"Well, he said something that got me thinking. I mean, I knew my work in prison ministry was a clue to the whole *help this man* thing, but when the guy said *seventy times seven*, it got me thinking about Jesus and what he told Peter about forgiveness."

"You know in some translations Jesus says to Peter, 'In light of your own life, what do *you* think it means?' I love that. Jesus throws the ball right into Peter's court, as it were. 'Do I forgive five, six, seven times?' Peter asks. And Jesus says, 'More like seventy times seven.'" Father Rayford immersed himself in the essence of that for a long moment, letting himself get lost in its profound meaning.

"That's right. Yeah. Did I tell you this already?" Jack asked, his gray brows knitting together at Father Rayford's immediate indulgence.

"No, no you didn't. I guess I just. It was something someone said recently. Go on. Forgive me." Realizing his pun on the scripture, he and Jack both burst out laughing.

"Good one, Father." He nodded hard and then he was shaking his head. "Okay. Okay, so, back to Inmate Services and this boy who's needing help getting a job. He's an ex-con and he's had a real rough time of it lately, and as I sat there, listening to him talk, hearing about how important it was for him to get out of the life he'd been living, it hit me -- hard.

"You know, my childhood was not easy to navigate. It was pretty rough for a time. I grew up with an alcoholic for a stepfather, and he wasn't within a hundred thousand miles of being a father to anybody, much less to me. Most times, he drank and beat my mother, my sister and me." He paused, staring off at nothing in particular. "I'm sorry. I didn't mean to get off on that. What I'm trying to say is, I don't think I would have made it through that time in my life without some of the people who helped me, guided me and made me who I am today.

"I think I told you about my Uncle Pete, Doc Sevrenson, Mr. Leonard, and Mr. Jacobs?"

"Yes, yes, I remember. They helped you quite a bit."

"They sure did. Anyhow, it occurred to me that maybe me going through all the," he stopped to clear his throat. "The things I experienced at the hands of Mitchell Lawrence. Well, maybe the bad stuff was a preparation of some kind, for … I'm not sure exactly." Jack stared blankly.

"Now you're talking. Go on." Father Rayford lived for moments when parishioners put together why bad things could be good. He learned early on in his ministry that the clarity, like he sensed Jack was about to expel, was nothing that could be told to anyone; it had to be discerned. Otherwise, the profound meaning was lost.

"Well, I overcame more than I ever thought I could and I know my faith in God was at the root of it, but the people who mentored me were also part of the whole process.

"As far as this young man is concerned, I guess I saw something in him. I can't really put my finger on it, but I saw it. It was more than just a plea for help getting a job. There was so much pain there. I don't know how I know that. I just know.

"He seems haunted, and even though he wants out, there's much more to it than that." Jack was hearing his own words and a bit surprised he had taken so much of Ryker in. He stopped, took a moment. *How do I know all this?*

"It's okay," Father said, sensing Jack's sudden discomfort. "The Holy Spirit doesn't usually send us a memo to notify us when it's going to work through us. You're good. What else?"

"Well, that was it. The director out at Inmate Services told me she thought, given my experience in prison ministry and all, I could be of assistance to this young man. And, when I saw him, I knew. He's the *one*. I feel it. I'm going over to his apartment first thing in the morning and we're going to find him a job. And I guess we'll go from there."

Amazing, Father Rayford thought, as Jack left the parish hall. He was lit up inside. Not knowing who the man was had been so hard, but now, he had a name, a face, and a mission. It was good.

He watched Jack get in his car and drive away. Looking up at the sky, he said a quick prayer, grateful his job had such wonderful perks. *Sightings of the Holy Spirit never cease to amaze.*

◆

Ryker had come back to an empty apartment, minus one reclining chair in the center of the room, left by the first tenant. He had nothing to put in the apartment when he was released from Bradshaw. He had a few clothes and his toiletries. He had a couple pairs of jeans he had gotten from Goodwill and a few shirts. He washed them in the sink every other day.

When he saw the empty place, he smiled. It was like a clean slate, and today, at the meeting with Jack, he felt he had been given a clean record. Jack didn't ask about his past and it felt good. *No givin' a voice to what been*, he thought. *He seen me first; not my record. He seen me. My whole life, my own father ain' seen me. Nobody has 'cause I been somebody who always takin' cur a them, not someone who gots needs and wants. I feel it. I don't git why, but I feel alive, for the first time.*

When he sat down in the chair, he leaned it back and drew the one blanket he had over him, thinking he would catch a nap and then see what kind of food he could get with the few dollars he had. He closed his eyes and he lay back in the chair. *Thank you, God. Thank you for giving me Kailey and now, Jack. I feel like it gon' happen. If I git this job or two, or three, I could turn thangs 'round. I could stop the sellin' and the violence and all that come with my old life. I could be free. Lord, please help me do d'is. I know I can. I know I can be free.* And then he fell into a deep sleep.

Thoughts of his family and what this would mean for them stirred his sleep. They didn't know this side of him. His subconscious wandered back in time to when he used to hang out with his childhood friends, Ronny, T.J., Bam, Run, Joey, and Cowboy. They bonded over stale beer and cigarettes, the only sustenance they could find around the house to take when they snuck out at night. They smoked, blowing rings like they had seen their parents do, and if someone was hurting from seeing something go down, they talked about it and tried to chase away the pain.

He saw Ronny's face the night his father was beaten to death in front of him, just outside his house. He had been under the stairwell, playing hide and seek with his brother, when his dad came home and some guys jumped him. He heard something about his father being untrustworthy and then he heard his father's screams, and then coffin-closed silence. His heart was beating so hard they could all see his skin pulsing; b'boom, b'boom, b'boom. Cowboy had said, "You pee yo' pants?"

Just asking the question broke the tension. Joey said, "Naw, Cowboy, he didn't wet his self. You thinkin' a Run. If Run was there, it would a been *runnin'* down his leg."

"Shut up Ronny," Bam said, standin' up to bump chests with him. "You think you can make fun a my brother just 'cause he have a accident a long time ago. He was three, man."

"Easy," T. J. said, always the peacemaker. "Ever'body know Ryker gon' grow up to kick all they butts one day."

"Ryker," Bam said. "Ryker ain' gon' waste time kickin' nobody' butt. He be thinkin' a how to take they money.'

"Take it and leave," Ryker clarified. "With no one the wiser."

Before the night was over, their crazy antics had distracted Ronny for a time. He still had to go home and get through the night, but Ryker had hoped he would remember their voices in the midst of the pain.

If he could think of their petty arguments or the fisticuffs Bam and Cowboy nearly came to over Run, maybe the images flashing through his subconscious, when he *did* sleep, would be colored by a few memories of his friends, being there for him, helping him through the initial shock. Nothing would soothe him when it came to losing his father, but the bond between them all held strength, solace, maybe even threads to begin healing.

"Leave? Where you think you gon' go?" Bam asked. "Ain' nobody ever leave, man."

"And, what we 'pose to do when you gon'? Or, don't you cur?" Cowboy chimed in.

"I know what he gon' do. He gon' die like ever'body else," Joey said, his voice sullen and let down. "You d'man." Ryker felt it, the responsibility.

He slept on into the evening, through the night. He was still sleeping when he heard a bam, bam, bam at the door. Jolted awake, he reached for his piece. *Habit.* He'd thought he might go by Daddy D's house to get it before he got the call from Ms. Simpson. *Jack*, he remembered. *What time is it?* Seeing his phone on the floor, he picked it up and saw it was 7:25 a.m. *What? I ain' slept like that in years. It's mornin'?* The banging resumed.

"Ryker? You there? It's me, Jack."

Shit. "Comin', Jack," he said, his voice calm and easygoing, though he was hurrying, trying to find his jeans and a decent shirt. Random flashes of his old life were still in his head -- the time he found his cousin, almost dead in an alley, having scored a bad stash, or the day he carried little Samuel out of the street when he was gunned down in a drive-by shooting. Samuel's father took him from Ryker, while his mother pounded him with her fists, striking blow after blow on his chest, his head, his shoulders and his back. He stood, letting her, not once shielding himself or backing away. *She didn't know what she was doing. She was scared.*

Samuel lived because Ryker walked into the line of fire to bring him out of a blood bath. Firing ceased when Ryker walked out, glaring in their faces, daring them to shoot him. He seemed to walk an invisible line that was shielded from any harm.

When Mrs. Whittaker calmed enough to see Samuel would make it, Ryker was gone. She was in an ambulance and the EMTs were saying he was lucky. The bullet grazed his ear, appearing to have penetrated his neck because of the blood on him.

She remembered how she pounded Ryker for taking her boy's life. She tried to go to him and ask his forgiveness, but Ryker dropped out of sight for a time after that. When she saw him again, their eyes met and he said two words, "Forgiven. Forgotten." She hugged him so tight, he could hardly breathe.

It was moments like those that made him wonder, *How I gon' walk out these people's lives when I been there for so long? Where I gon' go?* He looked down at his chest, standing in front of the mirror in the bathroom. He saw the fists hitting him, the agony of Mrs. Whittaker's face; he heard the sound of bullets firing. He saw the blood on Samuel's neck, his mother's blood, his own. *So many voices in the blood.* He gripped the bathroom sink and tried to shake free.

"Ryker?" Jack called, his fist softer as he pounded the door once more.

He opened the door in his jeans and Jack saw him wipe at his face. He looked deeply saddened, no -- bludgeoned by something. When his eyes met Jack's, the haunting moment passed, bringing a spark of relief, perhaps a hint of regret.

"Jack, I be ready in a few minutes. I didn't wake up when I thought I would. I'm so sorry." He left the door open and left the room. Jack could hear water running so he raised his voice so Ryker could hear.

"You all right? You looked like you saw a ghost."

Ryker returned his button-down shirt on and open to the waist. As he buttoned it to the second button, he nodded.

"I'm good. Sometime I 'member flashes a my life and it like I's seein' it for the first time, 'cause when it happened, my mind shut down. I's there, doin' what got to be done, but it ain' 'til later, I 'member how it was. It's like watchin' a movie I seen, but bein' shocked I's in it," he explained.

"Do you want to tell me about it?" Jack asked, not sure he wanted to know.

"Naw. Let's get movin'. I don't want to get behind. I really appreciate you helpin' me. I still don't know why you want a do it, but it don' matter. I'm ready."

"Well, let's head out. We're gonna stop and get something for you to eat, then we'll be set," Jack added.

"It's okay, you don't got a do that," he said, surprised Jack thought about him needing food.

"Nope, not negotiable. A man's got to eat if he's going to get a job. So, let's go. Grab your driver's license and anything else. Shoes would be good," he said, looking down at Ryker's bare feet.

"Oh, yeah." He turned and grabbed some ratty-looking tennis shoes and a pair of old, worn socks. As Jack looked around the apartment, he wondered how this boy was sleeping at all. He had no bed, no table.

"How long you been livin' here, Ryker?" Jack asked, thinking he had just moved in.

"About six months."

"You've got no furniture to speak of," Jack said, his eyes still roaming the empty space. Ryker looked up and Jack could see it in his face. He'd told Jack all he had were the clothes on his back. Seeing it brought it home hard.

He really doesn't have anybody, Jack thought, swallowing hard.

"They just things, Jack," Ryker said.

"That's right. You're right. You're getting out and getting a job. That's what's important," Jack said, in agreement. *His focus is spot-on.* Jack had to give him that. *Why invest in things when you're trying to change yourself?* "Makes sense, but I think we can find you a bed though," he had to add.

They left the apartment and stopped for breakfast at a Denny's. Ryker ate every bite of a large breakfast. Afterward, they started looking for places he could apply. They hit Brookshire's grocery store, Wal-Mart, Target, Albertson's, and Kroger. Jack helped him fill out the applications and Ryker walked them inside and gave them to the managers. Several of them *did* say they were concerned about hiring a man with a felony on his record.

Jack and Ryker broadened their scope over the next few weeks, which turned into months, trying nursing homes, auto shops, car wash places, vehicle detailing; they covered as much territory as they could. They went to Weatherford and tried the unemployment center there, but Ryker was referred back to Project Rio, which was a job placement program for parolees. That would have been okay if Ryker was still on parole, but he wasn't so he couldn't file an application there.

Jack was relentless. He decided he would walk into places with Ryker, introduce him as his friend and personally endorse a recommendation. Jack had worked in so many places in the city of Fort Worth. Surely his contacts would help Ryker in some way. There had to be someone who would hire him. He called close friends, asking if there might be a maintenance job or any kind of minimum-wage opportunity, but he soon learned there was nothing doing.

Jack and Ryker saw each other every day, talked about prospects, walked in and out of businesses with the hope of Ryker being hired. Ryker, still amazed that Jack was putting himself on the line this way, watched him. Jack's stride was confident, purposeful, but not arrogant or assuming.

When Jack introduced Ryker to his friends or family or a potential employer, Ryker noticed he always put his right hand out to shake, while patting the other man's arm with his left. It was a kind gesture and Ryker wanted to try it. Jack got a good reaction from folks, whether he was greeting someone he knew or someone he just met.

When Jack walked into a store, he didn't wait to be greeted. He raised his chin to the store clerk or the secretary or the maintenance man and said, "How are you doin' today?" He smiled, genuinely, and if a conversation evolved from it, Jack took time to talk. Ryker finally said, "Jack, how you know all these people?"

Jack's eyebrows drew together, causing all the lines on his forehead to deepen, "I don't know 'em, Ryker, but I appreciate them. If it weren't for them, I wouldn't be able to go on about my business, whether I'm buying a stick of gum or asking to see my lawyer or whatever. These people may be the minimum-wage earners, but they are the support for all the people above them and below. Their job is important, too." He stopped when he saw this was intriguing to Ryker.

"Ain' nobody do that where I'm from," he said. "People think you up to somethin' if you gittin' up in they business. You could be tryin' to distract them so somebody can take they cash or steal they car."

"I see," Jack said. "So, how do *you* walk into a place? Show me."

"What? Right here?" Ryker looked around the mini-mart.

"Yeah, go back out and come in the way you do if you're in the 'hood," Jack quipped.

Ryker laughed at the way Jack said it.

"Go on," Jack pushed his shoulder. Jack walked over to an aisle and stood at an angle so he could see Ryker come in. Ryker went all the way to the car and Jack angled his head in order to watch his every move.

First, Ryker turned his head and scoped out the parking lot. When he got to the door, he threw it open with confidence and when he looked back to see a lady walking up the sidewalk, he caught it just in time to see her through the door. He glanced around the mini-mart. His eyes were serious, no smile; and when he walked, there was a swagger, almost like he was gliding, but with a confident bounce; a rhythm. Jack saw him round the end of the aisle. He stopped a couple feet from Jack. He held out his hands as if to say, "Well?"

"Confident, a gentleman with the lady; probably for the younger ones to take note of and a 'don't mess with me or I'll take you out' attitude," Jack assessed. "You see anybody you need to fight in here?"

Ryker looked around. "Naw. Not really."

"Okay then," Jack said, punching his shoulder. "Lighten up, son."

Ryker laughed out loud.

"That's good to hear. Don't think I've heard you laugh much since I've met you," Jack said.

"Can't 'member the last time I did," Ryker said. Jack gave him a side hug and turned to walk out of the store. Ryker watched him go. Jack's shoulders were broad, as he rolled them back and down. He remembered to thank the clerk and call him by name. Two people came in and he said hello, graciously, kindly. Each time, he patted a shoulder, said hello and asked how they were doing. He stood and listened to their responses; he was genuine. When Jack started to press the door open, he turned and said, "You coming?"

"Yeah. Say, Jack, how you know when to put yo' guard on and when to chill?"

"You said it before, son, *I feel you*," he reminded Ryker. "It's about letting the spirit of the situation be your guide. I guess I pay attention. I notice folks and try to be present in the moment, even if it's just getting a cup of coffee, understand?" He raised his cup, took a sip and walked toward his sedan.

"I don't know man," Ryker said. "You go to da south side and they ain' many people gon' git that."

"What's that got to do with it?" Jack stopped, mid-stride. "You tellin' me people don't want to be treated respectfully?"

"I'm sayin' you gon' git robbed on the south side -- robbed, beat and left on the street."

"Okay, you're probably right, but this," he gestured to the mini-mart, "isn't on the south side. So, what's stoppin' you here?"

"I got 'choo, I'm 'on do it, but I'm just sayin' it ain' for ever' place you gon' go."

"It is for me." Ryker shook his head, opening the driver's side car door for him. "Besides, you'll have my back on the south side, 'cause, I'm old and out of touch, right? Oh, here you are," he handed Ryker the key to his apartment.

Ryker patted down his pockets. "That key was in my pocket. How'd you?" Jack shook his head, smiling.

"Old, my ass," Ryker muttered.

"This world moves pretty fast, in case you hadn't noticed. All I'm saying is take time to care about people, even when they don't deserve it or ask for it. Use those keen observation skills you have, from being on the streets, to scope out the good in people too. I'm not saying ignore the bad. Just keep an eye out for the good and offer it from time to time, no matter what you receive in return."

Ryker nodded. He thought of the people in his life. Bagman John was one of the first people Ryker got to know when he moved to Fort Worth from Cooper. John had the word on the street, knew everybody's business.

Ryker met Bagman when he ran errands for his granddaddy. He was eight or nine years old. Things had been tight when he first came to live with Daddy D. His mother had trouble finding a job and Ryker wanted to help out so he started carrying small packages to and from the night club, just down from where they stayed on Powell. He had to meet Daddy D's friend, Charlie, in the alley with a brown package; it was illegal for Ryker to be in the club, being that he was a minor.

The first time he saw Bagman, it had been raining and he thought he saw a large garbage bag move. Knowing that rodents frequented the alley, he wasn't scared, but when the whole bag moved, he started to run. Curiosity, and instinct told him to stick; feet planted, right where he stopped.

"Hey little man, what's goin' on?" a voice said.

Ryker looked around, trying to figure where the voice was coming from, not completely sure he should trust his gut. It had led him to trouble more times than he cared to count.

"It's okay little man, you a'ight. Just move along."

"Who d'ere?" Ryker said, wanting to see a face, whoever it was.

"The name's Bagman. Bagman John. Now, move along," he said.

Ryker did as he was told, but he asked Daddy D about him the next day. Daddy D said his name was John Casey. He'd lost his family a long time ago to some kind of tragic accident. After that, he didn't see a purpose in having a home, where he would be reminded of what he'd lost, day after day, week after week. He said he'd rather be out on the street, watching over people, keeping an eye out to warn them if trouble was coming. He'd been doing it for fifteen years.

Once Bagman decided to care for you, he became your eyes and ears. Daddy D said to be cool with him. He called him "Diamond." When Ryker asked why, Daddy D said, "because he rough 'round the edges and he gon' cut you if you gon' mess with anybody he cur 'bout, but inside he as real as it gets. Give it time, you'll see."

Daddy D had been right. Bagman John had warned him off trouble more times than not. At eight years old, it couldn't hurt to have someone watching his back on the street. When Ryker needed ways to make cash, Bagman introduced him to a guy named Gerard Fuller.

Stripping cars and selling the parts turned out more cash than carrying packages to and from the club for Daddy D. In time, he became the fastest Gerard had. The extra cash made it possible for him to buy groceries and put them in the refrigerator before his mother came home from work. He and Daddy D figured she couldn't throw away good food if she didn't know where it came from.

He wouldn't have had to resort to this if she hadn't caught him putting cash in her purse. It had been the one and only time she gave him a spanking. She told him, "You may be the little man in this house, but you ain' gon' buy no groceries. You a kid and you need to be yo' age. I worry 'bout the food and the bills. You hear me?"

Daddy D heard the whole thing and that's when they came up with their plan; if she didn't know where the groceries came from, she couldn't be mad. It worked well. It was the beginning of him assuming an important role in his family. He became someone his mother and grandfather could depend on and that was a good feeling amid all the bad he had been through.

The friends Ryker had come to know and appreciate, growing up, were the ones who had his back on the street. The everyday, surface chatter that he saw Jack having with the people he ran into seemed meaningless and unnecessary. He chalked it up to Jack being white and in the middle class.

He wondered if Jack knew what it was like to be poor; to not know where his next meal was coming from or how he would pay rent. Still, he liked the idea that everyone deserved to be acknowledged in their job or on the street. He could remember times when he had to ask passersby for small change, hoping they would have a dollar or two for bread or milk. He and his sisters were so hungry after school and waiting for supper was hard. Nine times out of ten, they passed by without a forward or backward glance, never really seeing them there at all. It hurt. They felt rejected *and* invisible.

"I think we need to stop for lunch and then get back at it," Jack said, pulling into a Wendy's. When they had their food, they found a table and sat down to eat. Jack was so hungry he could have eaten his hand off. He grabbed his burger and started to take a bite, when he looked up and saw Ryker. Eyes closed, he was saying a prayer over his food.

The boy never ceased to amaze and surprise him.

They ate quickly and were back on the road. Ryker looked over at Jack. As they continued to pound pavement in search of a job, his thoughts kept pulling him away from the mission; the days he found work on the streets, stripping cars and selling parts were long gone, but seemed present, all the same.

His thoughts wandered to how he got into selling cocaine and weed. His so-called contacts were temporary and often anonymous, everybody using names with one or two initials, not always standing for their real name. It was about proving yourself and staking out your territory, while defending it with your life. He looked at Jack, still driving. *He tryin' to give me a chance to prove myself in a honest job.*

Given his record, it seemed impossible, even to him.

Why you want to help me after I been where I been, doin' what I been doin'? He was there again, asking that question for the umpteenth time in his head.

"All right," Jack said, interrupting. "I think we've hit every place on the list for today. Now, we've got to give it time. Let's get some supper at the house and talk about your interview tonight, okay?"

"Jack, we been at this for a while now. You really think somebody gon' hire me?" Ryker asked the question they'd both been thinking.

"Yeah, I do. We just need to start changing things up a bit. I'm going to make some calls and see what I see. We're not dead in the water yet, son. This old man still has a few tricks left."

The truth was, he was becoming as discouraged as Ryker. He knew Ryker was getting help with rent from somewhere, but he wasn't sure he wanted to know where. Jack had been helping out with groceries and transportation, but when he discovered Big R had given him full custody of Junior the day he went to prison, this complicated things further than just whether or not Ryker had a job. His housing, through Inmate Services, was set up on the basis that Ryker was the only one living there. Mrs. Simpson warned him about letting people live with him. His mother had asked to stay a few nights and his sisters were in and out.

"Have you talked with your mother about moving back in with Daddy D?" Jack asked.

"Yeah, she goin' to move back day after tomorrow."

"What about your sisters?" Jack pushed.

"They already gone. Tiffany git a job and she gon' help mama 'til she git on at the nursin' home and Neka back with her boyfriend," Ryker said, looking at Jack's profile for some sign this was good news.

"What about your lady friend?" Jack was determined to free Ryker of his dependents. He would have no chance of really making it out if he didn't draw some boundaries for his family. Being their sole support had been one of the reasons he couldn't get out, the times he tried in the past.

"Angela?" Ryker asked. Seeing him nod, still keeping his eyes on the road, Ryker went on to explain. "She been helping with Junior. How I s'pose to find a job if I ain' got nobody to watch him when he git out a school? He five years old."

"Could he stay with his mother?" Jack asked, no inflection in his voice. He was trying to guide Ryker without telling him what to do per se. He knew what it was like to be where Ryker was. Jack was no stranger to caring for siblings or a parent. His mother married two alcoholics, and her second husband, Mitchell Lawrence, damn-near put them all in the hospital more times than Jack wanted to remember. His only thought was to protect his mother and sister from another occurrence. If he had been old enough to get his own place, he wouldn't have thought twice about letting his mother and his sister stay with him, so he could keep his stepfather from putting his hands on them ever again. Family was extremely complicated, he knew.

"Doris ain' right in the head," he said. "She still on the powder and drinkin'."

"Okay, well, I know Angela has been good about keeping him. Could she possibly take him to her mother's house while we're out looking for jobs?"

"Yeah, I gon' talk to her 'bout that. You know she ain' just babysittin' Junior, right? We together. She think she may be pregnant, too," Ryker added.

Jack was silent; this was hard for him to understand. Jack believed a man and a woman should be married before sleeping together and living in the same house. He knew the world had evolved quite a bit since he was out there, dating and seeing women, but here was Ryker, trying to get out of his criminal life and he's got his father's illegitimate child to care for, two boys with a lady in Oklahoma and now, a baby on the way with an eighteen-year-old girl. *What're are you thinking, son?* Jack almost said it out loud.

Forcing himself to take a moment, he tried to imagine walking in Ryker's shoes, if only for a minute.

He doesn't know any different. His father is still married to his mother, while having affairs and children with other women. His mother has never remarried or asked for a divorce from his dad. She's having her own affairs and the kids have no role models, other than Daddy D, and he's living with a lady he's been together with for twenty-something years, but never married. How's Ryker supposed to believe in the sanctity of marriage or in any relationship? You're together and you have a few kids and then, one day, when things are different, you separate and go your way. Sometimes you meet up for the sake of the kids and other times, you move on, but try to stay in touch.

One last possibility hit him, hard – he's lonely.

Unable to resist, Jack asked, "Are you planning to marry this girl, Ryker?"

"Ah, I don't know. She young and I'm the first man she love. She's so inexperienced. I don't know, Jack. She like a good friend, the best friend I got. I just want to protect that somehow."

Yeah. Jack thought. *Real friends are hard to come by.*

"Well, see if she'll understand that you have to abide by the rules of the housing contract. If she can reside with her mother and help with Junior, then maybe we can get everything else worked out. You think she would consider that? Could you talk to her?"

"Yeah, I can do that," Ryker answered, hearing the relief in Jack's heavy sigh the moment he said it. "Thank you. I know things is a lot more complicated than 'xpected. I gon' get a job. I am," he said.

"I know you will. We just have to keep on it. Let's have some supper with Sarah and then you can take the truck to your interview."

"What?" Ryker said, incredulously. "You gon' send me out on my own?"

"Ye-ah, I sure am," he said, sounding almost like he'd said *yeehaw!* "I think you need to take this one on your own. Maybe you need to ditch this old man – I could be crampin' your style." Ryker snorted out a laugh.

"Doubt that, Jack."

"No. Let's see what you've got. I've been with you for a while now. It's time for you to go solo, don't you think?"

"Okay, if you say so." Ryker smiled at him then. "You think I ready?"

"Yep, sure do. You've got the interviewing process down. We've gone over all the tough questions about your record and all. I've seen you answer well for yourself in every interview you've had. I don't think you've really needed me all this time. So go on with your big bad self," he said, smiling back.

"Hey guys. How'd it go?" Sarah greeted them at the door. "Supper's ready if you're hungry." As Ryker followed them inside and saw their supper laid out on the table, he thought how grateful he was for Sarah and Jack. *How'd I get so blessed? First, they was Kailey, then Ms. Simpson and now Sarah and Jack. Lord, I don't know how I got to be so blessed, but I's so grateful.*

"C'mon now, fellas," Sarah said, smacking their hands when they reached for a biscuit. "Go wash up. You guys need to mind your manners," she said.

When Ryker returned to the table with Jack, Sarah smiled. As he sat down, he noticed she was looking him up and down, eyeing his clothes and his hair.

"What?" Ryker asked. "Do I got somethin' on my face or my shirt?"

"No, no. Um, are you planning to go to that interview tonight, looking like that?" she said, still smiling sweetly.

"Uh," Ryker looked at Jack for help. "I don't know. Somethin' wrong?"

"Well, yes dear. After supper, why don't you jump in the shower and I'll get you a fresh shirt. You'll tuck it into your jeans and we'll let you borrow a belt. Yes, that will be much better. Go on, eat up. And you're going to run a brush through that puff you call hair, right?" she finished, still smiling just as sweet.

Looking at Jack, who was shaking his head and smiling too, he said, "Yes, ma'am. Thank you."

Chapter 5

It's not clear if waiting for the fish to bite or actually
hooking the fish is the best part of being a fisherman.
I can remember seeing one of the guys on the lake
catch something and this was both exhilarating and
frustrating to me.

"Well, now. Look at you, dressed like you somebody,"
Esther Ross cocked her head to one side, looking Ryker up
and down, "Are we tryin' for respectable or responsible?" She
stepped aside when Angela came running up to hug him. His
eyes on Mrs. Ross, hers on him; it was a stare down of wills as
he wrapped his arms around Angela. She folded her arms
across her chest, straightened to her full height, raising one
eyebrow when he tightened his embrace with Angela.

She was an attractive woman, he had to admit. Her cocoa-
colored complexion, the high cheekbones and slight lines at
the corners of her mouth and around her eyes, gently defined
her; she was incredibly beautiful, her stint of being a single
mother of two in her early forties barely showing.

Eyeing him, she wanted to yank his arms off her youngest
daughter. She was so sheltered, having few experiences in
dating, much less love. Her oldest, Mia, was living on her
own and seeing someone Esther had met with open arms.
Lincoln Bradley had a good job, a decent family; all the
elements that make a good man. When he came around, she
reached out to wrap an arm around him, as he gave her a peck
on the cheek. It felt right and good.

Mia. Her demeanor was so much like hers; she was the
spitting image of Esther when she was a young girl. She loved
to watch Mia with Lincoln; imagine she'd made better choices,

fallen in love with a better man. Lincoln held promise, purpose, something that could lead to happily ever present with the hope of happily ever after.

Stop Angela, she wanted to scream, as she rubbed her cheek against Ryker's. Her eyes beamed up at this rogue man, as if he'd reached up and pulled a star from the velvet sky just for her. She was giddy with indescribably energy and vivacious curiosity; she was her father, or *is she me all those years ago?* She was entranced. This mysterious man had already consumed her; he'd swept her up and there was no going back.

"You look so… mmm, mmm, mmm," Angela said, a huge smile spreading across her face at the sight of him. He had cleaned up like Sarah instructed and he looked amazing. Her dark eyes lit up and her smile was so full of utter delight, he could almost ignore her mother's obvious disdain, emanating from her demeanor.

Esther Ross rolled her eyes, part of her remembering the thrill of seeing Chester for the first time. She'd met him at a street light, both of them waiting for it to change so they could cross to the other side. The light changed three times before their eyes unlocked. *Dear God, how did we get here? She met him at the McDonald's off of White Settlement Road for Pete's sake. She come home all lit up inside.* Esther remembered the first she'd heard of him. Her daughter looked so beautiful when she talked about him. Her eyes sparkled in a way that she didn't think possible. *Mine did too,* she shook her head. *Mine did too all those years ago.*

Angela had been such a bookworm in high school; painfully shy and uncommonly calm in attitude and behavior. Esther often wondered if she would ever find love. When she came home talking about Ryker, it was as if she had come to life.

"Mama, he's so good-looking and he's got this dark, mysterious thing goin'. But, he a gentleman, too," she added, when she saw the concern in her mother's eyes. "I think I's fallin' for 'im." At first, Esther had been elated to hear her talk about him. She'd loved seeing Angela so happy. Then, he came by to have dinner with them. He had swagger and confidence, seductive eyes and a smile that melted Angela the moment he stared into her eyes.

Esther felt the butterflies of the past, swarming her insides; only they turned quickly to bees and she felt like she was waiting for them to sting. Every moment he and Angela spent together, the buzzing became more pronounced, as if warning her of the pain coming in spades.

Even so, she'd seen the adoration in Angela's eyes and the hopefulness. *What if this boy was the real thing? How could she deny her baby girl if he was the one? What gave her the right to impose her experience on Angela?* So, she agreed to keep an open mind. She understood when Angela said she was going to babysit his stepbrother during the day, at that dingy apartment with no furniture, despite what her instincts were screaming in her ears, daily. *Am I crazy? This story' so familiar, like Chester and me happenin' all over again. But, I can't say no. What if it's real and I don't let her try?*

"Don't freak out or nothin', mama, but Ryker's father went down for possession several months ago. His daddy have a child by another woman. Her name' Doris. And, his mother know 'bout him, even though they still married. Anyhow, when his daddy go down, he ax' Ryker to take cur a Junior 'cause Doris messed up on pills and alcohol. Ryker been tryin' to find a job for a while. Until he do, I gon' help him out. So …." Her voice trailed off.

Esther's heart sank with every word Angela relayed to her about Ryker James Jr. He *was* her ex-husband all over again; the dark, haunted eyes, the confident, broad shoulders, the swagger. Angela fell into his arms and into his bed several nights a week. *I can't say why I let it go on. I know'd my baby girl was gon' end up pregnant.*

She had been right about that, too, hence her unmistakable disdain for him at present.

"Angela, could we talk some place?" Ryker's silky voice startled Esther from her walk through the many signs, the red flags.

"Yeah," Angela's smile widened, reminding Esther of when she was little. *Her cheeks were so full; we said they look like she have a mouth full a apples on either side.* Angela wrapped her arm in his and led him to her room. When they were inside, with the door closed, she looked at him, expectantly.

"We need to talk about Junior. The place I stay have a clause in the contract. It say I can't have nobody stay there but me and, if I don't mind the rules, I could git kicked out."

"What we gon' do?"

"It'd help if instead a watchin' Junior at my place, you could watch 'im here. Maybe I could come here and spend time with you, instead of us bein' at my place," his voice was a murmur of sensuality, as he pulled her close. "How my baby doin'?" he said, stroking her stomach.

"Good. He good," she said.

"How you know it gon' be a he?" he asked, smiling because he was hoping for a boy, too.

"I just got a feelin', that's all," and she was kissing his cheek and moving toward his mouth.

"I can't, baby. I got to go to my interview. We good?" he was asking about the new arrangements.

"Yeah, we good. I talk to mama," she smiled.

"I'll be back. I'll try to come see you later tonight. It gon' depend on whether I have a way back. The truck been actin' up. I don't know what wrong with it. I'm hopin' I can git to interview and back with no trouble."

"Okay, I'll be here," she said as he put his hand on her cheek. "Do what you got a do and I talk to mama."

When he walked back through the living room, he turned to say goodbye to Esther, but she was on the phone. The call seemed intense so he kept moving, out the front door.

Esther turned to hear the door close. Finishing her call, she sat down and stared at the door. *How could this happen?* She had done everything she knew to keep her daughters from falling for bad boys and the first one Angela sees. *Ah*, she sighed.

Just as she was about to relax into the chair, with her book, the phone rang.

"Hello?"

"Hey Ez," Chester Ross breathed into the phone.

"I told you not to call here," she said, sitting up straight as a board. "But, since you have, you'll be happy to know our little Angela is pregnant by that gangster she's seeing. He's like you, twenty years younger and a hell of a lot better looking." She let her words hit him hard, hoping he would hang up.

"Now, Ez, I didn't realize you still curred 'bout me at all and here you are, all riled up and anxious 'cause some boy done stole our girl's heart. You sure he's better lookin' d'an me?" he blew out a laugh, "what're we talkin', Denzel Washington-goodlookin' or…."

"Stop it. That idn' what I meant. *Denzel.* Was his father hooked on pills? Has he been in prison?" her tone hushed him up hard. "His father' in prison, his mother's livin' off her father-in-law and he's got a felony on his record for possession a cocaine. You good with that?" she spit out each word, undeniable resentment dripping from them. He couldn't tell if her disdain was for him or the boy. "That boy don't cur about nobody but hisself."

"Ez, Ez, listen to me," he said. "I know you hate me for getting involved with pills, but we've been over how it all went down. This boy's been sellin' white candy, probably since he could walk. I hardly think you can compare."

"It's worse. He's probably using, too? He's puttin' our girl in danger," she said. "He keeps tellin' her he's gittin' out, but what if he's lying?"

"Maybe he's on the level," Chester offered.

"Unbelievable. Are you naïve or just plain stupid?" her temper seemed to ignite with every word he said. Searing pain stabbed at her chest the longer the conversation dragged on.

"If he was usin', you'd know the signs, Ez. If you would let me back in the girls' lives, maybe I could help more. I been clean for almos' two years now. Can we talk 'bout me at least seein' 'em on special occasions?" When the phone went silent, he said, "Ez? Are you there? C'mon, honey. You know I love the girls. You know I do."

"I know. But I can't trust you, Chester. I just can't…." her tears falling as she clicked off.

Angela had been listening as best she could but couldn't make out everything being said. Tired of straining to hear, she came out from behind the wall, threw her hands up in surrender. "It was Daddy, wasn't it?"

"No child. Wrong number," Esther wiped at her face. The love she'd shared with Chester was still so present, his voice bringing back all the good times – the times she'd thought they could get through anything, with a little humor and a lot of love. *As long as they were together.*

"It was Daddy. I know it. Mama!" her voice relentless. "What did he say?"

Gathering herself and wiping at her face one more time, she whipped around, her eyes once embers turning cold. "Yes, it was him. You're right, baby girl."

"Did he ax 'bout me? What did he say?" Angela's heart skipped at the thought that her might still care; that he was sorry he left. He might have called to tell her he was sorry – he still loved her.

"No, child. We been over this. The only person he cur 'bout is hisself. You know it. I know it. If you must know, he wanted money. He probably ran out a his drug a choice and now, he needs somebody to give him cash flow."

"He loves me, Mama," her voice was pleading, like the little girl she'd been when he left. Making her own truth, she went on, "I 'member when I was little, when he left, when you made him leave. You told him to get out. *You* made him leave." She was crying now, destroyed by her mother's words about her father. "He loved me before you had that fight. He loved all of us. He left because a you!" and she stomped from the room, slamming her bedroom door behind her, as she'd done all those years ago. Some things hadn't changed.

Esther stood there, shaking from the emotion washing over her. Her memory of the night he left was ever-present. He was out of his mind on pain pills and begging her to see him through re-hab. Her parents were livid that he'd lost control on the job. Her father had taken quite a risk when he hired him to sell cars for him. He'd had no sales experience and then the accident; it simply confirmed he had no business working there.

The police report stated he'd taken a potential buyer for a test run, on the access road, near the car dealership, when he lost consciousness. The car veered off the road and into a clearing. No one had been hurt, but the customer had been severely traumatized by the incident, trying to steer the car to a safe stop, his leg stetching across the console to put on the brake.

When Esther's father, Terrence Vaughn, came to the scene of the accident, he managed to explain the situation by saying Chester had suffered a serious back injury and must have had a reaction to the medicine his doctor prescribed. It was all he could do to avoid a lawsuit and possible slander if word got out that he allowed his son-in-law to work at Vaughn Motors Inc., knowing that he was unstable and addicted to pain killers.

Esther had begged her father to keep him on staff, promising he would get clean and make a fresh start, but he had already proven to be a liability Vaughn Motors could not afford.

"He's done," her father voice was unforgiving, unyielding. Either you deal with him or I will."

If this had been the only incident, it would have been different, but Esther knew her father had been generous beyond reasonable expectations. So she checked Chester into a facility the next day. She told him that unless he stayed committed to rehab, he would not see his daughters ever again.

He walked out of the rehab at John Peter Smith Hospital hours after Esther and the girls left him there. The next day. The girls got up early, asking to see him. Not knowing if he could have visitors, Esther called for an appointment.

"Yes, ma'am," the physician on duty said. "But, he left shortly after you did, last night."

Esther changed the locks on the doors and got a restraining order, stating he was a danger to himself and couldn't be trusted alone with his daughters. Her father signed a statement as a witness, as did other co-workers at Vaughn Motors.

Even though he had been sober for a couple of years, she could not bring herself to trust him again. She'd moved on and the emotional pain associated with the entire experience was beyond repair. She told the girls he didn't want to see them. Any cards or gifts sent to them were thrown out, giving her story authenticity. Mia accepted everything without question, but Angela held out, hoping her mother was wrong about him.

Thinking about the hurt in Angela's voice and the sadness in Chester's was unbearable. She hated lying to her, but she couldn't take a chance on Chester. He'd broken her heart, her trust, and there was no going back; no second chances.

◆

Ryker was on I-30 headed west. The interview had gone well, or at least he'd thought so, until the end.

"Mr. James, I would like to hire you, but I have to be honest. I'm not comfortable hiring an ex-convict. I need to be able to trust my employees. I appreciate you coming in, but there's no job here for you."

As he drove, he prayed about the interview. This man was trying to do right by the people who had been loyal employees; Ryker could respect that. He was being cautious and Ryker understood that too. There were a lot of people who wanted in on the action when he was selling to the Bloods and working simultaneously with the Crips. Trust was the most important element in working with people. Ryker could think of four men he could trust. Their bond was stronger than the blood that ran through them; it was the blood they'd shed to survive that bound them and loyalty ran deeper still. *They's only me and mine; ain' nobody else gon' git inside that bond. How can I 'xpect a employer to feel right 'bout bringin' me into him and his?*

Other dealers let people in, people they hardly knew. They got greedy.

Thinking back on some of the tough calls he'd made, he felt a sense of pride. He'd mastered the game; he'd faced down the demons and lived another day. It was amazing that he was looking for a job and because of one felony, the managers were skittish. In his world, his one felony was like a trophy; an impressive feat. *I could a gone down so many times, I lost count.*

He handled things and came out alive. Part of him had trouble accepting that he was supposed to feel humbled and sorry for his record when he went into an interview. *How I s'pose to feel sorry for keepin' me and mine alive?*

At any time, he could have crossed the line, the one where power was more important than human life, but he didn't. He never took more or dealt more than was absolutely necessary. He'd remembered his mother's words, *control. If there's no other way, then upend their world. But, if you can leave peace in the wake a war, it's easier to carry. I done that.* Didn't that count for something?

He thought about the devil he knew. Time was passing him by and still no job. He watched the cars coming at him, each one a statement of status. He'd traded a stellar car for a rusty old pick-up. *I'd be fine with it if I had a job, a way to be useful, productive,* he decided.

Jack believe it gon' happen. What make him believe? He looked out at the night sky. *God. God make him believe.*

He knew there was cash waiting, his cut from deals being made in his absence. All he had to do was make arrangements to pick up his share. Romey was collecting from the apartment on 7th and Ace had the drop on the action on the south side, near Daddy D's. He could make a call.

Thinking about it felt wrong; his clean slate turning dark, shadows falling across it.

Jack and Sarah believe in me, he rubbed hard at his eyes, feeling the strength in the spirit washing over him. *I just don't want a be a burden to carry,* he argued with himself. *I ain' used to axin' for help or dependin' on nobody.*

Lord, I want to do what's right. I do. I just don't feel right taking from Jack and Sarah. They good people. They seem like they really cur 'bout me and my life, but ain' no way I want Jack to spend his retirement money on me. He have enough to take cur a, with him and Sarah. I know I'm a burden and it seem like I can't do nothin' 'bout it. I ain' got no way to pay him back or help myself, unless I go back to what I know.

I's grateful for Jack. I's grateful for the chance he give me. I just can't take from him like this. It ain' right. I could turn this truck around and grab my cut from Ace and Romey on my way to Cooper. It wouldn't take long to git back with my people. I ain' been out a the game long and I could git back in. The boys know to hang on to my cut, but I could go on and collect, git lost for a while.

Confusion permeated Ryker's thoughts. Driving usually calmed him, soothed the fears and kept things moving forward. He looked ahead, not back. Seeing the new coming toward him was comforting, being that it was fresh and untainted by his thoughts.

He felt a thud bounce the truck. He'd hit something. Another jolt came and a loud pop, like a gunshot. The truck swerved from the left into the right lane. There was a loud scraping sound and the smell of burning rubber wafting in through the vents and his driver's side window. He grabbed the steering wheel with both hands and was able to regain control, enough to get off the highway, onto the shoulder. As the car came to a stop, he looked back and saw a swirl of rubber flapping around the rim his tire was supposed to be on. He'd blown out his rear tire.

Looking down the road, he saw the Las Vegas Trail exit. His phone was dead so the only thing to do was leave the truck and walk to the nearest gas station.

Feeling the warm air on his face, he glanced up at the sky. *Diamonds in the dark, haunting sky,* he smiled. *Anything seem possible when all the glory blink down like d'at.*

Glancing back at the truck, he couldn't help but think there was a reason for the breakdown. As the gravel crunched under his feet, he drew confidence from the sound. It felt like he was physically burying the fear pertinently present just moments before. The black velvet cover overhead beckoned him to look up once again. Pinpoints of light, shining brighter, drew his eyes open, wider. He cast his gaze up ahead, mesmerized.

Lord, I don't know what's happening, but I ain' worried about this blow-out. I gon' walk to the gas station up ahead and see what's what. Wait, da't ain' no gas station. It's a repair shop. Lord, what you be doin'?

As Ryker came within a few feet of the door, the sign, Pro Auto Group, shone on the door. Inside, he could see an older man at the register. He walked around the end of the counter to straighten a few things, a pencil tucked over his right ear. He looked to be closing up for the night.

Ryker swallowed hard before he pressed open the glass door.

Greet them kindly, Jack's voice crept into his thoughts. *Look 'em in the eye and ask how their day's been, tell them something you appreciate in them. Be professional and show respect.*

"Good evenin' sir. How you doin' tonight?" Ryker said, clearing his throat.

"Well, hello there, son. I'm all right. I was about to close up. May I help you with anything?" he asked.

"I just want a say I sure am glad to see you still here. I don't want to be a bother, but my truck just broke down on the highway.

"I can see you put in a long day. I understand if you want me to walk on to the next place. You may need to get home," Ryker said, trying to remember how Jack said, *You have no idea what their day has been like. Maybe they need you to care about what's happening in their life for a moment.*

"No, sir. I wouldn't hear of it. I'm at your service," The man stuck out his hand and said, "Forgive my manners, I'm Steve Johnson. I own this shop and I'm a little short-handed, but I'm sure I can help you one way or another."

"Did you say you're short-handed?" Ryker perked up at the man's words.

"Yeah, I had a guy quit on me, mid-shift yesterday," he replied.

"Really?" Ryker paused, trying to steady himself. *Lord, you be workin'. I can feel it.* "D'at's too bad, uh, do you s'pose you might be hirin' somebody to replace him? I've been lookin', but haven't come up with …."

"What's your name, son?"

"Ryker. Ryker James, sir," he said.

"Ryker, have you done any detail work?" Mr. Johnson was looking straight at him, waiting for his answer.

Ryker stood tall, his six-foot frame straightening to its full potential. He rolled his shoulders back and removed his ball cap. Looking directly at Mr. Johnson, he said, "Yes, sir. I done cars, trucks, SUVs, boats. I used to detail boats for

Texas Marine Company over off the highway, Southwest Loop 820."

"Texas Marine is a good place. Why did you leave there?" he asked, still eyeing Ryker.

"Well, sir. I worked long hours and double shifts and I couldn't make enough to pay my rent and keep food on the table. My manager thought I deserved a raise but she was transferred and the raise didn't happen," Ryker said, shifting his stance to balance his weight on both feet. *Jack said stand tall, ready to work.*

"I see. Well, son, if you work hard for me, I'll raise you right up. But, I can't promise how much work there will be. Can you start part-time and go from there?" Mr. Johnson said, shifting his own stance and letting his hands rest on his hips, his thumbs hooked inside his belt loops, as he bounced on the balls of his feet, rocking forward, then back again.

Ryker tried not to lose his cool. He put his hands on his hips and looked down to gather his composure. When he looked back at Mr. Johnson, a smile pulled at the corners of his mouth, "Yes, sir. I would like that."

"Well, all right then. Let's get your truck, sign some paperwork and you can start tomorrow. I'm damn tired, so help me close up. We'll grab the truck, bring it back here and if you can call a friend or something, then we'll see what we can do with your truck in the morning. If you can help us fix it, maybe we can figure out a deal to pay for it, something that works for both of us."

"How do you think he's doing?" Sarah asked.

"He's going to be fine." Jack was turning his coffee cup, back and forth, back and forth.

Sarah poured Jack more coffee. He stopped, leaned back and watched the dark liquid go into the china cup. The English tea cups had been his mother's. The one in his hand was one of two that were not broken when he was a boy. Sarah was drinking from the other one, the sweet flowers unique to each cup, but the pattern unmistakably matching in style.

Flashes of how the other four tea cups broke, one by one, surfaced. He was ten years old and he came home to eat supper after playing a baseball game at the Fort Worth Boys Club. As he walked home, he'd hoped it would be a good night. He had helped his mother with the housework before he left for the game. He would help with his baby sister when he got home.

Walking up to the back door, he could smell her amazing baked chicken. His stepfather would be home soon. If he could get inside and wash up quickly, he could make sure he was sitting closest to him, just in case.

He walked into the kitchen and his mother was humming. This was a good sign. She always hummed when things were peaceful in her heart and in the house. She turned to see Jack come in. She smiled and Jack's heart skipped a beat. He wished it could be like this every day.

"Let's call your sister to the table, and could you get the baby?" she asked.

"Sure, Mama. I'll be right back," he'd said. When he came back, he put his baby sister, Jenny, in her high chair. She was so happy, her cheeks rosy from having just awoken from her nap. She reached for Jack and said, "Dack." He loved to hear her try to say his name.

Laura came into the room slowly. She was holding her baby doll. "Mama, the chicken smell good," she said.

When they were all seated, Jack asked if there was anything else he could get for the table. "Thank you, sweet boy, but all we're waiting for is your dad," she said.

My dad. He was no dad. My friends had Dads. I had a monster who beat us every other day of the week, unless we got lucky and he was too drunk to do it, Jack thought.

They waited for almost an hour. Jack played with Jenny and gave her little bites of cracker to keep her from getting fussy. His mother was tired. She was up late the night before. Her eye was not as swollen from the other day. He wondered if her arm was still hurting. The monster twisted it and Jack couldn't be sure if it hurt from the bruises he left when he held onto her or if he pulled it so hard, it was sprained. She wasn't using it to cook and he knew she had trouble holding Jenny.

"Okay, let's just start. I don't know where your dad is," she said, a half smile starting in the corner of her mouth. "C'mon, sillies. Let's eat."

When Laura grinned and Jenny giggled, his mother's smile spread so wide, her dimples showed. Jack wanted that moment to last all day. *If he had just not come home,* he thought.

When they were about half-way through eating, the door flew open and hit the wall. He was drunk and Jack could feel the anger emanating from him. He picked up the tea cups one by one and smashed them to the floor. Jack stood up, putting himself between his father and his baby sister. In one blow, Mitchell Lawrence knocked him to the ground. He didn't remember anything else until he woke up and saw Jenny. She had blood on her cheek and her face was white with fear. He slowly sat up and saw his mother was lying on the floor by the stove. Laura was crouched behind the television, shaking.

He stood up and felt the broken china beneath his feet. His skin prickled as he looked around the room, listening for him. *Where is he?*

"Jack," Sarah's voice blundered into the memory playing in his head. When he didn't answer, she looked over at him, setting her tea cup down a little hard. The crash had his face draining of blood, turning his complexion ashen, a stark contrast from his usual rosy cheeks. "Shug, are you all right?" She reached out to him, touching a hand to his arm. Jack's hand slipped, knocking over his own cup, his hands shaking as he tried to recover the coffee with his napkin.

"Oh, good gracious. Look what I've done."

"Where were you just now?" she asked.

"I, uh," he paused, a shudder running through him. Forcing himself to focus, he stared hard into Sarah's kind eyes. "I just don't understand why we haven't heard from him," he managed.

"He's fine."

"No, he should have called by now."

"Maybe no news is good," Sarah gave a half-hearted shrug of her shoulder.

"I could use some good," Jack was getting his bearings. "I haven't had much luck with the guys I called. There's just nobody hiring right now and I'm sad to say, Ryker's record is not easy to defend. I've done everything but sign my name to his application and swear he will be a good employee if given the chance.

"I was looking in the paper and right now, the rate of recidivism is at 67 percent. I can understand why, too. From what I know from Ms. Simpson, ex-cons are dropped off in the same community they committed their crimes in, given fifty dollars, with no place to live, no form of transportation and no job. How could anybody make that work, just out of prison?

"If we consider where Ryker would go, he would be at his father's door, asking for help. His father is a known drug dealer. If he went to his mother, she's barely able to keep herself employed. If he went to his cousins in Cooper, he'd be back with the Bloods. If he stayed in Fort Worth, he'd be back with the Crips. His sisters could be clean but chances are they'd have no way to help him either. That would leave Daddy D. Daddy D's been living with a woman whose daughter Ryker used to get into trouble with, which is what led him to deal drugs in the first place.

"So, if we can't help him," he said, now seeing the concern in Sarah's eyes, as he had not told her all of this until now. "Oh, Shug. If he doesn't get a job, how are we going to do right by him?"

"Well," she said, swallowing hard. "We just have to pray. We need to ask Father Rayford to pray. We can ask the church to pray. We are not in this alone. Let's makes some calls."

◆

Father Rayford sat across from Jack in Starbucks on the corner of highway Southwest Loop 820 and Trail Lake. As he took a sip of his double espresso, Father Rayford looked at Jack. Jack's normally carefully combed silver hair was disheveled and hanging in his eyes. When he put his cup back on the table, he sat back in the deep, leather chair and smiled.

"Jack, let go. You've chosen to be a servant of God. He knows your heart and more important, he knows Ryker's heart. Whatever happens, it's going to be right for him and you."

"I just can't understand how folks are supposed to get a second chance when they are given so little to work with when they get out." He was running his fingers through his hair again and Father Rayford put a hand on his arm.

"Jack. Jack," he said firmly enough to get him to look up. "Wait for him to get in touch. It's not even ten o'clock in the morning. He'll let you know when he knows something. In the meantime, remember he has to walk his walk. You have offered to walk with him, but you cannot take the steps."

"Yeah, I know," Jack said. "You know Elizabeth and Charles think I'm crazy to help him. They think I'm a fool to think a man so deep into criminal activity could really change his stripes. What if they're right? I mean, my gut tells me I can help him. My prayers tell me *to* help him.

"When I pray, I feel a peace come over me and … I'm basing all this on a feeling, my *gut* feeling. Am I crazy?"

"I thought you were one of the best fishermen around. Didn't you say you won state championships in casting at one time?"

"Well, yeah, but what's that got …."

"Didn't you spend an entire weekend trying to catch a twenty-eight pound catfish? You named it Charlie or something like that."

"Yeah, yeah. I did. It took me darn near two days to get him, but I …."

"You caught him," Father Rayford said. "Did you listen to your fishing buddies when they told you Charlie had you beat?"

"Nope." Jack sat back and felt his heart relax as he breathed a deep sigh. He nodded, understanding Father Rayford's point. "Okay. Okay."

Jack walked out of Starbucks with Father Rayford, shook his hand. He nodded to himself as he got into his sedan. He put the key into the ignition and started the car. As he backed out, he felt it, grace wrapping around him in a warm embrace.

———◆———

Ryker was pacing outside Jack's house. He had been waiting since he got off work at four. *Where was Jack?* He sat on the top step of Jack's front porch. He thought of how close he had come to going back to the life he knew. He thought about how hard he prayed while he was driving and then the car broke down and things seemed more hopeless. The next thing he knew, he had a job.

He woke up early, hours before he was supposed to be at work. He was so excited he had walked from his apartment. He didn't care how far it was. He just wanted to get there and start. He knew he could have called Jack, but he wanted to get there on his own. Besides, if he had gotten there and filled out the application, only to find out Mr. J had changed his mind when he discovered he was an ex-con, it would have been worse. He had to be sure it was going to happen. Thinking back over it, he was still reeling from the outcome.

"Mr. J," Ryker had said as he walked into the shop.

"Hey Ryker. C'mon in son." He was grabbing a cup of coffee. "The application is on the desk over there. Go on and fill it out. I'll be right with you."

Looking down at the application, Ryker was suddenly frozen. His heart raced, pounding so hard it felt like it could burst from his chest. He sat on a dilapidated chair near an old gumball machine. He began writing his name, address, and phone number. When he got to the part where it asked for references, he wrote Jack's name and address. *I hope I can tell you I got this, Jack,* he thought.

When he came to the part where he had to disclose his record, he wrote carefully, legibly. If he was going to get the job, he didn't want any confusion. Finishing, he handed it to Mr. J. He read through it and when he came to the part about his record, he looked up and met Ryker's gaze. He seemed to search for a moment.

After what seemed like hours, Ryker looked down. It had been thirty seconds. When he looked back up, he said, "It's okay, Mr. J. I can go." He almost made it to the door when he heard his voice.

"Ryker, if you're ready, I could sure use someone on that SUV outside. Could you get started on it right away?"

Ryker stopped mid-stride, turned and said, "Yes. Yes, sir."

There was no way to describe that moment. *The closest I can say was it like God just wrap me up; give me courage.*

The day had flown by. Car after car, truck after truck, he'd cleaned them, shined them up like brand new. He could hardly wait to get to Jack's house so he could tell him all about it. *Where is he?*

He stood and walked over to the car Mr. J had loaned him while his truck was being fixed. Opening the car door, he sat in it for a few more minutes. When he reached up to put the key into the ignition, he heard a car. Jack and Sarah were pulling into the driveway.

He was out of the car as quick as could be. He ran to the other side of the car and shouted, "I got it. I got a job! Jack, I got a job!"

"You what?" Jack thought he heard him, but he needed to hear him say it again.

Sarah insisted he come in for dinner. When Ryker told them the story, Jack couldn't stop smiling. Sarah was thrilled and told Ryker it was all because he looked presentable, going over all the things she'd told him before he went.

Ryker listened to them banter over who said what and who could take credit for him getting a job. He thought, *is this what it sound like to have a mama and a daddy who cur 'bout ever'thang that happen? They's white people who know me a little over six months and they actin' like I's been here all my life. They believe I could do d'is. They make me believe it. And, I done it. Dear God, I done it.*

Thank you, Lord. I gon' keep going. This a good start, but I got to git more work if I gon' really git out.

Ryker didn't stop looking for more work after he was hired at Mr. J's shop. A few weeks later, he saw a sign in the window of another auto repair shop just down the street from the Pro Auto Group that read "Hiring: need part-time help. Apply within." Ryker stopped by immediately after work and filled out an application. The manager said he appreciated it and if he could come in the next day for some training, he was hired. Ryker had two part-time jobs and was finally feeling like he could breathe a little. He was still behind on the rent but in a few paychecks, he hoped to change all that.

Once he was able to square the rent with Ms. Simpson, he told her about Junior and Angela. She understood things were changing for him, but couldn't offer him the same deal at the apartment. He told her he would be out by the end of the month.

Jack and Sarah offered their guest bedroom and rollaway bed as a temporary place to live. Ryker could hardly believe how supportive Jack and Sarah were. Angela's mother had been less than agreeable about Junior and Angela staying with her, so the move was going to be better in many ways.

◆

"What's this?" Sarah asked Jack one morning.

"It's an application for a job at State Farm, shooting pictures of vehicles for 'em," Jack said.

"I can see that, Shug. Why are you filling it out? Is it for Ryker?"

"Nope, it's for me," he said, looking up and seeing her confused expression. "I'm coming out of retirement for a while. My pension isn't really enough while I'm helping Ryker and Angela out."

"Well, that's absurd," Sarah said. "Jeff left me more than enough to live on when he passed away and what's mine is yours."

"Sweetie, I appreciate you saying that, but this thing with Ryker was something I took on and I don't feel right about asking you to help with it. You've already opened your heart and now, your house to them. I can work a little every day and it will take care of incidentals with them, okay?"

"I think you're silly. But I know there's no use arguing with you."

Jack smiled, looking into her beautiful blue eyes, her hair feathered about her cheeks. She returned his smile and patted his shoulder, mumbling, "Silly, silly man."

Jack thought of what Charles and Elizabeth said at church a few Sundays before.

"You know you're throwing your money down the drain, don't you, Jack?" Charles asked.

"Aren't you the least bit concerned about Sarah?" Elizabeth chimed in, knowing Sarah had some medical issues. "You should be thinking of your health and hers. Aging happens and you don't get to choose how well you do it. I've had to have a couple of surgeries myself. You never know what's going to happen."

"We're fine," Jack assured her.

"What's this we hear about you taking a part-time job?" Charles asked.

"Oh, now. C'mon. There's nothing to worry about. I'm helping my friend Frank out of a bind at State Farm. It's temporary. Nothing to worry about.

"Charles, how're things at the office? I hear you're spending a pretty penny on some remodeling." That was all it took. Charles and Elizabeth lit up.

"Fine, fine. Elizabeth and I are getting the plans ready for my new home office. We're choosing the colors and comparing swatches of material for the loveseat we're looking at recovering."

He turned to see Elizabeth nodding. "It's coming along so beautifully," she cooed.

The moment passed easily enough, but Jack wondered what other people were saying at church. He found it a little hurtful that many of them were so judgmental when it came to Ryker. It was true that helping him had been more than he'd expected, but he couldn't help but smile, ear to ear, when he saw Ryker on the day he got his job. *Why can't they see God working?*

Still, as he looked at Sarah, he didn't want to compromise things if there was any truth to what Charles was saying. If he subsidized their income with this new job so there was no concern, then it was his money to "throw away" and Sarah wouldn't have to hear about it from anyone at church.

There were several folks that were very supportive of Ryker's situation and of Jack's mission to help him. Jessica

Murray was one of them. When he told her about Ryker's predicament, she suggested that the church come together and work on bringing Christmas to Angela, the new baby, Junior and Ryker.

Jack's daughters joined in too, saying that in lieu of Jack and Sarah giving them Christmas presents, perhaps Jack could take any money he would have spent on them for Christmas and put it toward Ryker and Angela's "surprise Christmas." Sarah's son and daughter offered to do the same.

People who responded so generously made it easy to disregard the concerns of the others. Ryker had turned a significant corner and it was becoming evident. The parishioners of St. Timothy had a chance to talk with him, get to know him. No one pressured them to bestow Christmas on him and his family; it had been their idea. They were seeing something in him too.

When Christmas came, Ryker and Angela had gone to bed early. Angela was so tired, having been up with baby Malcolm several nights in a row. When Jack woke them the next morning, they seemed to drag out of their rooms.

Junior woke up early and was excited to go to church just because everyone was so kind to them when they went. Ryker told him that they would try to get him something after Christmas when the sales were on. Presents were the furthest from his mind. Junior thought he had already had Christmas when he saw all the lights on the Christmas tree in Sarah and Jack's living room.

Sarah had made gingerbread cookies and a Christmas tree cake for after their main meal at lunch. The tinsel Sarah wrapped around Junior's lamp, by his bed, was so sparkly; the twinkle lights woven into it made him feel as if Christmas was everywhere he looked.

"Is it time for church yet?" he asked, ready to go.

"Not yet, lil' man," Ryker had said, still trying to wake up.

None of them knew what was waiting in the parish hall. When Jack pushed them to get ready so fast, Ryker began to suspect something, but it was nothing like the surprise he walked into at the church. There were so many people waiting there, with Santa hats on their heads, presents in their arms and a tree that seemed to light everyone up inside. Leroy Anderson's Sleigh Ride played in the background, while members of the congregation presented Ryker, Angela, Junior, and Baby Malcolm with presents. Junior stood behind Ryker, wondering what was happening. Angela and Ryker could not speak. They just looked at each other and shook their heads, as if they had walked into a dream.

Ain' nobody ever done nothin' like this before," Ryker thought. *Dear God in heaven, how this happen?*

"What's goin' on in that head of yours?" Jack said, clapping Ryker on the back.

"I don't know what to say, Jack. I ...." He stopped mid-sentence. Seeing Junior riding around on a bike with training wheels, he raised his hands, gesturing at everything. Awkwardly, he stuck his hands in his pockets, turning to look at Jack, eyes brimming with emotion.

"Thank you," he kept saying to anyone and everyone he talked to.

Chapter 6

The hook, by design, is meant to keep you from reversing your path. It may hurt on the way into the trap but getting out is designed to hurt even more, often tearing you apart as you try to fight for release. The hook will invariably take some of your softest tissue with it if you should manage to get away.

"Hey Lil' R," a voice from his past said behind him, while he was detailing a Mazda four-door sedan.

Without turning around, Ryker said, "What's up, Ace?"

"Stuff goin' down," Ace said, walking around to the side of the car Ryker was detailing. "The word is you out. I's comin' round to see if … uh."

"Look it, I'm on the job, man. Why you here?" Ryker cut him off.

"What?" Ryker pressed when Ace didn't leave.

"Ain' nobody know if you really gone for good," Ace said. "It makin' it hard to run d'territory. Thangs is goin' down and…."

Ryker didn't answer.

Ace was standing there watching Ryker rub the chrome edges of the grill. He rubbed so hard, thinking about everything coming down on him, that by the time he finished, the chrome gleamed, catching the light and sparkling. A mixture of pride and irritation shone on his face. *Hard work bringing this beautiful shine. No tarnished edges. No rotten, rusted insides that can't be renewed. Clean, pure shine.* One thing he'd loved since he was a little boy was making things shine; making them look new.

"Eh, I think you passed brand new," Ace slammed through his thoughts. He glared at him.

What do you know about shine? What do you know 'bout brand new?

Ace raised his dark eyebrows, his mouth spreading into a knowing grin. The expression on his face reminded Ryker of the thrill of the score, the near-miss arrests, the good coming through the bad. *Fine lines; some white, some black, mostly gray.*

"You in?" Ace asked. Still no answer. "A'ight."

Ryker turned to watch him go. His head was high, shoulders broad and strong, the swagger still there. Just as he reached his ride, he took out his cell. He eyed Ryker, his stare intense and intentional, and answered the call. He cut his eyes away, his face void of emotion. *Business was business.*

◆

Years of knowing his brother flooded his mind. Ace wasn't the only one he left behind. There were so many. He was out of the fire, working a job and everyone he knew was in it.

He tried to shake it off. He still had to find a place he could afford. Working full time, between the two shops, was barely enough to make rent; this didn't include food and necessities, not to mention Angela being pregnant again.

"We 'posed to be protectin' ourself," he'd said when she gave him the news.

"We was," she whined. "It's just, I didn't know I got to worry 'bout it right after I had Malcolm. Nobody say nothin' 'bout it. I figure I's nursin' Malcolm so they ain' no way I could git pregnant. I couldn' be takin' no pill – that gon' be bad for the baby."

She had been different since she'd had Malcolm, needy and more insecure than ever. She accused him of seeing other women and flirting with girls at work. He had little patience for her because he was so tired all the time. *When would I be with another woman?* He wanted to scream at her. *I'm workin' ever' day, all day. I ain' got no time to go have no affair.*

A few nights ago, she told him she was late. He stared at her and she knew what he was thinking. They had talked about protection and how they needed to wait to have another baby when things were more stable. *Did she do this on purpose, knowin' I didn't think we needed to be havin' 'nother baby?*

"You don't want the baby?" she whined, knowing that was not the case.

She was adding more pressure to an already difficult situation. How was he supposed to support her, Malcolm, Junior and a new baby? He still didn't have a place to live.

Accepting financial support and even emotional support from Jack and Sarah was almost painful, given the obstacles became more every day. He knew Jack was working again because he didn't want to take money from Sarah to help him. Knowing that they were making sacrifices like this was eating him up inside. He could turn a few scores and no one would have to suffer.

No, it wasn't right for him to sell, but how many folks do things that are wrong in the moment, for the sake of what's right overall? He wanted to spare Jack and Sarah. They had done so much for him already.

Ryker ran his hands over the workbench, the dents and discoloration made him smile – *character,* he thought. *Life lived well, scars to show.*

He thought of his last customer, Mrs. Calwell, her face so delighted, when he handed her the keys to her Cadillac. "You are a miracle worker," she'd said. "I didn't think anybody could make this car look so good." When she opened the door and sat in the driver's seat, she saw the detail. She looked up, eyes swimming. It felt amazing to see how happy she was.

He looked around the shop, everything in its place, the concrete floor swept, ready for the next day. This felt good too. He turned out the lights.

Jack called every day, checking how things were going. It was comforting, kept him focused. He worked double shifts, saving enough to move into his own apartment again. Jack helped with the deposit so he'd have time to get the first month's rent.

Though things were finally starting to come together, he thought it was strange he didn't *want* to go home to the apartment. The kids were usually asleep by the time he got home and Angela was exhausted. He'd end up taking a drive, not really knowing where he was headed and end up in Jack's driveway. He'd sit for a while, wanting to knock on the door, maybe sit on the back porch and talk. Hearing Jack talk soothed his discontent; kept him from feeling so lost. Going home to Angela was draining, somehow. They had all the basics – food, water, a roof over their head, but she wanted more. He was making it, in an honest job, paying his bills and it felt amazing, until he had to face her. Her wants and needs weighed him down. What made her happy was heavier than anything he'd had to carry before. It felt like she was missing the way he used to be.

C'mon, man. Just one more score and you could stop all the complainin'. Ain' nobody got to know how you make it happen. Just one last score.

His thoughts were becoming more complex. It was as if he was two people; one was Ryker, who wanted to stay in this new life and find a way to make it; the other was also him, except he was torn, knowing Angela seemed to want him to go back to dealing. He hadn't considered she'd been attracted to the "bad boy" in him.

When they met, he'd just finished scoring on the south side for the last time. She'd been riveted when he told her how close he'd come to getting caught.

When he told her about Jack, she looked disappointed. "What 'choo mean you gon' git out and hang with Jack?" her tone irritated and tense. "He ain' like us. He ain' got no idea what it's like to be poor. What about yo' family and yo' friends? Or, don't they matter no mo'?"

"I ain' forgotten where I come from," his temper flared.

Even so, his thoughts turned to Ace – *he was axin' for help,* the thought crossed and hit hard. *He ain' never ax for help from nobody. He in deep and it's got to be bad or he wouldn't a come axin'. Ah, man. Ace done saved my life mo' times d'an I can count.*

Maybe Angela speakin' d'truth. He ran a hand over his face, scrubbed at the stubble on his chin. *Ace sayin' somethin' 'bout how it hard to handle the territory. What he mean d'at?*

He looked at the time on his phone. There was a message from Angela and a missed call from Jack.

Flashes of time with Jack and Sarah's went through his mind. *How was your day? Would you like me to fix you a little breakfast? How 'bout we sit on the porch and you can tell me what all you did today?*

He'd felt at home in the spirit of those moments. When he went to the apartment, he wanted to somehow transfer the essence of that to Angela and the boys. Only, the moment he stepped in the house, the noise of reality hit him hard; a freight train screaming its way to him. In seconds, his thoughts were scrambled and fragmented.

He was at a loss as to what to say; how to handle it. He reverted to habit. *Just do what gotta be done. Take the screamin' baby, go to the kitchen and try to give him a bottle, while yo' stomach growlin'. You can wait. Listen to Angela' complainin' 'bout ever' damn thang'; tell her it gon' be a'ight. Fall asleep sittin' up on the couch, no food in yo' belly, no peace in yo' heart. Start all over when you wake up;* the sharing of a meal or thoughts from his day shattered by the barrage of demands.

His co-workers talked about getting drunk or getting high; they imposed their lifestyle on him, which often triggered his temper. He couldn't imagine going over to their houses, spending an evening around them. It could send him spiraling into the demeanor he displayed around the funnymen in jail. *Not good. Not good on any level.*

Who then? Where do I fit? He wondered. *I can't go back to Pop's house. They's even more temptations there. The talk gon' be 'bout why I left and how come I's tryin' to be white on the other side a town. If I tell'em how great Jack and Sarah been to me, the word gon' be d'at I don' cur 'bout my own family.*

I do cur. I cur a lot. Ain' nobody git d'at. Ain' a day pass d'at I don' ax myself what make me think I's deservin' a gittin' out — why I so special?

I could try livin' in both worlds.

As Ryker headed toward his apartment, he was thinking about his connections; his mother coming by and asking to stay, Ace showing up, asking for help.

Ace, he considered. *They was more going on with that. He was axin' me to git back in the game. He'd a crawled over broken glass before he'd come axin' me d'at.* His gut tightened, as more knots formed. *He could be in trouble.*

What I s'pose to do? One last score ain' gon' end me. Just letting these words penetrate his thoughts felt as if someone else took over his body for the next few hours.

I ain' tryin' to put the blame on nothin' or nobody. It was my call. I's caught at a crossroad and I made d'choice.

Lookin' back, I think I know'd I's gon' get caught. Only, it was different 'cause it was the first time I know better. Jack all up in my head too.

It went down like this. Ace give me my half the candy. I's baggin' it separate and seein' the powder bringin' it all back. Times when I's with Trina. She my first for a lot a things. I done my first line with her. I's thirteen and she was older. We spend a lot a time together, messin' around and getting' high. It been a long time.

Man, you need to stay focused. No time to get caught up.

I could a made a run for it, maybe taken it to Cooper and scored there. I could a gon' for a drive, rolled down the window and let the wind carry it off. D'at would a been playin' it smart, takin' d'bad choice off d'table.

I mean, I had a life with Angela and the boys. Jack and Sarah would a been there for me. I could a just walked. Dumped the stash and walked. I wished to God I had.

I felt for my .45. It was pressed against my waist. I had to shift it so it fit more comfortably against my belt. A cold sweat sent a chill up my back. It make me think bringin' d'piece a bad idea.

Oh yeah? How you know you ain' bein' set up for a fall? I mean, check it, who's to say Ace ain' in over his head and you 'bout to take the heat? Wake up, man. Focus. You got to be ready for whatever come.

The piece a necessary evil. Yeah, if you git caught, this mean double felonies, but d'at's part of it. If you packin' d'candy, heat comin' too, less

*you want a take d'chance somebody gon' git d'drop on you. If you 'bout
to freak, pack up and go home to yo' white Pop.*

Eh, you hearin' me, man?

I just wanted to end the scene.

Then again, I know d'drill. A part a me already have it
mapped out in my head. Motel 6? Check. Scopin' buyers?
Check. Contacts for word on the street? Done. I ain' sure
how I go from thinkin' 'bout it to bein' in d'motel room. It
like I's walkin' and I end up there.

My stomach full a knots. Whatever I done didn' feel tight;
not even. I knew the risk. I knew worst case. I done
weighed d'cost a thangs. Walkin' in blind ain' ever been my
style.

They ain' no choice. It's either help Ace and make some
green or go home to Angela and the boys, empty-handed.
D'at ain' no choice. I don' cur who lookin' at it; they ain'
seein' a choice. This, right here right now all they is.

Jack gon' say they is but one day, he gon' have to stop
helpin' us. He ain' no rich man. He either gon' stop the
support or go under with me. I ain' havin' that.

I closed my eyes for a second; I didn't expect to sleep. I
couldn' say how long I's out. I's havin' that dream again. It's
d'one where I's lyin' on my bed and the window' open. It like
I's watchin' my own self on the bed, while I's sleepin'. I feel
d'is breeze from the window and I think, *somebody need to close
it. Somebody could git to you, man. You in danger. You leavin' yo'self
wide open. Somebody comin' man. Git up and close that window.
Hurry man. Git up! Freakin' git up and close that window! Right
when I git to the window, they's somebody comin' at me, then they's two,
then three, then ten, then a hundred -- all out for blood.*

The pain in my chest' so strong, it jolt me awake and I
looked 'round for 'em. Instead I seen a light blinkin'. It take
me a minute to git it's my phone. I'd put it on silent but it like
I woke just in time to see it light up.

It was Angela. I picked up and while we was talkin', I git
this feeling in my gut. *Run, man. Git out a there.* Still a little
freaked by the dream, the way it wake me right when my
phone ringin', I's thinkin' I done lost my mind. Angela talkin'
but I can't hardly hear her. She sayin' somethin' 'bout what I

gon' bring for dinner and I's like -- *my boys*. I's out here 'bout to run a score and my boys' is needin' me, axin' fo' me; they needin' they dinner. I felt like I's two people. I's they daddy an I's Little R. I couldn' think straight. *Focus, man*, I heard a voice say. *Focus on what' goin' down right now. You ain' no daddy right d'is minute.*

I told Angela I gon' meet up with her later and I hung up. I grabbed the ibuprofen bottle with my stash inside and listen at the door. I looked' out. Ain' no one in the hallway but I had a bad feelin' somethin' 'bout to go down. I walked past d'rooms next to mine. I thought 'bout ditchin' d'stash, just in case d'is feelin' dead-on. I heard footsteps at da end a the hall so I head for d'back stairs. I's out d'motel and in d'back alley in seconds and on my way to find Angela. I's walkin' away 'an I heard 'em, d'sirens.

Shake this off, man. You're good. This proves your instincts workin'. Stay with 'em, man.

Next thang I know I's in my truck, headin' to Daddy D' house on East Powell, 'bout 20 minutes away. The power rush was comin' hard. *This gon' be sweet if you stay in the game. You can ride the ride and walk away. Let's do this.*

I's almost to Daddy D's house. I's thinkin' of d'old gray porch and the swing-close screen door. *I used to climb on the railing and hide in the bushes. Mama would come out and fuss at me, and I'd wait until the last possible minute to get down from the loose porch railin' she was worryin' 'bout. We was barely makin' it then.*

One time, I axed my mama how come we didn't leave. She say some people was born lucky. They have all they want, all they need, but we was born poor and it is what it is. Sometime we have money and we have to enjoy it while we can — live in the moment —'cause it ain' never gon' last. Ain' nobody ever gon' git free.

I s'pose they's people who choose it. Fast money, no responsibility or work to do; just money changin' hands like water through fingers. Nobody know where it been or where it going. All the wrong that go with it, untraceable.

I seen Lelah's house -- Trina' house too. I wonder if she home. I done had some good times in 'at house. Like it or not, we been together, Trina and me, on and off for twenty years. I 'member so many times we try different kinds a white candy; crack, H, weed. We thought it was all d'same 'til it wadn'.

Trina was out her mind. I's glad I stuck to what I know'd and didn't git caught up.

I's lookin' at d'old neighborhood. Daddy D' house just down a street from Lelah's, the rent house me, mama and my sisters used to live at. It feel like I ain' never leave.

The thrill a the game fly through my head like a rush a cocaine. *How could that be? I done been gone almost three years and ever thang feel d'same.*

Trina. I ain' thought a her in a long time. I wonder if she' home. Maybe I stop by, see what's goin' on. I could get a idea a what's happenin' on d'street. She gon' have word.

Focus, man. We ain' got time for you to git off track. This gon' be quick and painless.

Something wadn' right. I could feel it. So, I drove 'round 'til I could think what out a place. If I's caught, I's goin' back to prison. *Lil' R, you thinkin' too much.* This wadn' just a few years if somethin' went wrong. *Yeah, okay. You right, you right. Concentrate on d'score, man. D'at's all you got a do.*

I know'd I had to ditch my .45. I couldn' take a chance on double felonies. The drug charge I could handle but bein' caught with a piece mean a third strike. I needed mo' time to scope out d'street.

Angela Ross

"Hey Jack, it's me. Um, I, uh." Angela was trying to think how to tell Jack that Ryker had been gone since he left for work at 7:30 a.m. that day. She stretched against the weight of her belly, now almost seven months pregnant with her and Ryker's second child. Her head was pounding, her feet ached. Pacing back and forth for hours hadn't helped with swelling.

She'd been debating whether to call Jack. She didn't dare call her mama. Something was wrong. She could feel it. Ryker had not called back to ask what she and the boys wanted for dinner. He was mixed up because he said something about meeting somewhere. He knew she didn't have a way to meet him. He had the truck.

When she talked to him about 4:30, he said he would see her in a bit, but he sounded anxious, like something was off. She knew he didn't like some of the guys at Pro Auto. They were a close-knit group and Ryker didn't do groups. He was a loner. He said he could tell several of them were gay and this was not a concern for him, until they wanted to slap and touch and flirt between jobs. He gave a look that warned them off but it hadn't done him any favors. The group was irritated he was not a "team player." Mr. J paid them no mind.

Ryker was a good, hard worker. Maybe something had gone down between him and the group. It was possible. Ryker was nobody's boy, never had been. Angela knew not to hold on too tight. Ryker needed his space and his independence, but when it got to be seven o'clock, it didn't much matter how much space he needed. She couldn't wait any longer. She dialed the shop.

"Hey Mr. J.," she said, clearing her throat.

"Hey there, Angela. How're you feeling?" Mr. Johnson said when he heard her voice.

"I'm okay. Thank you for asking. I was wondering if Ryker was still working. Did he pick up a extra shift?" she closing her eyes, praying he had.

"No. He took off about three o'clock, at the end of shift, honey." Mr. Johnson heard the concern in her voice and thought she might be having problems with the baby. "Are you sure you're all right? I'll be closing up in a bit, but I could get someone to close if you need something." He heard her breathing and it was ragged.

"No," she sighed. "I'm okay. I just, uh. Could you have him call me if you hear from him?"

"Absolutely. Look, I can tell something's up. What is it?" he pressed.

"Oh, no. I'm fine. I'm just tired, you know. Thank you, though," and she hung up quick.

She couldn't say why she was worried. Mr. J had never asked about Ryker's record. It had been an unspoken blessing, a present unopened. She couldn't risk opening it, not when it felt like everything was on the line; they couldn't afford not to have work, not now. Any suspicion could lead to Ryker getting fired. It only took a hint of trouble.

As she walked around the apartment, she tried to shake the bad feeling hovering over her. *Maybe if I just fix some macaroni and cheese for the boys, Ryker will show,* she'd thought. They were out of milk but she could stir up some powdered milk, using tap water.

As she cooked the pasta, Malcolm came running into the living area.

"Where Daddy?" he asked, seeing Ryker's jacket was not on the back of the door.

Soon Junior trailed behind him. "Yeah, ain' Little R 'posed to be home by now? What about dinner?"

"I'm making mac and cheese," Angela said, tapping the box with her spoon.

The boys stared at her, intently. Ryker had come home at the same time every day for months and they were used to the routine of having him bring dinner. The boys loved the way Ryker wanted to know what happened at school, from playing on the playground to doing math and spelling. He loved the way Malcolm said the days of the week. *Mmmday, Twoday, Weeday, Fiday.*

"Where's Thursday, little man?" he asked nearly every day. Malcolm would throw up his hands and shake his head hard, side to side. Ryker would look at Angela and say, "Okay, no Thursday," and Malcolm would burst out laughing; then, they were all laughing.

Then they would ask Malcolm his colors, which was even more endearing. At first, they teased him about pronunciation, but it too became a game of the sillies. He knew better. He just liked to hear everyone laugh. *Wed, boo, gween, lellow, pupple, ornj,* Angela shook her head, hearing them like he was saying them out loud at that very moment.

Once he'd gotten all the news from the boys, he'd always turn to Angela, rub her shoulders, then hug her from behind, wrapping his arms around the mound of belly in front of her. He'd whisper, "How's your day, baby?" She didn't know if he was talking to her or their baby on the way.

Even though her mood tended to be grouchy and irritable, she felt like they'd been doing better; she hoped.

She loved those moments when they were all together, wrapped up in Ryker's arms and attention. *Where is he? He's not answering his cell. It's been almost three hours. Where could he be?*

"Angela? You there?" Jack said. "I'm sorry I had to put you on hold. Sarah and I were making a list for the grocery and we needed to finish up. What's goin' on?"

"Jack," she stopped, trying to fight back tears. "You seen Ryker?"

"He's not working?" Jack heard her voice break and he could tell she was scared.

"No, Mr. J say he off at 3 o'clock and he ain' come home," she said.

"What about dinner?" Jack said, knowing their routine. He and Ryker talked about him making sure the kids and Angela knew they could count on him.

Big R had never been home, always out and about. It was one of the reasons his parents fought all the time. It was Ryker's idea to make sure they had a meal together every night. He'd been so adamant about it that he wouldn't let Angela cook dinner. He brought it home to ensure they didn't start without him. If he was going to be working a double shift, he usually got in touch early-on so she could make something.

"I fix some mac and cheese," she said, sniffling. "The boys ain' gon' eat 'til they know where he is."

"All right, I hear you. I'm getting my ..." Jack turned to see Sarah hand him his keys, "keys. I'll go out and see if I can round him up, okay? Now, just sit down and put your feet up. I can feel the swelling through the phone."

"Okay," she said, laughing a little too loud, as if it burst from her chest on accident. Jack knew her so well. He'd told her he would be there for them. She hadn't really believed it at the time, because she knew he thought she and Ryker should be married before they lived together, but here he was, honoring his word. *Thank God,* she thought.

When Jack hung up, he turned to Sarah.

"I know. Get out of here. Let me know when you find him," she said. When Jack seemed to put on a heap of guilt, along with his jacket, she told him, "Hey, he's my son, too, you know?" Jack smiled a half-smile. Sarah knew him well. He needed to hear that. Taking on Ryker and his family had been hard on the two of them, even though he said it was his responsibility. He knew better than that. Sarah was hesitant at first, but she'd come around. When she did, she fell hard for Ryker. She too thought of him as her own.

"I'm calling Father Rayford," she called after him as he walked to the car.

"Okay, Shug. I'll call when I know something."

This wasn't the first time Ryker disappeared. Jack knew there would be moments of doubt for him. Doubts were part of it. The job at Pro Auto was not easy for him to take, even with Mr. J being such a good boss. The guys there wanted Ryker to join in what they called "bein' on the down-low." Ryker couldn't, no, wouldn't, be part of any kind of male-to-male sexual interaction.

It had started with them smacking each other on the butt and grabbing asses from time to time. The first time they tried to include Ryker, he told them in no uncertain terms to back off. The tone of the group changed from then on. Ryker said he felt like an outcast, like they were trying to get rid of him somehow. His shifts began to get covered without him knowing and he'd show up to work, only to find someone else already working his shift. Mr. J always found something for him to do, but it made things hard.

This was just one of many adjustments Ryker was making daily, moment by moment. He hadn't expected to be having another baby, though he'd tried to accept his responsibility in it happening.

When he felt homesick, he'd go see his Pop or his cousins and it invariably set him back. They'd say things like he needed to be proud of who he was and stop trying to be white. They'd throw out jabs about his relationship with Jack. "Who this old cracker to you? He yo' sugar daddy? How come yo' Pop and yo' uncles ain' somebody you gon' turn to?

You know, hangin' with the crackers ain' makin' you no lighter."

The worst of it was when his boys, like Ace, came around. They knew how to get him interested in the latest on the street. It was like the bond they formed as kids honed in on his loneliness, his sense of loss for the life he lived before. Where he came from, your word was your bond and few had been able to maintain it as long as he and his four street brothers. It was Ace, Boxer, Terrance, Romey and him. When Ace came by, he felt him before he saw him. He knew what Ace was coming about. Despite their connection on the street, the guys were trying to respect Ryker's decision to get out. They had an agreement. The only way they would have come calling for help was if a life depended on it.

Ryker trusted these men to his grave, but it concerned Jack, the connection being so strong. He knew when Ace showed up, there was more to it than the score. Jack wondered if there was a part of Ryker, who didn't want to let go; who still wanted to be in on the scores.

Jack was not naïve, when it came down to it. He simply wanted Ryker to know he had a choice. Before he and Ryker met, Ryker didn't see one. Statistics showed that sixty-seven percent of ex-cons return to criminal activity within three years. It was a given, according to some studies on recidivism. Jack had done his homework. Minimum wage, judgment from society, the same community, no place to live, not enough money to pay for rent, food, and utilities, urine screens every two weeks with no transportation to and from and costing seventy-five dollars a pop was a lot to overcome and stay clean.

As Jack drove, he felt concerned about Ryker's state of mind. He feared Ryker was getting too close to freedom for comfort; too much too soon could make the confines of the familiar magnetic, reminiscent of good times instead of portraying it realistically. He could be questioning what he deserves, weighing his part in what was past. *Choices.* Jack knew this feeling well; he'd lived it too, years ago. *Only the chooser can choose. No one can do it for him. For a caretaker like*

Ryker, the lines blur – they did for me. I thought I had to save everyone. Can't save someone who doesn't want to be saved.

Walking the line was not easy with so many odds against. *He's ten days away from his three-year mark*, Jack realized. *This boy has tried so hard. He's just a few days away from making it to three years. We're here, son. What's it gon' a be?*

As he drove, he felt his stomach tighten and the acid inside churn. *Ryker, choose freedom, no matter how scary, how unfamiliar. Choose to live, son. No matter what happens, I'm sticking. I'm sticking with you 'til you say go. Never let go. I'll never let go, unless you force my hand.*

Chapter 7

I didn't see this hook coming. I saw the bright red
color of blood and I couldn't swim away.

Officer Payne of the Fort Worth Police Department walked to his squad car with his coffee in one hand, a donut in his mouth and keys in the other hand, as he reached to open the driver's side door. He could hear the scanner report coming through on his hip attachment.

"Please respond to East Powell, possible drug bust. Suspect is Ryker James, son of Ryker James, Senior, otherwise known as Big R. Drug lord father went down for possession in August of 1998. Son, aka Little R...."

"Copy that. Unit 79 responding. Could you send logistics?" Payne said, scrambling to get to his receiver.

Punching up the information on Ryker James Junior, he read the data.

Suspect Ryker James Junior, AKA Little R, is believed to have taken his father's business underground when his Pop went down. He took up with an elderly Caucasian man, claiming he was going straight. Word on the street is he's been running the business all along, while keeping up appearances as the black sheep gone white. Two of his powder pads were raided a couple of weeks ago; one was a rent house on 7th, the other an apartment off Sylvania. One of the whores slipped up and said he might still be in charge.

An officer on I-30 was pumping gas and saw Ace Jackson at Ryker's day job, Pro Auto Group, this afternoon. Informants followed Ryker to a Motel 6 off Vickery. Suspect a score going down. His room was empty when the officers got to the scene. Word on the street is he's been out for the last two and a half years. Let's pick him up and see what we can shake out. He surfaced on East Powell, driving a blue Chevy Truck. <end report>

Officer Payne spilled his coffee and his donut broke away from his mouth, sending it tumbling down his uniform navy blues. Trailing down his shirt in a dust of powdered sugar, the donut ricocheted off his recently dry-cleaned pants onto the floorboard of his patrol car. Instinctively, he started to brush his shirt, making matters worse.

"Oh, good God," he mumbled while trying to chew and brush the powder off his front. Pieces of donut sprayed from his mouth. *Ain' nobody gon' take this call. Ryker James is mine*, he thought as he waved his partner, Corbin, into the patrol car and, at the same time, threw the vehicle into reverse.

This wouldn't be the first time James had been taken in by Payne. In fact, most of the Fort Worth Police Department officers had taken a shot at charging James with drug possession. It had become a running bet as to who would actually get to book him on charges and make them stick. He has been brought in as many times by the Cooper police but nothing stuck to the man.

This time it's gon' be a new day, yes sir. I'm gon' to make sure these charges stick. Payne opened his glove department, eyeing the brown package. *There ain' nobody gon' miss this and James' gon' finally go down, just like his sorry excuse for a father. Tonight, Ryker, yo' luck done run out. And, I mean out!*

Payne's partner got in just as the dispatch sent a few more details.

"All right. It's time," Corbin said. "Let's do this."

"Copy that."

As the police car sped off in the direction of East Powell, the officers couldn't help but tense up. This had happened so many times before. Ryker was caught dealing or in possession and somehow he managed to ditch it. Or, procedure had been botched and the lawyer cut him a break on search and seizure. It was always something.

In all fairness, Ryker had circumvented the law so many times, most cops just wanted to catch him in a minor violation so they could get him off the street if just for a day or two, hoping that when they questioned one of his cohorts, they would slip up and corroborate evidence of a score and give them reason to charge him. They tried just about everything, but the most he'd gotten was eighteen months a couple years ago.

"You know what we're up against, right?" Payne said.

"Yeah, I know. This ain' my first rodeo. If he wants to be caught, he will be. If not, it's another joke on us," Corbin knew the drill.

"James ain' no fool. He knows his rights and the law. There's only one way to make this stick. Go around both. You feel me?"

"Yeah, I feel you. I don't like it but he ain' given us much choice."

"This how it's gon' go down," Payne glanced in his rearview mirror then looked to the right and left, scanning the area as he drove. "We gon' stop him for a violation. It looks like he's up for vehicle registration. His plates say he's due. Once he's out the truck, we gon' press him 'til he pops. With any luck, he'll have his stash with him. If not," and he tapped the glove compartment, "we gon' make sure they's somethin' on 'im," Payne said, his voice almost a low growl.

Corbin opened the glove box and eyed Payne, a little unsettled by the package he saw. This was never what he signed on for as a police officer. He'd sworn to uphold the law and hold criminals accountable years ago when he graduated from the academy. It had been different then. Things were done by the book and this kind of thing wouldn't have come up.

In 1997, Fort Worth had been named murder capital of the United States. Crime had escalated to an all-time high and the criminals were turning good cops bad, raking in the cash from drug scores like nobody's business. The Crips and the Bloods were battling it out in the streets, not much different than what happened on the streets of the bloody Fifth (Ward) in Houston. Officers were under tremendous pressure to stop the mayhem.

When the usual strategies and procedures didn't cut it, the pressure to bring the criminals to justice increased exponentially. Officers resorted to bending, sometimes breaking the rules to bring about arrests. The lines of justice were blurring and it became difficult to discern necessary tactics from abuse of citizens' rights.

Years later, progress was being made, but the means to meet the end had deteriorated from what was taught in the academy. Even so, the results were not impressive, given the magnitude of the problem. They needed to making a bigger dent in the number of arrests leading to charges that would stick.

Remnants of the last city council meeting flashed through Corbin's mind. The police chief stood there and all but demanded officers in the field bring drug-dealing to a screeching halt. It was like they were ordering in the fast food line and expecting the streets to be clean and the drug lords jailed within minutes.

Manson Shepherd had taken all he could stand, after the mayor and the mayor pro tem laid him out for not taking care of crime, he recalled. *He stood with his shoulders back, winding his head around to the right and left, as if about to step in a boxing ring. He looked at all of the officers, as if deciding something*, Corbin had thought at the time.

When he spoke again, Corbin remembered his words falling on deafening silence. He proposed a city-wide sting, geared to lull drug dealers into a false sense of complacency.

"Let's give 'em the apartments off Boca Raton Boulevard, the Villa del Rio and Oak Hollow apartments over there. They can do their business out there and keep the inner streets of Fort Worth a little cleaner. When the small-time dealers get comfortable and pass the word that they can deal without conflict, the bigger fish will join in. We let it ride for a while and when they're all nice and cozy, we take 'em down. We raid 'em and line 'em up for prison by the busloads."

Corbin was in shock. *Who did Shepherd think he was dealing with? Even the kids sellin' the candy were smart enough to see through that. They were gon' take things to a higher level and run all over the force. Didn't he know there were officers who already joined the ranks of the criminals?*

The cops who got busted down to traffic duty for not making their quota had families to feed; the chicken feed they were paying them wasn't cutting it. How did he think they were getting by? I'd bet my paycheck for the next ten years there were good cops who turned to the dark side because they felt they had no choice. If Shepherd put this sting into action, there would be someone telling-all when the showdown was set to begin. Something had to give on this before heads started to roll. Otherwise, everyone was goin' down and it was gon' be hard to tell who was on who's side. If we could get Ryker off the streets and bust some of his partners, we'd be set, he decided.

His thoughts switched back with the hard right Payne took toward East Powell. *I guess it's the only way. Beat them at their game.* He opened the glove box again, looked in the brown paper bag. Cocaine, pure. Two kilos. *Time for Ryker to go down. He's been running the streets for most his life, locked up for less than five years out of the nineteen he's been dealing. It's time.*

The hundreds of arrests they'd made over the years, trying to convict father and son was wearing on the police force in Fort Worth. Every time they came close, the charges were dismissed, even with hard evidence. Cooper PD finally took Big R down in 1998, but no one had been able to convict Ryker Jr. since then and they knew he was dealing.

Corbin remembered when Ryker got caught in Cooper, blatantly *caught,* and days later, the cop who found him in possession was a no-show at the hearing. The bust was supposed to put him away but Little R was back on the streets in no time. The officer mysteriously took a leave of absence. Not long after that, he supposedly transferred out of state, but he didn't resurface in law enforcement. He took his family and was gone.

Guys on the force suspected Ryker's people in Houston had something to do with it. Without the officer on duty or the evidence of drug possession, the judge could only charge James with evading arrest and breaking probation. He got time in prison, but nothing compared to what he deserved.

Payne's disdain for Ryker went much deeper. Payne's daughter, who was 14 when she met Ryker, had been going through a rebellious time, smoking weed on occasion, trying to impress her peers in school. Payne came down a little hard on her instead of taking time to see what was really troubling her. What started out being a way to get back at Big Daddy, the police officer, spiraled into much more.

Celia Payne went to a Rave with a few friends. One of her girlfriends brought a flask of vodka and she ended up on the dance floor, her inhibitions nearly non-existent. Ryker saw her dancing and their eyes met. She looked a lot older than she was so he responded to her when she began to dance just for him. There were hundreds of people on the dance floor, but she was fixed on him, showing him how much she wanted him, her body moving to the music, beckoning him to come out on the floor. He started to move with her and when he noticed she trembled at his touch, he knew. She was too young.

"Baby, how old *are* you?" he said into her ear. She laughed and kept dancing. When he caught Ace's eye, he gestured a rocking cradle. Pulling her arms from around his neck, Ryker said, "Come find me when you grown."

She stomped off the dance floor, sulking. Her moment with him was ruined. He followed, catching her arm and swinging her around. He leaned in, whispering in her ear, "Don't think it has anything to do with you," and he pulled back so she could see his eyes. "You're beautiful. Any man can see that. I just ain' gon' take advantage a you, not now, not ever. We can be friends though," he said, hoping she would understand.

When she yanked her arm free, he called out after her, "Hey, I got sisters and I wouldn't want them at the mercy a somebody like me. Get yourself home. Stop dancin' like that. You gon' catch something you can't handle."

Ryker ran into Celia several times after that, but he thought of her as a little sister, one he wanted to protect. If he had known she was Payne's daughter, he would have had good reason for resisting her, but he was unaware. It was a feeling he had. Something told him to leave her be.

Still, Celia was not one to let go of him so easily. She started seeing a Crip, thinking she would run into Ryker from time to time. Eventually she did.

One night, she saw him close to the Crips hangout. She didn't know, but he'd been out, collecting on some unpaid debts on the south side. One of the guys he called on got in a lucky shot, popping him in the eye. It swelled a bit, looking a lot worse than it was. The guys who clipped him went down hard for it.

When he left the scene, he saw Celia. She immediately jumped to the wrong conclusion. She was trying to talk him into coming with her, letting her take care of his eye. She begged him to let her help; claiming friends do that for each other.

He finally gave in and he agreed to let her come to his house for a bit, telling himself it was better she was off the streets and away from the Crips. She sat beside him on his couch with an ice pack. She leaned in close, lightly pressing an ice pack to his eye. She smelled so good and her voice was sweet and seductive. Still, nothing felt right about it. Unable to say what he knew would hurt her yet again, he feigned sleep. Not realizing how tired he really was, it wasn't long before he was out.

Celia was pretty upset. She slipped away from him and went through his things, hoping to find something, anything to ease the rejection. When she came across a bag of cocaine, she used a razor from the bathroom to cut a few lines. Ryker woke up and she was gone, the remnants of her steal still on the bathroom counter.

Despite his effort to protect her, she'd found a way to use; to get back at Big Daddy. He checked his sources on the streets, trying to find out how bad. It didn't take long to learn she was hooked *and* hooking. Even though she never fingered Ryker as the one who started her on it, Payne assumed it was him.

Ryker saw her several times after. She'd come to him, jonesing for a fix, but he refused to sell to her, forcing her to go elsewhere for her habit; she felt rejected by Ryker on all counts. Though Ryker's intentions were good, she got addicted fast and began to confuse how she was introduced to the drug scene.

What Ryker didn't know was there were several Crips who didn't really know who she was or care whether or not she was Payne's daughter, much less if she was too young. Most of the Crips saw her as a customer and a good one at that. As long as she paid, one of the members made sure she got her fix. By the time Ryker knew how bad it was, it was too late.

◆

"Ryker's going down. I don't care what it takes," Payne said over and over, as if that alone, could make it so.

Corbin saw the fury in his partner's eyes. He knew Payne had not seen his daughter in several months. They'd heard through a friend of a friend that she'd started seeing a Crip. She'd changed her hair, her clothes. The innocent girl she'd once been was gone. A couple of times, they thought they'd seen her hooking on the south side, while they were out on patrol, but by the time they'd doubled back, she was gone. She'd been nearly impossible to find. They knew. They'd tried.

"You know we're gonna find her, man" Corbin said, reading his partner's thoughts. He wondered if Payne had any objectivity left. He harbored so much hate for Ryker; he was sure he'd been the lure for his Celia. Even though Corbin knew it wouldn't do any good, he had to say it. "You know, the word was a Crip got her hooked, not Ryker."

"Doesn't matter. It *doesn't* matter!" Payne spat. "He's going down! I don't care what he's taken in for; he's going down for life, if I have anything to say about it. He's where it all started. Cooper police caught Big R and we're going to get his son."

"You sure about this, man?" Corbin asked. "How you think Celia gon' take it? When Payne was silent, he pressed on, "She gon' suffer if we don't go by the book –she gon' know you ain' no better, a common criminal. Maybe we do this fair and just, show her what's right."

"Fair and just," Payne mumbled. "Fair and just. Was it fair and just when he let a 14- year-old girl stay the night with him? Was it fair and just when she got into drugs and he assumed he had nothing to do with it? Who'd he think gave her the drugs? He was the one selling to the Crips. He'd been selling to teenagers for years and no one could nail him. My question's why? We couldn't we get charges to stick. Why?"

"I'm with you on this, man, but we have to have proof and we need to get it the right way or else we ain' no better than him or his dad," Corbin said, reluctantly.

"Do you have the file?" Payne was reminded of their continued investigation of priors on Big R and Ryker. "Everything's backed up and protected, right?"

"Yes, of course," Corbin said, running his pale white hands through the tight curls of salt and pepper strands that were falling into his line of vision. "But considering recent events, there's a chance Ryker is still trying to sell in Fort Worth since they couldn't nail him in Cooper. I'm telling you. We're gonna catch him if he's here, dealing."

"You really believe that? After all the times we've set there, waiting for sentencing, knowing that the drugs were confiscated from Ryker, filed and committed to evidence, only to discover that they magically disappeared when he was processed. Please. It took Sheriff Foster dying to catch his Pop. You know some of the officers involved in the whole Foster cover-up left the Cooper PD and transferred to Fort Worth. This could mean we have some dirty cops in our midst, ready to help him out for a price."

"You're saying you know for sure Sheriff Foster was dirty?" Corbin was trying to think it through objectively. "Some say Foster and James' friendship was just that. His hands were clean. His only crime was that he knew James was hosting 10-day parties out on his farm and he didn't bust him.

The word was, since Cooper was a dry county, James would go two counties over to get the booze. He fixed mouth-watering barbeque and offered folks a libation and held to a strict policy; no one could leave the farm while under the influence. Big R even provided a place for people to crash if necessary. And, several times, Foster crashed the event, only to find folks dancing, drinking and having a wonderful time. There was no sign of drugs at the scene."

"Whose side are you on? I don't believe that for all the money in the world. And I'm not talking about Big R. I'm talkin' 'bout bustin' his boy. There was a reason Big R went down hard, be it dirty cops or Foster dying. And both of them deserve life in prison. Waiting for the law to get it right is a joke. It's time to do what *they* do. Circumvent the law and git 'r done. Taking Ryker down, set-up or not, will give me some peace of mind and I dare say a lot of other people too. So, what's it gon' be? You in or out?" Payne pulled over and stared Corbin down, waiting for his answer.

Chapter 8

*I had to look. I saw the ones caught. Their eyes
were lifeless and a long, silver, slender spire was
connected to a fishing line that ran in and out of each
one of their mouths and gills, neatly sewing them
together into a bundle of dinner for someone.*

Ryker James, Jr.

Ever' thang was all messed up in my head. The guys at work, actin' funny. They was wantin' me to join in they fun. I ain' like that. I don't go both ways and I wadn' gon' pretend just to keep my job. I had Angela thinkin' I's flirtin' with other women when I wadn'. She pregnant and her hormones' talkin', but I couldn' take much more.

The boys' was the best part a things. I'd come home and they was waitin'. We'd talk 'bout they day, what they been learnin'. They was no expectation, 'cept to be d'ere, playin' with 'em. I could do that. I *did* do it.

Then Ace come to the shop makin' ever thing complicated. He playin' on all my guilt, bringin' the word from da others. He wouldn' a brought it if'n he didn't have to. Then, he seen the funny men. It make me want a prove I'm a man or somethin'. I ain' no queer, but how's it all look? How was I s'pose to keep goin' with all this goin' on?

I couldn' believe I was back on East Powell, packin' and carryin'. When I's talkin' to Ace, all I could think was how them funny men makin' me look. I should a walked on it all, but I start thinkin' how I used to pull down a couple three g's in a weekend and I's stuck workin' this job, defendin' myself 'gainst guys gone gay. They's slappin' each other' ass 'n highfivin', shakin' theyself and actin' all crazy, up in my business. Next thang I knew, I'd joined up to do the score.

They's granddaddy' house. I keep passin' it by. *What the hell I doin'?*

The candy in d'bags, up my sleeve. My arm itchin'. I could let it fly; just roll down the window and let it go out the window.

Never let go, Jack say. He wasn't talkin' 'bout the candy.

I done let go a what he talkin' 'bout and now it pullin' me back in. I don't know how I let it happen. I know'd I's stronger 'an that. It like I's on autopilot and it all come at me, all at once. The guys at the shop, Angela and the kids, Jack and Sarah, Ace comin' by, me makin' less than ten dollars an hour. D'next thing I know, I had my .45 hidden in my jeans and my hands on the wheel and powder to sell or lose, *what the hell was I doin'?*

I didn't know. I didn't know who I was no mo'.

I stopped thinkin'. My hands was sweatin' and da acid in my stomach' churnin'. I's 'bout to score. If I could pull it off, it was gon' mean rent, food, things for the babies.

I could a stopped and axed Jack for money to help out, but I didn't want a owe him. I wanted to be independent, doin' my own thing, countin' on nobody but me.

Like it or not, that's what I's used to. I ain' never had family like Jack and Sarah. My father hardly talk to me when we was livin' together. Mama always have her own problems. My sisters wadn' 'round, less they need somethin' from me. Ain' nobody ever come 'round 'lessen they needin' somethin'. Still, I was the man a d'house, man a d'family, in a way. When I's that man, I wadn' defendin' myself against funny men or barely makin' it ever' day, tryin' to stretch paycheck to paycheck.

Part a me was jazzed. It felt good to have my piece on me. It feel like control in the middle a all the confusion. *Home.* Home wadn' with Jack and Sarah, no matter how much I like it there. They house wadn' mine. I didn't never fit there and they people wadn' my people. They nice and they act like I part a things, but I know'd the truth. I didn't have no home.

I's never part a the drug world neither. I done what I had to, to survive, but it wadn' a home.

When I meet Jack, I thought I's home, but I ain' been standin', side by side, like a man. He always helpin' me out a somethin'. He done had to come out retirement to help with some a my stuff. That ain' bein' my own man. That's bein' a burden. I ain' nobody's burden.

Bein' back in the game tonight mean I ain' nobody's problem. I's gon' be part a the solution. I had the stash that was gon' give me the green. Ain' nobody have to worry 'bout me no mo'.

What did I want? I wanted to go back to when I's little. Mama call me little man 'cause she say I come out smart, calm and cool. I didn' never cry like some babies. I's the kid solvin' ever'body' problems. Pockets a time wadn' missin' like now. Ever'thang clear and I know'd who I was. Ever thang make sense. I ain' done nothin' wrong. I had ever'thang ahead a me.

My first experience with God happen when I's little too. I used to hang out by a convenience store near our house. They was this old woman who used to sit outside the store. She tell me to ax Him for my blessings ever' day. I didn't really git her so she told me this story. She say that one day, when we gone and we finally with God, they gon' be a angel who show us 'round heaven. She say they gon' be streets a gold and angels singin' to God's glory, mansions ever'where and then we gon' see this buildin'. She say it gon' be so high, we can't see the end in the sky above.

When the angel take us inside, we gon' see boxes floor to ceiling. She say we gon' see the ones with our name on 'em and the angel gon' say, "These be all the blessings you didn't ax for while you on earth. If 'en you had, you would have received all these."

I 'member lookin' in her wrinkled, tired face and they was this good feelin' come over me, a kind a peace. From that day on, I ax God for my blessings ever' day. I prayed ever' day. It all make sense, how God want us to seek him. I's little, but I git what the old woman say. I think that's why I ain' afraid to die. I's stared death in the face ever'day since then and if my time come, it come.

Tonight ain' no different. If it my time, it my time. Sometime I think I pray for it to be my time. I know God know my heart and that be enough. I's tired too, real tired.

What the hell? Mama?

Ryker's mother was waving from Daddy D's house. She came to the end of East Powell, motioning him to stop. He slowed the truck and she climbed in.

"What are you doin', son? You've got to get out of here. Give 'em to me," she said, reaching for his sleeve.

"What? What you talkin' 'bout?" Ryker said, pushing her hands aside.

"I know you tryin' to score," she said, her voice shaking. "It ain' gon' happen. Get rid a the powder. Give it to me and I'll flush it. It ain' worth you goin' down. C'mon son, give 'em to me."

"Okay. All right, calm down, Mama. I give 'em to you if 'en you git out my truck," he said, knowing it was the only way to get her out of danger.

As she stepped out, he rolled down his window, as if to hand her the packages. Just as she reached for his sleeve, he sped up and left her there, yelling for him to come back. He looked in the rearview mirror and she was still screaming, her arms outstretched, begging him to return and leave the score behind. He drove on.

She ain' s'pose to take cur a me. I been takin' cur a her most my life. She think I gon' hand her a bomb and drive off so she can deal with my mess. No. That ain' me. I can't believe it come to this.

Check it. The police 'bout to reign you in. Someone, somewhere, done served' you up? You feel the breeze, man? The police been huntin' you down as long as you been alive. Now, they comin' for you. Somethin' up.

Ryker sobered, as if suddenly aware of where he was; what he was about to do. His mother was trying to save him. She'd never stepped into the line of fire for him before; he'd kept her free and clear of his business, but there she was, waving him down, trying to take the fall. *Maybe God showin' me somethin' here.*

Maybe lettin' 'em take me in is the way to go. I could go down for the last time and be done. The only question is whether Angela be d'ere when it all over. How long befo' I see Malcolm and Junior? Ah, man. The baby.

I was drivin' back toward Daddy D' house. When I turned onto East Powell, I could see his house up ahead. I kept driving, going around the block once, twice, a third time. I's tryin' to think. Me bein' by my granddaddy' house, I gots reason to be in this part a town.

Daddy D. Howard D. James. Thinkin' a him, make me think a the times me, Mama and my sisters stay there.

The porch where he like to sit in the late afternoon have a ramp now. He add it when it git hard for him to do the steps. I can almost see him openin' the screen door, while trying to hold hisself up with his cane, balancin' until he can git in between the screen and the front door.

I 'member stories he used to tell about my grandmother, Aileen James. We used to dangle our legs off the porch in the heat a the summer, when they was barely a breeze. He'd tell funny stories 'bout her. He call her a "tough old bird."

He rarely smiled but some a her antics raise the corners a his mouth like nothing else. She died a cancer at 68 years old, leaving him to finish raising my dad and his eight brothers and sisters on his own. Of course, we had to hear how he worked so many jobs, from sun-up to sun-down, to take cur a ever'body. He say d'at was how Aileen would a wanted it.

When she alive, she spend most a her days angry with him. He was drinking and not helping her with the kids. But it was because he couldn't face her leaving him. She knew the cancer would take her and he couldn' stand the thought of it. She finally decide to take the kids and raise 'em alone if he wadn' willin' to face the truth. This shook him to the core. After, he beg her to come back and promised to do right by her and the kids. When she agreed, he got a job at a feed mill and worked another job at night to take cur a the nine kids. They got by.

Daddy D know my father have issues with his temper and the drink, but he say my father have a good side too. It wadn' 'til I live with Big R I seen the side Daddy D talkin' 'bout, hard-workin' and responsible. Big R love his family on some level. The other side a him, the one who beat my mother within a inch a her life, came to the surface whenever he drinkin'.

Daddy D know'd his son better than anybody. We'd show up on his porch, in the middle a the night. He'd look down at us kids with sad eyes and open his door. Then, he'd see my mother; he called her Resa, and rows a wrinkles be all over his forehead. We didn't talk about it. He just fix us something to eat and we'd go to bed.

Me drivin' by his house, doin' this last score, probly make Big R proud right about now. Daddy D' be disappointed. He wouldn' want me to take no more chances with my life. I could knock on his door and he'd take me in, no questions ax. But, that wadn' my way, just like it wadn' my way to take from Jack and Sarah.

Jack and Sarah. How I gon' 'xplain this if somethin' go down? Jack say I's a good father. He say I come a long way in almost three years' time. I doubt he gon' say that after this.

Hey, Ryker! 'scuse me for interruptin' this whole Oprah-Dr. Phil moment you got goin' here, but we kind a under d'gun. Wake the hell up! Score happenin' or not?

My head all messed up. Nothin' makin' no sense.

Chapter 9

*The spire had been plunged into the soggy, lakeside
dirt floor, making it impossible for them to wriggle
free. Still alive, they wiggled against each other, using
each other as momentum in hopes of freeing
themselves.*

Ryker was in trouble; he could feel it.

Jack walked into the house three hours later. As the
grandfather clock struck on the half hour, eleven thirty p.m.,
he sat down at the kitchen table. Rubbing his hands over the
stubble on his face, he felt his stomach tightened and needles
pierce his chest from the inside out.

"Hey there, Shug," Sarah said, setting a bourbon and water
down in front of him. She sat across from him with a glass of
Zinfandel and stared into the pale pink liquid.

"He's nowhere to be found. He's not answering his cell. I
don't know what to do," Jack said. "I can't bring myself to
call Angela, but I need to do it."

"I already talked to her," Sarah's smile didn't make it to
her eyes. "I knew if you took this long, it wasn't good." She
reached for his hand. Smoothing the purplish veins on his
rough, dry skin, she tried to soothe him. When she looked up
and saw the shadows around his eyes, she knew he was sick
with worry. She could feel his pulse and his blood pressure
was up, his hands shaky. *Crazy. What were we thinking?* She
thought. *He's a career criminal. That's what it said in the thirty-
something pages. It's public record.*

As if he heard her, he said, "I don't know why I thought I
could help him. I just can't work it out in my head. I mean, I

know when I'm being sold a load a bull. He was sincere about wanting out, I know it. I felt it.

"What's he doing? Where is his head?"

"I'm not sure," Sarah wanted to reassure him, but couldn't think of a thing to say.

"Maybe he went out for a drive," he grasped at hope, "but, my gut's tellin' me different. I don't know what to do."

"He *could be* out, driving around," Sarah wanted to hope too. "Angela's praying he is. Apparently, he's done this before and come home okay. She says sometimes he just needs to think, sort things through."

"Did you call Father Rayford?" Jack asked, suddenly remembering Father Rayford could have heard from him. "I don't know if I told you, but Ryker has been spending time with him at the church. After we surprised him with Christmas, Ryker went to see him. He said something about not feeling he deserved the outpour of generosity from the church."

"The presents?" Sarah was surprised.

"Well, he's never had anyone do something like that before," Jack said. "I get the feeling he's been the sole provider for his family since he was a young boy. He's the one his mother comes to every time her paycheck isn't enough. He's the one his sisters come to when their money's tight or they need a place to stay. He's the one his Dad calls to take custody of Junior, even though Junior has a mother and several relatives who could take care of him. Ryker is the one they all come to -- his cousins, friends, and family. He's sustained them for almost twenty years. Even if Ryker wanted to change this habit, he has to untangle himself from them and all their issues and problems."

"That sounds familiar," Sarah quipped. "Who else could we say did that about?"

"What?" Jack had not heard her. He followed the path he just recounted aloud; it was like a map with tiny roads winding him through the twists and turns of Ryker's family ties. "You know, I'm not sure Ryker can ever really leave his old life. How are you supposed to walk away from the only family and friends you've ever known? That's like asking someone to deny they existed; to forget where they came from or how they grew up." Jack stared into his bourbon. "No one forgets. You move past it, but it's not forgotten, at least not for me anyway." Jack was rambling and still had not noticed Sarah had answered him.

"Jack," she said more firmly. "*You* did it. You left an abusive stepfather who could have destroyed you. You got a job at age nine and you worked your way up, until you were working for Leonard's Department Store in downtown Fort Worth. You got your mama out of that house and away from that horrible man. She stayed with your Uncle Sim and Aunt Joan, while you went to live with your Uncle Pete and Aunt Rachel. You rode your bicycle to work and caught the bus to school.

"Not to mention all the statewide casting tournaments you participated in. You were the apple of Uncle Pete's eye with all your awards for fishing and casting. Honey, you're the man you're talking about. You got out and you did it in the midst of the aftermath the world called the Great Depression. You got a scholastic scholarship and finished college in three years and then served in the United States Army for another three – you served in the Korean War, for goodness sakes. You're talking as if what you and Ryker have attempted can't be done."

"I didn't leave my family. I separated from them, but I was around, I checked on them. I saw my mother marry another alcoholic.

"You know, I thought when my sister and I got her and Mason to go to Alcoholics Anonymous that we had them on the right track. She'd found someone who was going to be good to her. They lived sober for twenty years as far as I knew, and I would have known, trust me," Jack said, his voice lower and affirming.

"I thought I had finally caged the animal that had attacked my family again and again. I checked on them all the time, making sure they were going to meetings and working the programs. I was so convinced that Mason and she were committed, doing the steps. I even co-signed on a house they set out to buy." Jack shook his head and pressed his fingertips to his eyelids.

"What? What happened?" Sarah said, understanding Jack was struggling with what he was about to say. "Was there a reason to believe Arch Mason wasn't sober?"

"Well, you know my mom died rather suddenly," he began, rubbing his eyes harder, feeling the tension get worse and needing relief. "Now, I've got no way of knowing what really happened, but oh, hell. I'm just going to say it. Laura and I went to see her when Arch told us she had fallen ill. We thought it was a little strange that he said she wasn't well. She was healthy as a horse, aside from her arthritis.

Mason said she was on several medications and he was concerned she was not taking her meds properly. I could've sworn he was saying she was in danger of overdosing.

"Anyhow, we went down there as soon as we could get away because his comments were a bit strange and he kept going back and forth about her exact condition; his story didn't make sense with what we knew about her.

"By the time we got there, she was lying on her bed, hands folded over her chest and the Bible upside down, turned to the 23rd Psalm; it was her favorite passage in the Bible. She was dead." His brows furrowed deeply and Sarah came closer to him, now putting together what he was implying.

"You think Mason might've had something to do with her death," she said, her eyes growing wide as saucers.

"Not then, I didn't, no. But later, when we were getting her affairs in order, I heard, through the grapevine, that Mason had been living in the house with another woman. My mother was not even in the ground and he'd already moved another woman in.

"Turned out, with a little digging, I found out he'd been seeing her for months, even before my mother passed."

"So, you think …." Sarah began again.

"Hold on. The worst of it was, he'd met this woman, Inez Chambers, at AA, but they both had stopped going to the meetings. My mother was not even dead and he was cheating on her and skipping out on meetings.

"There wasn't anything I could do. Mama was gone and I didn't have any proof of all he'd been up to, but that wasn't the worst of it. Mason and Inez often got together and drank and one night, they had a fight and supposedly, she was yelling and screaming at him," he paused, wiping a hand across his cheek, not wanting to say what he'd read in the newspaper.

"Oh, dear God," Sarah said, covering her mouth.

"As the story goes, he felt so threatened by her, he grabbed a kitchen knife and stabbed her twenty-seven times. That's what the paper said and that's when I suspected he might have had something to do with my mother's death. The courts let him off with a slap on the wrist for Inez; he claimed self-defense, but I had a God-awful feeling about it all when I read it in the Star Telegram. I guess I figured he was going to sell the house and disappear with the money, so I went back to the house, thinking he might try to sell the house out from under me; I had co-signed on it so I had a right to some of its sale.

"I walked up the sidewalk and there was a guy outside the house, dressed in a business suit, very professional looking. I thought *who is this guy?* Turns out he was Mason's attorney, Nelson Jones. I asked what he was doing at the house and he said he was checking it out, trying to get an idea of what kind of shape it was in so he and Mason could sell it.

"I told him whatever the house brought would have to be between me and Mason, since I co-signed on the house. Long story short, he and Mason were out to get the full sale of the house and leave me out of it, even though I had put the down payment on it and helped with the mortgage throughout the time they were there.

"Funny thing was, this was about the same time the famous criminal lawyer, Richard "Racehorse" Hanes, was defending T. Cullen for the murders of his wife and a 13-year-old little girl. Cullen walked because Racehorse used his acclaimed courtroom theatrics to get him off. Remember that?"

"I think I do," she said. "It happened in August. What was it? 1976?"

"Yeah, that's it. Of course, I didn't know Racehorse from Adam, but I mentioned his name all the same because this lawyer was thinking I had no recourse and the truth was I needed some leverage, so I fudged a little. I told him that I was going to talk to my brother-in-law, get him to take a look at the case." Jack laughed a little. "I said, 'I'm sure you know him. His name's Richard Hanes, goes by Racehorse.' Next thing I knew he was backing down off the whole matter. It was fun to shake him up a bit after he looked down his nose at me.

"The worst of it was that if Mason was capable of stabbing Inez over and over, 27 times, he could have forced my mother to overdose. How would I ever know what really happened? No sale of a house would ease my mind about that. I just prayed she went on her own accord.

"Anyhow, the point of all this is I know how hard it can be to let go of your family. No matter how many times they disappoint or fall short, they are your family. I couldn't turn my back on my mother and I spent twenty years trying to make sure she was safe and in treatment. It was never enough. I don't know how someone breaks so deeply they can't recover. I guess it was by the grace of God I didn't break. Scars that deep can sever hope."

He looked into Sarah's eyes and saw himself through hers. *Dear God, this is the reason isn't it? This is the reason God asked me to help him.* He sat back and raked his hands through his hair. *God chose me to help because I get it. I've been there.*

Seeing that Jack registered all he'd just disclosed to her, she reached for his arm and squeezed. The gentle gesture reminded him of a good memory, one he needed at this very moment. His eyes lit up at the thought of it.

"This is like that catfish, Shug," he said, his eyes brightening as clarity took shape and his previous confusion started to dissipate like a foggy windshield wiped clear. "I can't let go of him now. I've got to hold on tight, support him, get him through whatever is happening so -- so he can get strong enough to fight. What was I thinking? This wasn't ever gon' a be a walk in the park. It's a fight for his life."

"Well, yeah, it is, but… where are you going?" Sarah released his arm, as he got up, leaving his drink untouched and grabbing for his jacket.

"I have to get out there and find a way to help him. I'm going over to Angela's and see if we can brainstorm where he could have gone. If we put our heads together, I might be able to help before it's too late."

"Wait for me. I'm not sitting here all by myself, waiting for you to bring our boy home." She grabbed her sweater and her knitting needles.

"What are you going to do with your knitting bag?"

"I think better when I'm knitting and you said brainstorming, right?"

They walked out the front door with plan and purpose. Jack's stride was strong and determined. As they drove to the apartment on White Settlement, he and Sarah talked more about it. Neither had really considered the emotional aspect of it.

"He's been the man of the house since his mother packed all of them up and left Big R that night," Sarah was struck by the thought. "He was five years old and there he was, gathering his sisters' things, packing all he could in a bag, dressing those girls and holding their hands as they walked on the highway in the middle of the night. I still can't imagine that. Freezing cold, they were walking on the highway; the wind slicing through their clothes and no coats."

Jack let out a bawdy laugh, "He asked the police officer, who picked 'em up on the side of the road, if he would run the light bar when they got to the train station. He must have loved seeing all the red and blue lights flashing. Remember? He said his face hurt from smiling for so long.

"I don't know why I didn't see this before. I imagine separating himself from the role he's had in their life all these years isn't easy. He's been like a," Jack couldn't think of a word that described it. *Caretaker? Man of the house? The protector?*

"Le guardien," Sarah said in a goofy French accent. "You know, in French, gardien means warden too, protector of a minor. Shoot, from what we know of his family members, it fits. I mean, every time we talk to Ryker, one of them is camped out in his house because they've had something happen, whether they're needing money or a place to stay or worse.

"Remember when his cousin, T.J., was strung out on meth? Angela told me how they had to take him in and nurse him through withdrawal. He was so sick, throwing up everything they gave him to eat. He and Angela kept vigil over him until he got through it. I think T.J. was out of it for over a week."

"And Ryker was working the whole time," Jack shook his head, realizing this was why he looked so exhausted every day. He hadn't complained or let on that he was helping T.J. until they were through it. "Angela watched over him and the kids during the day and Ryker came home to take over at night. He never said a word. He just did what had to be done."

"Can't imagine," she said. "I think I'd have been tempted to take him to a hospital, slap him in rehab. Used to be a family member could sign you in and you had to stay until you were clean. Now, people can sign themselves out whenever they want. I bet that's why they just helped him through it. It takes a good person to go through that with you."

"I imagine it does. We can't abandon him, no matter where he is tonight," Jack said.

As they pulled into the parking lot of Ryker and Angela's apartment complex, they didn't see his truck. Jack and Sarah looked at each other. Both nodded. They knew what they had to do.

Angela came to the door in her pajamas, rubbing her belly. Her eyes were like a raccoons, shadowed and heavy-laden.

"Did you find him?" she asked, hopefully.

"Nope. Feel like brainstorming? No matter what's happened, we've got to come together on this and help him through," Sarah put her arm around Angela, walking her to the living area. She dragged a nearby chair over and grabbed a few pillows, propping her feet up as high as she could. "First thing is to get that swelling in your ankles and feet down. Circulation," she smiled. "Two birds with one stone. We'll keep you company, brainstorm a little and before you know it the swelling will be down *and* we'll have a plan."

Jack sat down beside Angela and held her hand. "Where are the boys? Are they sleeping?"

"Yeah, I finally got them to go down, but they want him home. They don't understand," she wearily pushed her hair out of her face.

"I know. You must be exhausted."

"No, this is good. I need to *do* something or I'll go crazy."

"Okay, maybe if we think this through, we can figure out what's going through his head. You said he called about four-thirty this afternoon, is that right?"

"Yeah, he sounded strange, distracted. I axed him if he was okay and he start to answer, but then he said he had to go and that he gon' meet up with me later. Before I could say anythin', he was gone. I tried to call back, but it went straight to voice mail."

"Meet up with you? Did he say when or where? How would you meet him anywhere? He's got the truck." Jack shot out questions so fast, he could tell Angela was a bit overwhelmed, but it got her thinking. She sat up quick. "What? What is it?" Jack asked, moving closer to her.

Chapter 10

There is no reason. I am swimming in close and taking in the sight, knowing all the time that I could be caught and in the same predicament. The sight draws me in and I am fixated.

I got a do somethin'. I can't be caught with the candy and my piece.

Ryker circled Daddy D's house one more time, still driving carefully. He had been going over everything in his mind, his gangster-self debating with the man he had become over the last eight months or so. He thought of Sarah and Jack as he rounded the corner and Daddy D's house came into view. He rolled down his window and let the powder fall from the packages, clouds of cocaine dissipating into the warm breeze as he drove. With the powder gone, he eliminated a potential felony. *One down, one to go.*

The .45 was still tucked in his jeans. If there were some way he could walk it into Daddy D's house and crash there for the night, he could sleep, get perspective and maybe see things differently in the morning.

He'd gone two streets over from Daddy D's, still trying to decide if he should knock on his door or go home to Angela, maybe find Jack.

Just as he came to his decision, red and blue lights swirled in his rearview mirror. The siren followed. Instinct took over.

Don't cop to anything. You forgettin' they got nothin' on you if you don't give 'em a reason to search the truck or you. Play it cool. You the master a the game. Head in the game man, head in the game. You can do this. They ain' got no reason to stop you. Take your time, Little R. Do what you know. Don't lose focus or you goin' down. R'member, you done ditched the drugs. They can't git you for nothin' but packin' heat. And, if you cooperate, then you could skate. No one got a know you packin'.

It's true. I can do this. I can. They can't detain for me for no reason. All I got to do is remind them of my rights.

Wait. Vehicle registration due. *Shit.*

Ryker pulled his truck off the road, onto the shoulder. *I ain' caught yet. I gon' do what they say, remind them a my rights and hang tight. It could still be okay.*

When he rolled down his window, Officer Payne walked up.

"May I see some ID please?" he said.

"Is there a problem, officer?" Ryker asked, calm and cool.

"I said, let me see some ID," Payne repeated, now angry that Ryker questioned him.

"Officer, is there a reason you stopped me? I was going the speed limit and …."

"Little R, you gon' do whatever we say 'cause we got cause to stop yo' ass. Yes, it's called vehicle registration renewal. Ever hear a that?" He was cocky and belligerent.

Ryker handed him his driver's license and his insurance card. "You know I got a couple days to git my registration done. I's gon' take cur of it tomorrow." Ryker tried to stay calm, though his heart felt like it was pounding out of his chest. His piece was pressing against his groin.

"What are you doin' over here in this part a town, this time a night?" Payne asked, as he started to write up a warning for the vehicle registration.

"My granddaddy live over here," Ryker said easily. "I's comin' to see him."

"At midnight?" Payne's tone was accusing. "C'mon, man."

"Yes, sir," Ryker looked Payne in the eyes.

Check yourself, man. You could walk on this if you chill. Don't press yo' luck, he thought, as the officer stared him down.

"Why don't you step out the truck?" Payne countered. "Now."

Ah, man. Look what you done. Now you gone and pissed him off. Calm down, man. Do what he say. Just chill."

As Ryker started to open the truck, he said, "You know you got to have probable cause to search me or my truck."

"Did you see that Corbin? Did you see him knock my arm away when he opened his door?" Payne said, dramatically, throwing himself back, as if Ryker had pushed him.

"Yes, yes I did see that," Corbin said at the same time Payne grabbed Ryker by the collar and yanked him from his truck. When Payne threw him on the hood, his piece was pressed into his groin, a painful reminder that he had to get rid of it. Payne began to pound him on his backside while his arms were spread across the hood of his rusted-out blue Chevy. Racial insults were flying back and forth between the officers.

When they turned him around, his oversized t-shirt hung low, covering the bulge in his belt. The "pat-down" started to become more intense and he was hauled upright, the hits to his chest harder and harder. His pulse was racing. He could feel his blood pressure rising higher and higher. He felt the accusations with every strike to his body.

"We gon' make sure you ain' carrying. Yes sir!" Payne yelled in Ryker's ear so loud he pushed his shoulder higher to try to shield his ears. "That's right, nigger! You hear what I'm tellin' you? We gon' make sure you ain' gon' slither yo' way out a this. You gon' be looking' at charges tonight, if I gots anythin' to say 'bout it. Watch and learn, watch and learn," he said, patting harder and harder, coming closer and closer to the 9 millimeter.

Hearing the officer's voice so close to his head, it reminded him of a near-arrest a long time ago. He hadn't seen Payne's face; his cap came down low, covering his eyes, when Ryker rolled down his window just moments before, but he knew the voice. *It's Payne. This gon' be payback for Celia. He gon' take you down, whether it violate yo' rights or not. Git the hell out, man.*

Ryker pretended to stretch his torso, pushing his shoulder blades together. He slowly collapsed inward, as if in submission. Lowering his head, he let the weight of his body fall, his arms came across his chest as Payne wrapped his arms around him, grabbing his wrists to subdue him. In a matter of seconds, Ryker reversed his wrists and threw his arms down hard, his elbows shooting into Payne' ribs, his fists hitting him below the belt. Breaking Payne's hold, he grabbed Payne's nightstick from the holster and struck out at Corbin. As soon as Corbin felt the blow hit his shin, Ryker was free to run.

Seeing the park nearby, he sprinted toward the trees, shielding him from possible gunfire. With every pounding step, he was scoping out the area ahead. Looking both directions, occasionally glancing behind him, he saw Payne and Corbin coming up fast. When he turned back to see what was in front of him, he spotted a fence ahead in the distance. Almost to it, he saw there was an alley with bushes to the left and a concrete path to the main street on the right. He could climb the fence, jump down, and run either way if he made it over the fence before Payne and Corbin got to him.

His heart pounding out of his chest, he reached the fence, scrambling to the top, his feet slipping a few times in his struggle. His adrenaline was pumping hard. He was invigorated. It'd been a while since he'd felt this kind of rush; it was a pure adrenaline high. No more contemplating right and wrong. His only motive was escape and survival. He felt his muscles strengthen, his senses more keen under pressure. His arms and legs synchronized in a fast, fluid motion. At the top of the fence, he looked over his shoulder to see Payne coming up fast. Payne pulled his service revolver and just as he aimed, Ryker jumped, landing hard on the pavement.

The officers screamed, "Freeze or you goin' down!"

When he hit the ground, Ryker rolled to the right, into the bushes. Realizing he could make a break for the main street or take his chances in the alley, he stopped and took a few seconds to think. *I could let 'em catch me. They got nothin' but resistin' arrest. I done dumped the powder. If I ditch my piece and run far enough down the alley, I could … I could be on the run for the rest a my life. I could ….* His thoughts turned to Jack. "It's all about choices, son. If you choose to stand for yourself, against the odds, you've got a chance. If you run, you'll always be running."

He lay on the pavement; the last thought in his head coming to him with absolute clarity, *what's done is done. Accept the consequences and move on. No more runnin' from it, no more. Give yo'self up. Beg Jack to forgive you, whatever it take. You don't want the rush no more. Maybe this be the grace Jack be talkin' bout. Most people say if you gon' change yo' life, you got to make a clean break. This it. This gon' be it.*

As he waited to be cuffed, he felt electric shocks course through his body instead. Over and over, blows from a nightstick were coming fast and hard. He lay there, taking it all. The Taser hit him again, even though he wasn't moving or resisting.

Bruises formed and bones cracked, with each strike of the night stick and each steel-toed kick to his ribs. He resigned himself to the excruciating pain. He felt his insides sear, as the pain soon paralyzed him. He plunged into darkness.

Memories flooded to his brain. He saw his mother. She was anxious and wringing her hands. It sounded like sandpaper rubbing against itself.

Then, it was night. He could see her hands shaking, her face translucent. Blood drained from her face as she lay there, unconscious. She'd been beaten again and he had to find a way to help her. He tried to get up and go to her, but his legs and arms wouldn't move. He watched the blood draining from her face, turning a pasty white -- a sharp contrast from her dark, russet complexion.

He felt his insides begin to stretch and contract with equal force, leaving his stomach churning like bubbling acid, the lining started to burn. His blood pumped so hard and fast that it welled up, causing a ringing in his ears. He couldn't focus on her.

Another flash brought a shadow of a man. It was him. He was hovering over his own body, watching himself use every ounce of strength to give his mother cash. The money was enough. She just had to take it. *Take it, mama. Take it now.*

He held the cash in his hands, feeling the crisp bills. When will she be strong enough to handle things? He felt the cash slip through his fingers. *She gon' be okay. She gon' be okay, now.*

Then he saw Angela and the boys and his fingers clutched at the bills, just before they were completely gone. Holding on, he felt searing pain tear at his heart. Angela stroked his head, the baby in her belly rubbing against his shoulder. He turned and saw his mother again, pale and fading. His heart was slicing in half, blood spilling, voices calling. *Who do I save? Who need me most?*

There were more flashes. He saw himself on a mountainside, a tight wire between him and his boys, his new life. *No looking down*, he told himself, but couldn't resist a quick glance. He swayed and teetered, seeing jagged edges of rocks below. Righting himself, he fought to regain his footing. Another glance down and the scenery changed, flash after flash. *Where am I?*

A voice narrated the thoughts in his head. The tape was loud and blaring like a bullhorn.

Scenes played: him selling drugs, enforcing payment on orders from the Crips, hanging with the Bloods, running his father's business, hitting the ground when a task force raided his father's barn for narcotics, hearing his boys cry when the police ripped them from his arms, cringing at the sight of a young boy gunned down in a drive-by shooting, his father beating his mother to a bloody mess, his uncles on Bloody Fifth working over pimps who didn't deliver, white powder veiling faces of dead bodies, rivers of blood flowing from his hands. Nothing making sense. He was tired of trying to focus. So tired.

Chapter 11

*The pull is overwhelming. I swim closer and though I
see the hook shimmering beneath the bait, the taste
keeps my attention. I am now biting at the hook, no
longer careful of the tremors to the line. I cannot turn
and swim away.*

"Mr. James? Mr. James?" Nurse Blanche of John Peter
Smith hospital said, her voice growing louder each time.
When she couldn't get a response, she turned to the doctor,
standing in the doorway. "I think we're losing him."

"No, we're not," his heels clicked on the hard, white tile.
"Let's get some nitroglycerin in him and check his vitals. If
we have to do a pressure ventilation, we'll know soon
enough." Another nurse administered the medication into his
IV, as Blanche pumped the blood pressure meter vigorously.

"His BP is dangerously high," she warned. "He could
arrest again any second."

Ryker James, Jr.

*If I die, what I gon' leave behind? What gon' happen to my family?
I's the one they turn to when they in trouble. Even though I know they
ain' there for me, I can't leave 'em. I can't leave. Who gon' be there for
'em?*

"Let me tell you somethin' I heard long ago, Little Man," a
voice said. "God give us blessings ever' day, but they ain'
nothin' like what we gon' have in heaven."

There's a heaven?

"Of course they is boy. They's a road a gold with d'most
beautiful trees. They's leaves of ever color and the flowers. I

can't even describe how perty. It like walkin' through a gorgeous countryside, all green and lush. They's an angel leadin' the way. She gon' take us to our blessings. They's so many with yo' name on 'em."

My name? Can't be.

"You wrong. They's the ones I told you 'bout. 'Member, Lil' Man?"

The darkness pulled him further down.

———◆———

"Mr. James, Mr. James, please. Can you hear me?" Nurse Blanche said. Ryker groaned.

She turned to the doctor and said, "His blood pressure's coming down. I think he's coming out of it. That was close, a little too close."

Ryker awoke in his hospital room. There was so much pain in his chest and in his head. The longer he was conscious, the more the pain spread throughout his entire body.

Falling into the alley was the last thing he remembered. He heard an officer tell the doctor he would be transported to Mansfield jail as soon as he was able to move around on his own. He'd been charged with possession of cocaine.

Cocaine? Can't be. I dumped it. How did I get charged for possession?

Angela Ross

"He said he had to meet somebody," she said slowly, trying to remember exactly what Ryker had said. "His tone change and I, I thought he was…." She turned to Jack, the pain on her face saying it for her.

Scoring cocaine, Jack thought. Sarah closed her eyes and Angela did too, rubbing her belly and shaking her head slowly, tears falling, one by one, down her cheeks.

Jack wanted to hold her and tell her she was mistaken, that Ryker would never go back to dealing. He believed that and he was quite certain she would be grateful to hear the words, but Ryker had been in this life for almost 16 years; he was a career criminal when he met Jack; nearly three years straight or not, Jack couldn't give her false hope. The truth was, he wasn't sure how much Ryker was retaining from their time together.

"I think we have to face every possibility," Sarah's words seemed to force Jack to take a deep breath. When his lungs filled, he felt every part of him relax, if only for a moment. Shaking his head back and forth, he eventually looked at Sarah and Angela, the disbelief evolving into a nod of affirmation. "But, that doesn't mean the worst has happened. Let's focus on the Ryker we know, pray he's okay.

Sarah was right, Angela knew. *The old Ryker could have slipped up and said those words without meaning anything by them. Or, maybe he did mean them, but that didn't mean he'd acted on them. Every second can change the next.* "We have to pray he will be strong enough to remember what he's learned over the last several months," she resolved.

"That's right. You're right," Jack finally said. "God can work through us, even when we're going bass ackwards and blind."

His play on words had the three of them laughing, as tears spurted from her eyes, landing on Jack's shirt. She wiped at them and fell into his arms. Sarah leaned in to embrace them both.

"You know, he told me he never want a disappoint you," Angela said, looking from Jack to Sarah. "I know he mean it. We been friends a long time. He say I ain' like all the other women 'cause he wadn' never friends with 'em. I know when he lyin'. I do. And, I think he really mean it when he say he gon' bring us food. I know it look bad now, but somethin' wrong, I'm tellin' you. Somethin' wrong. He wouldn't go back after all he been through, not in his right mind."

"I know that's true," Jack said. "We just have to pray him through it. Now, you lie down and close your eyes when we go. Pray for him. Okay?"

Sarah nodded and Angela did, too. She and Jack got up to leave. When they were almost out the door, Angela called out, "You know, he say you like the father he ain' never had, Jack. And you like a mama to him, Sarah. I can't tell you what it mean to him. There ain' words." She waved goodbye and walked into her bedroom as Jack and Sarah smiled and closed the door behind them.

Jack tried to lie down, close his eyes and pray, but thoughts of another time, long ago, kept seeping in, diluting his conversation with God. He got up and paced. When this didn't help things, he lay down again for a few moments. But when he closed his eyes, he kept remembering what Angela said about him being the father Ryker never had.

Exhaustion married images under the dark canopy of his eyelids, forming a random sequence; there were snippets of turning points throughout his life. One was when Mitchell Lawrence came at him with his belt because he moved from the spot on the area rug in their living room. He'd stepped in front of his sister, knowing he could take the beating better than she.

He saw flashes of Uncle Pete teaching him about casting with live bait and lures, Doc Sevrenson making a funny comment to match every serious one Pete was trying to make.

He saw Mr. Leonard coming to him when the manager of the sales department, Jake Landers, tried to pin a lost sale on him.

He saw Craig Jacobs, assessing his work on the fence he had asked Jack to paint when he was ten years old. They stared at the fence for such a long time. "You've done a wonderful job, son," he finally said and relief washed over Jack's entire body.

There were flashes of his mother, lying dead, her Bible turned to her favorite Psalm, and of Daddy Conner, the day they signed the papers to buy the farm.

The images surfaced at random, some washing peace over him, lulling him into a light slumber, and others causing his body to jerk with fear and anxiety.

When he woke, it had been twenty minutes. Giving up on getting a few hours, he got up and walked to the kitchen to turn on the coffee pot. Just as he pressed brew, the phone rang, startling him.

"Mr. Lawrence?" the voice said. "This is Nurse Blanche. I'm a nurse at John Peter Smith Hospital. Mr. James put you on his list of people to call in case of …."

"What?" Jack interrupted her, his heart starting to race like a thoroughbred out of the gate. "Oh, my God, he's not, he's not …."

"Mr. Lawrence," she said more firmly. "Mr. James is stable, but he has been asking for you. He requested I call and see if you would come down to his room in the Intensive Care Unit."

"Oh, dear God, I thought you were calling to say, to tell me," Jack collapsed into his recliner, holding his chest, willing his pulse to slow down.

"Are you there?" Nurse Blanche asked.

"Yes, yes. I'm here. I'll be there as quick as I can." Jack hung up and woke Sarah. "Shug, we got to go. Ryker's in the hospital."

Sarah got up quickly; they dressed and were in the car and on their way within minutes. Silence filled the car, a heaviness weighing down any thoughts that might have turned into words spoken aloud. Jack wished he were still lying down and this was merely a flash instead of the living nightmare it was.

As they walked into JPS, he smelled the familiar and pungent odor, a combination of stale sweat, Clorox bleach, and Lysol.

"We're here to see Ryker James," Jack said to the receptionist.

"Yes, could you sign in?" she answered without even looking up. "He's in room 351. Take the corridor to the elevators. Go to the third floor and his room is on the right."

"Thank you," Jack said, looking at Sarah.

When they walked down the corridor, there was no mistaking his room, as an officer stood outside. Jack verified he was Ryker's in-case-of-emergency contact and the guard let them pass. Ryker was lying on the hospital bed, his eyes swollen shut, his arms covered in bruises. He was hooked up to a heart monitor.

Dear God, what in the world happened to him? Jack thought. A doctor came in momentarily.

"Are you Jack Lawrence?" Doctor Heideman asked.

"Yes, uh," gesturing to Sarah, he said, "This is my wife," and he slipped his arm around her, more for his own comfort than acknowledgment.

"Mr. James has been asking for you and he said if he was sleeping when you got here, to let you know his status. Mr. James suffered multiple shocks from a Taser gun when he resisted arrest last night around 1 a.m. An ambulance brought him to us about 2. He was in pretty bad shape. He was severely beaten and," he paused, "He almost died on the table. He was damn lucky to have made it to the ER at all."

"I don't understand," Jack's thoughts were reeling with questions. The doctor, registering shock and confusion on Jack's face, realized he'd been remiss to consider how it would affect the old guy. Jack was losing color in his face.

"Sir, how about you have a seat over here," and he gestured to the chair beside Ryker's bed. "I'm going to get you some water. You too ma'am." He reached for another chair and dragged it over for Sarah.

"I don't want a chair," Jack was irritated, when he saw pity in the doctor's face.

"Okay, well, if you're sure. Mr. James should be awake to relay the rest of the story in a few hours. He's not quite out of danger so try not to upset him when he wakes. We need to keep him as calm as we can. His heart needs to recover from the events of last night. Like I said, he's lucky to be alive. Most people would have died, given the brutality he suffered."

When Jack and Sarah took a seat by the bed and surveyed the wires attached to his head and chest, the doctor excused himself and left them alone. The dark patches on Ryker's arms and legs were like camouflage on his dark skin. His eyes were tiny slits, surrounded by swollen mounds. His mouth was deformed by the swelling on both his top and bottom lip. Sarah sat beside Jack, tears falling one at a time down her face. *Dear God, help us.*

Jack's face was solemn, but determined. As he watched Ryker sleep, he thought of how many times Uncle Pete sat by *his* bed, after he'd suffered a severe beating from his stepfather.

He thought about the times Lawrence didn't come home before bedtime. His mother stayed up cleaning, scouring every inch of the house in hopes of staving off a beating and when she finally gave up and went to bed, Jack remembered how he assumed the position. He'd snuck out of his bed and laid on the floor outside the master bedroom door. If he could be the first thing Lawrence tripped over, maybe he could spare his mother the inevitable beating.

The last time, he tried to fight back, getting in a few hits; it only made things worse. When he woke, his eyes puffy, his lip split, and his arms bruised from the old man's knees pinning him down, Jack remembered being surprised that Uncle Pete was sitting at *his* bedside.

"Hey there, slugger," he'd said so Jack didn't have to open his eyes to see him. "You know I'm here. I'll be here all day so you rest. Know that, son. I won't be leaving you any time soon. You're stuck with me, boy."

Jack remembered feeling so grateful for him. Uncle Pete stayed with him all that day and all the next. It was only a few days later that he told Jack he had arranged for his mom and his sisters to live with his brother and sister-in-law, Sim and Joan.

Jack was thinking, *where does that leave me?* When Uncle Pete said, "You're stuck with me sport. It'll be closer to Leonard's and school."

"Mom's okay with all this?" Jack managed to ask, trying to fight back tears.

"Yeah, sport. It's all worked out." He rubbed the top of Jack's head, the only place that wasn't sore from the likes of Mitchell Lawrence.

Jack didn't move from his place by Ryker's side. He waited several hours before Ryker woke. The nurses came in and out, checking Ryker's vitals; the sound of the blood pressure gauge reminded him of his own breathing after Lawrence's wrath, labored and shallow. He remembered lying on the floor, his body crumpled unnaturally. His breath was ragged and he wanted to move, but was too afraid. His mother had to wait until Mitchell passed out before she could call for help; her injuries were almost as severe. She managed to crawl to the telephone and dial 9-1-1, feeling for the right buttons, her eyes too swollen to see.

Each time Lawrence made a sound, she'd freeze, praying he wouldn't wake or catch her before she could make the call. She had a searing pain coming from her side. *My ribs must be broken*, she remembered thinking.

Though Lawrence did not wake, even when the sirens of the ambulance sounded, Maggie was frozen in fear until the police arrived. She insisted that the ambulance see to Jack first. When they finally got to her, she had lost consciousness.

Jack did not remember much after he was lifted into the ambulance. He thought he was still in the ambulance when he awoke and saw Uncle Pete beside him, his hand on Jack's wrist. His words were soothing and kind. He'd said, "I won't leave you again. Never again, son. If that monster comes near you again, you won't be the one in the hospital. I'll wrap my hands around his throat and never let go," Uncle Pete said.

"Stop. Stop," Aunt Rachel told him. "Please, he's been through enough."

"Never let go," Jack whispered. "Never let go…."

Jack was lost in his thoughts when Ryker came to. He tried to squeeze Jack's arm, but his strength was minimal. His voice raspy, he said, "Sorry, Jack. So sorry."

"Don't talk, son. Save your energy," Jack assured him.

"It's my fault. Bad choices. Got confused," Ryker tried to explain.

"Stop. You don't need to explain. I'm here. You're stuck with me, Ryker. I'm not going anywhere. No matter what you say, I'm here, so just rest."

Later that evening, the chief of police came by while Ryker was sleeping. Jack stepped in front of Ryker's room door. His shoulders squared, his hands on his hips and his feet firmly planted, he said, "May I help you with something?"

"Step aside please. I'm here on official business," Police Chief Raymond Doss said.

"I don't mean any disrespect, but you're going to have to go through me. Ryker James was beaten within an inch of his life by your officers. I guess you missed the sign back there.

I-C-U? His status is still touch and go. If you want to say something, I'm the only one you're gonna see," Jack side-stepped to match Doss, when he tried to go around him.

"Are you aware you can be charged with obstructing justice?" Doss barked at Jack.

"Yes, yes, I am. Are you aware I'm prepared to sue the department for unjustified, nearly fatal police brutality? I'll be glad to step aside and call every reporter in the Metroplex, tell 'em what your men did to my son." Jack was almost growling at Doss.

Doss looked into Jack's determined eyes, shadowed by lack of sleep and he guessed, worry. He decided to cut him some slack, not to mention that Jack's allegations weren't far off the mark. He had already spoken to Payne and Corbin. He'd actually come to check on Ryker, assess the need for damage control.

Doss was a little confused when Jack said Ryker was his son. *Who was this old white man, defending scum like Ryker James? Had he not seen Ryker's record?*

"Sir, let's take a moment and calm down. Who are you exactly? You said your 'son' and you and I both know Ryker James is not kin to you, so …."

"He's my son in every sense of the word. He's been trying to change his ways and he was doin' just fine until your officers decided, because of his past record, he needed to be beaten to death. I'd say that was taking the law way past fair and just, wouldn't you?

"Haven't you noticed he's been off the radar for a while? Or, don't you pay attention? He's been living in minimal housing, caring for his stepbrother, his little boy and another baby on the way. Part of the time, he's been living with me and working two, sometimes three jobs to make ends meet, and here you stand, saying you're going to charge *me* with obstruction of justice." Jack looked at the floor with disgust. "Don't that just beat all," Jack said under his breath. "I'm the one person who gives a damn. All *you* want to do is lock him up."

"All due respect to you, sir, James has been in the drug business for most of his life. It may be true that he's been making an effort to change as of late, but…" he shook his head, seriously doubting James had changed at all. He squared his shoulders, looked into Lawrence's eyes; considered the possibility. The old man wasn't budging, all four-feet-six inches of him. He looked like a burly version of Matlock.

Sifting through the last couple of years, he considered. *He could be right. One of the reasons they haven't been able to find Ryker could be because he's been with this guy. He sure as hell hasn't been in the community circles he usually runs in or he would have been easier to track. Come to think of it, his men had told him James was not just flying under the radar, but that it appeared he wasn't even on the grid. Maybe he has been with this old man. It would certainly explain a lot. Was he taking this man for a ride so he could lie low?* Clearing his throat and beginning again, Doss asked, "How long has he been in your acquaintance?"

"I don't see how that is any of your business," Jack spat out. "What of it?"

"Sir, James was caught with 27 grams of cocaine. We're not talking about a minor charge. He also struck Officer Corbin so he could make a run for it through the park. Why was he runnin' if he's innocent?" Doss pressed.

"Yeah, good question. I'm thinking your officers are makin' things up as they go along. We'll see about those charges, won't we? I've been a citizen of Fort Worth my whole life, made contributions in the community, served in the Korean War, worked my way up the blue collar chain to management at General Dynamics, which is now Lockheed Martin. Do you think I was born yesterday? I'm no spring chicken and I think I know Ryker James better than you ever will."

"Be that as it may, the charges have been filed, and when he's well enough to stand on his own, he'll be transported to Mansfield until bond can be set."

"Yeah, and we'll see about that, too. Until then, I don't think you have any business coming around here." Jack folded his arms, his legs spread apart. His body was virtually blocking the entrance to the room.

"Well, just let James know I was here when he wakes up. He also needs to know his truck was impounded last night. His wallet was found on the front seat. The keys are with the attendant at the impound yard on North side Drive." Doss trailed off.

Clearing his throat, Jack started to think he might have just been killing the messenger. He nodded and managed to say, "Thanks for letting me know. It saves me a call, I suppose."

Returning the gesture, Doss said, "Well, I need to get back to the station." As he turned to go, he couldn't help himself. He turned back. "Mr. Lawrence, at the risk of making things worse, I must say that Ryker James *is* a career criminal. We've been after him for the past 15 years and his crimes are nothing to snuff at. Tigers, stripes and all that." He tipped his hat and walked away before Jack could respond.

As Jack watched him go, he breathed a deep sigh. Doss was speaking the truth. Some of Ryker's choices cost others their lives, whether it was through addiction or through gang violence. Jack knew who Ryker James had been. He knew Ryker had a long way to go before he would be free of the man he was. He said a prayer as he walked back into Ryker's room. As he prayed, the image of the old man he and Luke had seen at the prison kept flashing in his mind; and his words, *seventy times seven.*

Sarah was on her cell phone, talking to Angela.

"He's in rough shape, but he's stable," Sarah explained. "I know. I know you want to come up here, but what about the babies? Oh, you're mother's coming over? Well, good. Then, I guess we'll see you in a little while then," she said, trailing off.

Jack resumed his place by Ryker's bed, took a sip of his coffee, now gone cold. *Seventy times seven.*

"Have you talked to Brock Kingsley?" Sarah said, as they waited for Ryker to wake.

"Every week. You know that," Jack said.

"What about Daniel Barton?"

"Yeah, I've written 'em both letters. I need to get them in the mail," Jack said, remembering he meant to put them in the mail a couple of days ago.

"You know, what you did for Brian was amazing," Sarah pressed on.

"Stop," Jack said, knowing she was trying to remind him of the people he'd helped. They were prisoners who'd had similar situations, not unlike those facing Ryker.

"No, I won't stop. Tell me what you did to help Brian," she insisted. "He'd been in prison, out at the Michael Unit, at Tennessee Colony. What was he in for? Twenty-one years for armed robbery?"

"No, attempted armed robbery," Jack snapped. His fatigue was wearing on him.

"That's right, and one night he heard a couple of his cellmates talking about that poor woman, Ann Hicks, who was killed and chopped into pieces and spread all over tarnation so nobody could find her. They'd been trying to find who murdered her for five years," Sarah continued.

"Well, actually, she had been dead for 14, but they didn't know until five years ago. The assistant criminal district attorney, who was the inspector of record, and an officer in the Tarrant County Sheriff's office couldn't get a lead to save their lives, but Brian knew who was responsible and I told a Texas Ranger friend of mine, Chase Landers, to check where Brian said the murderer scattered her body."

"Didn't they all come down to the prison and talk to Brian?"

"Yeah, I remember because Brian was afraid when they called him to the warden's office. He wouldn't say a word in front of the warden, so they kicked the warden out of his own office." Jack chuckled a bit in spite of how he was feeling about Ryker. "But, the upshot of it was, in exchange for Brian telling them where Boulware had buried that woman, the Assistant Criminal D.A. McElroy, Inspector Thomas and Lancaster in the Sheriff's office wrote letters on Brian's behalf to get him transferred out of that terrible prison he was assigned to at the time; and that woman, and I use that term loosely, on the parole board, gave him a two-year set off."

"Set off? I've forgotten what that means."

"It means the letter we wrote and all the ones the other guys sent to help him get transferred were ignored and he couldn't come up for parole review for another two years. It's a game, I tell you, a damn game. The governor decides he wants to lock 'em up and throw away the key and this woman wants to impress him, so Brian is screwed out of his transfer for another two years."

"He did get transferred though," Sarah gently reminded him.

"Yeah, he did."

"At least he's serving the rest of his sentence in a better place," Sarah said. "And he wasn't the only one. How about Daniel Bronson, the son of the state representative from where was it? Richardson?"

"Tyler," Jack corrected, surprised Sarah was remembering all of the men he'd helped over the years. "He was given a life sentence for impersonating a doctor. A life sentence," Jack said, shaking his head. "Then he was attacked in prison and they broke his back, injuring his neck, too. He couldn't hurt anybody the way he is now, but his daddy won't lift a finger to help him because he doesn't want the governor to know his son is in prison. I think it's more about the expensive medical care and medication he has to have now. I'm sure Big-Daddy-State-Representative doesn't want to pay for all that. It's a racket, I'm telling you," Jack said.

"But, they have you. These men have had you to come see them and encourage them to keep going. You've prayed for them, believed in them. You've been their advocate, their mentor."

"Yeah," Jack admitted. "I just wanted to help 'em get through. People need someone to believe in 'em."

"It's helping. And, we're going to help Ryker, too. You'll see. Ryker's been the hardest one to help, but it doesn't mean we can't do it."

"You're right," he said, reluctantly. "I know you're right," his voice more resigned the second time he said it.

By this time, another hour passed and he heard Ryker stirring. When he could tell Ryker was awake, he said, "How are you doin', son?"

"Sore," Ryker grimaced, as he tried to sit up.

"I had a visit from the Fort Worth police chief. Doss was his name. You feel up to tellin' me how this all happened?" Jack asked.

"Yeah," he said. "Could you maybe help me sit up?"

Pushing the button on the side of his bed, he watched Ryker's bed raise him to a sitting position. He swallowed hard and sipped from a cup of water. When he got rid of the dryness in his throat, he said, "I's worried 'bout bein' a burden to you and Sarah. I thought if I scored one more time, I'd be able to get ahead a my rent and take some of the pressure off. I don't know what made me think I could go back. I didn't want to. Everything in my head all messed up. I kept hearin' two voices in my head. One was you and one was the old me. Things was just hard to figure out.

"Ace come by the shop and the guys was doin' they gay stuff. Ace already think I done walked out on him and the others and for what? To work for a bunch a gays for minimum wage? I ain' judgin' 'em. I just don't want 'em puttin' they moves on me.

"It got me thinkin' they right. I ain' able to make rent and keep my utilities paid, food on the table, and then these guys actin' like I done turned soft. I was trippin'. Then, Ace say he need my help with this score. He ain' never axed for help. He'd sooner cut off his arm than ax me for nothin'.

"I started to think 'bout the people I done left behind when I left. They's a lot a good people, people who put theyself on the line for me, time and again. I thought a my Pop. He went down not long after he warn me that I might have custody a Junior. I was so angry, about so much, I threw ever thang in his face.

"Somehow I git it in my head this last score could make everything right. I could keep from burdenin' you and Sarah. I could pay my own stuff and I could help Ace, somebody who help me more times than I can count. I ain' thinkin' a what could happen. I's just thinkin' like I used to, tryin' to protect ever'body else. I don't know how else to 'xplain it.

"I know'd it was wrong. And, I changed my mind. I got rid a the cocaine before the police stop me. I didn't have nothin' on me. All they could git me for was not havin' my vehicle registered. That was it. Next thing I know, I'm bein' pulled from the car and Payne is sayin' I resisted him and his partner's not sayin' nothin'. I'm bein' beat down so I duck and break free and I'm runnin'.

"I would a made it too, but I heard you, in my head, sayin' somethin' bout standin' and facin' things. I *chose* to let them catch me, Jack. I could a been long gone. Now, they sayin' I have cocaine on me. I was clean. I admit I's gon' sell that stash, but I cast it to the wind two blocks over before they stop my truck. Jack, you got to believe me."

"I do, son. I do. We'll talk about some of this later. Let's table it for now and we'll talk about it when you're better and we figure out what's going to happen with the magistrate. First thing's first.

"Now, Luke is going to come by once we get you settled at the house. If you're up to it, you can ride with us to get your truck. I don't think you need to be driving quite yet.

"A'ight," Ryker said. "What I gon' do 'bout the charges?"

"I'm going to hire a lawyer friend of mine, Isaiah Dexter. We'll see what the sentence is gonna be. I bet when the dust settles, we can plead it down." Jack's voice was like a very low rumbling, growing deeper with conviction as he spoke.

◆

The next night, Dr. Heideman released Ryker from the hospital. Jack and Sarah took him to their house for the night because, for some reason, the arresting officers had not yet filed charges on him.

Despite the horrific beating he took, he was doing okay. It was hard for Luke to see him, beaten up so badly. As they road to Fort Worth impound together, Ryker told him what happened.

"Sounds to me like the officers made it a racial issue," Luke said.

"I don't know 'bout that. One a them was black, just like me. I just know I didn't give 'em no cause to hurt me so bad.

"I talked to Dexter," Jack interrupted, trying to change the subject. "He's going to do everything he can to help you, but you're due in Mansfield so they can set bond." Silence filled the truck. The reality of the charges began to sink in. The choice Ryker made seemed to choke any words they might have said the rest of the way back.

Finally, Ryker broke the silence, "I don't git how you do it Jack? I done made a bad choice and you standin' by my side. What make you think I deserve it?"

"I don't leave when the going gets tough, son. You should know that by now. Besides, it ain' over yet. We're gon' get you out of this."

Ryker was his family and he was sticking. *Never let go.*

Chapter 12

*Being on the hook is exhilarating, even intoxicating;
the prey knowing it has been caught and still having
a moment or second of hope that it could still get
away; it's a rush.*

Several months later ...

"All rise," the bailiff said as the Honorable Harold Proctor swooped into the courtroom from a side door and took his seat. In his deep, baritone voice, he got right to the point. "In the case of The State of Texas vs. Ryker James Junior, has the jury come to a verdict?"

The foreman nervously stood and said, "Umm, yes sir, we have."

Judge Proctor impatiently responded, "Well, what say you?"

"Umm, yes sir. We the jury in the case of the state versus Ryker James, Jr. find the defendant, umm, guilty, of a second-degree felony -- possession of 27 grams of an illegal substance."

Judge Proctor turned to face Ryker. "Mr. James, you have been found guilty of a second degree felony. I have reviewed your record and the facts in this case and I hereby sentence you to serve two years in state custody at the Manuel A. Segovia Unit in Edinburg, Texas. Mr. James, do you understand the verdict and the sentence as they have been explained to you?"

"Yes, your honor," Ryker said and the gavel came down hard.

"This Court is adjourned," Judge Proctor concluded. He was out of his seat and headed toward the door as his gavel dropped on the bench.

———◆———

Jail. The experience is indescribable. It's rancid, smelling of sweaty bravado, anxiety, fear and weighted hopelessness. There's not been a disinfectant or a form of bleach made yet that can mask the smell of potential death emanating throughout the place. As the guard processed Ryker, flashes of his first incarceration came to mind. Not good.

He walked, carrying his bedding to his cell, his face a dead-pan expression. His eyes cut from cellmate to cellmate as he passed by, daring them to mess with him. They hadn't seen anything yet if they thought they were going to screw with him while he was there. His uncles taught him to defend himself under any circumstances, and to show no fear.

He heard the inmates call out to him, "Fresh meat, fresh meat, fresh meat," their chant finding a rhythm. He didn't react. He just kept walking, proud and defiant.

He was one of forty inmates in a large cell. He made his way in, the men intentionally shoving him as he walked by. He made eye contact, exposing a minimal dose of the rage that had been living inside him for years, recently resurrected during the beating he took from Payne and Corbin. He thought it was dead and buried, but as he lay there on the ground that night, taking it, he knew he it was more alive than ever.

When he dropped his stuff on one of the lower bunks in the mass of steel bunk beds, a guy named Stone knocked his bedding to the floor. His rage was stoked from flashes of beatings given and ones he received as he cut his dark eyes in Stone's direction. Stone swelled to the utmost height of his stature, revealing his bulk to Ryker. Ryker simply stared him down, daring him to start something. His mouth was tight, his jaw muscles clenched, his hands extending and forming a fist. He flexed his well-toned muscles, thinking *bring it.*

Stone's eyes narrowed as he returned the challenge, squaring his shoulders and planting his tree-trunk-size legs.

Ryker decided to show him how little his show of strength affected him. He pierced him through with one last hard look, then turned and picked up his bedding and dropped it back on the bed, lingering in a bent-over state, as if to say, "You could come at me from behind and I could still kick yo' ass."

Slowly, he stood to his full height of six-foot-two. He rolled his shoulders back, cocked his head to the side and back, then shrugged his shoulders. *Bring it.* He thought it so loud, he was sure it had been heard by the huge, hulk of a man. Stone rolled his shoulders and slowly backed away, still glaring, but not willing to chance what he saw in Ryker's dark stare.

Other cellmates witnessed the whole thing. Silence fell over the room like a heavy, wet, rank blanket. Ryker had forgotten how deep his fury ran; his thoughts turned to the time he spent in Houston, learning from his uncles. *He could do this,* he decided. *Just have to pick my battles.*

He was assigned to the laundry room the next day. Word on the cellblock was that he was fresh bait for rape or a "come to Jesus" beating. He didn't care. He was living through nightmares as he slept, walking through them as he worked. There was nothing he feared in this place. Nothing and no one.

He heard them coming up from behind in the laundry room. The hairs on the back of his neck prickled. He felt for the make-shift knife he'd fashioned from a utensil he stole from one of the cooks at breakfast, letting it slide down from inside his sleeve.

One of them grab him around his shoulders to secure him, he crossed his arms over his chest, turned his wrists outward and threw down his arms hard, the blade of the knife stabbing into the upper thigh, near the man's groin. When he screamed in pain, the others saw their accomplice's blood, still dripping from Ryker's weapon, and they started to back away, realizing they had picked the wrong man to attack.

The others left their man to suffer at Ryker's hands. The guy was shaking his head, pleading with Ryker not to finish him. Ryker grabbed him by the hair, holding the blade to his neck. Bending down, close to his ear, he whispered, "Spread the word. Laundry can bring stains you can't git rid of and ain' nobody gon' live to tell about it. You feel me?"

He felt Ryker's steel-like clutch, holding the back of his head. The man did his best to nod compliance, but when Ryker shoved him to the ground, the man clasped his leg, still bleeding profusely. He looked up at Ryker and said, "Why?"

"Why what?" Ryker nearly growled.

"Why ain' you gon' kill me? You had me, man. Why you lettin' me go? I'd a done you," he said, swallowing hard and gasping for breath.

"I got time. I got eighteen months to decide how it gon' go down; to plan it and make sure it happen slow and painful," Ryker whispered, his tone dripping with rage.

The man got to his feet as quickly as possible. He eyed Ryker, never turning his back until he was out of his sight.

Word spread like wildfire throughout the Segovia unit. Ryker sent a message and it was received. He wasted no time, networking with inmates to turn some cash. Once he found a guard who would get him smokes, he was in business. *Let the prison games begin.*

He thought about Jack. It had been weeks since he was taken to Segovia. Jack came out to the prison and visited him the first week, but he hadn't been back for a while. He said he had to get Dexter moving on his case and it could take some time. It seemed like it was taking longer than expected.

It didn't surprise Ryker. He had a rap sheet fifty pages long. He had no illusions about how much Jack would be able to do for him. He'd run. He'd cut and run.

Resisting arrest. Ryker slumped down on his bunk. Jail. No guarantees, no matter what messages you've sent. Inmates turn on people for just about anything. There were Bloods and Crips in their respective groups around the yard, challenging the weak, making them succumb. No one had made a move on Ryker yet, but he was bench pressing more than anyone in the yard in preparation. He had to be ready -- untouchable.

He thought about Jack and Sarah. He wanted to go back in time, make different choices; see the mistakes before he made them.

The truth was he'd questioned whether he was worthy of escaping the hell that had been his life. How could he go free when he'd hurt so many people? He'd broken the law over and over, living off peoples' addictions to cocaine, crack, and weed.

He'd had a front row seat to the agony of withdrawal. Smokes were some solace, but the ones on H and other intravenous drugs were suffering in a way no one can really comprehend unless they've been through it.

He slumped farther down in his bunk. Jack had probably seen his whole record: Delta and Tarrant County, Oklahoma. Maybe he decided Ryker was a lost cause. Maybe he *was* lost. How was he supposed to come back from this?

Jack Lawrence

I had just gotten off the phone. I was talking to Dexter and it wasn't looking good. I was supposed to meet Ryker to talk more strategy.

Luke stopped by to talk and he could tell I was in a bad way. He surprised me a little when he spoke of Ryker. I had heard all I could stand from some of the people at church, saying I was wasting my time and money, while Ryker was making a fool of me. I expected Luke to feel the same; heck, I was questioning myself, too. I thought he was going to ask about Sarah. He had to know I'd spent a good bit of money on Ryker and I figured he probably wanted to know how far we'd been set back, because of it.

"You know, I understand what you're doing for Ryker, more than you know."

"You do," I said, not sure what he meant. *How could he know? Half the time, I was taking it moment-to-moment.*

"You know, when my dad died, I knew he was a good man," Luke went on. "So many people showed up at the funeral; each one kept coming up to me, telling me stories of how my father had been there for them." He stopped, looking into Jack's eyes.

"I know. Your mother told me as much," I admitted, nodding. "Your father was as good as they come."

"Well, what I want to tell you is, after the funeral, I was home and people were still calling and bringing food by. It was good to hear from them and all, but by the end of the day, I was ready to just have it be over. Anyway, the phone rang and it was late, about nine-thirty. I hesitated a little. It rang at least seven or eight times and just as I thought it would stop, something told me to grab it.

"The man on the other end of the phone was black -- I could tell by the way he talked and, I'm not proud of this, but I didn't know my father knew anyone of color so I was preparing an excuse to hang up. But, before I could get it out, he told me he wanted to tell me what a hero my father was." Luke paused, swallowing hard.

I waited, seeing he was having a hard time telling me this.

"Anyway, he said that my dad had helped him buy a house, years ago. He said it was hard for African-Americans to get loans because the language was so hard to understand and not many folks believed they could make good on the loan, even if they got one.

"So, Dad helped him through the process and he said Dad took a lot of grief for it, but that he was the reason this man was able to get a home for himself and his family and he'd never forgotten it. He said my father was ahead of his time, way back then. He thanked me for having the privilege of knowing my Dad and I have to say *no one*, up until that point, had said anything that comforted me the way this man had.

"Anyway, if you're questioning anything right now, I just want you to know, I'm proud of you. I know my father would be too. It's amazing that my mother picked two incredible men to marry; two men so much alike."

I couldn't speak. The tears were so many I couldn't stop them from falling. *How did Luke know I needed to hear this? Dear God, I must be doing something right.*

"He's lucky to be alive." Luke abruptly changed the subject, giving me a chance to regroup. "What kind of person beats and Tasers someone nearly to death? A law enforcement officer, no less. Our taxes pay their salary for crying-out-loud. Passersby said he was not even moving and they were still zapping him, again and again. You know this was a racial attack."

"It certainly was discriminatory. I don't know about racial."

"Well, it doesn't much matter if the officer is black or not. He obviously thinks because he's a cop with a badge, he can do this kind of thing."

It was as if Luke was affirming my mission to help Ryker with every word he was saying. My one concern about being there for Ryker was my own children feeling displaced. When Luke told me the story about his father helping that man, it was as if God had removed all doubt from my mind.

"Thank you for telling me about your dad. I can't tell you what it means to me to know you understand. I have a feeling this will take some time. Ryker's in pretty deep. I'm expecting to wade through some pretty rough waters before we hit new land, if you know what I mean.

"You know, we filed his taxes this year. He had just received five hundred dollars -- his first refund, working in an honest job. It was gone when I checked his wallet. Damn shame. He can't win for losin'."

Dexter met me at the courthouse in downtown Fort Worth on Throckmorton. I had a chance to look at the police report and knew I had to talk to Ryker, hammer out more details if we were going to plead his sentence down any. I needed to get out to Mansfield prison. They'd taken him there, a few days after we got his truck from the impound place. Dexter was checking on a few things that might help.

When I got home, Sarah met me at the front door.

"Jack," Sarah's voice was tentative. "What are you going to do? I mean, twenty-seven grams. Could Doss have been right about Ryker?"

It took a lot for Sarah to ask me this. We'd talked about it after Doss claimed they found the drugs on him. After hearing the status of his arrest and the charges, there was no getting around the possibility he could be playing us.

"I don't know. I don't know," I said, sighing deeply. "I'm looking at the evidence, eyes wide open, but my gut's telling me to stick. That, and I promised him."

"*We* promised him," she said, reaching for his hand and squeezing tight.

Ryker James, Jr.

Sitting in the yard, smoking a Camel, he looked out through the double razor wire. He wanted to rewind the tape of the events that had transpired over the course of the last few weeks. *Jack*, he thought. *Jack believe in me like nobody ever done. He done give me his support and open his family to me and what'd I go and do? Fail him.*

At this point, he was looking at eighteen months in prison and having a hard time feeling he didn't deserve to serve every day of it.

Still, Jack was there. It was like God was working in both their lives, though he couldn't imagine why. What made God believe he was worth the effort?

———◆———

When his cell door opened, Ryker saw a very shaky, crazed-looking man stumble in.

He watched him for a time. The man was scratching at his arms and legs and moving in spastic, random motions. Ryker nodded hello but the man didn't respond. He just kept weaving.

Then he stood up and paced, his head jerking to the right awkwardly. He was agitated. He reminded Ryker of the junkies he'd sold to. *Withdrawal ain' easy*, he thought.

Ryker tried to talk to him.

"Hey, man, you a'ight?"

"Shut the hell up," he grumbled.

Ryker raised an eyebrow, looked around for anyone watching.

"It's hot in here," the man wiped at his forehead. "I'm burning up. Damn."

A few minutes later, he was complaining again, "I'm freezing. It's so cold, I can't get warm." Ryker knew his body was probably cycling through withdrawal at warp speed. The man held on to his arms as tight as he could. "It feel like somethin' cuttin' me from the inside out."

It gon' be a long night, Ryker decided.

"Hey, my name's Ryker. What's yo' name?"

"I know yo' freakin' name! You don't know me?" he said, spitting out the words.

"What 'choo talkin' 'bout?" Ryker said, taken aback. He mentally flipped through his people, then his dad's people, friends, relatives. Standing and walking over to him, he looked into the man's face. Pain stabbed through his chest, as shock took over, his pulse racing. *D? Dominik.* Realizing he hadn't said it aloud, he cleared his throat to speak.

"D?" his voice was ragged. "It can't be." Moving in for a closer look, he saw his eyes, "Ah, man -- naw. I," he stopped, caught up in his emotions. He backed away, giving him room, while flashes of memories flooded his mind. It was hard to believe they used to go to the park to play stick ball and climb trees together and now, he was so messed up. He shook his head, willing it to be a bad dream. D was the one who figured out how to string a line between the trees so they could zip-line from one to the other. Whoever touched the ground was out.

Narrowing his eyes at the skeleton D had become, he flinched when D started slapping at himself. It was like he was trying to kill a million spiders.

He leaned against the steel bunk beds, watching as his cousin struggled. He thought of others on the street he'd sold to, who looked just like him. *This what I done when I sold to people,* he thought, his tough exterior cracking at the sight of his cousin. *This the way I's makin' my livin', sellin' 'em what I think gon' let 'em escape the pain a they lives for a time, but the truth was, I's sendin' 'em down a long road to hell."*

D was pacing faster and slapping at his head. He was dripping sweat, not really responding to anything, not even Ryker's voice. He suddenly launched his body at the wall and bounced back, landing on the floor, where he scrambled to a sitting position. He rocked back and forth, screaming out when the pain was too much.

"Shut the hell up, you crazy mother!" other cellmates yelled.

"C'mon, D. Shut it!" said another.

Soon the yelling was so loud Ryker couldn't tell if it was coming from inside the cell or out. He prepared himself to protect D if anyone decided to come at him. Riding it out, as his cousin shook and slapped and screamed, he prayed silence would come.

When it finally did, he was listening, hoping D was still breathing. He was in a fetal position on the floor against the wall. *Please let 'im be breathin'. Breathe, man. C'mon.* Unable to wait any longer, he went over to him, placed his fingertips to the inside of D's wrist. He felt like he was waiting for his mother to breathe, like he did all those years ago.

After a few seconds, he felt a thready pulse. Relief washed over him and he sat down beside him, leaned against the wall.

He thought of the night D came to him. He had cocaine, talking about how he needed a hit so he could get through his initiation into the Bloods. Initiation required D to kill a Crip. Ryker tried to talk him out of going through with it, but D was convinced he had no choice. He said the powder would help him cope. When Ryker couldn't change his mind about the killing, he tried to take the cocaine from him; he wasn't giving it up.

Ryker tried to get the name of the person who sold it to him. He knew it was no one in his circle. Given all the greedy dealers out there, lacing the pure with the bad stuff, Ryker could only imagine what he was in for with the mystery stash he had.

Ryker watched him snort lines. Dominik shook his head hard. When he walked down Main Street, Ryker watched him for a time, not ready to let him out of his sight. Two hours later, he was still shadowing him. Every second, he considered forcing him home, locking him in until the lines wore off.

The last place Dominik went was into the Bloods' crib. Ryker waited for an hour or so, but D never came out. He thought about working his way in, calling in favors, but he knew D would never forgive him that.

When he left, he could feel it was a mistake.

After that night, Ryker didn't see him, even on the street, for a time. The ache in the pit of his stomach was constant. He worried D was lying dead somewhere. Weeks later, he saw him in an alley, pretty messed up. He tried to help him, but D wasn't having it.

Months went by and still no sign of him. He never expected to see him again. Part of him was glad he was alive, but seeing him in so much pain was almost worse than not knowing.

After his first kill, Ryker knew D would *keep* using; anything to get away from the hauntings.

He shouldn't have given up on him; he should have hunted him down and found a way to help him. D was no longer the cousin he knew. He was not in this world and he didn't want to be.

Ryker was surprised D knew him at all.

C'mon man, keep breathin', Ryker prayed. *Breathe. Dear God, let him make it through this.*

Chapter 13

It seems fair to assume that all fish try to resist being caught. The air is cold as it assaults the skin. Oxygen is sucked from its gills as a thin line attached to the hook unforgivingly pulls it toward the fisherman. If only their bodies could house the brain humans have, giving them the power to reason.

"They ain' no pulse," *D' in trouble*. "Guard!" Ryker called out. "They's a man in trouble. You got to git him help."

Dominik was taken from the cell. He was kept at Methodist Mansfield Medical Center for several days, until they could stabilize his heart. Ryker prayed for him every day until he returned. He lay awake at night, asking God why it hadn't been him. He'd experimented with cocaine, crack, and marijuana.

When he lived with Daddy D and his mother, the summer before he went to live with his dad, he'd been with Trina. She was the daughter of Daddy D's lady friend, Lelah. He and Trina were often left to fend for themselves when they were teenagers. They did lines of cocaine and experimented, like teenagers do. Ryker felt like he could do anything. Trina made him feel invincible.

She wasn't like any woman he'd ever met. She was strong, confident, independent, and wild; she wasn't afraid of anyone or anything. She taught him how important it was to be his own man. She said the minute you try to do otherwise, you lose part of yourself forever. "Nobody's worth that," she'd said.

This was probably why he *didn't* end up like Dominik. He wasn't about proving himself so he could join a gang or using to escape reality. He was about relying on himself. He never joined a gang for the same reason. He wanted to be the one people came to, someone who could take care of himself and others. This way, they owed him, which ensured him being in control. Once he gave himself over to someone, be it in love or in business, then he would be vulnerable to *them*. He couldn't let that happen, not in his world.

Ryker's perspective

I think I's untouchable 'cause nothin' was personal. It was business and I could work either side because I was in the know. That's how I ran the game, knowin' what make people tick, or not. Family and friends was part a the game. They was nothin' like the people in Jack's family or his circle a friends. They was all about operatin' purely on a need-to-survive basis. They was no love involved and frankly, that made it easier to deal.

Granted, ain' nobody want a be 'round me, lessen they need somethin', but at least I know'd what was comin' at me and why. I know'd more than I ever wanted to know 'bout what happen on the street -- gang violence was part a the life.

When we was littles, we seen it happen. They was no Crips then or Bloods, but my family was a gang of its own, if you git what I'm sayin'. We was always together, day and night, watchin' each other backs, twenty or so of us. In the late '80s, early 1990s, the Bloods and the Crips came through and the families who been the "gangs" before just joined up with whichever gang make sense to 'em. So, bein' in Mansfield wadn' much different than bein' back in Ag-Land -- Aggravated Land on the South side a Fort Worth. I done been in the pressure cooker where gangs fester. Bloods was who my family join on my daddy' side and Crips was who some a my cousins choose on my mama side. The Bloods on my cell block ain' that different really.

D'at ain' true. The Bloods a different breed in here. Ain' been here long, but I can feel it.

Ryker was telling the truth about the gangs. The Crips and the Bloods began in Los Angeles in the late 1960s. Crips was an acronym for Community Revolution in Progress. The Bloods became their rival because there were so many gangs coming together under the Crips' cause in the 1970s, making them extremely powerful in communities across the country.

A common misconception was that gangs formed in the projects or the ghetto, but the reality was, gangs began on school campuses. This aligns with what Ryker experienced too.

Kids were treated badly in school and felt so unaccepted among other students that they did what they could to fight the peer pressure. One thing that did that in a hurry was violence and extortion, a means to show the "popular kids" who was really in charge.

As the Crips got stronger, the Bloods and the Piru gang realized they had to have allies. The Denver Lanes, the LA Brims and the Lueeder Park Hustlers were coerced into joining the Bloods in 1972.

The name "Bloods" came from the Vietnam War, where African-Americans, fighting for their lives, referred to each other as such. When they secured their allies, the East Coast Bloods soon followed, coming from New York City in 1993. A notorious gangster from Brooklyn, Leonard "Deadeye" Makenzie, who was living in a Ryker Island cell, hooked up with another prisoner, who called himself the "Original Gangsta" Mack; together, they started the New York chapter of the United Blood Nation in 1993. Deadeye was twenty-six years old then. He's in his late 40s now, still incarcerated in upstate New York.

It wasn't long before the Latin Kings' leader in New York, known as King Tone realized the Bloods were dominating the New York prison system. Because his own gang was leaning toward being political activists, he decided to join the Bloods, making them even stronger. At the same time, the Bloods spread throughout the prisons.

Ryker was about 16 when a lot of this was already in motion. He was learning how to steal cars and score drugs to sell, as opposed to convenience store shoplifting. He wasn't aware his father's side of the family was in the Bloods, until shootings and stabbings began to affect his family.

Ryker remembered hushed talk, late at night, about a shooting or a knifing. He sometimes woke up in the middle of the night and no one was home. He knew it was something gang related because some of his cousins from out of town talked about being members of the Third Gate Bloods in Fort Worth when they thought he wasn't around. At the time, he didn't really know how big the Bloods were across the country. He thought the Bloods in Cooper were it, but later learned the prisons had taken things to a whole new level of power.

Many believed gangs grew during the 1970s because there was still so much racial hatred around and no one wanted to deal with it. Brothers were "turnin' white" by going to school and educating themselves. Those who could get scholarships did. Those who couldn't afford to pay for school and weren't eligible to get scholarships were left to the streets.

Gang rules in the Crips and the Bloods were different in each faction in cities across the United States. In Ryker's neighborhood, the Bloods and the Crips were sources of power in a state of poverty, where most felt powerless. Any group that gave them some control over their meager existence was, in essence, heroic.

The Bloods in the prisons recruited the strongest, most evil inmates, trying to overpower the others. There was little choice about joining one gang or another, if you wanted to survive. Numbers spoke volumes. If you chose to go it alone, you significantly lowered your chances of survival in prison.

Fortunately, Ryker had connections in both gangs *before* he was incarcerated. He'd established a name for himself as an untouchable enforcer in the criminal world outside prison, which allowed him more freedom, regardless of where he was.

He worked both sides on the outside; he was an enforcer for the Crips, anonymously handling deals gone bad and, at the same time, he sold drugs to the Bloods in Cooper. No one was the wiser, which afforded him protection that most couldn't buy. Being born to the life and trained by drug Lords on Bloody Fifth had its benefits, even if it didn't feel that way.

Having informants in both gangs kept him in the know, but it was a fine line to walk.

Inside prison, all bets were off. He had to work the ranks, hope for the best and be ready, in case his information went south. This was where his ability to protect himself became paramount.

———◆———

The difference between me and Dominik was I's gon' find a way to overcome the life I's dealt. I wasn't gon' answer to nobody or live by they rules. Dominik just want to escape the pain in his head. All the thangs he seen was too much for him to handle, so he done the drugs to git 'em out his mind.

I's different 'bout pain. I faced it head-on, dared it to kill me. There wadn' nothin' special 'bout it, 'xcept I believe in God. I surrender ever'thang to Him and I know'd if it wadn' enough, then so be it. I know'd they was a higher power and I think it save me again and again. They was no reason I last as long as I done. I should a died ever time I's saved. D'at's how I know'd God ain' done with me in d'is life; they had to be a reason I survived.

I still ain' figured it out, but that's why I's so determined to git out this life. If I git out, I gon' be better able to see it.

———◆———

A new cellmate was brought in ten days after Dominik was taken to Methodist Medical. He was six-foot-six, with broad shoulders and huge hands. When he walked, it sounded like the giant Ryker's mama used to read to him about in Jack and the Beanstalk. "Fee-fi-fo-fum," she used to say in her lowest, scariest voice. Everything about him was big. His head had to weigh at least fifty pounds by itself.

His name was Roman Hawk.

He stood in front of the bunk bed, staring at Ryker, his face stoic and unyielding. Ryker was lying on the bottom bunk and he could feel the giant, hovering.

He waited for him to say something. When he didn't, Ryker cut his eyes up in his direction. They stared at each other for several minutes, the other inmates expecting a fight they would remember for the rest of their lives. Hawk finally reached for the back of Ryker's orange jumpsuit, close to the base of his neck, to pull him off his bunk. Intercepting his move, Ryker grabbed his wrist, twisted it behind his enormous shoulder blades, while shoving his face into the top bunk mattress. Pressing Hawk's twisted arm higher into the center of his back, Ryker grabbed his dreadlocks, pulling his head back hard, exposing his jugular. He held tight, waiting for the giant to say something or counter his move.

Hawk was still, eerily still, despite his painful, awkward position.

After several seconds, Ryker decided to release him. Perhaps Hawk was there to even the score. It had been three weeks, and in that short time, Ryker had not made any friends but had managed to make more than his share of enemies who had yet to find a way to take him down. As Ryker let go of his arm and let his head fall forward, Roman Hawk regained his composure and slowly turned around to meet Ryker's unremorseful glare.

"You done?" Hawk said.

Ryker rolled his shoulders, cocked his neck from side to side, preparing for the first blow.

He figured if he could withstand the first blow, he had a shot at holding his own.

Chapter 14

I wonder if people who have grown numb to the pain of existence eventually stop feeling everything. Fish have the excuse of not having a cerebral cortex that notifies the brain that the body is experiencing pain. What is the excuse for humans, who have the capacity to know better?

Jack Lawrence

"Good morning, Shug," Sarah said as Jack dragged himself into the kitchen. "Did you talk to Dexter about the charges?"

"Yeah, we're doing what we can to knock the sentence down. The officers had no cause for searching Ryker's car or him, for that matter. He was pulled from his truck and beaten. The officers are backing each other as to how it happened. No surprise there. What I don't get is Ryker says he disposed of the drugs before he was stopped. So how did they find 27 grams on him?"

"You think the drugs were planted?" Sarah asked, raising her eyebrows.

"Who knows? Ryker told them he knew his rights when they pulled him from the car. He said the only way he resisted was by telling them he knew they had to have probable cause to search his truck. He's right, damn it. You know, we found his wallet on the front seat. I know he had a five hundred dollar check in it because I helped him get his tax refund. It was nowhere to be found," Jack said.

"You're saying he was framed?" Sarah sat down at the table with Jack. Jack watched as she added sugar and cream to her coffee and stirred. As the spoon went round and round, Jack thought about Ryker's statement to Dexter.

"I'd say he was spotted on East Powell. They probably had no reason to stop him so they ran his plates, found out he was due for vehicle registration. The officers on duty decided to stop him, see if they could get him to pop on something.

"If Ryker's telling the truth, they *had* to have planted the 27 grams. It's not like there was anyone there to say otherwise. It's their word against his, but here's the thing. He had plenty of time to run. He *chose* to face the music. If he was carrying, why would he do that? What could possibly have been in it for him?" Jack scrubbed his forehead, his thumbs and fingers kneading the tension he was feeling.

"You're saying he thought all they could get on him was resisting arrest; that's why he didn't run," Sarah was thinking out loud. "If there was no evidence, and he had already disposed of what *he* had brought, then he'd have been right. What would it have been? What could they have done to him for not renewing his vehicle registration?"

"Not much," Jack concurred. "So, they bring the drugs, just in case he's clean, plant them on him. Who's going to believe he's innocent? He's a career criminal, a long way from the straight and narrow. I bet the officers were banking on him resisting arrest. If it smells like a set up…." he looked up at Sarah.

"Looks like a set-up, then it probably is a set-up," she finished. "Clearly, it's not just employers and his family and his friends having a hard time with him changing careers. Law enforcement isn't behind his rehabilitation either… heck, they're his biggest enemy."

Jack considered his own predicament, as he attempted to navigate his way to freedom from his abusive stepfather. Every moment was a gamble. If he came home with pocket money after working all day, Lawrence might be grateful and take it from him; clap him on the back and say "good job," or, if he was in a mood, it might be the reason he took out his belt and started swinging. *I was held captive, completely at the mercy of the man who made the rules. They weren't the rules, according to the law; they were rules he'd made up to suit himself. If these cops decided to make the rules that night, Ryker was at their mercy and it wouldn't have mattered what he did.*

Jack thought back to what it was like under Mitchell Lawrence's house rules. *Every day the rules changed. I could obey him, disobey him; it didn't matter. I still got hit. A lot of times, I felt like acting out or doing wrong. Why not? I was going to be punished no matter how good or bad I was.*

When Ryker started working, he wasn't knowingly doing anything wrong, carrying small packages to Daddy D's night club at nine. He earned about two or three dollars and didn't really know what he was carrying back and forth.

I was selling fruits and vegetables door-to-door at that age, I suppose. Then, I went on to odd jobs like painting Craig Jacob's fence. That was a real booger of a thing. I spent hours trying to get the strokes blended the way he wanted. I think I held my breath until he finally said I did a good job. I wonder how many times Ryker held his breath, hoping he had done the best job he could.

By the time I got a job at Leonard's, Ryker was learning to steal cars and sell the parts on the street.

I was selling sporting goods by then. Fishing equipment was my specialty because I learned so much about fishing and casting from Uncle Pete. Ryker learned from whoever was around, I guess.

His first attempt to sell drugs ended with him lying in the street, having been beaten nearly to death; someone had other plans for his stash.

By thirteen, I was out of my stepfather's house and my mother and sisters were away from him, too. I had made it. When Ryker turned thirteen, he went to live with his father and his criminal career had just begun. Big R taught him to be a professional drug dealer.

It took me from age nine to sixteen before I could manage things on my own. I had Uncle Pete, Mr. Bob, Mr. Craig and Doc Sevrenson teaching me everything they knew along my way. Seven years.

At sixteen, Ryker had learned the drug business from the ground up from his father in Cooper and his uncles on Bloody Fifth in Houston. He was essentially on his own, selling to the Bloods in Cooper and the Crips in Fort Worth and, all the while, answering to no one.

Mitchell Lawrence was in my face, day in and day out the whole time I was trying to find my way out. I fought hard to keep going as many times as he knocked me down. There were plenty of times I was confused and felt like giving up.

Ryker had a drug-dealer for a father, who used his best friend, the town sheriff, to cover his covert drug business while parading about the town of Cooper, pretending to be an honest, hard-working citizen. His mother was barely able to take care of herself, depending on Ryker to bring home enough money for rent and groceries however he could. His family on his father's side were members of the Bloods and some, on his mother's side, were in the Crips.

Still, Ryker found a way to survive for twenty-five years, about twice as long as I was forced to survive the two drunk bastards, who raised me to age thirteen.

I'll be damned. We're about half-way through if it takes Ryker as long to work his way out of this mess.

"Jack? Where'd you go?" Sarah pressed.

"What? I was just, uh," he felt a shiver run through him. "You're right," Jack said, coming back to the conversation. "Walking Ryker out of the life he's led is complicated, more so than I realized. I was thinking about my life just now. I didn't think it was possible to forget how long it took me to break free of Mitchell Lawrence, but I've been so caught up in Ryker's situation, I suppose I'd forgotten it took quite a while, about seven years. Can you believe that?"

"You did the best you could, Shug. You were a little boy," she smiled. "You should have been allowed to be a little boy.

"Yeah, I was," he took a sip of his coffee, now cold. "The grace of God is something else, isn't it? I guess it takes stepping outside your own fire and into another's to receive it, but I'll take it. I'll take it," Jack said, smiling and shaking his head.

"I wonder if Ryker had a place to go," Sarah said, as Jack gathered up papers for another meeting with Dexter. "You had the boys' club and Uncle Pete."

"I tried to lose myself in fishing," Jack mused, remembering. "I'd have come up with darn near anything to get out of the house, away from Lawrence. I wonder how Ryker got away, or did he?"

"I imagine he coped the best way he knew how. He's talked about his childhood friends," Sarah said.

"You know, he mentioned his father to me when we first met. Big R had just gone down for possession. Ryker didn't look at me when he spoke of him. It was as if he was embarrassed by him, ashamed maybe. I understand that. It took me years to come to terms with my father and even longer for my stepfather."

"You met Big R. What did you think of him?"

"Well, there wasn't much to it when I visited him in jail. He could hardly look at me. I tried to talk to him, but he was preoccupied with the vending machines. He wanted an orange soda and some kind of chips or something. I tried to have a conversation with him, get to know him, but he was only interested in getting change for the machines," Jack said.

"Ryker said they had very few conversations, even when he lived with him."

"Yeah, I guess that's true," Jack stroked his chin, feeling a little stubble he'd missed shaving. "I'm glad to be seeing Ryker tomorrow. I feel like it's been months and it's only been about three weeks or so. It's strange how he fit right into our lives. Even the kids accepted him as part of the family. I was so glad they welcomed him and Angela into our family gatherings so easily -- no awkward looks or strange comments. I love our kids," he said.

"Well, I haven't wanted to worry you, but I've wondered how he's doing in jail. I've heard stories. Ryker's pretty tough looking, but I just hope he hasn't met his match, if you know what I mean." Sarah didn't want to think about it.

"Well," Jack said with a half-laugh, "Whoever thinks he can go up against Ryker and win, uh, let's just say I'd hate to be the other guy."

Chapter 15

*Fish may have a built-in defense relative to the fight
against the Fisherman and his hook. Its central
nervous system can detect painful stimuli, but the
brain does not have the cerebral cortex to translate
the message. Saving grace or handicap in the fight?*

Ryker stepped forward, into Hawk's space, baiting him
into a fight by doing it in front of the other cellmates. He had
nothing to lose and the way Hawk stared at him, he
remembered thinking he *should* be scared, but his instincts told
him he could handle anything Hawk dished out.

Hawk made no move as he looked down at Ryker. The
inmates were getting impatient and they began to yell out,
"Check it, a stalemate."

"I got bets on the giant," another said.

"I'll take that bet 'cause Ryker gon' kick his ass," said
another.

Finally, after several seconds, Ryker was tired of the
staring. He bumped his chest into Hawk's once, then twice.
Hawk didn't budge. Just as Ryker was about to throw the first
punch, a guard came through. It was Ryker's source for
cigarettes. He called Ryker over to the bars. Banging his
nightstick in their code, yelling, "break it up animals" to the
others.

Fortunately, Jones' words carried weight, as several of
them had met with his nightstick and ended up losing several
teeth or not walking well for a couple of days. Ryker cut his
eyes at Jones and back at Hawk. Jones clanked the bars
harder, raised his chin to emphasize. Ryker looked around,
cocked his head, side to side, and then walked over to Jones.

The others spread out, giving Jones and Ryker space, still eyeing Hawk.

"What's the deal with Hawk man?" Ryker asked.

"You don't want a go there," Jones said. "I'm sayin', keep your distance, but maintain. You feel me?"

"Yeah, I feel you'," Ryker said.

"Naw, man. It ain' what you thinkin'. He strong and can take all ya'll down, but he been through it, if you git me. Show respect 'cause in a one-on-one, he a force. He ain' one to go lookin' for trouble. He a loner, like you. So don't think you gon' make friends," Jones explained.

"I done showed him I could take him," Ryker said.

"Then, you 'bout to git hit hard. Trust me, man. Don't mess with him. Let him save face in front a the others." Jones laughed. "If you make it, you got a bond for life -- respect," Jones whispered and disappeared around the corridor.

Ryker heard the door buzz; signaling Jones was off his cell block. He looked back at Hawk. He was done waiting.

Ryker felt a blow knock him back against the wall. He didn't react, still glaring at Hawk like he expected as much. Ryker threw his arms back against the wall, propelling himself forward, and in two lightning jabs, he knocked the giant's head back and forth.

Hawk spit out a tooth and blood smeared across his chin as he grinned and wiped it away. As fast as Ryker struck, Hawk slammed one fist into Ryker's ribs and reached down, before Ryker could double over, Hawk grabbed his neck, shoving him back against the wall.

Ryker's vision blurred and he lost his capacity to breathe. Hawk pinned him with little effort, his fingers and thumb closing around Ryker's jugular. Ryker forced himself to keep his eyes open, his rage emanating as he started to lose consciousness.

When he was almost gone, he blinked, clearing his vision for a half a second. Hawk's expression had changed. He released him, letting him collapse to the floor. Ryker refused to give him the satisfaction of dropping him so he didn't gasp for breath. He steeled himself against the pain in his ribs, slowly taking in what breath he could and managing to sit up against the wall, still feeling the rage, full throttle, as if it was erupting from his insides out. Pulling his legs up under him, he braced himself against the wall and pulled himself upright, using one hand, while the other held his ribs. He felt the break and groaned once as he forced himself higher. *You goin' down, motherfucker, if I live through this. I'm 'on take you out, nice and slow, savor ever painful second.*

The cellmates in the room backed up. They had seen the rage Ryker rarely unleashed. And, hurt or not, they could tell he had a death wish, but he wouldn't go easy. Hawk saw the darkness take over and for the first time, he backed up, too. The hairs on the back of his neck stood and prickled down the length of his spine. Chills spread, icily stabbing every pore, one by one like instant frost-bite.

Chapter 16

He is not the prey. When he bites, he is surprised he
tastes nothing but his own blood. Shock ensues but
his fight does not wither; it strengthens.

Crash! Metal broke into pieces like shurikens launched at a
mirror, the shards slicing through the air. Light blinded him
as he tried to cover his face. Jagged metal penetrated his
arms, random pieces piercing his scalp. He felt hot liquid
make its way down his head to the edge of his chin. *Blood or*
sweat, he wondered. *Doesn't matter.*

Rolling for cover, he braced himself for the next blow,
knowing the shelter he took could shatter under the rage-filled
animal. He prayed for a miracle, something unexpected --
anything.

Before he could assess his options, more metal broke over
his head. His face hit the floor. The last thing he
remembered was the taste of his own blood.

He woke in semi-darkness, his head throbbing. Swinging
his feet to the edge of the bed, he rubbed at his temples, his
vision clearing slightly as he reached for his glasses. Sparkling
pieces, caught by the morning light coming through his
bedroom blinds, startled him.

He put his glasses on and picked up his bare feet, when he
saw that more chards blanketed the carpet. *The bedside lamp,*
he thought. *What happened? Where am I? How did I get here?*

Turning, he noticed the florescent numbers on his alarm
clock read 7:45 a.m. *Oh, dear Lord, I fell asleep. I have to get*
moving. I'm supposed to be at the Segovia Unit by 9:00 a.m. When
he stood, Sarah opened the bedroom door. "Are you all
right?" she asked, seeing the lamp on the floor.

"Yeah. Uh, yeah. I'm fine," Jack said. "I, uh."

"Your arm is bleeding. You're not all right. And how did the lamp get broken?" she said, walking over to pick up the pieces.

"It's just a scratch. I tried to pick it up and, well." Jack was still disoriented.

"You cut yourself" Sarah finished. "I knew I should have moved that dad-blamed lamp. It barely fits on the end table. I should have switched it out for the smaller one in the living room. You must have knocked it off the table when you reached for your glasses. I'm sorry. I had the water running and didn't even hear the crash." She was now picking up all the glass and the broken pieces of the light bulb.

"No, it's not your fault. I just wanted to sit for a minute, after I got dressed."

"You poor thing," she doted on him. "You had that meeting with Dexter yesterday and I know you didn't sleep a wink last night. Are you sure you're up to the meeting with Ryker today?"

"Yeah, I just, I leaned back against the head board and closed my eyes for just a moment and, I must have fallen asleep, because I had this terrible dream. A nightmare really, and I think I threw my arms out," Jack said, wiping his hands down the contour of his face.

"Let me guess. Your stepfather," she said, turning to him. "I'm sorry, honey. I'm so sorry. Good Lord, you're as white as a sheet. Do you want to tell me about it?" The nightmares he'd been having since Ryker went to Segovia were vivid. He had described some of them, but it seemed they were getting worse and she wasn't sure she wanted to know about this one. *Why couldn't Mitchell Lawrence leave him the hell alone? You'd think he did enough when he was really here*, she thought.

"No, no. I don't want to talk about it. I have to get on the road. I promised Ryker I would visit him today and I can't disappoint. It's been too long and I could tell by his voice last week that he needed me there, in person." Jack walked to the bathroom and checked his arm where he'd been nicked. Looking back at the room, he said, "I'm sorry to leave this mess, but I have to get out of here."

Following him out of the bedroom and into the corridor, Sarah grabbed his wallet from the entry hall table and handed it to him. "Wait right here," she said, disappearing into the kitchen. He put his wallet in his pocket. Then he patted his other pockets, looking for his glasses. Hearing his keys jingle instead, he reached in and brought them out, thumbing through the ring until he found the one for his Mercury Grand Marque.

"Your glasses are on your face," Sarah teased, knowing he was looking for them, but trying to lighten his mood.

"Sarah," he said, more gruff than he intended. "Have you seen my …."

"Jacket," she said, handing it to him, as well as a brown paper sack and a thermos. "I know you're in a hurry, but sip this coffee and there's a bagel in the bag. Don't tell me you're not hungry. Just eat some of it, any of it. For me. Okay? Or else you owe me a lamp, mister," she said, patting his cheek and giving him a quick kiss.

He smiled. *I love you,* he thought.

"I love you, too," she said, as if he'd said it aloud.

After he slipped on his jacket, Jack juggled the paper sack and his coffee as he opened the car door. When he got in, he checked the map for the quickest way to get to the Segovia Unit. After looking a few minutes, he tossed the map on the floor board and put the car in reverse.

He backed out of the driveway onto the access road. *Why did they have to bring the dad-blamed freeway into my living room?* He thought every time he pulled out. He threw the car into drive and sped onto highway Southwest Loop 820, taking the left lane, headed I-20 East. As the speedometer gradually climbed to sixty, his mind flipped through chapters of his life again, paralleling Ryker's in contrast or complement, as it happened, to his own. More similarities surfaced and he was surprised again at how similar their childhoods read.

Decades apart, a few circumstances and cultural aspects notwithstanding, the symmetry was a lot to take in. Ryker saw a lot of violence come down around him as a small boy that escalated as he got older, though he wasn't the punching bag like Jack had been. Most of the trauma was from witnessing it.

Not much different from me. The scars left behind from emotional abuse are not much different from the physical. Sometimes the manipulative mind games are worse. I think I suffered from both, if I'm honest about it. Ryker doesn't know that, though. No need. I don't even like to remember myself.

Jack thought about the violence he suffered. It was random and impossible to detect, no matter how hard he tried. There were times Lawrence was drunk and Jack was certain he would erupt and start swinging, but there were also times when Jack waited for it to happen, having sensed the same scenario, and there was no incident. Alcohol could be highly unpredictable, depending on the individual's genetic make-up.

Still, Jack knew it was worse when he had to endure Lawrence's attack on his mother and his sister. When he was able to manipulate the situation, he positioned himself between them and his stepfather. *I wanted to be the one hit if I could force the bastard to do it. I assumed this was normal until I joined the Fort Worth Boys Club. The guys saw the welts on my back and shoulders and told the director. I had to beg her not to do anything about it. I knew it would only make things worse.*

Later, Jack discerned things from what his Uncle Pete said during his weekend visits to the lake house, that there was a name for the way his stepfather treated him -- *child abuse.* He wished he'd had the courage to voice his experiences sooner, hindsight and all. *Uncle Pete sometimes cast his line over or around my shoulders. It took a while for me not to flinch or dodge it; I was used to being hit. He just wanted to spend time with me and fish but I had to work through the instinctual reaction every time. I couldn't help it.*

Thinking about this struck a chord in Jack's perception of Ryker. *Come to think of it, we've had to work through a lot with Ryker. He's had a difficult time processing Sarah and I paying for expenses. He keeps thinking he owes us somehow. Or, that I might Lord it over him to make him do my bidding.*

Of course he thinks that. That's all he knows. The truth is he has never actually asked for money. I've seen the need and given it, but he didn't ask. He'd go home hungry if I forgot to offer him dinner or check he'd eaten sometime during the day. He'd go without, simply because it slipped my mind. It's crazy the way we are taught to think, not even by words. Actions tell all.

Thinking about all this, Jack nearly missed his exit. He quickly signaled so he could get over. He shook off the memories and the analysis. He needed to focus, be supportive, and give Ryker a reason to keep the faith. *Keep the faith -- doesn't get much harder than this.*

Just as Jack got off at Heritage Parkway, his cell phone rang. He pulled into the Exxon at the intersection. The incessant ring continued until he could get the car in park. Finally, he answered. "Yeah. Hello?"

"Hey, Jack," Isaiah Dexter said. "You with Ryker now?"

"Hey, Dexter, no. I'm just about five miles north of Edinburg, about to turn off highway 281 and head into Hidalgo County."

"Good, I'm on my way, too. I'd like us to talk, the three of us. I think I may have a way to get Ryker's sentence down," Dexter said, when he was interrupted. "Hang on."

Dexter's administrative assistant handed him some paperwork. In it was a note for him to call a man named Bagman John. Looking at Shana, he said, "Witness?" She nodded.

"I've got to go. I'll see you in about an hour. Keep the faith," Dexter said.

Jack let the phone slap shut with a half laugh. *Keep the faith. You're reading my mind, Dex.*

The rest of the way to Segovia, Jack felt his chest relax. He breathed in deep, and felt his body grow calmer, when he blew out the breath. He prayed that he found Ryker in good spirits. *It can't be easy in jail. No tellin' who he's had to deal with there.*

Ryker sat up when he heard Jones call for him outside his cell. The pain in his ribs was still rough, but not as bad as it could have been. The last thing he remembered before Hawk came at him again was the voices of the other inmates screaming Hawk's name, like a chant.

When he woke in the infirmary, his ribs had been taped up and he was hooked up to a heart monitor. His blood pressure had been so high, they thought he arrested.

He had been back in his cell for a few hours. He was glad to see Jones. Maybe he could get some answers about what went down after the screaming. Making his way to the bars between him and Jones, he took hold to steady himself.

"Hey man,"

"Well?" Ryker was a little irritated at Jones. He was looking him up and down, cautiously, instead of giving him the word. "What?!" he snapped, tired of waiting.

"You must be the luckiest son of a bitch I ever saw," Jones said. "The guys said Hawk-man look like he seen a ghost. How you manage to stand up after?"

"After what?"

"That slice to yo' ribs. The boys say he backed off a you when you stood up. The way the guys described it, you shouldn' a been able to move, much less stand after he dogged on yo' ribs. Whatever, they said his eyes went wide and he stepped back.

"Then, the guys was gon' finish you off and he threw six of 'em 'gainst the wall. Once they slid to the floor, he turned and looked at the others, like he was sayin', 'anybody else want a piece?'

"Nobody move. That was when he call for me, tellin' me to get help. Word has it, he ain' nobody's friend, but if anybody come close, you it."

"How you figure that?" Ryker said, completely baffled by the entire account.

"I done some checkin'," Jones turned to see who was listening, or not. "Hawk-man been through it like I said, but it was a lot worse than I thought. He in for killin' his mother *and* his father. The story was his old man came after his mama and Hawk-man was handcuffed to a wrought-iron bed, forced to watch or some shit.

"Anyhow, he couldn't take it no more so he dragged the bed over to where his father was beatin' his mother. He rammed the frame of the bed into the back of his daddy's legs pinning him to the wall, then ground him in, breakin' both his legs and, at the same time, causing him to fall over the front rail of the bed backwards. The force of it broke the bastard's back in two. Only thing was, Hawk-man was in such a rage to protect his mother he didn't realize she'd fallen to the floor.

"When he forced the wrought-iron bed into his father's legs, he didn't see her. She'd slid down the wall, unconscious. Part of the bed hit her, too -- crushed her skull, when he rammed the bed into his daddy. Some nasty shit, man. Anyhow, somethin' change when he seen yo' face. Maybe he seen his mama face, who knows? Alls I know is he's the one who save you and he ain' gon' let nobody near you, from now on.

"I talked to him after. All he said was, 'Ain' nobody look right through me like that before.' He say you look at him through and through, and you didn't back down. He even say, when you twisted his arm up and tried to take him down before, he couldn't believe you had the balls. Weird motherfucker say it felt good to be the one in pain.

"Then, you let him go and faced him, head-on. He say he knew then he had to fight you to save face, but he had no intention a hurtin' you. He knew you was strong and shit, so he knew you could take it.

"Didn't matter, though. His anger got the best a him when you popped him with both barrels. He said you pack a powerful punch. I knew that.

"Anyhow, he said he lost control. When he seen your eyes, he seen his self in 'em or some shit like that. He say the rage inside you was some kind a whack. Whatever, he snapped out of it and that's when he call me, tellin' me to git help."

Ryker just stared, not knowing what to say. *That's it. That's the grace of God in prison*, he thought.

"Hey," Jones barked, snapping his fingers in front a Ryker's face.

Ryker glared and narrowed his eyes, squared his shoulders.

"Ease up, man. Just tryin' to git yo' 'tention. Don't forget, you got a visitor today in twenty. Clean yourself up. You look like shit. And tell yo' cash man he need to step it up, or I gon' sell these smokes to somebody else."

Jack got out of the car and stood for a minute, looking at the entrance to the Segovia Unit. Seeing the jail up ahead, he felt his chest tighten as he walked toward the entrance. He knew he would be searched, processed, and watched from cameras in every room of the facility.

I feel like I'm back in my stepfather's house, standing on the area rug, trying not to move a muscle. The evening news is blaring behind me and all I can think about is keeping my sister and me safe from the monster who sits in the recliner. Lawrence used to watch his stepfather breathe, taking sips of whisky that stirred his inner rage, feeding it like lighter fluid to a flame. He hated the company that fired him after ten goddamn years of service. He hated his boss for choosing to keep a wet-behind-the-ears, snot-nosed adolescent to work his job, instead of appreciating a dedicated, competent and loyal company man, who'd spent a decade of his life working long hours, overtime and double shifts. This was how he was repaid for his life's work.

All I felt was anxiety and fear. If I breathed wrong, he would come down on me with a vengeance. If my legs shook, he would yell and scare my little sister. If I stood between my sister and him, I faced his raw, unrestrained wrath. There were no shackles to stop him, no handcuffs to bind him, nothing. We were at his mercy, the whole experience washed over Jack.

"You okay sir?" a guard asked, when he saw Jack's obvious discomfort, walking into the building.

"Oh. Uh, good morning, I'm here to see one of the inmates, Ryker James, Jr.," Jack managed. "His lawyer will join us in a little while. My name is Jack. Jack Lawrence."

"All right, Mr. Lawrence."

"Jack, please. Call me Jack," he smiled and nodded, not able to stand being called Lawrence, mister or otherwise.

Looking at Jack with concern, the guard acknowledged his request and took a more gentle approach. "Jack, we'll need to see some identification. Then, you'll need to put your cell phone, car keys, wallet and any other personal items in this bucket. You can retrieve it on the other side of the scanner, which you will need to walk through, when you're ready." As if reading from a script, the guard continued, "Please be advised that no pocket knives, jewelry or items that may be used as a weapon will be allowed past this point, including pepper spray, nail files, etc. When you empty your pockets into the bucket, some of them may be confiscated until the end of your visit today. Some may not be returned at all. If you would like to deposit any of the aforementioned items into your vehicle at this time, it would be advised that you do so now."

Jack heard the guard's words and checked his pockets. He had the army knife Uncle Pete had given him when he graduated from high school. He excused himself and took it to the car. When he returned, the same guard ushered him through. He was taken to a visitation room and told to wait. He glanced around the room, surveying the other visitors. He was the only white man in the room. There were African-Americans, Hispanics and Asians, but he was the only Caucasian.

He noticed he was overdressed, considering the others, who were wearing jeans, workout clothes, and t-shirts. He was also the oldest person in the waiting room. Everyone else looked to be under thirty years old. He ran his fingers through his silver hair, combing it away from his forehead. He was also the only one in the room *without* a nose ring, earrings, or multiple tattoos.

"Jack," he heard the guard say. "It's time for your visit."

He rose from his chair and followed the guard down a long corridor. When he reached the actual visitation room, he saw others, sitting across from their prisoner, talking into a telephone.

Ryker sat on the opposite side of the strong, glass partition. Jack sat down in front of him. When he looked into Ryker's eyes, he relaxed; head to toe. Ryker's demeanor was grateful and appreciative, humble.

"Hey, Jack," he finally said into the mouthpiece, after looking around, eyeing the guard assigned to him.

"Hey there, son," Jack said. "Lots of supervision here, huh?"

"Yeah, you could say that." He shot a half-smile to Jack.

"You're sittin' funny. You all right?" Jack asked.

"Yeah, just a few minor altercations," Ryker said, revealing his taped ribs by opening his orange jumpsuit so Jack could see the wrapping.

"What the heck happened?" Jack said, immediately concerned.

"It's a long story. I'm fine. How's Sarah? How you doin'?" he asked, trying to change the subject.

"She's good, sends her love. She would have been here, but I asked her to let me come alone. I wanted to spend some time with you," Jack said, looking down. He almost felt selfish about his request of Sarah.

"You a'ight?" he asked. "I know. I know I screwed up, disappointed you. I'm sorry. I'm real sorry," he said.

"Ryker, I came alone because I wanted to talk with you, man to man." He paused, trying to choose his words carefully. "I know what happened the night you were arrested and I know you were trying to do the right thing. I wanted to come and tell you Dexter has some news. In fact, he's supposed to be here in a little while to give us the latest on things."

"You think he can git me less time?" Ryker said, hoping for some kind of reprieve from the week he'd been having.

"He thinks he can get your sentence down to six months," Jack said.

Ryker looked up, surprised. "Really?" he said, swallowing hard, hoping he hadn't heard Jack wrong.

"Really," Jack confirmed.

Ryker sat back in the steel chair. "I don't know what to say." His eyes filled and brimmed with emotion he could not afford.

"There's nothin' to say. I made you a promise and I aim to keep it. Can you hang in for the next five months?" Jack asked.

"Yes sir, I can…I will," He turned his head, not believing what was happening. He had to ask. He needed to hear Jack say it. "You believe me, Jack. You believe I's tryin' to do right?"

Seeing Ryker's raw emotion toward him, Jack stiffened, forced himself to exude the strength Ryker needed him to emanate. "Damn straight. No doubt in my mind, son. Now, Dexter will be here soon and we're going to put our heads together and find a way to get you out of here."

"I don't know how to thank you. I'm just," he paused. "So grateful," he said.

When Dexter arrived, he was ready to work the case. He brought the information Shana provided when he was talking to Jack and shared it with them in visitation.

"Bagman John called your office?" Ryker asked in total disbelief.

"Yes he did, and we have his statement. He was in the alley and saw the beat-down. He can verify that you were incapacitated and the officers in question were needlessly brutalizing you," Dexter said, nodding over and over as if to reaffirm the statement again and again, given the shock on Ryker's face. "I figure we go in, talk police brutality, illegal search of your vehicle, of *you*. Did they read you your rights?"

"Yeah, when they threw me on the hood a my truck," he said.

"Jack, this case is going to be a walk in the park. I could get the whole thing thrown out if the officers hadn't found the cocaine," he said, looking at Ryker and raising his eyebrows.

"I told you, it wadn' mine. I didn't have nothin' on me. It was planted," Ryker said.

"Well, I'm just sayin'," Dexter quipped, still a little peeved he couldn't find a way to prove that. "I wish Bagman John had seen 'em planting it."

When the visit was over, Jack stood and nodded at Ryker. They had a plan and Jack was going to see if he could secure Ryker's jobs until he got out. Ryker had recently applied for the nightshift at Wellington Nursing Facility and he was planning to continue his detail work at the auto shops as well.

He was supposed to start at Wellington the week he was arrested and Jack hoped he could help him hold on to the job until Dexter could get him out. God must have been working over time because the manager had a soft spot for ex-cons, trying to turn their lives around. The guy agreed to hold the position for Ryker.

Though the auto shops couldn't hold his job for him, they gave him letters of recommendation for the good work he'd done; his work ethic had been exemplary and they were happy to help.

Jack also spoke with a construction company that had used Ryker for a few jobs here and there. The manager said if Ryker could be on-call, he would try to get him working as soon as possible to make up for him losing his day jobs.

The best part was Ryker's work ethic spoke for him, loud and clear. He'd come in any time they called him. He was never sick, always on time and seldom said no to a double shift. He had developed a reputation among the people he'd worked for; his dedication and competence spoke volumes. Jack came away proud and never more sure he was doing the right thing, standing by Ryker.

Chapter 17

There are extraordinary fish like the Hawaiian Goby. The female undertakes one of nature's most daunting journeys, climbing massive waterfalls to find safe pools for breeding before bringing the young into the world. What makes certain species more protective than another?

Two months later

"Jack," Angela said quickly, followed by a deep groan. "Jack, it's time. I know it's time."

"What? Angela? How far apart are the contractions?" he asked, while she yelled out in agony. "Sarah, we've got to get over there and help her. She's having the baby. Angela, take deep breaths. We're on our way. What hospital?"

"John, uh, Peter, uh, Smith, uh," she breathed between clenched teeth.

"Breathe. Breathe, Angela. We're on our way."

When they arrived, they found her water had broken. She was screaming into Jack's ear as he helped her to the car. Sarah had her things and they were only ten minutes from JPS. Upon arrival, Angela began to cry, but not from the pain. "I can't believe he's not here. How can this happen? I need him," she sobbed.

"I'm here and Sarah's here. We won't leave your side," he said.

She looked at Jack and her head dropped into her hands.

"What?" Jack said. "What is it? You okay?"

"He said it, but I didn't believe him. He said you would be here for me, too. I didn't believe him. I just …." She stopped, unable to finish when the next contraction hit.

Turning to Sarah and lowering his voice, Jack said, "Say something, Sarah. She needs to calm down, she needs to breathe for goodness sakes."

"Angela, dear. Do you know the sex of the baby, sweetheart?" Sarah said, shrugging her shoulders when Jack threw up his hands in frustration.

"No. Heh, heh, heh, hoo, hoo, hoo." She did her breathing exercises, trying to cope.

"Want me to breathe with you?" Sarah said, grateful for the exercises. "Just until we get you to the hospital, okay? Heh, heh, heh…."

Jack was looking in his rearview mirror, shaking his head, as he drove. By the time they reached the emergency room, Sarah and Angela had become somewhat of a team.

"Angela, we're going to take you to your room," a nurse interrupted them, "check you, okay? Is this your family?"

Angela looked at Sarah and Jack and they nodded, as if to confirm it one more time.

"Yeah, they are," she said, smiling before she grabbed for her belly, another contraction hitting.

"Okay. Let's get you into this wheelchair and then to your room. You folks can sit in the waiting area, while we get her situated. We'll come get you in a few minutes, when there's more news."

"Okay," Jack was relieved. "Sounds good."

When the wheel chair disappeared behind the maternity ward's automated doors, Jack and Sarah stood there, wringing their hands.

"How's she doing this while he's in jail?" Sarah asked aloud, not to anyone in particular.

Jack stood beside her and did not answer. He had no idea.

"Excuse me," a voice sliced through their thoughts. "My name is Esther Ross. I'm Angela's mother. This is Mia, her sister. We went by the apartment to check on her and the door was open. Her bag for the hospital was gone so, we…."

"Oh, thank God," Sarah thought; only she said it aloud.

"She's in labor," Jack blurted out to distract her from Sarah's comment. "Room 131. I'm Jack and this is my wife, Sarah. Jack and Sarah Lawrence," he clarified when there was no recognition.

"Oh, my word. You are the sweet couple who has been helping my daughter and her … uh, yes. So, nice to meet you finally," she said. "What room did you say she was in?"

"131," Jack said, nodding and trying to smile.

Angela gave birth to an eight-pound, one-ounce baby boy that night -- Rycobi KeVon James.

Angela stayed in the hospital for twenty-four hours and then took Rycobi to her mother's to stay for a while. She couldn't handle taking care of Malcolm, Junior and the new baby by herself. Without Ryker, she had no way to make enough money for rent or food. Her mother wasn't easy to live with, but she was all Angela had until Ryker was released.

Esther Doss walked into Angela's bedroom while she was changing Rycobi. She breathed a heavy sigh and cut her eyes at Angela. She didn't have to say anything. Angela knew her thoughts. *I told you he was just like your no-good father. I don't know why you didn't listen to me ….*

Angela endured the heavy sighs and the lectures from her mother. She met them with silence, not really having an answer for what had happened that night when Ryker didn't come home. She knew what Jack had told her and she believed he was innocent too, but he still ended up in jail at Segovia. *Why had he decided to risk everything that night?* She couldn't understand it. *Why? When everything was going so well?*

Her mother made it hard for her, saying she wouldn't be able to watch the children, if that was her plan during Ryker's absence. She told her it was her responsibility; no excuses. Angela sent messages through Jack and Sarah because her mother refused to watch the children so she could visit him in jail.

"I'm so glad you're waiting for me, Angela," he had written in letters to her. "I don't know what I'd do if you weren't there at the end of this." Angela crumpled the note, not sure how much longer she *could* make it without him. She was lonely and exhausted.

By the end of Ryker's sentence, Angela felt drained. She had not slept, wondering if he would come home to her. Anything could happen in jail. She'd tried to hold on and pray for him, but it had been hard.

When he was finally released, Jack brought him to her mother's house. She had packed and was waiting for him, so they could go to the new apartment Jack found. When he walked up the sidewalk, she could see him from her mother's front-room window. He was skinny and his face was rough-looking.

When he stepped inside the house, she saw his eyes when they fixed on Rycobi. He looked at her and she could feel the sadness pouring out, as he reached for the baby; a sharp, quick sigh escaped like she'd punched him hard in his gut. He had missed Rycobi's birth and the first days of his life.

She held him out to Ryker and he took him, cradling him in his arms. He put his finger inside the tiny fist and said, "Hey little man, Daddy' home." His voice broke a little and Angela opened the door so Malcolm and Junior could rush through and wrap themselves around Ryker's legs. When he felt their arms embrace him, Angela circled her arms around them all, making it a group embrace.

"Let's go home," he said.

"Hey Jack," Ryker said when Jack opened his front door wide.

"You're just in time for some dinner. You couldn't have planned it better."

Ryker laughed. Seeing Sarah bringing some hot dishes to the table, he called into the kitchen, "Hey, mama."

"Hello stranger. Grab a plate and belly up to the table," she said, obviously glad to see him. "Where are the babies and Angela?"

"They at her mama' house," Ryker said.

When they sat down at the table, Ryker looked from one to the other, wanting to tell them what was on his mind, but not quite sure how to say it. When he couldn't find the right words, he just blurted out his question, "Jack, how you know you was gon' really git out?"

"You mean, how did I know I would get away from Lawrence?" Jack inferred. He thought about it for a moment. "I'm not sure I know the answer to that. I can tell you what I did know. I was in a really bad situation. I knew I hated my stepfather for hurting me and my family. I guess I figured if I was going to get him out of the house, I had to get a job and prove we didn't need him. I worked hard so I could prove it to my mother. That was the hard part."

"I kind a done that too, I guess."

"You sure did," Jack assured him. "You were working for Daddy D."

"Yeah, but it wadn' legal," he said, hanging his head and breathing a heavy sigh."

"But, you didn't know that at the time. You were doing the best you could, son," Jack said, seeing he was troubled by it. "You know, I had a lot of support. I've told you about my Uncle Pete and Doc Sevrenson, Mr. Leonard, and Craig Jacobs. They steered me in the right direction. A lot of people did. Can you think of anyone who was there for you?"

"Naw. Just my uncles and my cousins, but they was doin'," he stopped, looking ashamed.

"You know, the adults in our life do the best they can with what they know. My mother did the best she could," he continued to think through it aloud. "She got me up on Sunday mornings, me and my sister, and sent us down the way to church. She might not have been strong enough to leave Lawrence when she should have, but she wanted me to know God and that was a kind of grace in my life, when I needed it most, I'll say that. I learned the comfort of prayer and the power in it. I prayed all the time, still do," the words hung in the air a few seconds.

"My mama done that too," Ryker perked up a little. "We used to go to church on Sundays. We'd leave for service at 9 a.m. and sometime, we didn't git home 'til eight o'clock at night. We be singin' and praisin' the Lord. I could a stayed at church all day, ever'day. It felt like home."

"That's what got me through too," Jack said, a mouthful of cornbread keeping him from saying it clearly. He swallowed quickly so Sarah wouldn't know he'd pinched off some of it and they still hadn't said the prayer. "It's what kept me from giving up. It helped to go every week. I'd listen to the sermons and try to pick out things I could use to help me get through. The fishing and casting tournaments helped too; working at Leonard's. I tried *not* to have time to dwell on the bad stuff."

Sarah sat down and began to pass the food, offering Ryker a Salisbury steak, then an ear of corn and some sweet peas. She snatched the bread basket, already on the table, out of Jack's reach since she could tell he'd already helped himself.

"Do you have a hobby or something you enjoy doing, honey?" she'd been listening to their conversation and Jack made a good point. He kept busy.

"I didn't when I was young," he said. "Now, I like workin', doin' stuff with my hands. It don't matter what it is; yard work, cleanin' the house. I just like to be…."

"Useful," Sarah finished for him. "Well good. Make yourself useful now. Go get the butter from the counter in the kitchen. I forgot it. Then, we can say the blessing," she eyed Jack, making her point.

When he came back, and sat again, Jack gave the blessing and for some reason, he couldn't make himself bow his head and close his eyes. He watched Jack and Sarah do it, their wrinkled faces so earnest and obviously sincere. *They the real deal,* he thought.

When the prayer was over, they began eating. He pushed the food around his plate, struggling with himself. "I could a done somethin', found a way to do different than I done," Ryker said, reasoning in his mind that he should have.

"See, now that's where things get murky, as Uncle Pete would say about the lake water sometimes. How old were you when you started working? Seven? Eight?"

"Yeah, 'bout that."

"How did you get a hold of the drugs you ended up sellin'?" Jack asked.

"They was always around. My Daddy sold'em and my cousins did; my friends did too."

"Did you know it was wrong to have it in the house?" Jack pressed.

"Not at first," he answered. "I just knew it was something that was around. Nobody really talk about it."

"Okay, and how old were you when you tried it?" Jack asked.

"About 13, I think."

"And, did you know the danger in using?"

"I knew it wadn' good to be takin' pills or snorting things that alter yo' state a mind," Ryker said, starting to wonder where Jack was going with this.

"Did you know that taking these drugs could damage pathways in your brain and trick your mind into believing that the only way to feel better was to increase your dosage?" Jack looked hard at Ryker.

"No, I, I was fourteen and," he stopped when he realized the point Jack was making.

"Fourteen, Ryker. How could you have known?" Jack asked, cutting him off. "Be fair, son. Who was the adult who should have taught you about illegals? Who was it?" Jack said louder, his eyes snapping up to meet Ryker's.

"My Pop, my Mama."

"You did what you'd been taught. When you learned it was wrong, my guess is you were in over your head with no way out," Jack concluded.

"That's gen'rous, but you and I both know I know'd what I's doin' was wrong. I can't blame Pop for my actions and still be honest with you and myself."

"Good, because I'd a had to call bullshit on that," Jack said quickly, with a pretty damn good poker face. "My point is we can't choose our parents or guardians. We trust them because we are born to them and we are dependent on them for survival. Now, when we grow up and discover they were wrong about some of the things they taught us, then it's up to us to correct that. That's what you're doing now.

"You were living in an apartment with nothing but a chair and no job when I met you. You said all you wanted was to get out of that life."

"And, I ended up right back."

"No, you had a setback. There's a difference. Let's talk about what you had before you slipped. You spent almost eight months looking for a job, never giving up. When you finally got a job, you walked a few doors down from there and got another one, bringing you to full time. We had some trouble with rent until you brought home a few paychecks and then you and Angela settled into your new space, knowing you'd have to get a third job to cover rent and expenses. You'd just gotten the night shift at Wellington. All of this was good for you, for the boys, for Angela."

"I got scurred," he said, barely audible. "I couldn't see how I's gon' make it work, working double shifts, eventually night shifts, and never bein' home with them. Minimum wage ain' enough when you got kids and bills and rent. I'd just got that job at the nursin' home and it was gon' mean I hardly see 'em at all 'cause I's gon' work all day and then nights too.

"I started thinking about Daddy D. He had nine kids to take cur of. Most times, they took cur a they selves. Nobody spend time with 'em and that's when they start gittin' in trouble. I know Angela there, but I want a be there for 'em too. How I gon' do that if I'm always workin'? It's like I's gon' be the same no-show-father no matter what I do. That's why I try to sell that last score. I want a put some money back so I could have time off sometime."

"I know that makes sense in your mind," Jack nodded. "Let's think how it would be if you kept scorin' from time to time, because you know you won't stop with one more. There'll be something else you need or one of your family will ask for help or Angela will; there'll be added expenses. It's always something. You know that, right?"

Ryker sat back in his chair, nodded. Jack was right. *I done condition myself to the life. If I'm thinkin' I can walk back in at any time, then I ain' left. Damn. We got next to nothin' in the apartment; we barely eatin' and makin' rent and still, I got to keep it that way 'til I can afford to change it. That mean more work.*

"Let me tell you something. So far, since you left, you're taking care of your family, Angela and the babies. You're spendin' time with them. I know, I've seen you when you get off work. You just want to sleep, but those babies come runnin' up to you and you find the energy to play with 'em. I've seen you.

"Anyhow, you've kept up your end and it hasn't been easy. Balancing work, family and expenses, on a tight budget is a challenge and you're trying, despite your record. How's doin' a score going to help? Sure, the money will help, but what are you teachin' your family? What does it say about all the hard, honest work you've been doing?"

"D'at I'm playin' two sides to da middle," he said.

"Exactly. You're making your own rules, knowing the world, or the law, doesn't work that way."

"Just like my Pop done," he finished for Jack.

"Yeah. That's it," Jack held Ryker's gaze. "We're shooting for the long-run, son; going for the best life. Not making do in the short-run. We've got our children in our sights *and* our children's children. It's worth it. And, it'll happen, if we stay focused." Jack looked back at his food. He hadn't eaten a bite. He stood and took it to the microwave to reheat it. Looking back at Ryker, while it cooked, he could see some of what he said was sinking in, but there was still so much for him to adjust to and learn.

Ryker looked at Jack, his eyes staring hard at him. *How I gon' make it if I can't work things out with Angela,* he thought. *Ever' time I see her, I think a her maybe messin' around with some other guy. I done missed out on Rycobi bein' born. Her mama think I'm the devil and blame me for messin' up her daughter' life. It ain' gon' git better for a while. No matter how much work I git, it gon' be hard and they ain' much gon' let up for a while. I can't ax no more a Jack and Sarah. Check that. I don't want to ax no more of them. I want a do thangs on my own.*

What's more, I miss my friends and I ain' got nobody when there's an occasion for it. How I s'pose to leave the only family I know -- forever? Ain' t nobody I know'd ever do that.

Jack ain' done that. He still help his mama back when she alive. He said d'at. I need to git on the road and think. I can't do it when

I'm in Jack's house, eatin' his food. It make me want a live there, like I belong. As much as I'm grateful for everything he do for me, he ain' my blood-kin. What I gon' do? Try to be in his family? I got to think ….

"Ryker?" Jack said. "Did you hear what I said?"

"Yeah, I heard. I don't know, though," he said, putting his ball cap back on. "Nothin' add up."

"It will. You know, I know no one who has done what you are attempting. You're the first man I've met who was born to being a career criminal and set his sights on getting out. Do you know anyone who has succeeded?' Jack asked.

"Naw." Ryker said, thinking about where all of his friends were now. *Bam Morrison played football so well in high school that he ended up playin' for the Steelers. I thought he'd made it, but then I heard he and Ronny Brooks was picked up for possession a weed. They was just takin' it to a party. Neither one a them ever use or nothin'. They ended up gittin' stopped. Neither one would cop to it bein' theirs. D'at's how it is. Don't matter who in trouble. We a lot a thangs, but disloyal wadn' ever gon' be one a d'em. 'It ain' mine' was all they say. So both of 'em went down for it. Bam was kicked off the team and he had t'come home. Ronny had nothin' to lose so he was home.*

Then, Bam's brother, Run; he git on the Rams football team, but he bust his knee up and had to stop, too. He livin' at home and doin' nothin'.

My cousin, T.J., found out my Uncle Ray wadn' his real dad his junior year. Messed him up good. He know'd he was different than his brother and sister, but he couldn't figure how. One day, his dad ax his mama when they was fightin'. They didn' know he was there. She say his daddy' in the Marines. She have an affair when the man passed through on leave.

T.J. lose it. He git messed up on meth. He still ain' gittin' help with his addiction. The only one left is Cowboy, Joe Massey. His big dream was to be a bull rider in the black rodeo. He done it for five years and then he had a stroke while he on the bull. The rest a my people all still where they was when I left.

"I'm the only one," Ryker said, coming back to the conversation.

Jack stared at him, his eyes narrowed. He didn't expect Ryker to know someone in his criminal past who made it out - - not and lived to tell about it anyway. As he pondered this, he realized Ryker was incredibly brave to attempt it. It meant leaving everything he had ever known, to go straight. He wouldn't be able to go back if he made it and he could not have his family with him unless they went straight too. Not likely.

That's it, Jack thought. *Ryker said he'd known he had an important purpose since he was a small boy. He said there were multiple times when he looked death in the face, but somehow he was spared and that it must mean God had a purpose, a higher purpose. Ryker thought it was luck for a long time; a twist of fate, maybe, but it's more than that. I can see it as clear as day.*

"You know, if you're the only one who makes it out, perhaps that was what God intended. He chose you because he knew you were strong enough. You getting out *could* be the first step to helping others, people you care about," Jack suggested.

Ryker was messing with his ball cap and when it registered what Jack was saying, his eyes met Jack's and locked. He said nothing for several minutes. Jack motioned upward. "God may have bigger plans for you than you realize," and then he clapped Ryker on the back and turned to grab his plate from the microwave. Feeling it was cold again, he said, "Now, don't say anything else 'til I get this reheated and sit down, okay? Otherwise, I'll end up talkin' too much and it'll get cold again."

Sarah shook her head, smiling, because this was the second time he was heating his food. It was probably fried by now.

"You sayin' I could help some a my people?" Ryker asked, after Jack sat down.

"Yeah," Jack said.

"How?"

"Maybe, if we write it down, share our story, then others can break free too. I've done enough prison ministry to know there are tons of people, just like you, who would like the chance to try. We could be the ones to show 'em how it's done."

"How we gon' do that?" Ryker asked, intrigued.

"Well, I don't know, but our experience could make a huge impact on the world. Think what it would be like if more of us became mentors and helped people when they come out of prison. We've got five thousand prisons in the United States and not one of them has been good at correcting the bad behavior of the individuals who have been incarcerated. The rate of recidivism is almost 70 percent in the United States. Apparently, whatever rehabilitation programs the government has put in place are not cutting it. You and I have been working at this for going-on four years. I had no idea it would take this long, but having been through some of this with you, I'm starting to understand."

"Yeah." Ryker hung his head, feeling the disappointment in Jack's tone.

"Now, wait a dad-burn minute. I didn't mean it was your fault entirely. Sure, you've made some bad choices, but Ryker, we're talking about helping you untangle yourself from a life that you have been deeply entrenched in since you were born. It doesn't straighten out in a few weeks or a few months or even a few years. It could take a long time. But if going through this can help someone else, well, I think that could be worth something even better. Don't you?"

Recovering some from hearing Jack explain it the way he did, Ryker sat up straighter in his chair. "It would feel good to give back. I been takin' from you for so long. It'd feel great to give what I learn to someone who need it."

"I know just the person we need to see," Jack said. "Get up, son. We have some place to be and someone I want you to meet." Jack grabbed his wallet and his keys, his jacket already slung over his arm.

"Nice havin' dinner with you guys," Sarah said, as the front door closed behind them.

Chapter 18

*There is an interesting fish called the Weedy Sea
Dragon. It is found among coral reefs, sea grass
beds, and seaweeds off the south coast of Australia.
The male weedy sea dragon incubates the fertilized
eggs of the female in brood pouches located on its tale.
These pouches supply oxygen to the eggs by drawing it
from the father's own blood vessels. The father often
carries the eggs for months on his tail, in the brood
pouches, to secure the safety of the young.*

*Ain' nobody git what in my head, what in my blood and the blood
been spilled.*

As Jack drove, Ryker thought about what he'd said. He
could tell Jack understood how he really felt, to a point. It
was hard to imagine *anyone* could relate to the darkness of
violence and drugs. It had been easier to read from the book,
"Jack's Guide to Leaving the Criminal World." This way, he
didn't have to relive all the danger, all the horrific screams,
when justice was being dealt on the street. Listening to Jack's
assessment of what he had to do was simpler, less messy. The
road of broken bones, distorted faces and lost, dead eyes were
scenes from a life he couldn't explain or defend so it was
better not to give it a voice.

Ryker tried to absorb as much of Jack's version as he
could; fill the deep holes, where shock and horror threatened
to remind. If he could be useful with his hands, work hard
and be the Little Man his mother cooed over as a toddler,
then he was touching that part of him he believed God had
protected all this time; preserved for His plan.

He wasn't sure about writing his story down. He knew that would mean telling the whole truth, in that the power in the message could be diminished each time a lie disguised it, altering truth. His people were masters at altering their truth; it was often necessary to get through the next nightmare. When he spent the time in Segovia, he had to shove the God in him down, deep inside the shell he summoned for protection. *I wonder if that anythin' like puttin' on d'armor of God. Somehow, I don' think so.*

Keeping things less messy also made Jack more focused, more intentional about Ryker's path out. He laid everything out, like a map on the table. He pointed to the places Ryker had been and then redirected him to where he needed to go. When he saw his life on this map, there were no dead ends. He could go forward or backward or laterally, but at no time was he confined to the road he'd already travelled or committed to a path he didn't want to choose. There was no blood on the path, no dead bodies, and no voices in his head; in his blood.

Once you'd spilled blood of another, it became yours to carry, no matter the circumstance, no matter the intent.

He rubbed at his eyelids, feeling the tension release as he massaged. He was tired of thinking and talking. He needed something he could do, something that would give him a purpose he could feel good about. Jack said he knew where to start. *Let's hope so.* He couldn't help but think if Jack knew where he'd been, he wouldn't be helping him. *I's not sure I'd help me.*

Jack pulled into the parking lot at St. Timothy's. Ryker looked at him, but Jack was in motion the second the car was in park. Throwing his hands up, Ryker got out of the car and caught up to him, squaring his ball cap as he did so. Jack walked into the parish hall and there were about fifteen kids playing some game. He heard someone say, "The Lord be with you," and the kids responded, immediately stopping the game, "And also with you."

He and Jack bowed their heads, so as not to distract. Ryker removed his cap.

"Dear heavenly father, we're here in your name. We pray you will guide our thoughts and propel our actions to glorify you. No matter where we've been, help us see your plan for us. Alert us to your will. Bless this food to the nourishment of our bodies, so that we may commit our lives to your service. Amen."

As the teenagers formed a line to get their supper, Jack looked around the room. He saw Wayne Roark, standing at the back of the line. His wife, Anna Rae, was serving the kids. She wore a long sleeve, cotton t-shirt that read St. Timothy's EYC ROCKS! Wayne was wearing a similar shirt, only in a dress-casual, denim button-down. He looked like he'd just come from work.

"Wayne," Jack called to him.

"Hey, Jack," he looked relieved to see him. "Aren't you brave, walking into the youth group bible study. They're in rare form. Hey, we still on for poker Tuesday night?"

"You betcha. Hey, I wanted to ask you something," Jack said, stepping away from the line. Wayne followed and bent down so he could hear him, as the room was so loud and chaotic with the kids eating and chattering among themselves. Wayne was six-feet-six-inches so leaning down to Jack's stature was like getting down on one of his kids' levels.

"What's that?" Wayne said.

"I wonder if you know anybody who would be willing to write a book," Jack asked, raising his voice a little louder.

"What kind of book?" Wayne asked.

"Well, it's about being a mentor to ex-convicts when they are released from prison with no place to go, no job, etc."

"Sounds interesting. Who's it about?" Wayne pressed.

"Me," Jack said. "Well, Ryker and me." He turned and Ryker stepped forward.

"Oh, I'm sorry," he reached around Jack to shake Ryker's hand. "My name is Wayne Roark."

Ryker obliged and said, "Nice to meet you, sir. I'm Ryker. Ryker James."

"So? Do you know anyone who could do it?" Jack pushed.

"Sure do," Wayne said, waiting for Jack to get anxious when he didn't say who.

"Well?" Jack said, throwing his hands in the air just as Wayne expected. "Who? Spit it out, man."

"My wife," he said.

"Anna Rae?" Jack asked. "I didn't know she was a writer."

"Yeah, she has a degree in journalism and has written for newspapers, print media, magazines. She's been itching to write a book."

"You think she would write our story for us?" Jack persisted.

"I don't know. You'd have to ask her," Wayne said, realizing Jack was quite serious.

"Well, I don't want to interrupt. Maybe I could ask her another time." Jack said. "You know I've been a speaker for the youth group several times now."

"What? Did you teach 'em your best poker face?" Wayne smiled.

"As a matter of fact, I did," Jack said, laughing. "They're ready for Vegas, don't you know?"

"You could probably ask her now, if you like. She'll have a few minutes before the bible study starts," Wayne said, as he stepped back into line.

When everyone was served, Jack did just that. Anna Rae said she could meet with him the following Tuesday morning.

Anna Rae Roark, two years in.

"Hey there," Jack called out as he got out of his car. "I brought the background information you asked for, here in this folder," he said as the papers slid out and toppled to the sidewalk. I dove forward to pick up the pages and he was clearly disgruntled.

"Dad-blast it! I should have put these in an envelope, I guess," he said as he gathered a few of the papers the wind caught and carried to the bushes.

"Here. I've got them," I began stacking them, out of order. "No worries."

"I think sharing our story is really going to help Ryker," he said. "He's been trying to wrap his head around the idea that he's worth saving and, sometimes, if you shift the perspective just a little bit, make it about the big picture, it's easier somehow."

"I know what you mean. Changing the angle can bring clarity."

"Yeah. That's it exactly. We've come a long way and he doesn't see anything familiar. He doesn't fit with his family or his friends right now. I've opened my home to him, the church has too. Even my extended family has welcomed him with open arms, but ...."

"They're not the people he has history with -- no more than a few years, anyway."

"Yeah," Jack said, grateful I understood. "Writing it all down could give him just what he needs to finish the journey out."

"How so?"

"Well, Ryker has always been the caretaker among his family and friends. He's feeling a little guilty about getting a shiny, new life, while the rest of his people are still trying to survive in the same dark place he's getting out of. If he thought getting out would help them somehow, it might light a fire, so to speak. There's nothing he likes more than taking care of those who've been through a lot." I held up a hand to stop him.

"Jack, you understand that Ryker could be playing you. He's a career criminal. He's been taught to say what people want to hear, put them at ease and walk out with everything."

"Yeah, I know," and I could see the thought had crossed many times, from the way his brows furrowed and his jaw clenched. "But, that's where faith has to win out. You don't get far if you're not willing to take a risk. My gut says he's gonna do it, that he's sincere. It's gonna take time, but my prayers and my heart are telling me to help him."

"All we can do is the best we can."

"I know. I hear you," he said. "I won't give up though."

I watched him walk to his car. I had known him about five years. A father of four, a grandfather of eight and, he was supposed to be retiring from a life of hard work, but here he was, one-hundred-and-ten-percent committed to helping Ryker James and a few others, still in the prison system.

He was an impressive old man.

When he and Ryker came to me a couple of years ago, I started right away, gathering information and interviewing them, as well as many of their family members and friends. Given I had to keep working my day jobs, I couldn't devote all of my time to writing their story, but there were many nights I was up, praying. My instincts were telling me Ryker wasn't being completely forthright about his life; the truth was I didn't know if I wanted him to be.

I tried to interview them a couple of times a week, sometimes together, sometimes separate.

Some days I had a good feeling about Ryker and other days, I didn't. The first time we met without Jack was telling. I couldn't shake some of the things he'd said, "I learn to be whatever I had to, to survive. I could say whatever need sayin', be whatever need bein' if it mean gitin' somethin' to happen."

This statement came after long silences and one word answers. His deadpan stares were eerie at times, but looking away wasn't an option for me. If he was a master at duping people on the street, who's to say he wasn't doing this with Jack and I.

I surprised myself several times, when I said things like, "You do understand that when you say you could get people to do just about anything; that you can be anyone you want to be or anybody *I* want you to be in the moment, different personalities, whatever, all rolled into one – that this means you could be acting when you're with me, acting when you're with Jack – duping us."

It took a while to build a trust that would allow him to speak freely. When I cut through his bravado, he had to decide if he could trust me. Likewise, I had to decide if I could believe him.

I was two years into the project, still uncovering information about Ryker James. His history of being a drug dealer for the Bloods in Cooper, Texas, and his reputation for being an enforcer for the Crips in Fort Worth, were enough to raise a lot of questions relative to his commitment to getting out of the drug world. I couldn't wrap my head around his connection to the rival gangs; that he could walk the line between them and not be expected to join either gang.

"See, I had family in d'Bloods. They in Cooper. The Crips was in Fort Worth. Bein' they enforcer mean I'd git a call to go handle a situation, but it ain' ever gon' be in the same place as the gang livin'. Like, if d'Crips havin' problems gittin' a customer to pay for they drugs, d'en they gon' call me. I gon' leave town, go deal with 'em and then git back to my people in Cooper and lay low, so ain' nobody know who done the deed. Ain' nobody in that town know me, not even my name so when the beat-down happen, the police can't pin it on nobody."

"But, you have family in Fort Worth, too, right?" I asked.

"Yeah, on my Mama' side," he said, waiting for me to put it together. "But, nobody know I's the one enforcin' – see, they ain' nobody callin' me, knowin' my name. They just know if they need a enforcer, call this number. I'm a breathin' person at the other end, but I ain' gon' say nothin'. D'ey gon' say a name and I gon' pay d'at person a visit. I'm a ghost, you feel me?"

"Yes, I think I do. You sell to the Bloods and to the Crips, but as long as you're not living in either territory for any length of time, they don't know you're dealing to both of them."

"Exactly. When things heat up, I go to Oklahoma 'til they die down. They gon' call 'cause they need to score they drugs. It's 'bout bein' in da right place at d'right time and packin' d'heat ever where in between."

As I listened to him, the deception he'd mastered had multiple levels and the scary part was I could tell he was jazzed that he could and *did* do it; been doing it for years without incident.

He told Jack he was not meant to be in the life he was born to. He said he wanted to leave it years ago, but didn't have the opportunity to make it happen. At the same time, he boasted of his lucrative organized-crime-life, saying the money had been good and he had mastered the art of not being caught, with an occasional arrest here and there. I couldn't tell, from one interview to the next, if he really wanted out.

My stomach knotted each time we talked. I was trying to determine if he was being honest with himself, never mind Jack or me. Did he think Jack was loaded? Could Jack be his new cover for the business? The old saying, 'if it looks like a con, smells like a con, it probably is,' was a constant sound bite in my head.

I thumbed through the pages Jack brought. There was a passage that lay on top of the stack. It didn't have a number on either side of the notebook paper it was written on. It described a murder, and I immediately thought Ryker. *Why was this passage among the papers Jack brought?* I wondered.

I thought of Ryker's past, the gang violence, the history of his uncles spilling a lot of blood in the Fifth Ward, when they were dealing drugs in the '80s. I wondered if Jack really knew the man he'd sworn to help. Most people wouldn't take on a career criminal like Ryker if they knew where he came from and the people he was associated with -- not out of the goodness of their hearts anyway. There had to be something more.

I met Ryker in May of 2006. I began to develop a profile of him. My notes, which were often doodles I made as he talked, said 'guarded to extreme'. In all fairness, he'd sat down in front of me, slumped against the back of the chair, leaning to one side. His demeanor was calm, eerily calm, as he listened to Jack talk about their intentions to share their story. I kept trying to include Ryker in the interview, but he answered my questions in two or three words, careful not to offer any information that wasn't specifically asked. Jack often answered for him, if he paused for too long or showed apprehension. I got the feeling Jack had been told Ryker wasn't worth saving and he was concerned I'd heard the same from parishioners at our church.

At the end of the interview, I asked for one-on-one sessions. I needed to push for more details, more background on Ryker. There were moments when Ryker shifted in his chair, looked away. Some days, a darkness shone in Ryker's gaze; it was disconcerting. *What could Jack be thinking, getting mixed up with a dangerous man like James?*

Over the course of the next few months, I learned Ryker was listed in two counties, Tarrant County in Fort Worth, and Delta County in Cooper, as a career criminal with one felony under his belt for which he had served time and another charge for evasion of arrest and breaking probation, resulting in a stint at a half-rehab-half-jail facility, the Substance Abuse Felony Punishment (SAFP) program. Ryker had been a drug dealer for more than half his life. His rap sheet was in excess of thirty-seven pages long in Delta County alone. His sheet in Tarrant County was seventeen pages. I later learned he had another rap sheet in Oklahoma City.

In all those years of being in the game, he served fewer than five years in lock-up, and this was non-consecutively; we're talking a year, maybe eighteen months and then he was out on the street. Officers in Delta and Tarrant counties spent much of their time trying to take him down and they were looking to nail him for life. They wanted him to go down hard.

Jack depicted a young man, born into a dangerous world, who needed someone to believe in him. All I saw was a young black punk, looking to take advantage of a kind, elderly man.

There were so many people, just like him, poor and on welfare and food stamps, and they didn't choose to break the law, sell illegal narcotics or engage in violent acts of supposed justice. Given the depth of Ryker's involvement, he could still be "in the life," while telling Jack he was sincere about wanting out. *How would anyone know?*

Obviously, things have changed in the drug world since Ryker started selling in 1988. Technology evolved things quite a bit. Ryker admitted scoring used to be easier because people were giving him cash. He'd buy from his sources, flip the powder, double it and return with crack, making money off them and still having pure product left to sell. Pure meant no additives, like cooking it to increase the quantity.

To clarify, if he took money, say a thousand dollars, from the Bloods in Cooper and paid his source for the coke in Fort

Worth, he could cut the pure stash in half, pocket the first half and still have half to cook -- cocaine, a little water and baking soda over a hot skillet meant double the mass and voila, crack cocaine.

In the meantime, he sold the pure at high dollar, getting that score plus the thousand he got for the crack he made, and no one was the wiser. If he ran several scores, beginning with a thousand in cash, he could come back with seven or eight thousand over one weekend.

Back in the day, when Ryker was 17, 18 or 19 years old, he had a sweet set-up. All it took was a few people he knew he could trust, who also trusted him. By the end of the '90s, dealers had traded trust for greed and it resulted in excessive violence to secure deals. It may have been true that Ryker wanted out of the business, but maybe his reasons were about the same as the crack he was cooking -- half pure. Maybe the business was changing and it was going to be harder to deal and not face tougher sentences when he got caught. Only Ryker knew the answer to that and he was pretty tight-lipped. I had to determine Ryker's circumstances before he met Jack. I dug in and started grilling Ryker about it.

"I was workin' for da Texas Marine Company then," Ryker said.

"This was when you worked for Ms. Overstreet, correct?"

"Yeah, she said I's a hard worker and she recommend me for a raise. Didn't happen 'cause she leave. She transferred to another store, out a state," he said.

"Were you involved?" I thought maybe there was a personal connection that may have colored her impression of him.

"Naw, I s'pose we could a been, but it wadn' like that." He took off his ball cap and sat up straighter. "I told her I wanted out a dealin' and she, she uh, she the first person that believe me."

"And, Jack was next?" I added.

"Yeah. Ain' nobody ever believe me when I say it before. I been prayin' I could figure a way out and," he paused. "Forgit it," and he shook his head.

"What? You can say. You can say anything." I gently tried to get him to continue. Seeing he had shut down, I offered my own experience instead. "You know, I know what it's like when parents have expectations. They teach you their way and you don't have much choice when you're young. You're used to doing what's expected. I guess you could say I was a pleaser. I didn't want them to be disappointed in me or think I wasn't capable."

He looked at me for a long time. I imagined he was thinking, *You just some white girl, with a mom and dad who stayed together your whole childhood, then you git married, have kids and now you livin' in yo' lily-white house, takin' yo' kids to school and you safe and have food on yo' table. And then, you sittin' here, tryin' to compare yo' self to me.*

I started to defend myself, as if he had said the words. I stopped short. He must have seen me, because his eyes softened and he started talking.

"You ain' like nobody I ever met," he said. "You kind and you tryin' to understand. Thing is, I know'd drugs was wrong. I know'd it. I feel it, even when nobody git in trouble. My mama take me to church and I used to listen to the pastor and… I know.

"It hard to explain, but I's the one ever' body come to when they need money or help, and I's able to do it 'cause I know'd how to git things. I ain' proud of it and I don't expect you to git what I'm sayin'. I's tryin' to take cur a my family, even though they didn't cur. I guess I hoped they would.

"Then, I needed help and nobody there; not till Ms. Overstreet, then Jack, and now you." His eyes held a flicker of tears.

In that moment, I saw a young boy looking back. He had seen his mother beaten, almost to death in front of him. There was no telling what he had seen among the Bloods and the Crips. He sat before me, opening himself up because I gave a little -- not a lot, but I let him into my thoughts and it was enough.

"Are you still dealing?" I asked.

He looked at me and shook his head. "What make you ax me that?"

"You and I both know you've used before. No dealer sells and doesn't try it at least once, right?"

He cut his eyes away from me. "No, I'm not," he said. "I can't say I haven't thought about it. It ain' easy makin' rent and takin' from Jack. You know I just git out a Segovia. I done eight months and Jack help me git parole."

"Why did you sell again?"

"I didn't. I's clean. They plant those drugs." I narrowed my eyes.

"Yeah, okay, I know it was a bad choice. I don't know why I done it, but I could a got away and I decided to listen to Jack, stand for what I done, and I's almost beaten to death." His eyes met mine straight on. "What you want me to say? I screwed up. I told Jack I know I done wrong. I's tryin' to git used to bein' -- ah, I can't explain it."

"You're still addicted," I said.

"Naw, I ain' addicted to no drug," he said, a little too quickly.

"Maybe you're addicted to the life. Let's face it. You're walking away from your family, your community, your home. That's a lot to ask."

"It hard to make sense a things right now. Like, the night I's caught near my granddaddy' house. I can't say how I end up there or with the powder. I's so messed up in my head."

"Were you on something?"

"No, not d'at way," he said, searching for the right words to explain. "I'd just found out my lady was pregnant and I just git a third job. I had Junior to cur for 'cause my Pop in prison and Jack and Sarah done help me so much, I didn't want a tell 'em I couldn't take the pressure a things. I'm used to takin' cur a my own self and I ain' never had no help, much less ax nobody for it. I told Angela we had to be curful -- she said it was a accident, but I think she was worried 'bout hangin' on to me so she done it anyway. That ain' Jack's problem and I felt bad about it all."

"Why? What made you feel so bad you considered going back to dealing?"

"I's out a control. I's in a panic a some kind. I didn't know how to, to …."

"You didn't know how to cope?" I asked, not sure I understood him.

"I just wanted to fix what wrong. I's takin' too much from Jack. I's tryin' to help, the only way I, I don't know," he said, exasperated.

"You tried to help the only way you knew how."

"Yes, ma'am. That's it, I guess. Now, ever'thang start over and I's thankful for that, but when I can't turn to my family -- 'cause they gon' talk me out a my new life — and I can't go to my friends 'cause a the same thang, where I 'pose to go? 'Cause I know what you're thinkin'."

"What? What am I thinking?"

"You thinkin' I'm tryin' to take Jack's money and d'at I ain' got no plan a really changin'." He looked hard at me when he said it.

"I think you're still in the game," I said, holding my hands up, expecting him to get up in my face, indignant and all that.

"I ain'," he stared steadily.

"Maybe not directly, but you're getting a cut, somehow," I said.

He didn't respond. There was no emotion at all, which felt bad. His gaze was resigned, accepting of my accusation, but I couldn't be sure if it was because I was right or because he knew he had no way to prove otherwise.

After a long, very uncomfortable silence, I said, "I want to believe you really want out, I do. But if you're not being honest with Jack and Sarah, I will find out."

"I know. I can see it in your eyes," he said, cutting me off. "You ain' got to worry 'bout that. I know it gon' take time for you to believe me, I git it. Jack yo' friend and you tryin' to do right by him." He sat up straight and looked in my eyes. "I's tryin' to do the same thang. I thought I's protectin' 'im by not tellin' him I didn't know if I could handle thangs. I think part a me wanted a git caught so I don't hurt him. I'm messed up. I know that, but I want out more d'an I ever wanted anything. I just don't want a hurt Jack at the same time."

"You know you can't go back, among the people in your old life," I reminded him. "Even when things are tough, you can't."

"Yeah, I'm tryin' to git that. It's just that," he paused to think of an example. "Okay, I know. How you spend your birthday ever'year?"

"What?"

"Do you go out? Do you stay home and have a party?" he asked.

"I don't do the same thing every time. I just know I'm with," I met his gaze. He waited for me to finish my sentence, tears brimming, but not falling. "I'm with my family."

"When you was little?"

"Same."

"Yeah, so even though I don't want a go back there, I don't *want* to be with them, they …."

"They're who you know. But what about Jack and Sarah?"

"Oh, I want a be with them, but I ain' sure I deserve to be. You aren't either," he said, a half smile forming at the left corner of his mouth.

"Whatever you're doing, I know you're not telling me or Jack everything, so you need to know I would never let anyone hurt Jack. You get me?"

"Yeah, I git that. Neither would I," he said, a tear coming dangerously close to the edge.

◆

"Hey, man," Terrence Booker said as he walked up to Ryker, smoking a Cambridge. Terrence and Ryker went way back. He and Ryker used to hang out at Daddy D's when he was in town. This was when Ryker ran drugs through Cooper and Fort Worth in the late 1980s and the early 1990s. Ryker used to come in the middle of the night and leave before dawn, usually touching base with his trusted four, Terrence being one of them.

They lived on the Southside of Fort Worth in an area called Ag-land, short for Aggravated Land. In 1995, Ryker's trusted four were told that cocaine was coming across the border at a great price. Many believed this was due, in part, to the arrest of the hierarchy involved in the international drug syndicate, the Cali Cartel, which led to the dismantling of their empire and the sale of the confiscated drugs. The drug importers, who controlled the border, showed ingenuity when bypassing security at the border, allowing them to sell to dealers like Ryker and the trusted four.

In turn, Ryker's crew sold pure to good customers, giving them incentive to buy only from them. In time, Ryker and his people established themselves in the area and enjoyed immense power.

Because Ryker's trusted four had a good thing going, many outsiders attempted to kill them off and take their stash, creating a hostile, violent fight between Ag-Land and the other side, called the "Neighborhood" or "the Hood." The murders that occurred during that time increased to an all-time high, making it the most dangerous it had ever been in Fort Worth. It was understood that any trespassers into Ag-Land would be killed or, at the very least, severely beaten, ensuring they would never return. Ryker and his trusted four were enforcers of this unwritten law.

There was a band of rappers at the time, called the Bloody Nickels, who rapped about the violence, boasting that Ag-Land would always be in control. The surviving Hood members vowed they would lay in wait for the day of reckoning. It didn't matter when the day came, only that it came. Because Ryker had been out of action, he hadn't been back to Ag-Land.

Standing on the porch, outside the apartment Jack found for him while he was in Segovia serving his sentence, Ryker was trying to process some of the things he had been through over the eight months he spent in jail, in addition to everything he'd experienced up to that point. No memory faded much, if at all. He and Angela had made it through his incarceration and he wanted to talk to her about the things he'd been through, but he wasn't sure she was strong enough to hear them. He didn't know of anyone who was. She told him she prayed he would get out in six months for good behavior, but she also said she knew his temper and often awoke in the night in a cold sweat, thinking he had been killed in lock-up.

Ryker assured her he was okay, but he was still dealing with his side of it. Taking the beating he endured from Hawk-man was nothing he could forget so easily. It didn't take much for people to fight in prison. Though he had held his own, there was no forgetting what had gone down.

He was smoking a Merit, the second one in five minutes. He took a deep drag. Opening his eyes and seeing one of the trusted four walking up his driveway; it brought back a renewed strength he hadn't felt in a long time. At first, he couldn't be sure Booker was real. *Where had he come from? How did he know to come here?* Ryker thought. Then again, he knew how Booker found him. It was nothing *he* hadn't done before either.

"Hey," Ryker lifted his chin. "What's goin' on? What 'choo doin' here?"

"Do I got a have a reason?"

"Usually do."

"Give me one a those," he gestured to the pack of cigarettes Ryker was about to put in his shirt pocket.

Ryker held the lighter for him and then lit another for himself, taking a long, much needed drag and exhaling." He shook his head, a half-smile pulling at the corners of his mouth. It was good to see his trusted friend.

"I swear, I think you could find anybody, anywhere," Ryker said.

"Only the ones I cur 'bout. We go way back, man. How's yo' lady?" he asked, like no time had passed.

"Angela? Mad. She think I'm cheatin' on her."

"Are you?" he raised an eyebrow, knowing his street brother wasn't above it.

"Naw, not this time," he laughed, appreciating the exchange of familiarity. "She really insecure 'cause I's just released. She have her own set a nightmares while I's gone."

"How yo' kids doin'? I bet it' hard for them too.

"Yeah, it's hard all 'round, but they good. The baby, Rycobi; he amazin'." Ryker's smile widened at the mere thought of him. "Junior and Malcolm a hanful."

"Huh. Maybe we need to go out, do some clubbin', pay for it later," Terrence said, smiling and shaking another cigarette free and grabbing it with his lips. After he lit up, he said, "Let's get out a here and pick up some beer, just hang out." The words seemed to hang in the air like the acrid cigarette smoke.

Ryker looked at him, took another long drag on his cigarette and nodded.

They got in his truck and backed out of the parking space, near his apartment.

"How're the guys?" Ryker was referring to the trusted four.

"Why don't we git some beer and smokes and see if we can round 'em up, for old time sake?"

Ryker looked over at him, remembering old times, and said, "A'ight. Where to?"

"The hood, man. Let's hit Riverside and Robinson for the beer."

Ryker was soon driving down familiar streets, seeing the ladies lazily walking the corners, their thongs showing through their sleek, short dresses. He knew some of them and they offered their services. Hustling and clubbing had been two of the easiest ways to make a little on the side, aside from selling.

Driving helped. Terrence's suggestion to go clubbing on the south side was sounding better by the second. Feeling the familiar felt right, even though he knew it was a risk. Drinking and listening to loud music didn't sound bad either.

It was strangely comforting for him to be back. Riverside and Robinson convenience store was in the hood. There was only one way in and one way out. It was like gang territory but not as dangerous as Ag-land. He remembered the days he had been at the top of his game, in power. It would feel good to strut his stuff in the Hood. He could turn a few heads, remind them of his reign when he was there several years back. He had been untouchable then, and after all he'd been through, he wanted to feel it -- the intensity and the fear he used to induce, simply by walking through the door.

He had walked out of Segovia feeling all kinds of anger and resentment for the people he had been locked up with, while trying to get his head straight so he could return to Angela, Jack, and Sarah. He needed to feel in control and despite his best effort, he wasn't feeling it. Walking in and out of the hood, he felt the power.

When he walked into the convenience store, a woman *accidently* pushed him when she got in line to checkout. Dressed in a wife-beater, jeans, tennis shoes and a ton of gold bling on her hands and around her neck, she clenched her broad jaw, while staring him down through hooded eyes, heavy with black liner. Noticing her stance and attitude, Ryker tried to tease her a little. "Excuse you," he said.

"Excuse me?!" she exploded and pushed him again. "Excuse *you*," her voice a little loud. Eyeing her, there was something familiar about her, but he couldn't say why. Even so, he wasn't about to let her think she could handle him.

"Naw, you ran into me. Excuse you," he said, squaring his broad shoulders to intimidate her a bit.

"What? You think 'cause I'm a woman I can't take you?" She seemed to feel his arrogance and decided he should be taken down a peg.

"I know you can't take me, even though you dressed like a man. It don't matter. You can't take me so back off." He knew this would provoke her and that was fine by him. He was ready.

"Who you tellin' to back off?" She was now in his face, shoving her chest into his.

"I'm tellin' you, you outta yo' league." Ryker was trying to warn her. He was in a mood and he could feel his own rage fusing with the apparent chip on her shoulder.

"Am I?" she said, pulling her 9 millimeter from her backside and pointing it in his face. "You were sayin'?"

Out of habit, he reached in his belt for his .45. It wasn't there. He'd recovered it from Bagman after he went down for possession, giving it to Daddy D for safe keeping -- *Damn*. As he slowly brought his hand back to his side, an uncontrollable rage began to stir deep inside. No one got the drop on him, ever. His jaw muscles were clenched, his eyes bore into her. After a long, deadly silence, he spat out these words, "If you gon' shoot, you better make sure you kill me, 'cause if you miss, you good as dead. You feel me?" He was now coming closer to the barrel of the pistol, his voice a gravelly breathy sound.

She began to shake and the gun was blurring before him. She lowered the gun. He continued to stare her down, even as he turned and backed out of the store. He raised his eyebrows in clarification that he had reclaimed the "drop" she thought she had.

Following him out, she was shaking, but angry all the same. The rage in his eyes sent sheer terror coursing through her veins. Ryker heard her open the driver's side door of her car and happened to glance back at her, to make sure she was leaving. Then, he heard a gun click, and he launched himself around to the driver's side door as quick as lightning. He reached in, yanking her male friend from the car with one hand while grabbing hold of the gun with the other. The man tried to angle the piece back at Ryker for a shot. Before he could manage it, Ryker thrust his knee into the man's ribs, growling, "You goin' down. Both a you gon' pay," just as a police car rounded the corner into the parking lot.

Ryker almost had the gun free when the bright lights of the patrol car blinded him, causing him to loosen his grip. The officers were out of the car, yelling "Freeze! Police! Drop your weapon," but it was too late. The gun went off.

Chapter 19

*There is stillness when danger is close; some mistake
the tranquil calm for peace. The bait is moving,
flicking itself, begging its prey to take the risk. If
only fish had a cerebral cortex that could register fear,
pain, or danger, then the decision to risk would be
easier to make.*

Anna Rae Roark

Why didn't they meet me? Why won't they answer their phones?
It had been a few days since I met with Jack and Ryker.
We were supposed to meet at St. Timothy's on Wednesday
around 1:00 p.m., almost three weeks since my last interview
with them. I waited thirty or forty minutes. Neither of them
showed. It wasn't like Jack or Ryker.

I called Jack's cell phone and got his voicemail, then
Ryker's and there was no answer. I kept trying, intermittently,
throughout the day and into the evening, hoping for an
explanation, but there was no answer. I thought about the
intense interview Ryker and I had the last time we met.
Maybe he was insulted by the implications I made about him
using Jack, although I didn't get that impression. He seemed
surprised I was so blunt, but not especially concerned. My
instinct told me he was fascinated with my insightfulness
about his life, but knew enough not to open up until he was
entirely sure he could trust me.

Something had to have happened. I couldn't shake the
bad feeling that Ryker was in trouble. Jack mentioned Angela
was pregnant again, the last time we talked. After Ryker and
my conversation about Rycobi being a surprise, I was

concerned he wouldn't take the news well. Once was an oops, but twice? It put a lot of pressure on him before and it made no sense to have it happen again. He'd been back in his job for a few months and already they were adding another child to the mix? *Not good,* I thought, but none of my business.

Still, the first time he found out she was pregnant, he freaked out and ended up trying to score because he didn't think they could make it on his paycheck. *Had he lost it when she told him she was pregnant again?*

I asked Jack why she told him before telling Ryker and he said they hadn't been getting along. Since he had been released, his temper flared more often than before, and she was so tired from being up with the baby and taking care of Junior and Malcolm too, she was out of patience. When he came home, she had hoped this meant she would have help. Jack said he had been distant and picking up extra shifts, as if to avoid coming home. My mind was rambling. This could just be a miscommunication. *If so, why do I have this terrible, sick feeling in my stomach?*

I called each of them again. No answer. My mind continued to take me through the scariest scenarios: Ryker disappeared on Jack, he's hurt or dead somewhere, he's been picked up for possession. *Where the hell were they? Writing the story had been like a lifeline for both of them, keeping Ryker on the right track and Jack inspired. What was happening?*

Several days passed and I still hadn't heard from them so I continued to leave messages on their voicemails. By this time, I hadn't slept much. I kept going over my notes from my last interview with Ryker. Accusing Ryker of selling through his people was bold. He had barely begun to trust me. Still, instinct told me he *was* still dealing, maybe not directly, but through his connections. His silence left me wondering if I had hit on something. *Ah. Where is he and why isn't Jack answering?*

Several days later, I got a call from Jack.

"Listen, I'm callin' 'cause I need you to pray for Ryker." His tone lowered with every grave syllable. I had been right, I thought. "He, uh. He's been shot," Jack said, his voice breaking. I was sure I heard him wrong. "Anna Rae, are you there?"

Swallowing hard, I felt my stomach lurch and my hand instinctively covered my mouth. When I could manage it, I cleared my throat so I could try to respond. "Wh-what? What happened? Talk to me."

"He was lucky. The bullet hit him less than an inch above his kidney, but below his spine. He was real lucky. If it had been lower, the bullet would have caused kidney failure. Any higher, he would have been paralyzed. Either way, he was lucky he didn't die."

"Who did this? What happened?" I was sure his gang connections or his enforcing days had caught up with him. Where had he been when he was shot? Who was he with?

"We don't know. Sarah and I were at church when it happened. We rushed over to JPS when we heard. It's bad. He said he didn't know the guy who shot him, but, I don't know. I just don't know. I have to go now. Pray -- for the love of God, Anna Rae -- pray."

What if I was right? I thought as I hung up the phone. *What if he was selling again and the deal went sour? Worse, what if I'm wrong and one of his people decided to off him because he left the business?* Nothing she was thinking was good.

Ryker James, Jr.

I didn't even feel the bullet when it hit. I was so angry. Ain' nobody ever git the drop on me befo'. Ain' never happen. It was a good thang it wasn't the kind a bullets we use. Hollow points' silver bullets that explode on impact. If he'd a been packin' h-points, I'd a been dead. I ain' come d'is far to die.

Terrence was pretty shook up. We know'd it wadn' no accident. He called the crew. He was pretty pissed off. He said he took cur of it. "Threats like this have to be dealt with," he said. I felt like I's standin' outside myself again, like in a' dream. Somebody tryin' to kill me and I can't lock out the rage comin' for me.

Jack Lawrence

I think he knew the guy that took him down that night. He kept saying it was a random thing, but it doesn't add up. I feel like I have taken Ryker as far as I can. He has a job and he's saying that merging my world with his is more than he can handle. I don't know where we go from here. There is something going on with him and if he won't tell me, I can't help him. Sarah and I have told him that we will be his family, but he keeps saying he can't turn his back on *his* family, not completely, and we understand that. We never expected him to walk away from them for good.

If I'm honest, the shooting was a wakeup call for Sarah and me. He was out clubbing and drinking with one of the guys he used to hang out with on the south side. My gut tells me this guy, Terrence Booker, was someone Ryker used to do business alongside. This shows he is willing to keep certain friendships, even if they could trigger his old habits. I reminded him that his choices affect every bit of progress he makes, but the line he walks between his past life and the new one he's trying to forge is getting harder to see. I feel like he keeps going back to what he knows and then he is slapped down, hard, by people he used to feel he could trust. Each time, he says he understands it was a mistake to try to stay in contact, but then he either can't stay away from them or they won't leave him alone. I don't know which it is. Something has hold of him.

Several months later

"Anna Rae, it's Ryker," he said, his words slurred.

"What? Ryker? Hello? Are you okay?" she said when she heard him trying to talk. She couldn't understand him so she talked over him. "Where are you? Ryker. Stop. Where are you?"

"I'm at the church," he said. She could hear him sobbing, but she couldn't make out his words.

"Are you hurt?" she asked. "Listen to me. I'm on my way. Stay at the church. Don't go anywhere, you hear me?"

She hung up, grabbed her keys and yelled for her kids. They came barreling down the stairs and got into the car. There was no time to even lock the door. She drove to the church more quickly than ever before. She was sure Ryker had been in an accident, that he was hurt, that he was …. She couldn't bear to think about it. She just had to get to him.

Remembering that Father Rayford knew Ryker, she called him and asked him to meet her there. If he was in trouble, then she could ask Father Rayford to help with her kids while she got help for Ryker.

Father Rayford answered and she explained quickly. He said he would be ready to grab the kids from the parking lot as soon as she pulled in and would take them into the church until she could talk to Ryker.

When she pulled into the parking lot, Ryker's truck was there. He was in the back of it, beer cans all over the bed of the truck.

"Tell me what happened," she said. "Ryker, look at me," she yelled when he didn't respond.

"You's was right," he slurred, rubbing his head and trying to get up. "I's needs help."

The rest of his words were slurred and nonsensical but she began to slowly discern what he meant. He was showing her his addiction. He was lying in the truck, forcing her to witness what he had been hiding.

She swallowed hard. It was horrific to see the intensity of his pain amplified by the alcohol and whatever drug was in his system. She feared he could hurt himself. She feared he was suicidal.

This was her fear talking. Calling Jack was the only answer, no matter what Ryker said or what he wanted. Calling Jack was the way to go. She grabbed her cell phone and dialed his number.

"Yeah, hello?" he said.

"Jack?" she said, her voice shaking and faint.

"Anna Rae? Are you okay?" and everything spilled out of her; the things she'd said in the interview, everything. "Okay, okay. Slow down and tell me," he said.

Chapter 20

In the ocean, the continental shelf drops off at the edge of the reef, about twenty to thirty feet. Even so, fish swim to the drop-off and beyond, exploring the coral canyons below. Predators frequent the edge of the reef, just waiting to attack.

"I's so tired," Ryker managed to say when Jack arrived and saw him. "I need help. Ever'thing too much."

"Then, that's what we'll do. I'm going to get Father Rayford. We'll drive you. Let's get you some help," Jack said, nodding curtly at Anna Rae. She waited for Jack to come back with Father Rayford. Together, they drove Ryker to John Peter Smith Hospital, and he signed himself into rehabilitation.

Ryker stayed in rehab until he was well enough to go home, about thirty days. Jack and Sarah visited him regularly, encouraging him to work the program. While he was gone, Jack was able to get Wellington Nursing Home to hold his job until he returned. He and Sarah helped Angela with the kids as well.

"Do you think he's going to be all right?" Sarah asked Jack, after they came home from Ryker's place. They had taken dinner to them.

"I don't know," Jack said. "He was different tonight, don't you think?"

"Yeah, I do," Sarah said. "He was calm and he seemed comfortable in his own skin for the first time."

"He was happy, too," Jack said. "I think he's getting very close to that place."

"That place?" Sarah asked.

"You know, the one our kids got to, where they don't need us to weigh in on everything. I've always known we could only take him so far. That's why I told him he had to be willing to help himself. I've given him the resources to stand on his own. He's got a place to live, transportation, and a job. Coming clean was the last step, I hope."

"You know," Sarah said, carefully. "I think we're there."

"I hear you," Jack said. "I can't take him much further. Beer costs money and so does whatever he's been using. I've been helping him with rent, food, and transportation, paying for gas when he needs it. Maybe it's time for him to understand we can't do it anymore. I'm not saying we won't continue to love and support him, but maybe we pull back on everything else."

"Well, if you weren't saying this, I would be," Sarah said, relieved. "I think we need to let him go."

Jack looked up, not quite ready to go that far. "You mean …."

"I mean," she interrupted, not letting Jack finish. "He's had six years of us being there for him. We need to think how we would treat one of our own kids at this point. For all intents and purposes, he's our son, and we wouldn't let one of our own kids keep up this kind of craziness. We would have cut the cord and told them to sink or swim," she said, folding both arms across her chest.

She didn't wait for Jack's response. She walked passed him and into their bathroom, closing the door behind her, abruptly.

Jack sat in his recliner, leaned back. He prayed. *Dear God, is she right? Are we at the end of our road together, Ryker and I? I feel like we have been on this road for so long, I'm not sure where he begins and I end. I want to do right by him, but maybe getting him through his second strike, a near-death shooting, and rehab is enough. Maybe it's time for him to pick up and walk on his own. I don't know, but Lord I'm tired. I'm so tired.*

Over the course of the next three months, Jack and Sarah began to disengage the amount of time they were spending with Ryker. Because Ryker's truck had become more of a liability than a form of transportation, Jack decided to help

Ryker get a vehicle that he could rely on. He sold his Uncle Pete's Remington 12-gauge shotgun for about $550 and his deer rifle with an expensive scope on it for about $250 so he could purchase a used van. Once he and Jack had the van looked at and some decent tires put on it, Jack told Ryker he couldn't help him any more financially. Ryker was grateful and he told Jack he appreciated all that he had done for him.

As Jack stood there, watching Ryker climb into the Econoline Ford van, a silence blanketed any words Jack could think to say. It was as if he knew God was saying to release him. Ryker looked back at him, nodded and swung the driver's side door closed.

"Jack," Ryker said, swallowing hard, not realizing the words he wanted to say would be so hard to get out. "I'm so grateful for you and Sarah, for all the people who have been helpin' me all this time. I don't mean to show no disrespect, but I need to try things on my own for a while. I gon' keep in touch, but Daddy D say Angela and me can rent the house on Evans, near his place, and I want a go back and live there."

"Okay," Jack said, not expecting it to be as easy as it was. "I reckon I understand."

"I think," he said, looking ahead, out the windshield of the van, "I need to know I can do it, even without you. I need to try to figure out some a my struggles on my own. I done well here but I feel like I ain' ever gon' know I can do this, stand on my own, if I don't go. I don't know if it make sense."

"Yeah, actually, it does," Jack said reluctantly. "Sarah and I have talked about it, and neither of us wants to see you go, but we know you need to be your own man, without our input or interference, as the case may be. I just want you to be okay and I want you to know we're here for you. Never forget that."

"Jack, you the father I never had. And Sarah been the best mother I could ever ask for. I don't know how to thank you but I *will* make you proud. I want to make you proud of all that we done together. Tell Anna Rae I said thank you for believing in me and understanding me so well, giving me a chance."

"I'll do it," he said, put a hand on his arm for what he knew might be the last time for a while. "You know she's going to publish our story, if she can."

Ryker nodded, rolled up the window and started the van. He waved at Jack, nodding again and putting his hand over his heart. Jack responded in kind.

As Ryker drove off, Jack let his head fall to his chest. *Dear God, watch over him.*

When he looked up and watched the van go, he felt tears sting his eyes and start to spill over. He took a cloth handkerchief from his breast pocket and wiped at his eyes and nose. He was not only crying because Ryker was leaving but because he knew Ryker wasn't out of the woods yet. This sudden need to leave brought about more concern. Jack could feel it in his chest. The muscles around his heart were tightening and he knew he needed to fight Ryker about leaving but he had run out of strength.

Jack hadn't told Ryker, but he had been having chest pains and his blood pressure had been unmanageable over the course of the last several months. The stress of Ryker being shot hadn't helped. Sarah finally got him to go see his physician, Doctor Gates, and after several tests, they determined he was going to need bypass surgery. The last visit was not good news. Dr. Gates recommended a triple bypass.

As Jack stood there, his hand on his heart, he began to feel the pain in his chest worsen. His arm went numb and he felt shortness of breath. When Sarah opened the door and saw him standing there, she knew, too, but didn't catch him in time.

Chapter 21

I want to swim back to the calm, serene waters, but I
feel an extreme pull from a strong undertow. It
makes my muscles strain; I feel strangely exhilarated,
stronger for being here.

Ryker stopped by the apartment and gathered the boxes he and Angela had put together for the move. Angela had taken the boys to her mother's house and he was supposed to pick her up later that afternoon. As he took the highway toward his granddaddy's house on East Powell and Evans, he thought about Jack. He looked in his rearview mirror, half-expecting Jack's car to come up on his left side, but when he saw the traffic behind, he shook his head, knowing it was crazy to think that.

I need to know I can do this on my own, he thought. *Is that really why? Or, am I just leaving 'cause things got too hard? I can't just act like my family don't exist. Daddy D been good to me all my life and he ain' sellin' drugs -- ain' never sold 'em. If I could just hang with him and Lelah, then I's gon' be fine. Angela and her git along good; Trina' another story, but I gon' talk to her; 'xplain thangs. We been over a long time. It gon' be good for her to meet Angela and try to 'cept it. Yeah, it gon' be good for all of us.*

As he got off the highway, he saw Daddy D's house and the field across from it. There, beside the field, was the rent house he said Ryker and Angela and the boys could stay in. It looked okay. It wasn't anything fancy, but it was the home he was used to. Daddy D was sitting on the front porch, waiting.

When Ryker got out, Daddy D said, "Hey boy, long time no see," and he smiled at him. Walking into his embrace,

Ryker felt the frailty of the old man. When he stepped back, Daddy D looked behind him.

"Where's your shadow, boy?" and he laughed. "You know, the angel. Jack?"

"He at home, Daddy D," Ryker said, realizing he had come with Jack almost every time in the past, when he *did* come for a visit, which had been few and far between as of late. Jack and Daddy D were good friends, as Jack was with all of Ryker's family.

Lelah stepped out onto the porch and took Ryker into her arms for a hug.

"Hey, Mama," he said. "How things goin'?"

"Not too good a couple houses down, but good from right here," she said.

"So, Trina not happy 'bout me movin' back?" he asked.

"Oh, she's happy you're back, but not with Angela," Lelah said.

"She know we over," he said, shaking his head and watching Lelah's expression to make sure she knew, too.

"That don't mean she accept it," Lelah said.

"Well, she gon' have to," he said. "Angela and me together and we got kids, too. She and I was a teenage thing and I know we been together since, but not no more."

"I can't go there with you. You gon' have to talk to her and spell things out," Lelah said, raising her eyebrows to clarify.

"A'ight, I can do that," he said. "Angela gon' be at her mom's tonight and I can stop by and square things. I don't need them coppin' attitude and scarin' the boys with all they fightin' and name-callin'. You know how Trina can be."

"Yes, I do, but boy, you need to be clear. No flirtin' or encouragin' her, like you done in the past. You git me?"

"Yes, ma'am. Loud and clear," he said.

Ryker excused himself and started unloading boxes and carrying them into the house across the street, diagonally from Daddy D's. As Daddy D watched him go, Lelah pushed her hair back away from her face. She had a beautiful, porcelain-doll-like complexion, still. Her auburn hair was graced with bits of gray, but her Caucasian-Mexican descent gave her face this beautiful olive complexion that brought out her green eyes. She was fortunate to have only a few creases here and there, revealing her age in subtle ways. Trina looked just like her when she moved in with her mother, next door to Daddy D, all those years ago. She was fifteen or sixteen at the time. Ryker had just gone to live with his dad, but visited often enough that Trina and he had become good friends. Then, Trina's wild side took them to a whole new level of closeness, using marijuana and cocaine together.

When Ryker heard Lelah's words, he knew she was right. It was time he explained things to Trina with no chance of a misunderstanding. The truth was he wasn't sure he could break ties with her. They went way back and some of the time, she was the reason he was able to deal with everything going on around him. He owed her, to some extent.

As he looked out of the front window of the rent house, he could see Trina walking through the front room of her mother's house and into the den, just off the kitchen. *How I gon' tell her she and I can't be nothin,'* he thought. *So much gon' down around us. She been like the one person who been in my life for the last sixteen years. We been through times when I was running, times when I was in jail, times when I couldn't talk to nobody 'bout nothin'. She seen me through. I seen her through. No strings. Now it all changed.*

His cell phone rang.

"Hey," he said, when he heard Angela's voice. "What's goin' on?"

"Where are you?" Angela asked.

"I'm at our place," he said.

"Are you alone?" she asked, accusingly.

"Yeah, why?" he asked. Then, realizing what she was implying, he said, "Trina and I are over, Angie. I told you. We over."

A month or so passed and Ryker and Angela were settling into the rent house. Trina wasn't around very often. Lelah said she was staying away on purpose. He needed to talk to her soon because Angela was convinced he was still seeing her.

Angela would wake in the night and he would be gone. A couple of times, she looked across the street, wondering if he was there, even though the van was gone and she knew he was probably out driving. His habit was to take a drive when he was restless and unable to sleep. Still, she envisioned him parking a street over and sneaking over to Trina's house. The next morning, she would question him, watch his reaction and dissect his answers.

He knew, with each day that passed, he needed to tell Trina the deal, explain there was no chance of them getting back together. He decided to go out one night and see if he could find her. She used to frequent a club just off Riverside. It was a dive, but Trina knew people there and he could almost always expect to find her there when he used to visit from time to time.

When he walked into the club, he looked around and there were so many familiar faces. Each one nameless, as this was the best way to do business. A nod or an inconspicuous exchange was the communication. There were code phrases they used to communicate a score would happen or not happen, based on the action and the word on the street. He sat down at the bar and ordered a beer. The bartender walked over and threw down a napkin. Seeing it was Ryker, he raised his chin in acknowledgement and cut his eyes to the back table. That was when Ryker saw her.

When he took his beer to her table and sat down, she didn't look at him.

"What's goin' on?" he finally said.

"You tell me," she said. "You back?"

"Yeah, but it's complicated," he said, still neither of them looking at each other.

"It usually is," she said.

"So we keep it cool, right?"

"Naw, you in or you out."

A long moment passed and he glanced around the room. Familiarity began to take on a comforting feeling that wrapped itself around him, awakening the power that used to go with it -- the game, the challenge, the danger, the thrill of the score. He tried to shake off the feelings, pretend he wasn't interested, but the flashes of the past played through his mind, reminding him of his days on the edge. They were good times, some of them. He glanced at Trina and she met his gaze, gave a half-smile. Neither spoke, but they knew those days weren't over, not yet.

Over the next few weeks, he jumped back in, full force. He worked from 7 a.m. to 6 p.m. at the nursing home and then ran scores from two apartments downtown. He had asked Trina to live part of the time in one of the apartments, meeting his people and sending them out to score, while another lady was living in the other apartment, doing the same. He took late-night drives to the meets, making the exchanges and returning before Angela was awake. As he drove toward the house from Evans Street one night, he looked across the way and saw Trina cross in front of the window in the front room of Lelah's house.

Flashes of the past few weeks were already haunting him. *What am I doing? I don't want this life.* Flashes of Jack and Sarah seeped through the cracks in his resolve, moments when he felt them asking about his day or if he needed anything.

He looked at his phone. Scrolling through the caller ID, he came across a call from Jack, then one from Sarah, another from Sarah. It was midnight. Too late to call, but the number on the screen brought on a sick feeling. They called three times within the same hour. *Had something happened? Jack and Sarah usually leave a message and there was nothin'.*

He sat, staring as Trina walked past the window again. She stopped for moment, looked out, as if she felt him somehow. *That's how we been all these years. It so natural for us to feel each other. I done walked right back into the darkness and didn't even feel it. Told myself I could deal and stay in control. What the hell am I doin'? I got to end this, now, before I lose ever thang.*

He parked a block down, got out and walked between the houses to get to her door. As he rounded the corner of the house to the patio outside the kitchen door, he saw her get up from watching television. When she started to open the refrigerator door, she glanced over her shoulder and she could see him through the window beside the door frame. She opened the door and he was leaning on the frame, his boot resting on the stoop.

"Hey," he said, his voice silky and a bit rough at the same time.

"Hey," she answered shortly, turning her head quickly, as if uninterested.

"Can I come in?" he asked.

She stood back and gestured with one arm, letting it fall to her thigh as if to let him know he was interrupting her show.

"I came to talk," he started in. "I'm done, Trina."

"You what?" she said, smiling with a wicked grin much like she used to when they were seeing each other all the time. "What? Your little lady can't handle you, the real you?" she smirked.

"Naw. It ain' like that," he said. "I just ain' the same man no more."

"What? You sayin' your new family' more important than what we have all these years?" Her voice had an edge to it.

"Maybe I am," he said, not sure if she was ready to hear what he had to say. When he saw her eyes, he knew he had started it and better finish it. "No, I am sayin' that. I left the dealin' for a reason, and I'm done. I never wanted this and I …."

His cell phone rang and he looked at the caller ID. It was Jack. He silenced the ring and turned back to her. "Look, I know we go way back and I cur 'bout you. I always gon' cur 'bout you, but …."

Before he could finish, she was on him, kissing him hard and pulling at his clothes, grabbing him and wrapping herself around him, pressing herself against him. He grabbed her arms and pulled her back. She smiled that wicked smile and licked her lips, raising one eyebrow.

Realizing he had been swept up in the kiss as well, he shook his head to clear his mind.

"I can't do this," he said. "Angela and me, we got a family together. Now, I know it's hard 'cause we livin' so close."

She broke free and swiped at his face, her nails catching his cheek and drawing blood. When he grabbed her wrists, she screamed for him to let her go. He did so, concerned he had hurt her when he clutched her wrists, but then she swiped at him again, raking her nails over his face and across his neck. He backed up and said, "I'm sorry. I can't do this. I'm with Angela."

She backed him up against the tiny windows that framed the side of the door, slammed her fist toward his chest, but when he moved away, her fist crashed through the bottom window. Seeing she was bleeding, he tried to come toward her, reaching out to help her, but she swiped at him again, all the while screaming that he had lied to her. They were supposed to be together and he had lied. He'd moved his two-bit girlfriend across the street and was forcing her to watch them be together. "You smug, son of a bitch," she yelled.

He backed away and walked out of her yard and back to the van. He drove the rest of the way to his house, opened the van door and started to get out. Catching his reflection in the rearview mirror, he tried to wipe away the blood. *It was a huge mistake to think I could go back home,* he thought. *Nothing can ever be the same once you leave, and I did leave.*

He looked down at his phone and saw Angela and Jack had called. Listening to the first message, he heard Angela's voice, asking him to come home. He could tell she had been crying because she woke up and he was gone. *How am I s'posed to explain things to her? I didn't know I had even fallen back into my ways. It was like I was on autopilot or something.*

He glanced out the window at Trina's house. He knew she was hurt and angry. He wanted to see if she was okay, but he knew he couldn't. It would just make things worse.

He stood and closed the van door. He needed to get inside and talk to Angela. As he walked toward the house, he flipped through his keys to find the house key and heard sirens. *Just like old times,* he thought. I'm not home for any time and there's already somethin' goin' down. He started to go inside, but the sirens got louder, coming toward their street.

Within a few minutes, the Fort Worth PD rounded the corner off Evans Street and blocked his driveway. He turned to see them coming up to the house. *What the hell was this? I*

*ain' done nothin'. Ain' no way they can charge me with nothin'. Ain'
nothin' on me or in the van.*

The officers walked right up to him and said, "Mr. Ryker
James, you have the right to remain silent, anything you say
can and will be used against you in a court of law."

"What're you doin'?" he yelled. "I ain' done nothin'."

As they forced his head facedown onto the back of the
police car, he pushed up and looked across the street. Trina
stood at the window, arms folded across her chest, her hand
bandaged from where she had broken the window. *She done
this. She done called the police on me.*

His phone was ringing again. It fell to the porch when the
officers cuffed him. It was Jack. It kept ringing and ringing.

Chapter 22

Who will survive this moment, you or the fisherman?
When I think of being on the 'hook,' my perception
is always depending on one thing. Who is the one at
the other end of the line?

Jack was rushed to the emergency room at Harris Southwest on Harris Parkway. Sarah was trying to stay calm as she rode in the ambulance. She called her brother, Charles, and his wife, Elizabeth, when she arrived in the ER.

"Charlie, it's Sarah," she said. "It's Jack. He's had a heart attack, I think. Please come. Please come now. We're at Harris Southwest."

As she waited, she tried to call Ryker. No answer. She tried again and again, but still no answer. Just as she was about to dial again, Charles and Elizabeth came through the ER double doors and immediately looked around the vast waiting room for Sarah. When they saw her, they rushed forward and held her tight.

"How did it happen?" Charlie asked. "What are the doctors saying?"

"He's being prepped for a triple bypass," Sarah said.

"Well, all right," Elizabeth said, calmly. She had been through this with Charles not so long ago. His situation had been touch and go, but she held it together and prayed him through it. "I'll call Father Rayford and get him on the prayer list. It's going to be all right. We're here and we're going to pray him through it. That's all there is to it," she said.

About an hour later, Father Rayford had come, along with several other friends Sarah had called. Within another hour, there were about two dozen of their closest friends, gathered in the waiting room, praying and quietly encouraging Sarah. It was another three hours before the doctor came out and gave any news.

"Mrs. Lawrence?" Dr. Gates said, interrupting her conversation with Charles and Elizabeth.

"Yes," she said, getting to her feet. "How is he?"

"He's going to be fine. He's still in recovery. I expect him to be out for several hours, but you're welcome to go sit with him. I don't think I need to tell you to limit his visitors and any stress for the next couple of days."

"No, no. I understand," she said.

It was about ten days later and Jack had finally been released. Sarah took him home and got him settled. She waited on him hand and foot, trying to minimize his stress, but he was as stubborn as an ox. She finally told him she would let him go to church, if he promised to take things really slow. It had been two weeks ago, Wednesday, when she promised that. He did well to make it to his follow-up visits with Dr. Gates. It took a little more than a month before he could get to the 10:30 Mass at St. Timothy's.

As he made his way up the walk, he turned to see Anna Rae and Wayne walking toward him. "Hey, Jack," she said, reaching to hug him. "I heard you had surgery. Are you all right?"

"Yeah, I did." His gravelly voice sounded like he was gargling. "But, I'm okay. I can't tell you how much I needed to see you here today. I didn't know I'd make it, but church isn't the same, ever, without you," he said, smiling through his tears.

"Oh, Jack. Thanks." She blinked hard so as not to join him, but as he cried she let a tear fall. "I had to check on you, you know? You're pretty special to me and I wanted to also tell you -- I'm almost done with the story."

"What?" he said, perking up a little bit. "I, I can't believe it. I knew you said you were working on it, or at least, Wayne said you were, but I had no idea …." His voice trailed off.

"Yes, I'm really excited about it. I think it's going to be good, and I promised I would make it happen."

"You've made my whole week -- my whole year! I can't tell you what this means to me. I, I guess you need to know Ryker is gone."

"What? Where is he? When?" she stammered, not able to believe what she was hearing. *Where would he go, and why?* She thought.

"Well, he decided to go live with some of his family. He's still in Fort Worth, but living over by Daddy D."

Anna Rae was silent for several moments, looking into Jack's eyes, hers darting back and forth. She knew this wasn't good news. Seeing Jack's face, still pale from his surgery, she could tell he wasn't happy about it either.

"Okay," she said, trying not to feel the anger well up inside.

"Yeah," Jack said, both their disbelief and frustration present though neither of them were acknowledging it. "He said he needed to do things on his own." Jack rubbed against his clenched jaw. When he realized he let some of his irritation seep through, he tried to quickly recover, saying, "But we're still keeping in touch and it's uh, it's going to be okay, I think." So much false hope reverberated in his hollow words that she reached out, hugged him, and held tight for a few moments. When she released him, he was smiling but it never reached his eyes or his heart, and she knew he was worried.

There was good reason.

On the way home, she was fuming. "What the hell is Ryker thinking?" she yelled out loud, needing to vent the rage welling up with every second she considered where he was and what he was doing. *What has all of this been for if he can just run off and go back to dealing. It doesn't matter. I can't worry about this. I've finished the book for Jack and that's what matters. I made the promise to Jack. Jack, not Ryker. Well, yes, Ryker, too, but I hate this. I hate this for Jack and Sarah. How am I supposed to finish this book and publish it, knowing that the man we have all been pulling for has gone back to -- okay, I don't know that for sure but I highly suspect it.*

What the hell? Gone to live with his family. WE, Jack, Sarah and I, are his family. How could he do this?

Chapter 23

I should go back to the bank. My mind plays tricks on me. Does swimming close to the stiller waters mean I am weak? Should I stay in the rougher climate to prove I can?

Ryker James, Jr.

"Jack, it's me," he said. "I need you to listen to me and before you say anything, let me git it all out, okay?"

"Okay, I'm listening," Jack agreed.

"I'm in jail in Fort Worth for burglary, and before you say anything, I'm innocent. You got to admit, all the times before, I's guilty a somethin' even if the cops git it wrong, I's still responsible for some of the things they sayin' I done, but this time, I didn' do it." Ryker tried to keep his voice calm. He couldn't believe he was saying all this either. He had to consider how it sounded to Jack. "Look it, I was tellin' Trina thangs was over 'cause she was given Angela a hard time and, I *was* givin' mixed messages, but when I went over there and told her, she went crazy, scratchin' and clawin' at me. I thought she lost her mind. So, I told her I's sorry and I left.

Next thing I know, the police show up and arrest me for trespassin', sayin' she reported me breakin' and enterin' her house and stealin' her television. I ain' done no such thing. I's tryin' to do right by her, explain I was with Angela and that we ain' a thing no more."

"Anyhow, I been appointed a lawyer. I'm in Mansfield, and I need bondin' out. My lawyer think I'm guilty 'cause a my record and he ain' even come see. I got these letters from him, sayin' he gon' visit me, but he ain' comin', Jack. This my third strike. If I go down, I ain' comin' out. I didn' do this. Please help me. I don't know what else to do."

"I'm gon' tell you the truth. I went back 'cause I thought I could deal with everything and git my life back with my family, not dealin' drugs, just check on things.

"That's who I am. It's what I do. Takin' cur a them is my whole life. How I s'pose to stop that?

"When I seen Trina, I realize she the worst part a my addiction to that life. She and I started everything -- the drugs, the sex, the craziness -- we done all that together. As soon as I seen her and she start tryin' to take me back to dealin', that's when I know. I know'd I had to stop. I felt it, deep inside. So I pull her off me and kind as I could be, I told her no. I told her I's with Angela. I know this may not make no sense to you, but I thought I's helpin' some a the people I done left behind. I thought if'en I help 'em, then I'd be more, more, uh ...."

"Deserving?" Jack finished.

Silence blanketed the conversation. Jack was hearing Ryker say he had gone home and ended up back in the same game. He all but turned the clock back to before they met and rejoined the life he led before. *I wonder what stopped him,* Jack thought. *Whatever it was, it was something deep-down. Maybe this was what had to happen,* he considered. *It would certainly explain why he had to go back into his old life -- he had to be sure he couldn't live the double life. As long as he had me, he had a safety net.*

He thinks I'm going to be that now. What do I do? Oh, Lord, what now?

"Jack?" Ryker said. "Are you there, Jack? Please, you have to believe me. I didn't break and enter or steal anything."

"I do," Jack said. "I believe that, son. What are you going to do about it?"

"I'm on fight the charges. I'm on prove I didn' do this," he said.

Jack smiled. It was the first time he had ever heard Ryker say he would fight for his innocence. All the times before, it was about pleading his sentence down. For the first time, Ryker had been charged with something he really hadn't done and he was fighting mad about it. *Well, all right,* Jack thought. *It's about time.*

He rubbed at his chest, his fingers tenderly feeling the scar from his triple bypass.

"Well, I'll try to get down there to see you. I've had a few things happen here and it may be a few days."

"Is you a'ight? I seen you called me. Sarah too."

"I've been in the hospital," Jack said.

"What? Jack. Is you okay?"

"I'm fine. Fine, fine. Just had a triple bypass." He tried to say it like it was just a thing he had to take care of.

"Oh, no. Jack." He pressed his fingers into his eyes hard. "Jack, don't, don't you worry 'bout me. Just take cur a you. You, you my family, Jack. You was who I was s'posed to be takin' cur a. Oh, Jack."

"Ryker, I'm fine. *Really.* I've been taking it easy and I'm okay. You hear me, son?"

"Yeah. I hear you," he finally answered, after several seconds.

"Who's your lawyer?" Jack asked.

"No. You needs to just …."

"Tell me who it is or I'll just have to find out on my own and you know I will."

"Bob Matthews," Ryker answered, knowing Jack wouldn't stop until he knew. "He think I'm guilty 'cause a my record, I know it."

"All right," Jack said, flatly. "I'll go by his office and see what I see."

Silence crept back between them, suppressing any judgment Jack felt, at least until he could talk to Matthews and see Ryker in person. The words *seventy times seven* broke through and lingered in his mind.

"I don't know what to say," Ryker said. "Just, uh, thank you."

When Jack hung up with Ryker, Sarah was standing beside him, arms wrapped around his shoulders. "What now?" she asked.

"He says he's innocent," Jack said. "All the times before, he was guilty and we were just trying to plead him down and teach him to do right. He says he didn't do it this time. He's fighting it," Jack said, incredulously. "That's something," he said, looking into Sarah's eyes. "That's something."

———◆———

It was 7:00 a.m. and Robert Matthews was sitting at his desk. The sign outside his office read, Robert L. Matthews, Attorney at Law: Criminal Defense. He stood about six-foot-two, with broad shoulders over a solid build. His salt and pepper hair was still wet from the shower he took after his 5:30 a.m. jog with a colleague. As he read through the file on Ryker James, he dictated a letter to be sent to Ryker, clarifying the status of his case. He also said he would visit Greenbay so they could discuss it.

Matthews had been on a court-appointed circuit for the last twelve or thirteen years of his thirty-five-year career in criminal law. His schedule was booked with back-to-back appointments, court appearances, and follow-up meetings. Sometimes his day began even earlier and lasted well past midnight. Matthews was thorough with his clients, no matter who they were. When he was assigned to someone, he did his absolute best to provide a sound, legal defense.

As he raked his hands through his damp hair, he thought about Ryker James. He saw him for the first time in Mansfield lockup. He was locked in a small holding cell with twenty or so other inmates. Every time a lawyer came to talk to one of them the other inmates chimed in with their "legal advice," spouting off legal jargon and just being a general nuisance. When Matthews called out to Ryker, he walked over, his shoulders squared and confident.

"Mr. James, my name is Robert Matthews," he began, "and I have been court appointed to your case. I trust you have received my letter and, given this is not your first rodeo against the law, I …."

"What?" Ryker interrupted. "You think I done this? I'm innocent, man. I didn't do this."

"Yeah," the other inmates shouted. "He's innocent. Fuck you, man."

Ignoring the others, Matthews looked at Ryker. "I would like to discuss your case and, as I said, you're looking at a minimum of fifteen to life. This is your third strike, according to your file," he said, trying to talk over the others and still communicate with Ryker properly.

"No way. I ain' doin' no fifteen years for somethin' I ain' done. I ain' guilty. Maybe you think I am 'cause all you lookin' at is my past, but I ain' done nothin' wrong and I ain' servin' no sentence." Ryker was yelling over the other inmates. The mood of the "jury" in the holding cell had turned sour, deciding Matthews needed to be raked over the coals.

"Look, Mr. James," Matthews said, calmly. He wanted to convey his next words in a clear and concise manner. "I need to speak with you about your case, but yelling at me isn't necessary. I'm here to defend you."

"I don't get that feelin'," Ryker interrupted.

"He ain' defendin' you, man. He tryin' to screw you over." The others added, yelling more obscenities and taking over the perceived fight Ryker was having with Matthews.

"I'm not here to," Matthews tried again, but didn't get to finish.

"Look it. I ain' done no breakin' or enterin'. You ain' been out to the place. If you was to go out there, you gon' see that!" Ryker continued yelling at the top of this lungs. When Matthews saw that he was getting nowhere, he turned and put the file back in his briefcase and ended the confrontation, while Ryker screamed from the holding cell for the next five minutes.

This was the first of three attempts Matthews made to talk to Ryker. He knew that the accommodations at Mansfield were limited. Other holding facilities allowed you to take your client to a smaller room, where you could discuss their cases one-on-one, without the audience he had at Mansfield, but Ryker was convinced Matthews had no intention of defending him. He attacked Matthews the second he walked up to the holding cell.

This was nothing new. Matthews had dealt with many clients who were pretty upset about their predicaments, but what made Ryker's situation a little different was that he had a history of repeat offenses. None of this was new to him and yet, he was acting as if it was his first experience being locked up. This had thrown Matthews. *What was it that made him think I wasn't going to defend him?*

Matthews rubbed his hands over his face, feeling stubble he'd missed when he shaved after his early morning run. It always annoyed him when he missed a spot. He glanced at the grandfather clock in the corner of his office; 7:20 a.m.

His thoughts turned to Eileen Jefferson and what she said the last time he saw Ryker in the holding cell.

"Bob, come with me," she said, leading him out into the corridor. Pointing to the top of her hand, she said, "I think you may need to consider that the reason you're not getting anywhere with this man is because he is of African-American descent. You have to know that many of these young, African-American men are often raised by single mothers or even grandmothers, and they aren't likely to listen to a white male. They simply don't trust you and it may or may not have anything to do with you. Perhaps it would be better if I take on his case," she said.

Matthews shook his head and recalled how surprised he was to hear her say that. *It didn't even cross my mind that his belligerence had to do with the color of my skin or my gender. I couldn't care less if he was black, white, Jewish, Muslim, Chinese, or Japanese. Still, that's what she thought. And, he did calm down when she came to talk to him. Maybe her being African-American and a woman did have something to do with it,* he thought.

Matthews had told her that he understood and would be glad to step aside, but for some reason, she didn't take on the case. He was still trying to talk to Ryker but he was so combative. He stood, getting up from his big leather chair and walked to the window. He loved the view of the sunrise over the Trinity River in the distance. This was the time of day when his thoughts seemed the clearest.

He watched a few joggers go by. Birds swooped low, gliding toward the embankment, where they spotted morsels a couple left on a park bench. Just as they came close, a squirrel was suddenly there, grabbing the crumbs. Matthews hadn't seen the squirrel; it had been in the shadows. Seeing the squirrel make off with the remnants, the birds swerved and flew away. Matthews looked back at the bench and his brows furrowed at what he saw. The squirrel hadn't taken all of the food, only what he needed. The birds had seen it too and were on their way back for a second pass. The remaining food was miniscule, but nevertheless viable. *Viable*, Matthews considered. *Synonyms of that would be feasible, possible, even worthwhile. Maybe I need to make a viable, second-pass too.*

Ryker had been transferred to the Green Bay Facility in north Fort Worth. Matthews needed to go to Green Bay and talk to Ryker. He had a little more than an hour before visiting hours began and if he could get him one-on-one, away from other cellmates, he might be able to really talk to him. *And, I would make time to do that, but I have no way of knowing if he's going to talk to me any different since he's been moved to Green Bay. The truth is the chances of him being innocent are miniscule,* he thought.

And as sure as he knew what he needed to do, he was also sure he wouldn't talk to Ryker today. He walked back to his desk and looked at his schedule. It was full, as usual. Glancing at his notes on Ryker, he saw something that prompted him to make one more pass through his file. *He's been arrested countless times for possession of an illegal substance, crack or cocaine in most instances. He's got two felonies under his belt and now this burglary. It doesn't play. Whatever his beef with me, I should have gone to see him. I guess I could try to get there early today. Looks like he's up against a $1,500 bond to get out. I could maybe get that down to $750. I know the magistrate and he's pretty fair.*

Still thinking things through, he picked up his empty coffee mug and headed for a refill. Just as he walked out of his office into the corridor, his administrative assistant, Grace Shelby, stopped him.

"Good morning, Bob. Here, I'll get you some more. I have a man here to see you," she said, taking his mug from him. "His name is Lawrence, Jack Lawrence. He says he wants to discuss one of your clients, Ryker James."

"Well, I guess, show him back to my office," he said. When she returned with his coffee, an elderly gentleman was standing behind her. Before he could introduce himself, the gentleman stuck out his hand and said, "Jack Lawrence," and Matthews felt obliged to take it.

"Mr. Lawrence," Matthews said, opening his mouth to speak again when Jack interrupted.

"Jack. You can call me Jack. I'm here on behalf of Ryker James.

"I'm sorry Jack, but I cannot discuss anything with you. Uh …."

"I know, client-attorney privilege," Jack added. "Still, you can listen to me, can't you?"

"Mr., I mean Jack, I have a full schedule today and one of the items on it is getting Mr. James bonded. So, if you'll excuse me," he said and gestured toward the door.

"I'm aware of that." Jack was not deterred. "This'll only take a minute."

Matthews saw that Jack was not going to be denied. He could see it in his eyes, so he sat down at his desk.

"Mr. Matthews, I met Ryker James about six years ago and to make a long story short, there isn't much I don't know about him. And, I know that his criminal record is extensive. I say this because I've been working with him to get him on a better path and help him turn his life around. I'm here to tell you that I've seen him through a felony sentence. Countless times he's been locked up for warrants or arrests and heck, he was even shot -- almost didn't survive that.

"Anyway, all of this is to say I thought you should know that in all the time he's been a career criminal, he's never said he was innocent." Jack let his words hang in the air. Matthews squinted, waiting for Jack's next words -- some kind of defense, or words of assurance, or proof of something to back up what he was saying, but there was only one more thing Jack added.

"I just thought you should know what all the noise he's making is about. For the first time, believe it or not, he's innocent," Jack finished. "Thank you for seeing me. I suppose I'll see you over at the courthouse." Jack turned to leave and heard Matthews clear his throat.

"It would help if your friend would listen to me. With all the yelling he does, I can't get a word in edgewise," Matthews said, raising his eyebrows to emphasize his point.

"I suppose that *is* considered disrespectful," Jack said, pausing. "But I must say, after all I've been through with him, and he is a good, good man, he has never shouted his innocence at the top of his lungs. I guess it's music to my ears," Jack said, shaking his head and chuckling. "But, I hear you and I'll relay your message."

Re: Cause No.1205163 -- Burglary Habitation
Court: Criminal District Court 3 -- Tarrant County
State of Texas vs. Ryker James

Dear Mr. James:

I am in receipt of your letter dated July 14, 2010, and received it in my office today, July 19, 2010.

I spoke to Jack Lawrence, your friend, who is planning to come and see you. **I did not and will not under any circumstances discuss the facts of your case with anybody other than you.** Your bond is set at $1,500.00 because you are a convicted felon and your charges of Burglary of a Habitation would have been 2-20 years in prison and up to a $10,000.00 fine if convicted; however, since you have been convicted of Possession of Controlled Substance and spent two years in TDC, the new charge is raised, if convicted, to no less than 5 years nor more than 99 years or Life in the penitentiary and a fine of up to $10,000.00. I am surprised that your bond is not higher.

I have enclosed a copy of the Complaint filed against you along with your Criminal History in Tarrant County, which is self-explanatory, and all that is available to me at this time until indicted.

Robert Matthews
Robert L. Matthews, Attorney at Law

Ryker James, Jr.

I received d'is letter from Mr. Matthews on the same day Jack come to see me. He say Matthews' was gon' try to bond me out and he's hoping to reduce it to seven-hundred-fifty dollars. Jack bring the police report and he was as shocked as me 'bout what it said.

"Jack, there ain' no name on this report. She didn't even say I's the one leavin' her property. Don't matter 'cause I didn't do anythang to her but still, there ain' nothin' on this report that say I done this and I'm sittin' here, in lock-up."

"Yeah, I see that," Jack agreed. "Matthews refused to discuss your case with me. He said you tore him a new one when he tried to discuss it with you."

"That's 'cause he was actin' like I done it. I didn' do this. He send me a letter, sayin' he gon' come see me when I'm transferred. Do you see him? He ain' been here yet," Ryker yelled, practically jumping down Jack's throat.

"Yeah, he said you've been yelling at him, just like you're hollerin' at me right now," Jack rolled his shoulders back, squaring them, ready for more of the same.

Ryker opened his mouth to let out another stream of anger when he realized what Jack had said. Nodding, he shut his mouth and banged his hand on the screen between them.

"I think you've got something here," Jack said, when Ryker put his hands on the top of his head, disappointed in himself for losing it. "You can prove Matthews hasn't properly represented you. The police report alone is evidence of that. But, I would stick with the paperwork and keep your voice down; *control* is important when you go before the judge; it shows respect, maturity. You don't have to listen to Matthews or me, but I think you've got a shot at getting out of here if you do."

Chapter 24

I suppose God's grace occurs in all species, sacrificing wants and desires in the moment for the good of someone or something else. Humans often take this to extreme, taking on the life of another and making themselves responsible for his or her choices. Strange, someone did that long ago at his Father's request.

When the hearing for the indictment took place later that day, Jack was sitting in the courtroom, waiting for Ryker to be brought in. He felt so much anxiety about what Ryker was going to say and do. He had done his homework and had every right to be upset, but if he didn't handle this right, it wasn't going to go his way. He wanted to understand why Ryker had gone back to Daddy D's house and even tempted himself with Trina.

Part of him knew, like Ryker had said, that he needed to be able to stand up to the people he had grown up with and yet, it was such a risk, given everything he had accomplished. Jack shuddered inside as the court was called into session. Ryker was standing there with his attorney and it was clear from the expression on his face he had not calmed down much since Jack last spoke to him. His eyes were intense.

Once the formalities were out of the way, Magistrate Anthony M. Rossetti turned to Matthews, waiting for his response. Matthews began to speak and Ryker listened to Magistrate Rossetti agree to a bond of seven-hundred-and-fifty dollars.

Just as he was about to move on to the next case, Ryker interrupted him.

"Excuse me, your honor."

"Mr. James, the bond has been set, down from fifteen hundred. Is there something else?" Magistrate Rossetti said, peering over his bifocals, perched atop his ample nose. The shadows under his eyes were reason to believe he was ready to get through his docket with little or no complications.

"Your honor, Mr. Matthews' not defending me," he said, evenly and calmly, reaching for his paperwork. "I got these letters d'at he sent me. They say he gon' come see me while I's at Green Bay. Ever' one a them say he gon' ax for no less than ten years and probation. Today' the first time I actually seen him since the letters was sent to me and he still ain' ax me if I'm guilty a the charge against me. The police report don't even name me for doin' the crime. It don't make no sense. I had to ax my father to get me a copy so I could be prepared today and I just wanted you to know that I deserve somebody who gon' fight for my innocence 'cause I *am* innocent."

"Your father," the magistrate said. "Is he here today?"

"Yeah, he right there," Ryker said as he pointed to Jack. Squinting, Magistrate Rossetti eyed Jack and then looked back at Ryker. Shaking off his instinct to question how this elderly white man could be the young black man's father, he turned to Matthews.

"Bob, is this true?"

Matthews felt a drip of sweat streak from the top of his head to the edge of his sideburns. He glanced at Ryker, unaware he took the time to read the letters in his hand, much less pay attention to the fact that Matthews had not come to see him. Thinking of the last few weeks, he started remembering scheduling problems and mishaps. He knew he'd missed a few things, but was shocked to hear the list being summarized by this young African-American man standing beside him. *He's telling the damn truth,* he thought.

"Yes, your honor," Matthews said, reluctantly. "I did say I would come see him, but we had some difficulty communicating three times prior to that. Still, he's right, I should have come to see him and talk about his case."

"Mr. James, are you saying you would like the court to appoint another attorney to defend you?" Magistrate Rossetti asked.

Ryker looked from Matthews to the magistrate and, with no hesitation, said, "No, your honor. I just want him to do his job and defend me."

Matthews turned and looked at Ryker, realizing he had every right to ask for another court appointment. Ryker returned the gaze and Matthews saw a slight nod, as if Ryker was giving him another chance.

"Mr. Matthews, how long have you served in this courthouse? Twelve years?"

"Yes, your honor, about that," Matthews answered, knowing his reasons for asking.

"I have to say, that in all my time on the bench, I have not heard anyone, who has a record like Mr. James', speak so well, *for himself,* in my courtroom." Rossetti paused, his right hand coming up to reset his glasses further back on his nose. "I would also venture to say this young man has expressed his concern, regarding his defense, quite respectfully, despite the fact that he hasn't received adequate representation. Quite frankly, he could have thrown you out with the bath water, so to speak, but instead, he's asking you to stick," Rosetti said, fixing his gaze on Matthews and raising his eyebrows for emphasis.

"Bailiff, is there anyone downstairs in the holding cell or the surrounding individual meeting rooms?" Rosetti asked, not taking his eyes off Matthews.

"No, your honor," the bailiff said.

"Well, Mr. Matthews and Mr. James, would you like to take some time and talk about your case, see if you two can make an effort to communicate a little better?"

Both men nodded.

"All right then," he said. "Mr. Matthews, why don't you and Mr. James take your time and talk through some of this, without the rest of us as a distraction."

When Ryker and Matthews walked down to the holding cells, the bailiff offered one of the smaller rooms, stationed around the large cell. Ryker looked at Matthews and walked into the large cell in the center of the room. Following, Matthews almost smiled because he felt the same way about being in small, confined spaces.

"Mr. James, if you would permit me to speak, without interruption, I would like to say something to you, okay?" Matthews began. When Ryker stayed silent, he continued. "I was wrong not to come see you and follow up on the police report. I should have gone out to the site and taken some pictures, looked at the statement and seen that you were not actually named in the accusations this Trina Jones made. I was wrong and I apologize for that.

"I also should have come out to Green Bay. There are no excuses for it. I guess I owe you an explanation. I, uh, tried to talk to you several times in the holding cell out in Mansfield and I know they don't have the same set-up as they do here, in this facility, but you kept yelling at me, no matter what I said. And then, Ms. Jefferson," he waved a hand in the air.

"Wait, who? The lady lawyer, who seen us fightin'?"

"Yes, that's the one," he cleared his throat and continued. "She said something to me, and, well, I need ask you about it."

"A'ight," Ryker answered.

"She said your attitude toward *me* may have had something to do with this," and he pointed to his skin. Ryker looked down at his arm and back up.

"Naw, it ain' about race, man. My granddaddy' been with a white woman the last twenty-somethin' years. Lelah' her name and her daughter, the one accusin' me a breakin' into her house and stealin' her TV, she white, too. We used to be together. That ain' never cross my mind."

"So, there's nothing about me, personally, that has offended you somehow," Matthews said, not really sure how to word what she'd said about him being male.

"Naw. My only problem was you thinkin' I's guilty and not comin' to see me and work out my defense."

"Well, all right then, because it didn't even occur to me that you might have a problem with regard to that, until Ms. Jefferson said her peace," Matthews said.

"*My* thang is, I'm innocent and I ain' gon' plead guilty to doin' nothin' I ain' done," he said.

"I hear you and after looking over your file, I'm going to make sure you don't," Matthews said. "I'm going to defend you, just like you asked. I know I was wrong not to do it before. I admit that and I'm sorry, Mr. James."

"Ryker," he said. "Call me Ryker. And, I'm sorry too. I should a listen to you."

As they went over the case, the stack of papers in the file being at least a foot high, Matthews was able to determine there were multiple holes in the story Trina told the police. It was agreed that Matthews would go out to the house and snap some pictures so they could show that it was impossible for Ryker to break in, steal her TV and carry the fifty pound dinosaur over a six-foot fence, sprint across the yard and conveniently stash it minutes before the police arrived to take him in, not to mention the fact that said TV was still in her house.

Within three hours, Matthews and Ryker had ironed out the details of the way they were going to proceed with his defense.

Given that this potential felony would have meant a third strike for Ryker, Matthews was determined to get the charge dismissed.

After seven years of giving Ryker every possible chance to live free, Jack sat in the courtroom that day, proud as could be, that Ryker fought for *his own life, for the first time*.

As Jack drove home from the courthouse, he thought, *He just may make it out*.

◆

"It was worth it to come down and bail Ryker out one more time," Jack said when he sat with Sarah, drinking a hot cup of coffee the next morning. "He spoke to the magistrate with respect, only asking for Matthews to do his job. It took guts to expose Matthews' lack of initiative with his case. Matthews knows practically every judge in that district.

"Ryker impressed everyone in the courtroom when he stood by Matthews, instead of asking the judge to get him another defense lawyer. Matthews wasn't expecting that," Jack said, chuckling a little.

"Sounds like he was well-prepared," Sarah clarified.

"That was it," Jack said. "He had his letters from Matthews, proof that Matthews hadn't come to see him at Greenbay. Can't beat that with a stick," Jack said.

"So, you think he has a chance of walking away from this potential third strike?" Sarah asked.

"Absodamnlutely!" Jack said. "He's out on bond and Matthews has done a complete one-eighty. He's seen the police report and knows Ryker couldn't have climbed that woman's six-foot fence carrying a fifty-pound television. I mean, how ridiculous is that?"

Chapter 25

*Now, I am swimming in different, unfamiliar waters.
I can still see the fisherman on the bank through the
clear water. I know he can see me. He is casting
sustenance into the clear water. There are no hooks
that I can see. Where are the hooks?*

I've got to call Anna Rae, Jack decided.

When he tried to talk to her a while back, she cut him off, saying she had finished the book and didn't want to know Ryker's most recent situation. She thought he had gone back to his old ways; either way, he'd taken a giant step backward.

What Jack didn't know was that Anna Rae had done some soul searching of her own while he and Ryker were sorting things out.

She'd spent five years interviewing Ryker, listening to his inner strife with regard to his past life and the one he was living now. When she learned he was trying to change his life for the better, she assumed he had tried professional counseling, but nothing had come of it.

After his addiction had been addressed, she learned that his going to the rehab facility at JPS was the first time he'd actually sought professional help for any reason and there had been no *real* counseling. With as many drug addicts who came through the rehab center on a regular basis, there was less than minimal opportunity for adequate counseling.

The truth was, she knew very little about addiction so she took a volunteer position at the Recovery Resource Center in Fort Worth. Her first day was a rude awakening to what Ryker's viable options were, whether he was there for physical or emotional addiction.

"Okay," the receptionist at the RRC said. "My name is Maria and I'll get you started in a few. I need you to listen to how I answer phones and then it's going to be you. Baptism by fire, honey. Focus, because I'm going to need you to jump in and learn everyone's extensions as well as procedure as quickly as possible. Oh, and F-Y-I, this may sound strange to you, but we have people who come to us strung out and using. They can be suicidal so wave someone over if you have to. There's no hold button for them, if you get what I'm sayin'," she said. Anna Rae started to laugh at the thought of it and then realized she wasn't kidding.

She watched for the first hour and a half, as Maria assisted the people who came in requesting services. There was a family of four, who came in. The mother and father seemed put-out the moment they sat down. The sister was on her I-Phone some of the time, then she switched to her I-Pad. The substance abuser came by herself to the desk. She signed her name on the list; her short, spiked hair almost as intense as her parents' glare. The girl smiled a half-smile and Anna Rae met it with an understanding return.

Anna Rae watched her return to her seat. She wore a men's t-shirt, a pair of Dockers shorts, huge combat boots and a men's running jacket. When Anna Rae let her gaze wander, inconspicuously to the rest of her family, she noticed her father was in business casual, her sister had on cheerleading shorts, everything matching from her hair bow to her cutesy socks and arm bands – bubblegum pink, with butterflies swirling about her bouncy pony tail. Ironically, her mother wore Capri pants, a tight, lime-green t-shirt and Cat-In-The-Hat socks and a matching hat. There were no words.

Maria interrupted her train of thought, saying "Could you call the next person back?" Anna Rae looked down, knowing the last person was this girl. She hadn't seen her name until this moment.

"Levi?" she called out to the waiting room.

"Leviticus," the Cat-In-The-Hat woman corrected. Anna Rae looked over at the girl. Her head dropped to her chest. Anna Rae wondered if there was any connection to the book in the Bible. *Sacrifice, significance of the anointed ones, clean versus unclean, day of atonement, ritual law, tradition, blessings versus punishments, vows… how creepy,* she mentally slapped herself. *It's a name. Yeah, a name that literally describes this poor child's need to escape it.*

"So, do you think you can handle the desk while I go to lunch?" Maria asked, when Anna Rae returned from taking Levi to the scheduling representative.

"Sure," Anna Rae said, her voice betraying her conviction.

"When I get back, Dr. Priestly, our director, would like you to visit with her in her office," Maria said over her shoulder as she grabbed her purse and sack lunch and headed for the break room.

"Excuse me," a frantic woman said, just as Maria stepped out of ear shot. "I need to know what to do. I was in last week and my son was given information from you people and he can't remember what he was told to do. Can you help me?"

Anna Rae hesitated. *Who do I direct her to speak with?* She was thinking. Before she could determine who, the woman continued.

"Look, I'm his mother," she placed a shaking hand over her heart. "I don't understand how you can keep information from me. I'm the one who found him."

"Found him?" Anna Rae wasn't following.

"Yeah, if I hadn't, he'd be dead. He took a lethal dose of heroin and what? I'm good enough to save his life, but I can't know what you people are instructing him to do? Withdrawal is a bitch and you say you don't have a bed for him right now so what am I supposed to do? Take a chance he could kill himself, again?"

"Uh, no, uh," Anna Rae stammered.

"Ma'am, could you follow me?" the scheduling rep interrupted. As they walked toward the office at the end of the hallway, Anna Rae turned to see Maria standing there.

"Doing okay?" she asked.

"Why can't a mother know her son's assessment and his information about recovery?" Anna Rae blurted out.

"Because said son is an adult. The law requires that we keep all of his information confidential, unless the patient signs a legal document, giving her permission to participate in the process."

"But he's not in," she held up a hand.

"His right mind, I know that's what she's told you, but we can only deal with facts. Until we determine she is not the problem, she is not allowed into his recovery."

"But, she said she found him, almost dead," Anna Rae said, incredulously. "Why would she sabotage his recovery? I mean, she's his mother…."

"She could also be his supplier. Wake up squeaky. Not everyone wants their child to grow up and be healthy and happy. Some parents want their kids to sell heroine and rake in the money. She may need him to stay addicted for a whole number of reasons and if she doesn't know how he's being treated, then," she stopped, when Anna Rae nodded.

"Then, she can't keep him addicted enough to sell, sober enough to stay alive."

"Hey, Pollyanna's got a brain," Maria teased. "Who do *you* think the law is coming after if we give out confidential info without that signature – a sober signature. 'You what? You gave Mommy his file? He's over eighteen. I'm so sorry, your funding has been cut. Liability is a real problem.' *I'm* going back to finish my lunch, okay? Okay."

Anna Rae made it through the lunch break, answering calls. She learned that there were an exorbitant number of addicts in a constant line for beds that were few and far between. The ones most in need of the bed won out. This meant if you were pregnant *and* an addict, your chances were much better of getting to the top of the list and it came down from there. *Where would Ryker be on this list?* She thought. *He's nowhere. He's not addicted or pregnant and emotional addiction doesn't even rate. He's doing pretty well, having had no professional help, ever.*

When she met with Dr. Priestly, she didn't expect to have sympathy for Ryker's situation, but after experiencing the way the state requires them to handle difficult situations related to alcohol and substance abuse, she suddenly had a much deeper understanding of things. *Ryker hadn't had access to adequate assistance and yet, he'd managed to get clean and sober. He's had some backsliding, but nothing that couldn't be turned around. He left the scene though. Didn't that mean he was going back to the life?*

"Anna Rae?" Dr. Priestly said, breaking through her mental recall of everything that had happened with Ryker up to this moment. "You wanted to ask about your friend."

"Yes, I've been quite concerned," and she quickly brought Dr. Priestly up to speed on everything leading up to Ryker's recent situation. "So, when Ryker said he wanted to go back to his family, should I have been concerned or not?"

"Well, it's not really that simple. Often, people in Ryker's situation need to face their family; confront the triggers so to speak. It's not uncommon for someone in his place to want to leave and start completely over," she said. "It's hard to start fresh if people aren't accepting of your new life."

"So, his leaving," Anna Rae pressed for understanding. "It isn't that he is going back to dealing or using."

"Not necessarily. He may just need confirmation he's making the right decision -- to leave. And you have to remember that it's painful to be around you and Jack." This took Anna Rae completely by surprise.

"Why?"

"Because no matter how much he wants the life he sees you having, he has to do the work. He can't just hang out with you and Jack and your families, assuming them as his own." Seeing that Anna Rae was about to ask why not, she went on, "For instance, in your family, you may have people join you for special occasions or even dinner once a week, but you eventually want to be with your immediate family, relaxing and free of any pretension, do you understand? Even in your most relaxed moments, cultures within a home are different, no matter who you are." Priestly sat back and let her words sink into Anna Rae's thoughts.

Anna Rae started to say something and then forced herself to think of their family routine at home. She thought of the visits her mom and dad made or when Wayne's family came to their house. She was right. No matter how familiar, she was always glad to be back to their own dynamic. It was a culture *they* created, within the culture they lived outside the house, within the culture of society, within the culture of the

United States, which was but a fragment of the culture in the world. *Wow.*

She thought of the interviews she'd had with Ryker. Sometimes they met at her house and talked while they walked her dog, Shakespeare. Sometimes Ryker came by and watched a game with Wayne and the boys. Sometimes he sat on her couch for hours at a time, describing the life he lived before he met Jack.

She remembered hearing about his experiences with the Bloods, the Crips, and his uncles. Her thoughts were so focused on getting the information that when she had time to process, she had a hard time seeing how Ryker had been this man. The Ryker she had come to know was nothing like this drug-dealing gangster he described. *Or, maybe they were one and the same and I had trouble processing.*

"Anna Rae." Priestly broke through her thoughts. "You are not his family. You and Jack and Sarah are giving him the chance to *have* his own family, free of the world he was unfortunately born into years ago. You are, and always will be, his friends; I dare say distant ones, when he is finally on his own two feet.

"You see, once he is completely out, he will want to forget how hard it was, how long it took. He will want to walk clean, into his new life. That bridge you gave him will always be precious to him and you may see him and communicate with him from time to time, but if he really makes it out, he will want people around him that only know him today. Do you understand?"

"A clean walk. Everything he went through in the past over. Eyes forward," Anna Rae resigned herself to it.

"Yes. He may even leave town and start completely over," Priestly said. "He will take his children and his common-law wife and give them a home, separate from what he was, *who* he was. This is good, really good, if he has the encouragement he needs." She eyed Anna Rae.

"You mean if Jack and Sarah and I let him go," she said, understanding. "I was so angry when Jack told me he went back to his family. I felt like they were the enemy, trying to take him back to something he didn't want anymore, with their emotional ties and guilt-ridden pressures, but if I don't let go of him when he finally breaks free, I'm no better. That's what you're really saying."

"Well, think about it.   He didn't go back to his connections in the Bloods or the Crips, even though they were family. He went where?"

"Daddy D."

"Was he a drug connection?" Priestly asked.

"No. Never sold them or used them," Anna Rae said.

Priestly nodded. She could see the pain in Anna Rae's face. She hadn't considered this before now. "You will not know, and neither will he, that all the effort you and Jack and Sarah have put into his new life was worthwhile if you don't let him stand alone.   And, I'm not saying he won't slip. Daddy D may not be a voice of reason, should he have to face others who will tempt him.

"For lack of a better example, an alcoholic gets through the program, goes out into the world and doesn't drink. Great, but that doesn't mean if he avoids all the bars and temptations, that he will be safe. If you don't face it head-on, aren't you just trading one prison for another? No, you don't purposefully test yourself, but should the situation present itself, you have to be able to *deal,* no pun intended. Otherwise, you're simply trading one prison for another, neither of which is healthy.

"From what you've told me, you've been the catalyst for getting Ryker to rehab, helping him face his addiction and bringing all the details to light that he and Jack didn't know about each other. It's not easy to step back and let Ryker take things from there."

"I think that's why I was so angry when he left. How could he leave us? We helped him get out of the life that was so dark," Anna Rae said. "Why would he want to leave us?"

"He doesn't," Priestly said, catching Anna Rae's attention. "He wants to be free to be him. Not even your children are yours to keep, if you consider what keeping them for yourself would do to their lives, their freedom, their spirit," her voice was gentle, yet firm.

"So, I need to let Ryker finish his story. His story, not the one I wrote," Anna Rae said, finally seeing what Dr. Priestly was saying.

"Oh, he'll finish it. The question is, will you tell it as it is or how *you* wanted it to be," Priestly said. "And, there's no letting him. He's doing it, with or without you."

"Jack? It's me," Anna Rae said. "Could you have Ryker call me? I think I need to hear what happened."

"I can't wait for you to talk to him," Jack said. "Oh, Anna Rae this is good news. He's doing so well. He's out of jail and …."

"What? Jail?" Anna Rae said.

"Hang on, hang on. Talk to him, hear him out. It's all good," Jack said.

"Yeah, okay."

When she hung up with Jack, she shook her head, not wanting to think about what Ryker might say when he called. *Jail for the last few months,* she pondered.

Anna Rae kept hearing Jack say Ryker was innocent this time. *How could he still believe in him when he was standing in a cell?* She thought, incredulously. *And, if he's in jail, he's facing a third strike. Jack said he was out so….*

She picked up the manuscript she'd written, finished only a week ago. A mixture of frustration and intrigue washed over her. She remembered what she told Jack the day he called, wanting to tell her the latest on Ryker going back to his family. *If God wants me to put it in the book, you and I both know it'll be there.*

A few days after talking with Jack the phone rang.

"Anna Rae," Ryker said.

"Ryker?" she asked, a little anxious because it had been several days since she'd talked to Jack.

"Hey," his voice changed from business to familiar, even concerned. "I'm glad you answer. I been wantin' to talk to you."

"Yeah, I wasn't sure I wanted to hear what you had to say."

"I'm gon' explain ever'thang, if you let me," he said. He sounded good -- different, confident.

"I'm listening," she said.

Ryker told her the whole story and left nothing out. When he finished, her eyes filled. Hearing how he asked his lawyer to do his job so he could prove he was innocent, moved her beyond words. He stood up to his past and stayed true to all he had become over the last seven years. He was really going to make it out. *Maybe he needed this third, potential strike to bring everything he'd learned full circle; to remind him of all the work he had done with Jack, and me. Maybe this was what Dr. Priestly was talking about. He has to do this on his own now. And, he is. Dear God, he is doing it.*

"Are you there?" Ryker said when he finished. "Do you hear what I's sayin'? I'm innocent and we gon' prove that and then I finally gon' be free. I'm comin' back to live near ya'll and I'm gon' be workin' again. Jack and I already work out a place for me to live. Angela and the boys be with me. We gon' make it," he said.

"What about your family on East Powell and out in Cooper?" she asked timidly, remembering not to hold on to him as Priestly had said. *Encourage him to move on.*

"Oh, they be there, doin' what they do, but I gon' do what I do, and it ain' good for me to be 'round 'em. So, I gon' see 'em when I can, but stay where my job is at the nursing home. I got to keep movin' forward. No lookin' back," he said.

"No lookin' back," she said, knowing it was going to be a good *ending or beginning.*

◆

"Anna Rae?" Jack said, not even bothering to say hello when his cell phone rang.

"Hey Jack."

"I really wish you would talk to Ryker. Please, he really wants to talk to you and, of all people, he has given *me* more reason than anyone to doubt him and I'm sayin' he's on the right track. If you could have seen him in the ...."

"Jack. Jack," she said, interrupting the litany of Ryker's last few months. "Jack, I talked to him. I talked to him," she said slower so Jack could hear her because he kept trying to run over her words. "I believe him. I believe you. I was wrong. Remember what I said that day when you called me, wanting to tell me what happened? I was about to print the final copy of the book and I didn't want to hear what you had to say, remember?" she asked, pressing Jack to think back.

"Well, yeah. I remember. You said, and I quote, that if God wanted you to hear the real ending to the story that there was nothing going to stop Him making you write it. Yeah, I remember," he said with a muffled chuckle.

"I remembered too and I talked to him. I listened," she said, a little regret in her voice that she hadn't sooner. "We had a really good talk and I, I can't," she said, her voice breaking.

"You all right?" Jack said, realizing he had gone off half-cocked, expecting her to fight him, when he asked her to talk to Ryker.

"I just. I thought he had taken all we had to give and run back to his old ways," she said, tears now falling one by one down her cheeks. "I thought he played me, Jack. And, when he left, I was so mad at him, not because he had played me, but because he had turned on himself. He had denied himself the right to freedom. He screwed it up.

"When we talked and I heard what he went through, I thought I had been right, but then he told me how he stood up to Trina, stood up to his past, and he even stood up to his attorney. I cried when he told me. He had been real all along. He really wanted out and you believed him.

"Oh, Jack. The kind of faith you have in him is indescribable. You had no guarantee, no net to fall into below. You were as a child, as Jesus tells us to be and you, you *believed*. Thank you. Thank you for letting me be part of this story. I'm in awe of your faith in God, in yourself, and in Ryker. I've learned so much just being along for the ride," she said, breaking off and letting more tears fall.

"I cast my line a long time ago, seven years. I was fishing for a man who needed saving," Jack managed to say, as his tears were falling with hers. "I wasn't sure if I could hold on much longer."

"Damn near took us both under, I'd say, if Ryker's the fish you're talking about," Sarah said. She had been listening on speaker phone and Anna Rae hadn't known.

"I made a promise, Shug," Jack said to both of them, as he thought about the old man outside the prison where Jeb still resides. He smiled. *Seventy times seven,* Jack thought as a tide of warmth washed over him. A little sadness followed, as his part in Ryker's journey was done. A lot of grace pushed at the corners of his eyes and he couldn't stop it spilling over. "And, God worked through me, every step of the way."

"I'll say," Anna Rae said.

Epilogue

Ryker James, Jr.

I wanted my children to grow up knowing they Daddy a good, honest, hardworking man, who love 'em. I couldn't a done it without Jack and Sarah. I know I ain' ever gon' be done. I pray ever' day. I take ever' day, one step at a time. I listen to my heart, to what I knows right. I ain' saying it easy. I'm just sayin' I don't freak out and take drugs or sell 'em or lose control like I done before. I know how to handle it now.

Father Rayford said it when he say, "seventy times seven." I thought it was about Jack, forgivin' me all I done, but now, I think it more 'bout me forgivin' myself — forgiving all the people, all the time. Jack teach me how to forgive. He do it so many times, I kept thinkin' it about him. Maybe that what Jesus mean when he say to Peter, "Look at your own life and then decide how many times to forgive." Lookin' at mine, I know it by the grace a God that Jack reel me in and then let me go.

I know I'll never be able to repay Jack and Sarah for bein' parents to me, but I gon' pay it forward so I know what it feel like to do what they done.

If you want to help someone like me, really change the life a someone who need you, call Inmate Services and be a mentor. It's a gift ain' nobody gon' appreciate more.

Jack Lawrence

Uncle Pete always said the key to fishing was in knowing when it's a keeper and when to let go. I told him I still thought the best part was the catch and I would never let go.

It wasn't until later I realized if you don't let go, you could end up caught yourself. Of all the fish I've caught in my lifetime, Ryker was the biggest, and letting him go so he could swim in his own current was both the most difficult and the most grace-filled blessing I have received in a long time.

Ryker's trial was held on June 13, 2011. Matthews proved that Ryker was innocent and he was given two years' probation and the charges of breaking and entering were dropped -- no felony of record and no third strike. He is still working at the nursing home and following his probation. His probation ends in June 2013. Angela recently had his fourth child and they are all living together in a rent house, near Jack and Sarah, but hope to move to a new place one day soon.

Ryker stopped by Anna Rae's one morning on his way to his probation check-in. She was about to start her car when he rolled into her driveway. She jumped out and hugged him tight, so glad to see him.

"You doin' a'ight?" he asked her.

"Yeah. How 'bout you?" she asked.

"I'm doin' what I do. I'm workin' and lovin' on my kids. I'm free, Anna Rae, free."

Looking into his eyes, she didn't have words. He was looking into the distance, telling her that he had heard from his family and they were asking for things, as usual, but that he would take care of his immediate family first and keep moving forward.

"I'm done freakin' out and tryin' to fix ever' body else. I got my job, a place to live and I ain' gon' do nothin' to mess that up. I'm gon' do what right for me and mine." As he talked on, she listened to every word. For the first time, she could breathe him in, with no concern for his future. He had come into his own. Letting him go was easy all of the sudden.

Jesus said it, "seventy times seven." Jack was a seventy-something-year-old man who set out to save a young ex-con and it took seven years -- 2004 to 2011. In that time, they forgave each other countless times, keeping sight of their own transgressions when they considered giving up.

Jack is eighty-something years old now and still visiting prisoners and sharing the word of God. He will probably do it until he is no longer able. Folks still give him a hard time about the time and money it took to see Ryker through. Its true people cannot know the ending when they set out to help someone. Jack said this is why blind faith is essential. *If you saw what was coming, there's no telling what blessings would be lost because fear stepped in.*

Every time he hears someone say he didn't make a difference, he just smiles to himself.

God knows I did. That's enough for me.